"Quirk returns to the thriller scene with a thundering bang . . . Quirk's latest feels like he's been churning out political thrillers for decades, hitting on a timely plot that starts out fast and only speeds up as the story unfolds . . . [A] high-stakes, nail-biting political thriller."
—TheRealBookSpy.com

"Lots of good, tense plotting . . . A real pleasure of espionage fiction is tradecraft secrets, and Quirk doesn't disappoint."

—*Booklist*

"*The Night Agent* is a compelling, high-stakes thriller, lightning fast, relentlessly suspenseful, and unsettlingly realistic."

—Hank Phillippi Ryan,
bestselling author of *Trust Me*

Also for The Night Agent

"*The Night Agent* rocks. Fast as hell, especially with Quirk's steady hand in control. This story is impossible to put out of mind once you enter this look-over-your-shoulder shadow world. Relevant and revealing, this is one of the best thrillers to come along in years."

—Michael Connelly

"Baldacci's debut [*Absolute Power*] kept me awake half the night. I'm still a fan . . . I had the same reaction when I picked up *The Night Agent* . . . Best to start this at the beginning of a weekend, as you'll be burning the midnight oil 'til you're finished."

—*Newark Star-Ledger*

"*The Night Agent* is a whirlwind of a book, a captivating narrative that takes us inside the White House's inner sanctum and the shadowy machinations surrounding it. A powerful and taut thriller."

—Mark Greaney, #1 bestselling author
of *Mission Critical*

THE
NIGHT
AGENT

By Matthew Quirk

The Night Agent
Dead Man Switch
Cold Barrel Zero
The Directive
The 500
Hour of the Assassin

THE
NIGHT
AGENT

MATTHEW QUIRK

HEAD
ZEUS

An Aries Book

First published in the US in 2019 by William Morrow

Published in the UK in 2020 by Head of Zeus Ltd
This paperback edition first published in 2021 by Head of Zeus Ltd
An Aries book

9 7 5 3 1 2 4 6 8

A catalogue record for this book is available from
the British Library.

ISBN (PB): 9781800243477
ISBN (E): 9781800243422

Typeset by Divaddict Publishing Solutions Ltd

MIX
Paper from
responsible sources
FSC® C020471

Printed and bound in Great Britain by
CPI Group (UK) Ltd, Croydon CR0 4YY

Head of Zeus Ltd
First Floor East
5–8 Hardwick Street
London EC1R 4RG

WWW.HEADOFZEUS.COM

For Peter

Prologue

Peter Sutherland stalked through the trees wearing a navy suit, white shirt, and black Oxfords polished to a high gloss. Everything about him was FBI standard, the code he had followed so carefully for so long. A perfect square.

The ax in his hand was new, though, as was the borrowed pistol on his hip with no serial number.

Bruises and cuts covered the side of his throat. He hadn't slept in twenty-four hours.

The ax was a beauty, its steel blade gleaming like a razor at the end of thirty-six inches of American ash.

He walked toward the red brick mansion, studying it. Peter knew how to get in and out of a home without leaving a trace. That was his job. Surveillance. Tracking. Seeing without being seen.

But the time for hiding was over. He moved across the soft grass of the lawn, toward the back of the house.

The day was cool, but his cheeks were flushed. His heartbeat washed in his ears like crashing surf. He welcomed it, welcomed the adrenaline flooding down his spine as he took the steps of the rear deck two at a time to the door.

The house surely had an alarm system, but he didn't care.

Let them come. All of them. Police. Secret Service. The cold assassins masquerading as intelligence officers.

Peter had always been so careful about the rules. He had to be. His father had betrayed his country. Suspicion had trailed Peter for most of his life. No matter how faultless he was, he couldn't escape it, and now they had branded him as a traitor, too.

He didn't break his stride as he tilted his wrist down and let the ax slip through his fingers to its full length, grabbing it at the end of the handle. He closed his left hand on the wood grain just above his right and swung the tool back, over his head, the four-pound blade arcing until it nearly touched his spine. He whipped it forward with every muscle in his body.

Fourteen years of anger repressed, fourteen years of playing by their hypocrite rules, all the fury of watching the helpless die at the hands of the powerful—he put it all into that blow. Enough with the Boy Scout shit.

The blade hissed through the air, hit the door near its edge, and blew it apart like a breaching charge. The lock and handle splintered out.

He kicked the door open. A camera was straight ahead.

Perfect. He wanted them to see. Raise the alarm at the White House.

He marched upstairs looking for the safe.

The traitors had murdered innocents and waged war against their own country, a quiet coup. Soon they would have control. Soon more would die if he didn't make his stand. It might cost him his life. He knew that.

He knew he might have to kill someone here. That would have been unthinkable just a day before, but he had never known treachery like this, never felt anger like this. He didn't know who he was anymore, but he knew what he needed to do. This ended only one way. Looking down the barrel of a gun.

1

Six Days Earlier

Peter's Oxfords stood outside the closet door. A freshly pressed shirt hung on the knob along with a navy suit. His alarm chirped. It was five P.M.

He rolled out of bed and opened the shades, then brought the sheet and comforter back up, and tucked them in with neat corners.

The sun dipped low in the sky and disappeared behind the trees and apartment buildings near the National Cathedral.

Night was coming and his day was just getting started. He worked for the Federal Bureau of Investigation, and through a series of events he still couldn't quite fathom, he had been detailed to the White House. He staffed a night action desk in the Situation Room, a twelve-hour shift from seven P.M. to seven A.M.

His job, in brief, was to stand by an emergency line all night every night, waiting for a call that might never come.

The bus took him down to Lafayette Square, and he headed south as the setting sun painted the White House red.

He crossed to G Street and ducked into Tonic, a bar in

Foggy Bottom. He scanned the room for a colleague of his from the West Wing, Brian, who had told him to come by.

Walking along the back wall of the bar gave him a clear view of the entire space. He caught himself studying the other patrons, noting height and weight, distinguishing characteristics and unusual behavior, silently recording it all.

He could never turn off the old habits. For years watching had been his job. He started out in the FBI as a surveillance specialist, known within the bureau as a G.

He slipped along the edge of the crowd. Peter stood out at six six and a lean two hundred and twenty pounds, but he liked to avoid attention and knew how to get around without drawing too much notice.

He caught the eye of Brian, who waved him over. "You want a beer?"

"Thanks," Peter said. "But I'm heading in. I wanted to stop by for a bit."

"You're still on nights?"

Peter pretended to sleep on his feet, then opened his eyes, startled. "Sorry, what?"

Brian laughed, then took a sip. His suit was well-cut, modish, too expensive for his salary. He was an easygoing Connecticut prep who worked days in the office of the national security advisor. They had played basketball together a handful of times. He had a habit of attaching the name of a person he had just met to the end of each sentence—"And where did you go to school, *Peter*?"—that Peter took as a sign of an inveterate networker, filing names away in his mental Rolodex.

Peter recognized the man next to Brian from a barbecue that summer. He worked in the director's office.

"Hey, Theo," Peter said and shook his hand.

"Go ahead," Brian said to Theo, who cast his eyes around the room warily.

"What's up?" Peter asked.

"Theo saw the promotion and transfer lists."

It was a favorite topic of gossip among the bureau drones.

"Do you want to know if you're getting one?" Brian asked Peter, grinning.

"Of course," Peter said, and as Theo leaned in, Peter held up his hand. "But don't tell me."

"What?"

"I'll find out soon."

"You don't want to know?"

"It's cool. I'll wait."

Theo straightened up, and the pleasant air of shared secrets disappeared.

"It's not a big deal," Theo said, defensive now. And it wasn't. Bosses would often drop hints, and most of the raises and promotions were telegraphed well in advance.

"I'm not trying to give you a hard time," Peter said. "It's fine. But I don't want to know."

"You're making me out like some kind of sneak? *You*?"

Peter was careful about even the slightest hint of impropriety. People had been watching him, too, for much of his life, looking for the slightest breach. Maybe that's why surveillance and countersurveillance came so naturally.

He'd always hewed carefully to those rules, hoping they might let him escape the taint of his father's crimes, might save him from who he was.

"No," Peter said calmly. "But leave me out of it."

Theo let out a nasty laugh. "You play it so straight, but everybody knows . . ." He looked away.

"Knows what?" Peter asked.

Theo scanned the room to his left as if he were looking for someone better to talk to. He muttered something about *dad* and *spy*.

Peter stepped closer and looked Theo in the eye.

"Is there something you would like to say?"

Theo puffed up and stared back in silence for a moment. The others went quiet.

"I don't mind, really. I've heard it all," Peter went on. He'd been dealing with this garbage his whole life. You just had to face it down, show that you're your own man, with nothing to hide.

A pleasant rush coursed through Peter's body, the kind he used to feel before a big game, or when a surveillance target tried to lose him. He'd been cooped up at a desk for months. He longed for action.

He ran his thumbnail along the side of his middle finger and then pressed it in, hard, at the knuckle. The stab of pain braced him. It was an old habit, a way to break himself out of the moment. *Easy, Sutherland. Easy.* He took two deep breaths and then smiled.

That unnerved Theo, who shook his head and stepped away without another word.

Brian grimaced at Peter. "Sorry about that."

"Don't worry about it," Peter said, as the conversations around them picked back up. "I should get going anyway."

"You sure you don't want anything? Cup of coffee?"

"I'm good. Thanks."

Peter turned toward the door, and Brian raised his glass. "An honest man in Washington."

"I know." Peter smiled. "I'm screwed."

2

That night in the Situation Room started like any other. Peter stepped into the West Wing and a Secret Service officer checked his badge for access.

"How you shooting these days, Bear?" Peter's nickname from college ball.

"A little rusty," Peter said. "I need to get out there more."

"They still have you in that basement?"

"Yes, sir."

He let out a chuckle. The guard seemed to find the plight of a big man in a small room a source of endless humor. "What are those ceilings down there? Eight feet? Seven?"

"Lower every night," Peter said, gave the desk a friendly tap, and started down the corridor.

Peter's boss, James Hawkins, marched past, reading something on his phone. A senior advisor and veteran of the FBI's national security division, he served as the president's in-house man on counterintelligence and terrorism. He seemed to catch sight of Peter, though his only response was a slight knitting of his brows.

Hawkins was big, built like a laborer, balding with black hair cut close to his skull and a trim beard.

Now that Peter was in the White House, so close to the

president, he noticed people watching him more carefully than ever, saw the concern flash across their faces when they figured out who he was.

Hawkins had known his father before the scandal, and it didn't help that Peter bore such a strong physical resemblance to his dad.

Hawkins—divorced, lapsed Catholic, workaholic—typically moved through the building like a black cloud. He greeted subordinates, if he greeted them at all, with a lift of the head and a faint "hey" that sounded like the noise he would make if he were moving an injured limb. Maybe it was the toll from a lifetime of classified work, of carrying too many secrets, but he seemed especially cold toward Peter.

There were times when the suspicions got to Peter, made him feel like an impostor, an inside threat that had somehow managed to cheat its way into the heart of the government.

But tonight Peter didn't let Hawkins's glare trouble him. He paused by the windows at the end of the hall and looked out over the Rose Garden, and the glowing windows of the White House mansion. This was why he had been so careful for so long. He had earned a spot here, trusted with the nation's most closely held confidences.

He loved these limbo hours in the evenings and early mornings, when the political staff had mostly gone home. The desks were empty, the phones silent, the hallways still. In those moments, the White House was no longer a field of crises and partisan battle. All he could feel was the tradition and ceremony of the place.

His blue badge gave him all access, and sometimes he would roam the White House at night, have the first floors to himself. Even after almost a year of working here and even knowing intimately the costs and treachery of political life—few knew it better than he did—it still filled him with awe to have a desk in this place and to be able to play his part, however small.

His father had once had trust like this, and when he lost it, it killed him.

"You look like shit, Sutherland."

The chief of staff, Diane Farr, came around the corner behind him, a mug in her hand. "Just because I already buried you down there doesn't mean you can die on me, okay?"

"Understood."

That kind of access to the chief of staff was unusual, but so was everything else about Peter's job, working an emergency line that went straight to her and Hawkins, that only they knew about. Farr had hired him, brought him to the White House, given him this chance to prove himself.

She worked tirelessly, seven days a week, with a sharp-tongued relentlessness that always made him think of a gruff newspaper editor in a movie from the thirties. She was striking, with chin-length black hair and bangs, green eyes, and fair skin with the slightest touch of olive.

Running the White House was a job for masochists—chiefs of staff often left the West Wing via stroke or heart attack—but she seemed to survive it with a faint air of amusement, like she was watching all of this drama from the mezzanine. She had cycled in and out of the private sector, never married. Whenever she wanted, she could bail out to a high-end finance gig in New York, and coast on her connections.

"Are you getting any sleep?" she asked, leaning in slightly to examine the circles under his eyes.

"Here and there."

"How long have we had you on the desk?"

"About ten months." He looked at her mug: black coffee, steam rising off the top like smoke. She was settling in for a long night. "Though I don't know why you need a watch officer if you never go home."

"Only a couple more hours." She smiled and turned to go.

Peter took the stairs down to the ground floor. A plaque on a mahogany door said White House Situation Room— Restricted Area.

Peter rolled his shoulders back slightly and stood his full height. Even after a lifetime of being careful, there was nowhere he was more vigilant than in this room, the sanctum of America's secrets.

He carried himself differently here, because he carried his own secrets, those special orders that could be shared only with his two superiors, Hawkins and Farr, secrets he didn't understand himself: why they needed him on the watch, and who might come calling on the phone line he stood by every night.

He swiped his ID and stepped inside.

3

Straight ahead, past the reception area, the watch officers sat at a long desk, eyes fixed on their triple monitors.

The night watch was all business. Peter's entry merited little more than a raised hand from Mark who worked at the CIA and "What's up, Sutherland," from Jessica, the watch officer from the Pentagon. She was from Puerto Rico, a former marine intelligence officer, who would often join Peter for midnight lunch.

The Situation Room isn't a room. It's a suite of offices under the West Wing, a warren of watch desks and displays and partitions. What people think of when they think of the Situation Room—the command center with the long oak table and the clocks ticking down seconds in time zones around the world—was through a door to his left. It's where they defused the Cuban missile crisis and planned the mission to kill bin Laden. For all its gravitas, down here it went by a simple name: large conference room.

Updates from operations streamed in from military and diplomatic sources around the world, fleshed out by signals intelligence and field reports from CIA officers and their agents. The watch officers' attention circled the globe with the rising sun, as adversaries woke up. Morning was hitting Southeast Asia when Peter arrived.

At any moment, President Michael Travers might walk in and all would stand. An officer could find himself or herself as POTUS's first source on a breaking crisis, taken aside into the president's breakout room with glass walls that turned white for privacy at the touch of a button.

Peter walked past the long desks of the main watch center, past the president's chair, and continued to the far end of the suite, to his cube, not much more than a shelf in the back corner with a waist-high partition beside it.

There was the phone, the emergency line. It sat on his desk in silence as it had nearly all of his last 284 nights on the watch. In those endless hours between dusk and dawn, he would stare at it, willing it to ring.

He took his seat, and put his ID card into the reader on his desk to unlock his computer.

Every night Farr or her deputy would send him a list of late-breaking events and questions, and he would scour open-source news and the intel databases and pull together answers and analyses.

He often wondered if that work was simply putting him to good use, and the real job was waiting, watching that phone.

Everyone in the Situation Room was cleared top secret, but they all had confidences they kept from each other, loyalties to their home agencies, special access programs and codeword intelligence that required even stricter handling than TS.

That phone was Peter's secret. If it rang, any information

that came through it was to go "eyes only" to Hawkins and Farr.

The Sit Room was built from the ground up for that kind of discretion. Each desk was fitted with a small button that activated a speaker overhead, and sent out a noise-canceling wave of static. It sounded like the faintest hiss, but it was so effective that as you watched the speaker's lips move and heard no sound come out, for a moment you thought you had been rendered deaf.

Along one wall ran the Superman tubes, as everyone referred to them, cylindrical phone booths, sealed off with curving plexiglass for calls that absolutely couldn't be heard elsewhere within the room. They made the place look like a sci-fi set.

Even Peter didn't know what his phone line was for. The callers were supposed to use codes to indicate priority and subject matter. His job was simply to be a voice on the receiving end, to route the messages to his superiors, and make sure they picked up in an emergency.

When Farr and Hawkins had first briefed him, they seemed surprised that he hadn't pressed them for more information about the phone line. Of course he wanted to know, but he was careful and strict, and respected the rules on classified information as if lives depended on it, because they did. He knew all too well what happened when those rules were broken.

The whole thing sounded like a thrill at the start. He had even imagined a true crisis coming on the line and saw himself making the long walk through the gallery to the residence to wake POTUS himself.

That was 284 nights ago.

The Situation Room was small, far drabber than the slick mock-ups on television, and every night it seemed to shrink a bit more.

Even the keyhole intercepts and Superman tubes had lost their novelty. Ten months of living on a vampire schedule wears you down until you feel like an automaton fueled by the thin, bitter, hours-old coffee from the White House Mess.

He missed action, the endless hard physical training of college athletics, the rush of the chase from his days as a surveillance specialist in Boston.

In all his time on the watch, the phone had rung only once. A man's voice came on the line, composed, but with a trace of desperation behind it: "This is a night action," he said.

"Can you verify that, please," Peter replied, as he had been instructed.

"Pen. Clock. Door. Fire."

It was a mnemonic key that confirmed the status and legitimacy of the call.

The caller hadn't said a word after that. He hadn't needed to. "Night action" was a standard term in the op centers and watch desks around DC. It meant a crisis, call, or cable that was so urgent that the principal, be it the CIA director or the defense secretary, needed to be woken up.

Peter had called Hawkins and Farr, and when neither picked up, per protocol, he went to the Secret Service office down the hall. They sent a car to Farr's house and woke her, and she connected on the line twelve minutes later. After that, Peter was off the call. On the desk for 284 nights and twelve minutes of action.

He'd passed almost a year of his life down here, a hard

year, chained to this phone that never rang for reasons he didn't understand.

The work had cost him more than he liked to think about. He still wore the Hamilton Field watch with the leather band, but he never looked at the inscription on the back: P+L, Forever.

His ex-fiancée, Leah. She had wanted him to get out of government. He had been lucky to get the White House job through Farr, but the FBI higher-ups would never fully accept him, let him rise through the ranks. Leah would always ask him why he worked so hard for so little for a bureau that didn't want him. He had his reasons. Peter remembered the night his father died, remembered an unanswered call.

He liked nights. Liked the discipline. He sat beside that silent phone, scanned on his monitor a satellite photo of a troop buildup on the Latvian-Russian border, and let the work fill his mind.

Nine P.M., ten. The minutes crawled by. Click, scroll, type, repeat. By eleven, he fell into a groove, and forgot the clock.

At 1:05 A.M. his phone rang. Peter stared at it for an instant as if it was a hallucination, then lifted the handset to his ear. It was the emergency line.

"Go ahead."

"Hello?" a young woman asked, her voice wavering, the terror plain.

"Yes. Go ahead."

"Night action. They told me to tell you that. That you would know what to do. My name is Rose Larkin—" Two muffled cracks broke out in the background. "He's here. He's inside. He's going to kill me."

4

At six o'clock that evening, Dimitri Sokolov took the cover off his metronome and slid the counterweight down to *molto allegro*. He brushed his finger against the arm, and it began ticking back and forth with the pace of a panicked heartbeat.

He raised the lid of a black case and lifted a violin from the velvet. He had received the instrument, an eighteenth-century Mittenwald, as a gift for his twelfth birthday. Along the neck, the dark varnish was completely worn away.

He rested it under his chin and looked over the music on the stand before him. It had been a long time since he had opened the violin case, a long time since he had tried Mendelssohn's Concerto. It had been his wife's favorite. Today was her birthday, the first since she had passed.

He took each step slowly, deliberately, like a priest at an altar. He started in the middle passage to warm up, a long lyrical section that was unforgiving to his out-of-practice fingers. The movements on the bow and fingerboard came automatically, though already the strain was growing in the muscles of his hands. He was used to working with his hands; it was his livelihood, but not in this way.

Dimitri knew what was coming, a fugue passage of

double-stops and runs, a difficult task even for a trained violinist in top form.

He slit his eyes and the muscles around his jaw tightened as he sawed the bow. That sort of intensity in his face would have shocked any of the few people who knew him, as would his dexterity with the violin.

He didn't hide here in the US. Purposely avoiding attention would only bring it. But he had a way of concealing himself in plain sight.

He was friendly enough with his neighbors, but if you pressed them to describe him, the response would be so general as to be useless. Medium build, medium height, regular haircut, tapered and parted on the left, not especially outgoing but not reclusive either. He would wave and say hello, but never offered much more than a few empty pleasantries.

He seemed to be a regular empty-nester dad and DC bureaucrat. The Americans had a phrase for it—a gray man. It was only when someone really focused that he would notice the only exceptional thing about Dimitri: his perfect nothingness.

A loose strand on his violin bow danced in the air as he approached the scherzo.

The music had him now, the early nerves giving way to focus as his eyes raced across the long, slurred progressions of sixteenth notes leading to the crescendo. It was a difficult passage, one he hadn't managed since she died, always giving up, fingers cramped, and slamming shut the case.

He could connect all the notes, but he needed more than that, he needed expression, feeling, and all he had been able to put together was a technical succession of sounds.

But tonight, it was coming, and as the violin sang, cradled between his cheek and shoulder, he remembered the first time he had played it for Carolina. He shut his eyes, and felt the tears welling inside them as he approached the climax. He knew it by heart.

His phone rang, a cheap electric warble accompanied by the rattling of plastic on wood as it vibrated. He disregarded it and tried to go on, but that was the encrypted phone, one he couldn't ignore. He put the violin down and answered on the fourth ring.

"BEECH?" he asked.

"Yes. It's time. They're at the Westin in Arlington. Henry and Paulette Campbell. They're undercover as contractors for the Department of Commerce."

"Do they have the red ledger?"

"It's in their possession. I don't know if it's on them or at the house or elsewhere. They might have family with them, a girl named Rose Larkin, their niece. What are you going to do?"

"You want to know?" he asked. With stakes this high, lives being taken and war at risk, people often preferred to keep their blinders on.

A pause, then BEECH responded: "No."

"I'll take care of it." Dimitri disconnected. A year ago, at the beginning of this operation, they had sent a Metro train off its tracks, an attack that had been made to look like an accident. They killed dozens. What were a few more?

The violin and bow went back in the case. He had been expecting the call, so his equipment was in the kitchen in a small range bag. He pushed aside the napkin caddy, the woven place mats, and the salt and pepper shakers and put the nylon bag on the table.

He had a middle-aged man's taste for simple, reliable tools. He reached into the bag and pulled out a pistol, then ran a quick function check on the Glock 17, racking it twice and dry firing it at the oven. He checked each magazine by glancing at the witness holes and pressing down the top round with his thumb; all were full, all seventeen rounds. In a side pocket, there were three pairs of flex-cuffs, nylon over a steel reinforcement, and a suppressor to fit the Glock. Finally, there was an inexpensive Swedish knife, a type favored by outdoorsmen and survivalists. He had put such a fine edge on it that it could cut skin without even being noticed.

The other bag, filled with electronics, was in the car. He zipped his kit shut, and switched off the light. He was halfway through the door when he turned, went back and double-checked that the oven was off.

On his way through the living room, he stilled the metronome, then stepped out the front door. The neighbors' kids were running around in their driveway in the waning light, playing street hockey in their sneakers with two upside-down trash cans for a goal. He waved to them as he climbed into his car, tuned in NPR, and headed for Arlington.

He parked in the lot of a diner across the street from the hotel, about two hundred yards down the street, and surveyed his surroundings. After twenty minutes, a figure appeared in his side-view mirror, a woman in her late twenties, in a skirt and blouse, and a black jacket with a high neck. Everything about her said LA or New York, not DC.

Dimitri knew her from his advance work: Rose Larkin, age twenty-eight. He rested his hand on the passenger seat, beside a road atlas that covered the suppressed Glock, as she passed just feet from him.

5

Rose strolled past the diner, moving quickly in her heels, sunglasses mirroring the passersby. She got a few looks from the men, but she was used to that.

She was here to pick up her aunt and uncle from the hotel, but they had texted that they were running late. To kill time, she had gone around the corner and had what passed for coffee in these soulless precincts of Northern Virginia.

As she walked back to her parking spot, she saw a chalk line on the tire of her car—her aunt and uncle's car, actually—a classic Mercedes SL convertible that her uncle had stripped down to the engine and restored.

She placed her sunglasses on top of her head as she strode toward it, and checked her iPhone. She had been parked there for two hours and fifteen minutes, but there was no ticket under the wiper.

She turned left and right, glancing up and down the street, blasé, looking to all the world like a young professional with her act together. But the Carolina Herrera jacket and the Prada shoes, the whole outward-facing persona, was carefully constructed. She wore it like armor. She couldn't afford a ticket.

She reached down, eased the four-hundred-dollar pump off her left foot, then crouched and used its sole to scrub off the chalk mark.

After a few seconds, the tire was clear, and she stood to find an older man walking a terrier and staring at her with a disappointed look. With the shoe still on her hand, she winked at him. Then she pulled her heel back on and headed for the hotel. Her aunt and uncle were ready.

She met them just inside the lobby and hugged them both. Her aunt was tiny, five two, with deep smile lines around her eyes. Her uncle was a beanpole, dressed in his usual uniform of a Lands' End shirt and jacket, and pleated khakis with a cell phone holster on the waist. They both looked exhausted.

"Thank you for picking us up," her aunt said. Rose was supposed to get them at the airport, but they had changed plans at the last minute. "You didn't have to."

"It's the least I could do. And I love driving that car."

"Oh good," her aunt said, as they started walking toward the Mercedes. "We had to hammer out a few things with a client and the legal team, so we came with them straight from the airport."

"What are you working on?"

"LTE data standardization for government services."

"Cool," Rose said, but she was barely paying attention, her eyes fixed on the yellow ticket under her wiper. She scanned the street, but the parking officer was nowhere to be seen.

"But I . . ."

"Did you rub off the chalk?" her aunt asked.

"Well . . ."

"They all use plate scanners. The chalk is a backup."

"I think it's a decoy, to lull you into a false sense of security," her uncle added.

"Twisted," Rose said, as if there was something unfair about cheating a cheat.

"You know parking in DC is a blood sport." Her aunt sneaked up to her side and pinched the ticket out of her hand.

"Wait!" Rose said.

"We'll take care of this. It's our car."

"It's my fault."

"It's the least we can do for you taking care of the house."

Rose relented. She climbed into the back seat of the Mercedes, and they started down the highway. Rose had been watching their place while they were on a work trip. They both had worked for the Department of Commerce, and after retiring, they went back as contractors.

Rose lived in Los Angeles, until recently at least. The startup she founded had gone under, and she'd broken up with her boyfriend, and "house-sitting for family" was a much nicer term than "homeless."

She had grown up around Manassas. Her mom had raised Rose on her own, but she had trouble with alcohol, and was always running from one guy to the next.

Rose went to work at Denny's when she was fourteen, forging her mom's signature on the permission form. They needed the money and the leftover food she brought home.

When she was young, her aunt and uncle's home served as Rose's sanctuary, cluttered with books, shelves lining every wall and even the hallways.

Rose didn't talk to her mother anymore. The last time

she'd heard from her, she was living in Belize with a guy she met at a boat show.

Rose's aunt had asked her to come look after the house, and the timing was so perfect that Rose wondered if somehow her aunt had heard about Rose's recent troubles. It was Henry and Paulette, saving the day again, making it sound like Rose was doing *them* a favor. It could have been eighteen years ago, with Rose in the back seat of this same car, at their house for the weekend while her mom was off God knows where, Rose finally letting her guard down, somehow feeling that everything would be okay. They were the only people she had ever truly trusted.

Her aunt's eyes kept going to the mirrors.

Rose glanced at the cars behind them. "Is everything okay?" she asked.

"Oh yes," her aunt said, smiling now, bright as ever. "I was wondering if I forgot a charger. How is the house? Did anything come up?"

"Smooth sailing. I caught the recycling guys this morning."

Her uncle looked at her in the rearview mirror. "How's the business going, dear?"

"Good," Rose said, drawing out the word. "I can take it easy for a while before we have to line up financing for our next phase."

"Expanding?" her uncle asked.

Rose shifted in her seat. "Pivoting a bit."

"Pivoting?" her uncle said, as if trying out the taste of the word, and finding he didn't like it. It was a tech euphemism for crashing and burning and starting over.

"Everything is going great," Rose said, with finality.

Her aunt turned slightly in the passenger seat and their eyes met. Rose gave her a half-hearted smile, and then looked down.

She had always had a knack for making people believe what she wanted them to believe, but these two could see through her.

At the house, Rose heated up pasta with chicken and vegetables that she'd made the night before. Her aunt and uncle went upstairs to change before dinner. As they ate, and Henry leafed through the mail, Rose could tell they were both exhausted, barely keeping up with small talk about what had been happening in the neighborhood.

After Rose and her aunt did the dishes, Rose picked up her computer bag, and started toward the stairs. "I'll let you all take it easy," she said.

Her aunt's face fell. "Do you want some tea?"

"Well . . ."

That was what they did here, sat around the table long after the meal was done, telling stories, cracking each other up. But Rose didn't feel like talking. She was tired of keeping up the facade.

"And I think I have some Girl Scout cookies left."

"Really?" Rose hadn't seen any.

Her aunt pulled a chair over and reached into the back of a high cabinet. She came out with a box of Tagalongs. "I have to hide them or else Henry will eat them all. I forgot to tell you they were up there."

Had she? They were Rose's favorite, and she felt like

perhaps she was being enticed, but she didn't care. Tagalongs were Tagalongs.

Her aunt put two bags of tea into mugs and started the electric kettle, then put the moka pot on the stove for Henry. He could drink coffee at any hour without it keeping him up.

He came back downstairs a few minutes later, and his eyes went to the box of cookies like a wolf's to its prey.

6

Outside, Dimitri waited in his Accord, watching the house, perfectly still save for his breathing. Through the earpiece in his left ear, he listened to the three inside the house, sitting and talking.

For a moment Dimitri remembered his own kitchen table, drinking smoky black tea with Carolina.

The radio on his lap came to life: "We're all set up to hit the house. We can kill the lights and telephones. Do you want to go in now?"

The rest of Dimitri's team was parked around the corner. He looked at the clouds, drifting over the moon, then lifted the handset. He would wait. He wanted full dark. He wanted them unsuspecting.

"Not yet. Stand by. On my order."

He put the radio down on the passenger seat, beside the pistol, and as he listened to the voices around the table, the conversation moving in easy rhythms as with old friends, he couldn't help but smile.

7

Rose sat back, laughing, her hand on her chest, as her aunt finished a story about being mistaken for an Uber driver in her Prius. For the first time in a long while, she forgot about the overdue invoices and credit card bills. It grew late, and as her aunt brought their mugs to the sink, she turned to Rose.

"You know, we have so much room here and we're at work all the time or traveling. I know you have a lot going on, but we'd love to have you stay for as long as you want. We could use the company."

Did she know? Was this a graceful way of offering up a refuge?

"Thank you," Rose said, and shut her eyes, surprised by the sudden surge of emotion. "Things are a little crazy right now. That . . . that might be nice."

Rose and her aunt talked for another hour. Rose vented. She could hear her uncle in the kitchen, putting away dishes, singing an old Stevie Wonder tune, their wedding song. She'd always rolled her eyes, thinking it was sappy when she was a teenager, how he would scoot around with a dishrag over his shoulder, humming "You Are the Sunshine of My Life." But she didn't feel that way now. It was familiar, sweet.

She hadn't realized how badly she needed to say it all out loud, to let it hurt. It was nearly midnight when she hugged her aunt good night, went upstairs, brushed her teeth and washed her face, and then climbed into bed and shut off the light.

8

A pulsing shriek pulled Rose from her sleep. She sat up and recognized the sound: the smoke detector.

She checked her cell—almost one A.M.—and slid to the side of the bed. Her feet touched the cold floor, and she made her way through the room by the glow of her telephone screen. The display said she had no signal. Weird. She always had five bars here.

She hit the light switch by the door: nothing.

The alarm rang down the hallway as she pulled on a sweatshirt, and walked out of the bedroom, guiding herself with a hand on the wall. Then the sound cut off.

In the silence, she picked up an acrid scent, like the fumes from burning plastics, but it was faint.

Her panic rose, every breath shorter and faster than the next, but she forced herself to move slowly, carefully along the hardwood.

Her uncle's voice echoed up the stairs.

"Can you get the call through?"

"I'm trying," her aunt answered. "The landline's out. There's no cell signal."

As Rose came down the stairs, her aunt said something

about protecting the sources. Rose tried to make out the words: "chemist," and "book," and "binder."

"You don't trust them?" Henry asked.

"It's a precaution. Keep them out of it."

"Fine." A door slammed.

Her aunt strode through the kitchen carrying a flashlight, the cordless phone to her ear.

"Hello? Hello?" There was panic and desperation in her voice.

She looked at the phone, stabbed a button, and cursed—a word Rose had never heard cross her lips before.

Rose stood in the hall outside the kitchen, knowing she needed to move, but her legs felt fixed to the floor. When her aunt turned, Rose saw the pistol, black and gleaming, in a holster clipped to her belt.

"Paulette," Rose said finally. "What's happening?"

Her aunt whipped toward her with the flashlight, stinging her eyes.

"Rose, sweetheart . . ." She looked at the picture window at the front of the house, took Rose's arm, and led her back to the kitchen.

"Is something burning? What the hell is going on?"

"It's . . . there's not a lot of time to explain." Her aunt's eyes flicked from window to window.

Rose stared at the holstered pistol, and shivered.

The door to the garage opened and her uncle walked in, wiping the inside corners of his eyes with his thumb and index finger and coughing. He held a sheaf of papers in one hand and two thumb drives in the other. The chemical smell intensified, and in the garage, Rose could see black smoke hovering near the ceiling. He was burning something.

"I couldn't get through on my cell," he said. "But I destroyed all the OSPREY source material. You didn't use any of the encryption keys on the Mac—"

He stopped when he saw Rose.

"Please just tell me what is happening," she said.

Her aunt walked to her uncle's side, and they spoke in whispers for a moment, then Henry turned to Rose.

"It's work. It's not safe here. There's some confidential material we have, and when I got up I thought I saw someone watching the house. There's a chance they may try something."

"A chance! Paulette has a fucking gun. Someone's outside. And why don't any of the phones work?"

"Rose. Listen. Listen very carefully. This is not fair and I'm sorry I can't tell you the whole story, but you have to pay attention because we want to make sure you stay safe."

She started to protest, then let her hands fall.

"Okay. Okay," she said. She didn't want to panic. She just wanted to get through this. "What is it?"

Her uncle tore one of the pages from the reminder pad on the fridge, and began to write.

"We have to stay here for a little while and finish something," he said. "You're going to go out the back door, to Paulette's car. Drive down to the Mobil station. There's a pay phone there. Call this number. And tell them it's a night action. They will know what that means and they will ask you to confirm who you are. Repeat this."

He put the note on the dining table, and pointed at the words as he spoke them: "Pen. Clock. Door. Fire."

"What does that mean?"

"It's just a way of verifying who you are, and how

important the call is. That will connect you to the people we work for. Tell them the code and where you are and that you need help, and tell them that OSPREY was right. It's happening in six days. We have the red ledger."

"What? Why don't you tell them yourselves? Why aren't you coming with me?"

"We will, but we need to take care of something first. We'll be right there. So if you can get to a phone, we can use the help. There'll be time to explain everything later, okay? Now what are you going to say?"

"Mobil pay phone. Night action. Pen. Clock. Door. Fire. I'll tell them where I am. That I need help. That OSPREY was right. We only have six days." She took a deep breath. "And that you have the red ledger."

"Good. Tell no one else. Just the people who answer the phone."

"Who's coming for you?"

"Rose. There's no time. Trust us."

Henry stared out the front window. "You need to go."

His voice was so grave, so alien, that Rose put aside her questions, and nodded. "Okay."

She took the keys, went to the back door, and slipped her bare feet into her sneakers. Her aunt and uncle exchanged a few quiet words in the kitchen, then her uncle joined Rose and opened the door. He stepped out, drew his own pistol, and moved silently, expertly, suddenly a stranger to her as he scanned the dark.

His attention went toward the front of the house, as if he were standing between her and the threat. The car was parked on the side street. He nodded his head to indicate it was safe, and she started across the lawn. The wet grass brushed cold against her ankles and the hems of her pajama bottoms.

Forty feet from the car, she heard a faint sound, like running shoes on the street. She stopped and held her breath. After a moment, she made out a black figure standing beside the car. The shadows moved to her left: someone getting closer. She thought he was coming for her, but then he passed in between her and the house. Her first instinct was to shout a warning to her aunt and uncle, but that would only put them all in danger.

She needed to get help, but she couldn't reach the car without getting too close to these men. She slipped into the backyard, skirting the tangle of blackberry bushes where she used to play hide-and-seek with the neighborhood kids. Crouching, she passed through a split-rail fence, and ran through a patch of tangled woods toward the Rubinos' house.

Rose rang the doorbell. With all the madness going on at the house, she was surprised how worried she was about waking these people up in the middle of the night.

She rang again and checked her phone. Still no signal. What the hell was happening?

No one answered. There was no car in the driveway. She peered inside, nose to the glass. In the glow from the red standby lights on the TV and cable box, she saw a rubber tree with a watering bulb stuck in the potting soil.

They were gone, and there was a cordless phone on the island leading to the open kitchen.

She had tried to be silent but had made so much noise

running through those trees. She looked back the way she had come. The Rubinos' house, with its long sloping roof, was the only property out here. It backed onto a creek. There was nowhere else to go. Those shadows would find her soon.

She looked under the flowerpot and the mat and checked a decorative stone with a Celtic cross carved into the top, but there was no spare key.

White explosions flashed down the hill, muffled, more like snaps than the crack of fireworks. They came from somewhere in front of her aunt and uncle's house, each blast silhouetting it in red. Gunshots.

Rose picked up the stone, faced the door, and shattered the glass.

9

Paulette stood in the dark near the front window of her house. She had turned off the flashlight so she could see better through the glass, instead of waiting, staring at her reflection, visible to anyone outside.

She flinched slightly as the door from the garage closed. Henry walked into the kitchen.

"Are they gone?" he asked.

"Or waiting."

"Why?"

"Surround us?"

"Let's go out the back."

"You're done?"

He looked toward the garage. "I did enough. You should have gone with Rose."

"I told you. I'm not leaving you here alone."

She walked toward the rear of the house, and stopped, her eyes on the sliding glass doors. "They're already out there."

"The garage?" Henry looked out the kitchen window and caught movement. He shook his head.

"How many are there?" she asked.

"I don't know."

They had the exits covered. They would breach the house at any moment—a door, a window, there was no way of knowing where they would enter.

Paulette drew her pistol, and Henry followed suit. They went back-to-back in the main hall, covering as many entrances as they could.

"OSPREY," Henry muttered. They were retired, though it was from FBI counterintelligence, not Commerce. OSPREY was the source who had started them in on this case, who had led them to the ledger. It began as such a small thing, a favor, an unofficial investigation, and now this. At least they had hidden the ledger. It was safe.

"I didn't hear the car," Paulette said. "What about Rose?"

"It's quiet. She'll be okay."

"How can you be sure?"

"She's a survivor. They want the book. They want us. Though I never pictured this. In our own house." He let out a dark laugh. "Retired."

"We'll be fine. Remember Orlando?"

"Is that supposed to make me feel better?"

"We made it out. We always do."

Stones crunched outside—someone moving through the gravel.

She pressed her back against his.

The doorknob rattled.

A flash of white light filled the family room window, blinding them. Glass blew in and rained down on the oak floorboards and Persian rugs. Another shot came an instant later, as Paulette turned toward the window. She cried in pain and fell back, landing on her hip and elbow. Henry fired through the shattered window as cool night air rushed into the house. Another explosion of light. Another shot, and he doubled over.

The kitchen door slammed open with the sound of splintering wood, and then the front door blew in. Armed men rushed into the house while Henry leaned over, his left hand held to his abdomen and his right, unsteady, raising the gun. He wheeled on the first man through the front door, but as his aim fixed on the man's head, another came from behind him, seized his forearm, and stripped the gun from his hand.

He broke away and tried to move toward his wife, fallen in the shadows, silent. He couldn't see how badly she was hurt. "Paulette. Paulette, talk to me."

Before he could reach her, a man stepped in his path. Even in the faint light, Henry could have sworn he had seen him before—medium height, medium build, a haircut just like Henry's own, tapered and parted on the left. But the figure before him looked so generic, like any father he might see on the Metro or pushing a cart at Safeway, that Henry might have been mistaken.

"Get away from her," Henry said with an animal growl, and moved on him with a sudden ferocity despite the blood leaking through his hand. The man seized Henry's lead hand and bent it outward, wrenching the elbow as his other hand went to Henry's neck and drove him against the wall, choking off the cry of pain before it could escape his mouth.

A flashlight came on behind him, and one man ran upstairs while another searched the shelves.

A slick red stain grew on Henry's dress shirt, about five inches to the left of his navel. The man's face was so close to his he could feel his breath. His calm in the midst of this violence was more terrifying than any threat.

"Where is it?" the man asked.

He eased his grip on Henry's neck, but still Henry said nothing.

"The ledger. Where is it?"

"Who sent you?" Henry kept his voice even.

"I'm going to give you one more chance to tell me," the man said. "Or else I will kill her."

Henry shut his eyes, and his chin trembled. Paulette lay on the ground behind the attacker, now lit by the flashlight's blue-white glow. "She's already dead."

A voice called from the stairs in Russian, a language Henry understood well. "The girl is gone."

Anger took over the man's face, the first visible emotion he had shown. He glared at Henry, then looked to the door to the garage, and then out the rear window, to the lawn, a split-rail fence, and a stand of trees.

"Find the girl."

10

Rose reached through the broken pane in the front door, and a shard dug into the back of her hand. She hissed. A bead of blood grew from the cut as she reached farther and opened the dead bolt.

The house's alarm let out an electric whine as she stepped inside, and the security panel beside the door read: "Entry active—Disarm system." She ignored it and went straight for the cordless phone.

When she lifted it, she heard no dial tone. A sick feeling twisted her stomach. But then she pressed the talk button, and the tone sounded.

She began to dial the number from the note her uncle had given her, and then caught a shadow moving outside. She could see a figure striding toward the house, a gun held out in front of him.

Looking down at the phone, she realized she had lost her place. She hung up and punched in the numbers again as she ran through the unfamiliar house. The first hallway she tried dead-ended at a guest bathroom. She turned around and ran upstairs.

The front door creaked open. The phone, pressed to her

ear, rang and rang. She stepped into a room, a child's room, dropped into the closet, and shut the door.

A musty smell filled the small space. She sat back on the floor against the wall, her side pressed into a stack of sweatshirts. The hanging jackets and shirts brushed over her hair.

The phone pressed against her ear. A man's voice came on the other end of the line: "Go ahead."

Rose knew that making a sound might get her killed, but she needed to tell him, she needed to get help. She had promised them that.

"Hello?"

"Yes. Go ahead."

"Night action. They told me to tell you that. That you would know what to do. My name is Rose Larkin—" Two snaps broke the silence, muffled gunshots. "He's here. He's inside. He's going to kill me."

"I'm here," a calm voice answered. "My name is Peter. You're going to get through this, Rose."

11

Henry leaned against the wall, wincing with every breath, his hand clamped over the wound. Two shooters covered him.

The lead gunman—his deputy had called him Dimitri—stood over Paulette's body and listened to his radio.

He turned to one of the men. "They have the girl cornered in the house out back," Dimitri said in quiet Russian, a Urals accent, then pointed to the rear window. "Go."

The man left, and Dimitri faced Henry. "I know you can understand me," he said. "Just tell me where the ledger is, and we can leave her out of this."

Henry looked around the room and noticed one of the attackers wearing an earpiece that was hooked up to a small black box, a scanner. They were listening to the police frequencies. Those had been encrypted for years, which meant that these people had serious resources behind them.

"Who are you?" Henry asked.

"A soldier. Like you. I take no pleasure in this, but I will do what I must."

No masks, using names, openly speaking Russian: Henry knew they were going to kill him, but as he watched the man with the scanner, and saw his jaw clench as he listened,

Henry believed he had time on his side. Had someone heard the shots? Called the police?

The tech with the earpiece came up beside Dimitri and whispered something in his ear.

Dimitri lifted the pistol. The dead eye of the muzzle pointed straight at Henry.

"Last chance."

"No."

Dimitri glanced to Paulette's body for a moment, with something like sadness. That look, on the face of the man who had killed her, was an obscenity.

"It's better this way," Dimitri said. "To go with her. The rest is . . ."

He shook his head and pulled the trigger.

12

Rose clutched the phone to her ear. She knew about taking cover in spots like this, her heart pounding in her chest. Her mother had a type. The type you hide from when they get angry, red-faced with beer breath. But she hadn't felt fear like this in years, had forgotten the awful way it dried the throat until you felt like you were choking.

"I need help," she whispered into the handset. "My aunt and uncle gave me this number. I have a code."

She pulled the paper from the pocket of a hooded sweatshirt, but it was too dark to read. She thought of cracking the door slightly for light, but then heard the creak of footsteps below her. The stairs? She closed her eyes and remembered the scrawl on the page.

"Pen. Door . . . Fire. Wait. Clock. Pen. Door. F-fire . . . Jesus . . ."

"It's fine. Forget the code. What's happening?"

"It's 1765 Euclid Terrace. My aunt and uncle are there. There were shots fired. I'm in the house behind it. I had to get away. It's on Bancroft. I don't know the address, but there's only one house back here. My aunt and uncle told me to call this number. They are Henry and Paulette Campbell. They need help. Now. They told me to tell you that OSPREY was right. It's happening in six days, and they have the red ledger."

"What is happening?"

"I don't know. That's all they said."

"I'll send help. I need to talk to someone here—"

"Are you going?" She could hear the desperation in her own voice. She felt so small.

"No. I can reach another phone. I'm not going anywhere. We're going to keep you safe, all right? I am right here."

"Okay."

The line went quiet. In the silence, she could hear only her breath, coming far too fast now, and then the faintest sound: the stairs flexed, and then the boards in the hallway. Her breath caught as the gunman moved toward her. He was searching the house.

"They're here," she said, in the faintest voice. "I'm upstairs. I'm in a closet. Please."

"I'm here. I'm talking to the Secret Service."

The Secret Service? Rose thought. *What the hell is going on?*

She felt oddly cold, but still a drop of sweat ran along her spine.

The door to the room opened. She turned the volume down on the cordless until it could make no more noise than a whisper and sealed the speaker against her ear.

"Rose. Secret Service talked to the DC police. Someone heard the shots and called it in. The cars are on the way. They are coming around for you. Hold on."

She didn't dare make a noise.

"Rose? Rose? If you're still there just touch the microphone twice."

She ran her thumb over the two tiny plastic holes of the phone mic. Her hand was shaking.

"Okay," he whispered. "I'm here with you, Rose. It's going to be okay."

The footsteps moved closer, and she could hear the rustling of fabric. Was he checking under the bed? The man crossed the last few feet, stood just outside the closet. She could hear him breathing now, feel the floorboards flex under her as he shifted his weight from foot to foot.

What was he doing? Looking out the window? Waiting on orders? Listening to some unseen voice on an earpiece, just like she was? Or readying his gun?

She pictured Peter out there somewhere. Something about his voice, his calm, made her feel like she could trust him, even in the middle of all this.

All she needed was time. A few more seconds. She felt like her heart had seized in her chest. She kept picturing the door tearing open and a gunman standing over her.

She hugged her knees to her chest with her free hand and thought back to her uncle singing in the kitchen, that old Stevie Wonder song. She fixed on that, let the melody fill her mind and push back the fear.

Two steps. The floor flexed beneath her. The shadows shifted under the door. She clamped her eyes shut. The man moved closer, and the knob rattled softly as a hand closed around it.

13

Staring at that phone for 284 nights, waiting for this moment. The call was the highest priority, a night action. But Rose Larkin was no professional, carefully following a coded script. This was the desperate voice of someone about to die. She needed his help.

Peter was ready. As soon as the emergency line lit up, he pressed the button beside his phone, and a faint sound like moving water surrounded him. No one else in the Sit Room could hear him.

While Rose was on one phone, he reached across and pulled another handset from a surge desk, dragging it close to his own.

His first call went to the Secret Service. Their White House office was about forty feet from his on the ground floor. The line was eyes only to Hawkins and Farr, but there was a young woman and a killer out there, and his first move was to get law enforcement on the scene.

"Have you run this past—" the agent started to ask.

Forget protocol. Peter cut him off. "I have a national security employee's family in danger. I need cars at that address."

That did it. They raised the watch chief, who was on the phone with the DC police as soon as he disconnected from Peter, and also sent two Secret Service uniformed patrol officers scrambling from the Indonesian embassy to Rose's location.

Hawkins didn't answer, so Peter tried Farr. He held a phone to each ear, and looked like a madman, he knew, but he stayed calm as he raised the alarm.

All the while, he could hear Rose's breath coming and going.

The shooters were close. When he told her that the police were on the way, she couldn't even talk, only signal with faint scratches across the microphone of her handset.

He finally got through to Farr.

"Peter, what's going on?" She sounded like she had been sleeping.

"A night action call came in. I don't know exactly what's happening, but I think we have a family member in danger, shots fired. A woman named Rose Larkin called, said her aunt and uncle are Paulette and Henry Campbell. There's a shooter at her location, maybe multiple. I talked to Secret Service first, to get some cars over there ASAP."

"What did you tell them?"

"Employee in danger. No details. I don't know how much was compartmented."

"Good. I'm glad you got them moving. I'll be there in six minutes."

The line clicked off.

★ ★ ★

Peter waited, the phone to his ear while Rose hid in the dark and they closed in on her. He could barely hear her breath, but he could tell it was coming too fast: panic taking over.

"Rose. Are you okay? Hang on. Any moment now."

Another scratch, a rustle on the line. He stood.

"Rose?"

Sirens sounded over the phone, softly at first, so he almost thought he was imagining them, but then louder, distinct.

"Rose. That should be the police. Rose?"

No answer. He put his free hand to the wall.

"Rose." He wanted to shout, but that might give her away.

A quiet sob, then she spoke: "I think he's gone."

Peter clenched his fist. "Hold tight."

The door to the Situation Room opened and Diane Farr strode in, her eyes darting around the complex until she caught sight of Peter at his desk.

"Is that her?" she asked. Peter nodded and put his hand over the mouthpiece of the phone. "The police are there."

"In the house?"

"Not yet."

The Sit Room door slammed open, and Hawkins walked in a moment later, looking pissed. Farr met him and they talked briefly in the hall, leaving Peter to the call. He heard shouts over the line.

"What's happening?" he asked.

"They say that they're the police," Rose said.

Peter put his hand over the phone and called to Farr. "Are the police on the scene?"

She nodded.

"The police are there, Rose. They know where you are. Wait for them to come to you."

"Thank you," she said.

Farr held her hand out for the phone, and Peter leaned away slightly without even thinking, a protective instinct.

"Rose," he said into the handset. "I have someone here. She's the chief of staff for the White House. She knows what's happening. I'm going to hand the phone over to her now. Okay?"

"Wait . . . oh . . . okay. You'll be there?"

A hint of impatience crept into Hawkins's face as he stood on Peter's other side.

"Yes," Peter said.

"Okay." He held the phone out and as Farr took it, he could barely hear Rose's voice: "Goodbye."

Farr stepped away with the phone. "Okay . . . okay . . . good . . . they'll take care of you."

Hawkins put his hand on Peter's shoulder.

"You called the Secret Service first?"

"Yes. She was in danger."

Peter was ready for a reproach. His instructions were to connect that line straight to Farr and Hawkins.

"All right. What did she say?"

Peter repeated what he had heard, the names and references to the ledger, the six-day deadline, and OSPREY.

"Nothing else."

"That was it."

"Okay," Hawkins said. "We're here for the night. You can head out."

"Sir?"

"You know the only sir in the West Wing is the president, right?"

"I want to see this through."

"You did well, Peter."

There was a tone of dismissal to it. Hawkins looked at him intensely, as if this were some kind of test, of whether Peter knew his proper role.

Peter said nothing.

"Get a decent night's sleep for once. You look like you could use it."

He started to push back but checked himself. "I will."

Peter emailed the intelligence briefs he had assembled and logged out of his computer. He grabbed his bag and started walking toward the watch desks. Farr and Hawkins were both in the breakout room now, and he walked past them slowly, hoping for another sign of what was happening, but the door was closed.

He was two feet past it when he heard his name. He turned to see Farr.

"Nice work tonight, Peter. The police wouldn't have found her, or the second house, without you."

"What else can I do?"

"Go home. Get some rest. We'll be here all night anyway, and we'll need you tomorrow."

He hesitated for a moment, and she raised her eyebrows. Peter nodded and turned.

As he walked past the watch officers, Jessica called over. "What's up, man?" she asked. A night action to the chief of staff: even for the Situation Room, that qualified as an interesting shift.

54

"You know how it goes," Peter said. They dealt with need-to-know information all the time.

"Of course."

He saw the others looking. They wanted to know what Peter did back there by that phone, why he had access to the top. So did he.

14

Rose gripped the handset as heavy footfalls shook the house.

"Police! Rose!"

They ran into the room. "The house is clear. You can come out!"

"They say they are the police."

"They are, Rose," said the woman on the other end of the line. She said her name was Diane Farr, and she had spent their short time on the phone together with Rose on hold or speaking in clipped tones to someone else in the room.

Rose reached for the knob and opened the door. The light blinded her. She took two awkward steps, stiff from being balled up in that closet. Three cops moved through the room, kitted out in black, guns drawn.

"They're here," she said, but there was no one on the other end of the phone. An instant later, a man's voice came on. "My name is Hawkins. I'm with the FBI. I'll be there in ten minutes. Rose, I know this is hard, and you have a lot of questions. But can I ask you a favor? It's for your safety. Don't mention anything your aunt and uncle told you to anyone but me. Okay?"

"But why? What is happening?"

"I'll explain it when I get there, but for now, don't say a word. It's not safe."

The call disconnected.

She squinted against the glare of the lights. One officer reached his hand out to steady her. She thanked him, thanked them all, while tears of relief ran down her cheeks.

They went downstairs. She didn't like the way they were treating her, talking to her like a child. All she wanted was answers, and a moment to breathe, to think. Her hands wouldn't stop trembling. Christ, she looked like a scared kid. She stuffed her hands into her pockets.

They brought her out the back, with the Rubinos' house blocking her view down the hill to her aunt and uncle's home. Suddenly she realized why. They didn't want her to see what was happening down there.

She pulled away from them and crossed the lawn until she could make out the carnival of lights in front of that house.

"Rose, listen," the man in the suit said. He had identified himself as Secret Service, but she couldn't remember his name now. "You're hurt and you're in shock. Your hand. We need to get you checked out."

Dried blood flaked off the cut from the windowpane, but she ignored him. There were two ambulances parked in front of the house. Why call for ambulances? Why would they come and not rush off? Was it because there was nothing to be done?

"They're dead, aren't they?"

"Rose, now is not the—"

"Just tell me the truth."

15

Peter walked past a Metro entrance. It was closed for the night. That was fine. He avoided subways as much as he could. He had been on a train that derailed a year ago, an awful accident that he escaped with minor injuries, though many others died. The Metro still set him on edge, still tightened up the muscles in his neck whenever he descended its tunnels.

He took the S4 bus up Sixteenth Street. Even in the early morning it was crowded. It ran only every half hour and was one of the few options for people like him who haunted the empty downtown on the late shift—janitors and security guards and the occasional bleary-eyed young staffer crunching to please the boss.

By the time he reached his apartment, it was two A.M. There was no chance of sleep. He was wired. Ten months on the night watch had turned him into a nocturnal animal.

They had sent him home. He knew the rules, knew he should stay away, but something out there in the dark was calling to him.

He stopped at the front door to his apartment building, keys in hand, then turned around and started walking.

His car was parked around the corner. Just a drive, he

told himself, some fresh air while rolling through the pitch-black reaches of Rock Creek Park or the George Washington Parkway. He loved driving through DC at night, cruising the empty streets around the monuments and storied buildings, like it was all abandoned, a city under glass.

But as he rolled down Columbia Road, with the last of the partygoers stumbling home like wraiths, he found himself turning toward the house on Bancroft Avenue like a compass needle drawn to north.

16

The police had closed off the block, so Peter parked around the corner and walked. It had been more than an hour since the gunshots, and the cops must have had time to disperse any neighbors who were bold enough to go beyond looking out their windows and actually approach the crime scene.

There were still DC police and Secret Service cars parked down the hill at the aunt and uncle's house, though they weren't running any emergency lights. The scene was cold.

He edged past the yellow tape on a sidewalk and scanned the two houses, replaying the conversation in his head, picturing it unfolding: the attack on the house down the hill, the escape up here, the room-by-room clearing while Rose was trapped in that closet.

He moved closer. In the driveway of the aunt and uncle's house, near the open back of an ambulance, a young woman stood. She had auburn hair, swept behind her ear on one side, and wore a hooded sweatshirt and pajama bottoms. A bandage circled her right hand. Hawkins stood beside her, half his face lit by the interior lights of the ambulance. She was facing him squarely, and even from here, Peter could read her body language: standing tall, sharp and engaged. Peter assumed that was her, Rose Larkin.

A flashlight beam slashed through the woods and fixed on Peter. He stayed calm, though he could see nothing but the light's glare as someone crunched through the trees toward him.

"Hey. Need you to back up. You can't be here."

It was a cop's voice, and as the officer edged into the circle of light from the streetlamp, Peter saw that she was with the DC police, the Metropolitan Police Department or MPD for short, here to post security.

"Sure," he said. He thought for a moment of badging her, but that would have been an abuse of his credentials. He wasn't supposed to be here, and the whole story—FBI, White House, night watch—would raise more questions than he felt like getting into at two thirty A.M.

He started to turn away.

"Hang on," she said, and there was an edge of suspicion to her voice. "You live around here?" In his suit, he wasn't dressed like a curious neighbor, like someone taking a whining dog out in the middle of the night.

"No."

"Let's see some ID."

"Listen . . ."

"ID." Now the politeness was gone. The light was back in his eyes, and someone else was walking toward them. It made sense they would be suspicious of anyone surveying the scene.

"I'm reaching for my wallet," he said.

The newcomer circled to the side, into the light. It was Diane Farr.

"It's okay, Officer Vazquez. He's with me."

She held on for a second, glancing back and forth from Peter to Farr.

"It's fine," Farr said. The cop nodded and walked toward the crime scene.

"Peter." Farr shook her head slightly. "What are you doing here?"

"I couldn't sleep. What can I do to help?"

She didn't answer, just appraised him for a moment. "You miss the street work? The action?"

"I do."

"I get it. We've had you down there a long time. You want to know what happened?"

She wasn't volunteering information; she was asking him if he was curious, if he was sticking his nose in. His father had sold secrets, or so the allegations went. This was dangerous ground.

"I don't need to know anything."

"Did you say anything to Vazquez?"

"Of course not."

"Good." Her face was pale and she looked out into the dark, focusing on nothing, clearly still trying to process this. "The aunt and uncle are dead. Rose Larkin is okay. Shaken up, of course, but considering what she went through . . . she's tough. She'll be all right."

Peter stared at the house. "She didn't see the bodies?"

"No. Separate locations. You were on the phone with her the whole time she was hiding?"

"I was."

"It makes sense, why you would feel so close to this. But there's a reason we lock down information. The wider a secret goes out, the more dangerous it gets for the people at the center of it." She looked down to the house where two people had just died. Case in point.

"I wish I could tell you more, Peter. You did good work tonight. You should be proud."

He knew better than anyone how secrets could take lives. But still, the questions pressed in. What could be such a high priority that the chief of staff would come out here in the middle of the night? What was that emergency line for? Why were people dying? He held them back, only asked one thing: "What happens to her?"

Farr smiled. "That's why you're good at your job, Peter. You care. We're going to put her up at a hotel, have an agent keep an eye out. She'll be safe. You don't have to worry about that."

"I appreciate it."

"Sure. I'll see you at the office tomorrow." She glanced at her watch. "Or today, whatever the fuck it is. And Peter, everything you heard on that call . . ."

"Eyes only," he said.

"Keep your head down and leave this to us. Be careful, Peter. It's not fair, but you can't afford to make mistakes."

Peter started toward his car, and after fifty feet, he turned. Rose was down there, still talking to Hawkins, but something had changed: now they were arguing. Rose threw her hands back. She looked like she was under threat. Peter stood there with closed fists, thinking of Farr's last words, the warning. He watched as the conversation seemed to calm down, and then he walked away.

17

Down the hill, Rose stared at the front door to her aunt and uncle's house as two EMTs emerged, carrying a stretcher. Hawkins tried to stand between her and the house, but she pushed past him. He reached for her shoulder, but she knocked his hand away.

"Rose, you don't need to see that."

There was a sheet over the stretcher, covering the still form underneath.

"We have people you can talk to. This is going to be hard."

She expected grief or some overwhelming sadness, but felt only a steely calm, a numbness that filled her like a chill. If this was shock, it was welcome. She felt like she was watching the whole scene in a movie, and there was no fear.

"Have you caught whoever did this?" she asked Hawkins.

"There will be time for explanations later."

"I want them now. My aunt and uncle, who were they really? Did they work for you?"

"I can't talk about it. I wish I could, but it would only put you in danger."

She laughed, something bitter in the back of her throat, and looked up the hill. "God forbid. Aren't I already?"

He didn't answer.

"Why did they die?" she asked. "OSPREY? The red ledger? What is all this?"

At that, Hawkins stiffened, and stepped closer to her. He was an imposing presence, and something about the way he held himself—leaning into her space, shoulders rolled forward—reawakened a hint of fear in Rose, but she didn't let it show.

"Please explain it to me. I don't want to have to go to someone else."

It was a threat, a hint of hardball. He took a deep breath and relaxed, rubbing his forehead with his thumb and index finger like a parent trying to deal with a tantrum.

"You have no idea how dangerous that is," he said, his voice cold. He stared at her, then softened slightly. "They died to keep you safe. To keep *all* of us safe. That may sound like corny bullshit to you, but it's true. They did dangerous work, gladly, and without a shred of recognition. And all these people"—he pointed to the darkened houses on the block, the families sleeping inside—"are safer for the sacrifices they made, the secrets they kept."

The ambulance doors closed. Rose didn't know what to say. The adrenaline was beginning to burn off like a morning fog. She felt shaky again, sick, exhausted. He was right. She had no idea what had just happened, no idea what she was in the middle of.

"If it was so dangerous, why would they tell me?"

"Because they trusted you. They knew you could handle this. You could do the right thing." He looked back at the house she had just escaped and to the bandage on her hand. "And they were right."

18

Peter arrived at the funeral for Henry and Paulette Campbell a few minutes before noon, slipping through the doors of Holy Trinity Church in Georgetown. It was three days after the call.

The pews were full. He found a spot in the back, on a bench against the wall. He caught sight of Hawkins, in a black suit like he wore most days at work.

Farr had warned Peter to be careful about this case, and he had been wary about coming today, being seen as meddling or overly curious.

He recognized many faces. Some had eyed him as he came in. The church was full of the old Washington FBI hands who had known his father.

Everyone rose for the opening prayer, and the words came automatically. The incense and candles and echoing voices brought him back to middle school, to that dark last year of his father's life, when his dad started going to Mass every Sunday—which was often for him—then Wednesdays, too, and finally every morning.

It was a surge of faith, from a man who most suspected of betraying everything he believed in.

Peter tried to keep the memories from taking hold of him, from reliving those days.

The scandal happened long enough ago that he had wrung much of the pain from it. Most of the time, when he thought about it, he could handle the facts of the case coldly, clinically.

His dad had been a section chief in FBI counter-intelligence. During his tenure, the Russians had turned one of his agents and picked up the crown jewels: the names of the Russian embassy staff in the US who were secretly sharing information with the FBI. It was a catastrophic breach.

The seven Russians who were working for the US were brought back to Moscow with their families. The Kremlin and SVR—the Russian foreign intelligence service—made a variety of excuses to get them on the planes: commendations, reports of sick family back home. Most were brought to Butyrka Prison and executed in basement cells.

Suspicions circled that Peter's father had played a part in the leaks, that he had been compromised by the Russians as well, but they were never proven. The scandal broke in February. By November his dad was dead. He'd always been a gregarious drinker—cocktails on the boat or wine at dinner, staying up late telling stories with family and work colleagues—but the stress of the investigation, or of his guilt, changed his habit into something far darker. And one November night, he drove eighty miles an hour into a highway divider on the Beltway, Exit 57.

He'd been drinking, but he was always drinking then. Was it an accident? Or did he point the car straight at that barrier? There was never a clear answer. And his guilt was never proven, never disproven. The truth died with him.

Peter never could believe the accusations, not against the father who had taught him his whole life to look out for other people. It was strange, how Peter inherited the suspicions, the presumed guilt, along with his father's name, as if it ran in the blood.

They had a funeral for his dad, but he never really was laid to rest, not with all those doubts still in the air. Peter had always hoped that his father was innocent, a bystander caught up in some larger crime.

It was a long time ago, but there were moments, like now, when the past would come at him so vividly, a stab of pain. It was like stepping on a tiny piece of glass a month after you thought you'd swept up all the shards.

He would remember his father's funeral, the scent of wood oil and flowers. He never got over it, how empty that church was, how the priest's voice echoed off the unfilled pews.

He would see the faces of the American sources, the embassy staffers who were executed. He would picture their children. He'd gone to elementary school with one of them. After the Russians rounded up their parents, the children were sent to homes, little more than prisons, in the Russian Far East, pariahs for life.

He would be thirteen years old again, at the kitchen table before school, careful to not scrape his fork, not to make a sound as his father read the morning paper in silence, his eyes red, the recycling full of empty bottles. Peter could barely recognize the father he knew, the man who went through the crossword with him every Sunday and was never too tired to shoot a few baskets after work.

As the Campbells' funeral mass went on, Peter's eyes drifted to the wooden screens of the confessional at the side of the church.

He remembered standing beside booths like those every week near the end, waiting for his father to finish with the priest. The questions consumed Peter then. They still burned now: *What did you do, Dad? What did you have to confess?*

The front row of mourners began to file out, and Peter stood quietly at attention through the recessional, as Rose Larkin walked by in a simple black dress. She moved with confidence through the middle of what was surely an intimidating crowd of strangers: bureau division heads, special agents in charge, justice officials.

Peter could tell she'd been crying, but there was still a brightness to her eyes as she looked in his direction. It was impossible—they had only spoken over the phone—but he thought for a moment that she had recognized him.

19

Peter filed out the door after Mass, then turned and walked toward the Potomac, past the pockets of mourners and agents talking in small circles outside.

He was fifty yards down from the church when someone grabbed his shoulder.

"Sutherland, I thought that was you."

He turned to find a friend of his from training at Quantico, standing a little too close. Vito had always had a weird measure of personal space.

"Wild, right?" Vito said and looked toward the church. "Did you hear anything about what went down?"

Peter shook his head.

"I heard the Campbells were CI-4, retired."

Counterintelligence, squad 4. It was a legendary crew, spy hunters working against the Russians on US soil. The elite.

Peter's mouth felt dry, but he hid any reaction from Vito. His father had overseen counterintelligence, and counterintelligence in turn had run the investigation into the leaks that had happened on his watch, had driven all the suspicions that he was a traitor.

Was it another Russian operation? Killing our people on

US soil? The muscles in his back tightened up and he took a deep breath in. It was anger driving him forward. Whether his father was innocent or not, it was ultimately a Russian intelligence operation that had brought him down, and Peter would give anything to hit back at them.

"Who told you that?" Peter asked.

"Overheard some guys at the Washington Field Office. I didn't even know the FBI had people undercover like that," he said. "I heard they came over from the CIA. Maybe it was some old score settling."

"Did you hear anything else?"

"No. You didn't pick up any info from the White House folks?"

Peter wasn't going to give up anything to Vito, especially not here.

Peter just cocked his head and gave him a *come on, brother* look.

"Who am I going to tell?" Vito asked.

"You just told me something, and I haven't seen you in six months."

"Come on, man."

"Not happening."

Vito shook his head and muttered, "Boy Scout."

The burial was at Oak Hill Cemetery, a beautiful stretch of woods on the other side of Georgetown, on a hillside above Rock Creek.

He didn't want to draw attention to himself, so as the last mourners streamed through the gates, he crossed the street and stood under a bare tree in Montrose Park. It was uphill from the cemetery, and he could see the burial through the crypts.

Rose stood in a place of honor beside the graves, but slightly apart from the other mourners. She stood still, in silence—stoic or in shock—for the entire ceremony, until the time came and she reached into the fresh earth and scattered some on the caskets.

A man with bagpipes strode out from behind the chapel, and Peter turned and started down the street. Bagpipes always wrecked him. They'd played them at his dad's funeral, and he didn't particularly feel like choking up in the middle of a Georgetown park.

He crossed the street as the piper started up, the opening bars of "Amazing Grace."

He proceeded slowly, letting the music fade as the graveyard disappeared from view behind the white brick buildings. He took a wandering route to his car. It was a blustery day, but there wasn't a cloud in the sky.

Still on edge, he checked the sidewalk behind him at every corner and in every window's reflection.

At Thirty-First Street, he picked up on the sound of someone walking close behind him, following. He stopped fast and heard the double scuffing noise as the pursuer stopped short.

"Peter?" A woman's voice came from behind him. He turned.

It was Rose.

20

Peter's eyes narrowed slightly. She was breathing fast. She must have moved quickly to catch up with him.

"I heard you, after the mass," she said. "I recognized your voice. Was that you on the phone? The night . . ." She nodded toward the church.

"Yes," he said. "I'm so sorry about your aunt and uncle."

"Thank you."

Such an empty phrase, a rote exchange after the intensity of what had happened on the phone, but the only words he could find were that worn-out funeral script.

"Are you all right?" he asked.

"I'm managing." She looked down for a moment, then fixed her eyes on his.

"Can you tell me why they died?"

Peter pressed his lips into a flat line, glanced up and down the street. He recognized a few bureau people. He stepped closer to her and lowered his voice. "I don't know." It was the truth.

She shook her head, and a glimmer of anger showed. Peter had a feeling that a lot of people had been telling her "I don't know" that morning.

"Night action," she said. "The red ledger. Pen. Clock. Door. Fire."

He put his hand on her upper arm. "I know this all must be strange to you, Rose, but you have to be careful about talking about it in the open. It can get people hurt."

"I'm the last person you have to tell that to. I need to know what's going on. I'm tired of people lying to my face."

"I'm not lying," Peter said. That charge, in particular, bothered him. "I don't know. I answer the phone and get it to the right people. I only wanted to make sure you're okay."

"Okay? No. My aunt and uncle were executed, and I was nearly killed, and now I'm under guard and no one will do me the decency of telling me what the fuck is going on." She checked herself, then went on, calmer now. "They gave me your number. You must know something."

"In the grand scheme, I'm nobody."

"Then why are you here?"

"To pay my respects."

"What were they doing?" She held her hands out to the side, a plea. "What did you have them doing that got them killed?"

He didn't answer. She stepped back and evaluated him. Her eyes seemed to work as slowly and surely as a polygraph.

"And if you did know?"

"I wouldn't tell you." It wasn't an easy answer, but it was the truth, and Peter hated deceit.

"Why?"

"Because there are rules about it. And when they are broken . . ." He looked to the church. All he wanted was to help her, to reassure her, to find out who did this. But that was a dangerous impulse, stepping out of line, taking matters into his own hands.

She moved her head slightly, back and forth, eyes fixed on him, as if weighing a choice. She sighed in resignation, as if accepting it, then looked over her shoulder.

"You should go," Peter said. "Isn't there usually . . ."

"A repast. Yes."

"Maybe someone there, someone who knew them, can tell you more."

"They're all strangers. No one will talk to me. They just need me here to stand beside the coffins, dip my head and say thank you."

"You don't live here?"

"No. I was staying with them." Her face fell.

Alone at a funeral. She was breaking his heart, and he wanted to console her, to do anything to soften the blow. But he couldn't let emotion cloud his judgment. Because she was sharp. She hadn't been able to break down his front door, so now she was slipping in through the window, playing on his sympathy. Maybe she was trying to draw him out more slowly.

He hated that suspicion, but he had to be careful. Maybe she was just scared and alone. He took out one of his cards and offered it to her.

"I can't talk about work, or what's happening, but if you ever don't feel safe, call me. I'll get it to the right people. I'll do everything I can."

She took it.

"Peter Sutherland," she said and tapped his title. "Nobody."

21

Dimitri picked his way through the ivy and fallen gravestones, inspecting the dates of birth and death and the Daughters of the American Revolution plaques. To all appearances, he was a widower or genealogy buff, or just a man approaching the far end of middle age and taking some time among the dead.

The gun rode on his hip, so familiar it felt like part of his body. It was invisible under his jacket. He had sewed in thick fabric on the lining near the holster. The added heft kept the weapon from imprinting, revealing itself to trained watchers, and let the coat swing back with more inertia for a smooth draw.

He had waited until after the funeral to enter the cemetery, knowing that security would be tight. Only the most observant watcher would have noticed Dimitri's eyes, glancing past the headstones and the fences and the locust trees, to fix on Rose. She cut away from the rest of the mourners, and Dimitri followed at a distance.

He strolled down the overgrown walkway and turned left on the sidewalk. She was moving quickly now, almost chasing someone, and he tracked her from the other side of the street.

She called out to a man, and they began to talk. Dimitri recognized him. It was Peter Sutherland. Dimitri's pulse picked up, but he showed no outward reaction.

He had seen Peter once before, on the night of the killings, loitering near the crime scene. Finding out Peter's identity hadn't been difficult. Dimitri had good sources.

He walked past them without breaking stride. His car was parked half a block down, on their side of the street. He crossed to it, giving them plenty of space, and then sat inside. It was a late-model Accord, with Lyft and Uber stickers on the windshield.

The taxi cover was a good one for surveillance—sitting in cars, double-parking, cruising at all hours of the night—but he had never been able to get away with it in Washington, even with its motley collection of independent cabs in the days when DC was on the zone system, not meters. The drivers were all Ethiopian or Eritrean back then, and he would have stuck out. But now it was easy enough. There's nothing strange about a bland-looking white man sitting in his ride-share car fumbling for directions while trying to make a little money on the side.

Dimitri read the conversation in their body language: far apart—wary at the beginning—then closer. He remembered the long-ago days when he believed he might be able to change someone's mind with an argument, might be able to change someone at all.

Peter handed Rose something, and she stepped away. Henry and Paulette Campbell had trusted Rose, spent their last living hours with her, and she had talked to Sutherland on the emergency line. How much did she know? And what did she pass on?

They seemed to be working together now. It confirmed his concern, and in his mind he moved both of them from bystander to threat. The bureau had Rose staying at a hotel in Dupont Circle, but her security wouldn't be an issue. It was little more than an occasional drive-by from a patrol car.

They seemed like nice kids. It really was a shame. But in the larger scheme two lives were a small price. A secret had come to them unbidden, like a virus, and like a virus it was indifferent to their fates.

They both knew about the red ledger, a handwritten record, evidence of a crime that dwarfed a murder or two. It was the sort of thing that can start a war.

The stakes. You had to keep them in mind when you had a gun in a crying girl's face. At least he had to at the beginning of his career. Now he didn't even bother with the rationale. Work was work.

He lifted the encrypted phone to his ear and called his source.

"BEECH?"

"Yes. Go ahead."

"I just finished watching Rose Larkin rendezvous with Peter Sutherland outside the burial."

"Are you sure?"

That wasn't even worth a response. "We need to draw a circle around this before it spreads," he said.

Henry and Paulette Campbell had the ledger. They had found witnesses. And now Dimitri had to find everyone who knew about that book, everyone who had worked with the Campbells, and silence them. No one could learn the truth about the Metro crash. Peter Sutherland had been on the train that derailed and had survived. Those deaths were just the beginning.

Dimitri needed to keep the secret for three more days, and then everything they had worked for, all the killing would finally pay off.

"I can handle it," BEECH replied.

"We can't take the risk."

"I have it under control."

Dimitri's eyes flicked back and forth between Peter and Rose as they walked away from each other. He and BEECH were on the same side of this affair, for now. They both wanted that information destroyed. But that didn't mean they trusted each other. The book was too powerful. No one could be trusted with it.

"We have to find out what she knows," BEECH went on, "and who else she might have told. More bodies are only going to make our job harder, bring scrutiny."

It was a fair point, though that sort of thing had never stopped Dimitri before. The gun ached against his hip like a restless limb. He glanced at Peter through the windshield and at Rose walking away in the side-view mirror.

"You have one day to find out what they know," he said. "Unless I see them together again."

"Hold on."

"One day. Then I move." Dimitri ended the call. He didn't like the tone he was getting from BEECH, the imperative voice.

Dimitri pocketed the phone and looked from Rose to Peter and back. Which one should he follow?

He knew about Peter: bright, ambitious, scrupulous about orders. He shouldn't be a problem if he stayed out of this, kept his head down as usual. But Dimitri grew uneasy as he watched him move along the sidewalk. The young man was curious, asking questions, crossing lines.

Dimitri waited for him to pass the intersection one block down and then began the pursuit.

22

The sun set over Foggy Bottom. Peter should have been at home, sleeping, getting ready for his overnight shift, but instead he was strolling through the trees alongside the South Lawn of the White House.

He had just changed into his workout clothes in the old pool house that stood in for a locker room when they played basketball on the outdoor court.

Peter glimpsed the columns of the executive mansion over the tops of the maples, and as he came around the corner, he saw President Travers walking by the hoop, a ball under his arm. This was his game.

Peter took a deep breath and stepped onto the court. Travers shot the ball to him with a hard chest pass and a smile. He was a creature of routine and played every Thursday and Saturday night if his schedule permitted.

Peter still hadn't gotten used to the oddness of playing ball with POTUS. He remembered his first game. One of the president's personal aides—a guy named Perry who had played for North Carolina and served as Travers's body man during the campaign—invited him the day before.

That night Peter spent twelve hours sitting, staring at that phone, trying to figure out exactly how you play ball with the leader of the free world. Word got around the Sit Room somehow. Jessica warned him not to take it easy on POTUS. "I heard he hates that," and the CIA watch officer, hearing that, raised his eyebrows and made a doubtful face.

It's hard to overestimate how intimidating the man and the place were. Peter was no big star in college, but he had played in the NCAA quarterfinals with eight million people watching on TV and twenty thousand in the stands. He was used to pressure, but the first time he walked through the entrance of the West Wing, he found his heart racing. That was a game. *This* was the big show.

Travers seemed to love these evenings, a chance to cut through the layers of bureaucracy that cocooned him as the head of a four-hundred-thousand-person enterprise, to drop his guard with some of the younger staffers.

He had been a walk-on guard at Indiana University, and he was still good, still worked out for an hour every night.

The president had spent most of his twenties doing missionary work in Central America: no TV, too dangerous to leave the compound, so they would just play basketball eight hours a day.

His habit of getting together pickup games at the White House and on the campaign trail fit in with his Hoosier-farm-boy-made-good image. Travers's father had started a string of outdoor retailers in the Midwest, and Travers and his brothers had expanded them into a holding company that turned around businesses—unglamorous Middle American manufacturers and industrial firms. He had quietly established himself as a financial sage, a low-profile Warren Buffett.

A consistent political donor, he had done a brief turn as US Trade Representative, where he hammered out a US-China trade pact that won him a lot of respect inside the Beltway. He had essentially been drafted to run for president, an outsider candidate without a lot of partisan baggage who would have a broad appeal in the general election.

No one thought Travers would survive the primaries, but sharp, understated performances at the debates brought him to the head of the pack of contenders that spent most of their time trying to shiv each other.

He won the nomination. The election was a wide-open race on both sides to replace a two-term president from the other party. His opponent was a former secretary of Homeland Security, a no-bullshit Oklahoman named Anne Gibson.

As the general election approached, a series of financial scandals hurt her team, and Travers's plainspoken propriety cinched the presidency.

Diane Farr, who ultimately became his chief of staff, was the first party stalwart to see his appeal and rally the rest of her camp around him. She, too, had an independent streak and had cycled between posts in politics, mostly behind-the-scenes work and general counsel posts for major American multinationals. She emerged as a key advisor, navigating deftly to guarantee Travers some independence from the party and Hill lifers while still maintaining their support. It was natural that he chose her as chief of staff—selfless, lived for the job, an honest broker who could keep everyone happy and all the trains running on time.

Peter liked watching them work together, perfectly in

sync, yet still keeping a bit of the shtick where Travers was the country boy and Farr the foul-mouthed boardroom bruiser.

On the court in that first game, Peter started out easy, taking his time to get a read on just how hard they were playing. He ended up covering Travers. The guy was relentless, physical, driving, never stopping to talk or catch a breath. That made it pretty clear that he wanted a real game, and Peter gave it to him.

Most power forwards were six foot eight or more, but Peter made up for his relatively small size in Division I by being ferocious near the net. That's how he got the nickname Bear.

After two years at the end of the bench, Peter had been put into a key game, the coach calling his name in desperation after four other players had been ejected. In the final minutes, he hit one clutch shot after another, surprising everyone, himself included. Two days later he had earned a spot as a starter.

Basketball had always been a release for him, a place where he could let his guard down. People barely recognized him on the court.

He went hard in his first game with Travers. The familiar terrain and the sheer straightforwardness of it—doing something he was good at, out in the fresh air—made Peter forget himself, forget the hollowed-out feeling from the graveyard shift, forget being careful. He moved through the key, and the president set a hard pick, but as Peter rolled to one side, Travers lunged to cover him. Peter's elbow caught POTUS in the lip, and he went down. It was Travers's fault, but for a second it felt like there was no oxygen in the atmosphere. The Secret Service moved in on the court, and Peter wondered if he was going to jail.

He held his hand out to Travers, who pressed the back of his hand to his lip and came away with a dab of blood.

"I'm good," Travers said, calling off the Secret Service agents. Peter helped him to his feet. "I'm glad they didn't shoot you," the president said, beaming, clapped him on the back, and offered him the ball.

The deal with that kind of proximity, of course, was that you were an outlet, a way for the president to feel connected to the staff on a personal level and to put politics aside for a moment. A lot of young Washington strivers couldn't see that. They got near the commander in chief, and once they pulled their heart out of their trachea enough to talk, their ambition got in the way.

Once, while warming up, a Senate staffer had started in on something about FAA regulations and noise complaints in a home district. The whole crew went silent, almost wincing at the kid's misstep.

"Why don't we play ball?" the president said. That may not sound like much, but getting even a shade of disappointment from POTUS was devastating.

Peter never saw that kid on the court again.

Tonight, despite the lack of sleep, Peter found his rhythm by the fourth point, looking for holes in the defense, left, then back right, faking a drive and then dropping back with a fadeaway jumper just outside the paint. It arced high, past the White House facade in the background and came down with a whisper, touching only net.

The call, the killings, the funeral: it had dredged up a lot from Peter's past. But now, with the cool air burning nicely in his lungs, he was glad for the game. The court had always been a place where he could lose himself.

On the next point, the president boxed Peter out, then pivoted left and bounce passed the basketball to Perry. Perry pushed through two defenders and sank an easy layup.

Peter got the ball, rolled left, and found, where there hadn't seemed to be one, a clear line to the basket. He accelerated, so quickly it looked like he was shot out of a cannon, and was four feet from the hoop when the president came around the point guard, sprinting to defend Peter. Peter jumped and finger rolled the ball into the net.

He wanted to dunk. He could have dunked. Dunking has been one of his favorite things in the world, ever since he was fifteen and saw *White Men Can't Jump* and then spent the entire summer practicing until he had it down.

But you don't dunk on POTUS.

The president eyed the shot, and maybe he knew what Peter was thinking.

"Nice," Travers said, with a sly smile.

23

After he showered and changed, Peter headed in for his shift. He walked straight down the West Wing hallway toward the Sit Room stairs, and past Diane Farr. She didn't seem to notice him as she strode by. She was flicking through her iPhone while somehow managing to have a conversation with an aide who was also staring at a phone. Peter was five feet beyond Farr when he heard her call out.

"Stick around here for a minute, Peter. Hawkins is looking for you. Did *not* seem happy." She shrugged and returned to her emails.

Peter checked his phone and saw the message from Hawkins, one line: "See me when you come in." He turned down the hall and walked toward Hawkins's office.

He was just outside the doorway when he heard the deep voice: "You went to the Campbells' house the night of the murders?"

Peter stopped. Hawkins was already in close, behind him. Peter expected to be ushered into the office, but apparently Hawkins decided this would be a good conversation for the hallway, a public dressing-down. He had a way of looking amused when he was angry, the kind of face that accompanies the phrase *you know you're a real piece of work*. He was wearing it now.

"Yes."

"And you were told to stay away from this."

"I was."

"Do you want to tell me why you were skulking outside the funeral this morning and harassing a woman whose aunt and uncle were just killed, a woman you were expressly warned to stay away from?"

"I went to the funeral to pay my respects. She recognized me . . . my voice. She approached me."

"And what did you tell her?"

"Nothing. And I told her there was nothing I could tell her. And she more or less told me to go to hell."

"What did the girl tell you?"

"Nothing."

"People saw you talking. You can't sneak around two hundred fucking FBI agents without getting noticed."

"She was upset that no one would tell her why her aunt and uncle died. She wanted to know what was going on. I didn't know and I said as much."

Hawkins's mouth drew tight. There was nothing worse, when you were about to lay into someone, than finding out you were wrong. Peter wondered if it would make any difference.

"Sit down there. Answer the phone. Go home. Get some sleep. That's it. Can you handle that? You are the last person on earth who should be acting shady. I don't even know how you got cleared to be here."

He shook his head and disappeared into his office. Peter glanced down the hallway, past the open doors and assistants' desks, where eavesdropping without letting on that you are listening is a fine art. At the far end of the hall, he saw Theo, the guy he had tangled with at the happy hour, beaming.

That was why he had to be so careful. Even the perception of mishandling classified information could destroy someone. He'd seen it with his dad.

Peter stalked back to the stairs and found Farr waiting for him.

"Did you talk to her?" she asked.

"Yes. But I did nothing wrong."

"Sometimes that doesn't matter."

Peter put his hand on the banister. "What am I in the middle of, Diane? What were the Campbells working on? Why is this all outside of the normal channels?"

"Peter—"

"The Campbells said whatever was happening would happen in six days. That's three days from now."

"I can't talk about that, Peter."

"Is Russia part of it?"

She lowered her voice to a stern whisper. "You know I took a risk with you. Don't make this personal. You, especially, need to be careful. That conversation may have been innocent, but that's how these things start, one foot over the line."

I'm not my father, Peter thought. But she was right. He had no idea what had started his father down the wrong path, how harmless it might have seemed at the beginning.

"You should get to work," she said.

24

Peter entered the Sit Room, cut right after the door, and made it to his desk without drawing the attention of the other officers on the watch. He pulled up his files. The sources scrolled by his screen. The phone sat in silence on his desk.

It was a long empty night on little sleep, and as much as he tried, he couldn't keep his head clear, couldn't stop thinking about that sideways accusation that he, like his father, couldn't be trusted.

It took him years to get hired by the FBI, and he could only manage a support role, as a surveillance specialist in the Boston Field Office. It was often a stepping-stone to becoming a special agent, but his colleagues told him not to bother, warned him that the senior people at the FBI would never trust him because of his dad, that he would be stuck in a support gig in Boston for the rest of his life.

They were right. He applied for special agent every time the window opened, twice a year, and every other job that might move him up. He had been up for an intelligence analyst spot in DC and made it to the second round, but the answer always came back no.

He loved the dark humor of the ex-cops and soldiers on

the surveillance crews in Boston, the pride in handling even the worst details. There were a lot of miserable nights, his back wrecked from fourteen hours crammed in a midsize car, peeing into Gatorade bottles, but he didn't mind the work. At least he wasn't behind a desk. He was out on the streets, looking for bad guys and protecting witnesses.

The others called him Giraffe and gave him shit endlessly. It was a good joke: a six six guy trying to be inconspicuous. One supervisor, who couldn't stand having Peter around, would send him to Chinatown on foot surveillance with helpful instructions: "Blend in." He was good: meticulous, disciplined, never complained. He learned to be invisible, to see without being seen, and lived up to the nickname people sometimes used for the special surveillance group: the ghosts.

Farr had taken a chance on him by bringing him to Washington. He first met her when he was a junior at Boston College. He ran a summer basketball camp for low-income high school kids. Farr was a BC trustee, and he had talked to her a handful of times at some of the community outreach events and photo ops.

That's why he was surprised when he got an email from Farr a few weeks after Travers was elected, asking him out to lunch in the North End while she was in town for a trustees meeting. They met at an Italian hole-in-the-wall, a place that made its own ricotta and served the best lasagna Peter had ever tasted, but the last spot you'd expect for a high-powered political meeting. Maybe that was the point.

She told him that an intelligence chief at the bureau had asked her about Peter after he applied for the analyst position and wanted to find out if she knew him from her time as a trustee. She recommended Peter for the job, but it went nowhere. When she asked why, she was told it was because he was Thomas Sutherland's kid.

"Do you have anyone looking out for you?" she asked Peter. "What do they call them at the bureau, a rabbi?"

She was talking about a mentor, someone with juice who paved your way. It meant picking sides, doing favors, sucking up, playing politics. Because of who his father was, Peter couldn't play the game like that, nor did he want to. Everyone was always looking for some sign of him being on the make, of bending the rules, some taint of his father's sins. Peter just put his head down and did everything by the book, worked twice as hard hoping that it would be enough.

"I don't," he said.

"Your father's friends? People you knew from growing up? There's no one you can ask for a favor?"

"I left a lot of that behind in DC."

She nodded, and he wondered if she was waiting for him to ask her for a boost, if this was some kind of test. It didn't matter. That's not how he did things.

"I looked over your file, Peter. Your background check, your work in Boston. I couldn't even find a sick day, a late arrival. Most people at least have a couple of youthful indiscretions, but this . . . it's . . . almost Mormon. It's the record of someone who spent his whole life trying to work for the bureau. It's perfect."

There were pieces missing from that record. He'd been a sixteen-year-old kid with no father, already six foot and one eighty, confused and resentful and shut out. He scrapped. The anger got the best of him sometimes. A chain-smoking basketball coach named Mr. Welsh saved him, channeled that ferocity into the game. The endless practice and predawn conditioning taught Peter discipline and control. He didn't know where he would've ended up without it. He didn't like to think about it.

He pushed back his chair and looked at Farr. He knew what was coming. With all that scrutiny on him because of his dad, he couldn't afford a single mistake. But when he played everything perfectly by the book, people assumed that it was some kind of cover, some way for him to worm his way back into the heart of the FBI like his father had, like a cancer. They'd never give him any real responsibility.

"Peter." She put her fork down. "The people at headquarters, they don't want you. You're going to have a hard time moving up."

He knew that. He'd heard the cracks when he was at Quantico for his training, seen the look on his interviewers' faces at headquarters every time he tried to climb a rung. The FBI is a family business; most special agents had a parent or close relative who worked there, too. It helped build trust, but family ties worked against him.

His fiancée would tell him the same thing, on those long-distance calls full of silences. He didn't blame her for it. They got together in college, track star and power forward, the perfect couple, and then he nuked his finance career to make forty-five grand a year as a G and at a moment's notice spend his nights and weekends in the saddest shitholes of New England.

Leah was good enough not to ask him why he was throwing himself against this brick wall, trying to make up for what his father had done, trying to work himself into a place where one day he'd be able to prove he was innocent. Or maybe he was getting revenge on the old man by taking down everyone who thought the rules didn't apply to him.

He didn't know. It could have been all three.

"You still want to try to make a career at the FBI?" Farr asked.

"I do."

"I read about what you did during the Metro crash."

Peter had helped the people on his car escape, forcing the emergency exit and guiding them out. The *Post* featured him prominently in an article about the crash, trying to find a positive note in the midst of an accident that killed twenty-one people. Peter could think only of the ones he couldn't save, trapped deep in the Metro tunnels. Their cries for help still haunted him.

"We need people like that," Farr said. "I'm going to be chief of staff now, and I'll have a lot of sway. I might have something opening up," she said. "It's nothing glamorous. What do you call them at the bureau—a night agent? We need phone coverage, graveyards and weekends."

Night agents held down the fort at local field offices while everyone else slept. Often for a first posting, the FBI would farm you out to the middle of nowhere, a place like Tulsa or Albuquerque, but that was part of the job. It would still be a step up.

"I'm interested," Peter said.

"We're trying to figure out where we would park you. It might be the Situation Room."

"The White House?" Peter asked.

"Yes. But you wouldn't be a full watch officer, more of a

backbench thing covering phones and open-source intel as needed."

She was almost apologetic. Peter couldn't believe it. He'd been trying to prove himself for years, to earn that kind of trust.

"I stay with the bureau?"

"If you want. We can detail you over to the West Wing. It would be night action calls to me or James Hawkins, the senior advisor."

"The FBI higher-ups would be all right with that?"

"It's in the White House; it's my call. I can make it work with the bureau. I understand if you need some time to think about it."

It was all he wanted, and still he hesitated. It meant going back to Washington, to where this all started, to the work that had destroyed his father. It meant being tested.

Peter rested his hands on the table. "When do I start?"

25

After his shift wrapped up early the next morning, Peter stepped through the southwest gate, squinting against the dawn light. He felt like a walking cadaver, working his way up Seventeenth Street, as all the fresh-from-bed West Wingers streamed by in the opposite direction.

He went home, still fuming about getting called out in the middle of the office. There was laundry to do and emails to send—his godfather had moved back to town and they'd been trying to get together for months—but as he stepped inside his door, all he could think about was sleep.

He lay down. The buses rattled by, and the fire trucks tore up the street, sirens blaring, but Peter drifted off before he'd even had a chance to put his earplugs in.

He slept like a dead man until two P.M., when his cell phone started rattling on the nightstand.

He didn't recognize the number: 310 area code. Los Angeles, he thought, or maybe Orange County.

"Hello?"

No answer.

He squinted at the screen, his eyes still heavy with sleep.

"1 missed call."

He put the phone down and swung his feet over the side of the bed. It rattled again, a short buzz.

"1 voicemail."

He held it to his ear.

"Peter. Hi. This is Rose, from yesterday. I wanted to thank you for the other night. I should have before. And listen . . . could you call me when you get this? I'm probably crazy, but there were supposed to be people here watching out for me, and they're gone, and I think I've seen someone hanging around outside. Okay . . . bye."

He sat on the edge of the bed, holding the phone in front of him. The orders were clear enough. Leave it alone. He'd been warned, for his own sake, not to take matters into his own hands.

But something wasn't right, and she needed help. He remembered watching Hawkins argue with her, the night the Campbells died. He looked so angry. Peter didn't know what was happening, but he couldn't stand to do nothing. Before he had time to second-guess himself, he hit dial and pressed the phone to his ear as it rang.

26

Peter stepped into the lobby of Rose's hotel. It was a flatiron building just north of Dupont Circle, and the last time Peter had been there it had been a dingy place, with an Irish pub occupying the prime views on the circle.

Now it was passing itself off as some kind of Euro lounge. There were lots of guys in suits, but none sporting an obvious law-enforcement haircut or build or bearing.

He walked faster. There should have been protective surveillance up on Rose. When he called her back, she told him there was no one. Her guard was gone.

The elevator opened on the third floor, and Peter stepped out and found room 304. He tapped his knuckles on the door three times. Footsteps shuffled inside, and the peephole went dark. He waited. The door opened a crack.

"Thanks for coming," Rose said. She was wearing a hooded sweatshirt, her hair held back loosely at her neck.

"Of course."

"Did you see anyone down there?"

"No. If you're worried about your safety, I'll help you get in touch with whoever is handling the investigation."

Peter had encouraged her to do the same thing on the phone, but she wouldn't go for it.

"I don't want to talk to them. And I . . . I didn't feel like being by myself anymore." She pursed her lips, as if that had come out wrong, too unguarded. She might have been used to men reading into everything she said, looking for an invitation. Peter didn't.

She stepped into the hallway and scanned in both directions.

"Was someone following you?" he asked.

"I thought I saw someone, but I don't know for sure. Every time I looked, he seemed to disappear." She crossed her arms. "I feel like I'm going crazy."

"Rose, I'm happy to help you, or just hang out if you don't have anyone else in the city. What you've been through . . . no one should have to go through anything like that alone. But I want to be straight with you, I don't know anything about this case, and I couldn't talk about it if I did."

"I'm not working an angle. I just . . ."

Peter raised his hand, as if waving it away. "I'm not saying you are. But I had to get that out there."

A housekeeper backed a cart toward them. Standing in the hallway was starting to feel awkward, but she hadn't invited him in, and he wasn't going to ask. Maybe she was rethinking trusting a total stranger based on that first five-minute conversation, however intense. He offered her an easy out.

"Have you eaten?"

"I'm not hungry, but I'd love to get out of here. I've been pent up all day."

"Let's take a walk."

She tilted her head up, and he knew she was measuring him, wondering if he was enough to stand between her and whatever threat was waiting. She smiled. "That would be great."

They went downstairs, and Peter's eyes searched everyone in the lobby. Again, he noticed no security nor any surveillance, friend or foe. If someone was watching her, or following her, he was good, able to blend in completely.

They started walking through Dupont Circle and passed a white mansion, one of the old private clubs. The area around Dupont was dotted with embassies and chanceries. Peter and Rose passed Egypt, and then Iraq. Embassy Row was a strange place, with its high walls and barred windows and black cars coming and going. You could have two states locked in a deadly border conflict overseas sharing a manicured hedge on Massachusetts Avenue.

They worked their way back past Dupont. Peter could have broken up the silence, but it was an oddly comfortable one. It seemed like they'd blown past the bullshit small talk phase the night her aunt and uncle were killed. The only thing they wanted to discuss, both of them, desperately, was off-limits: What the hell were they in the middle of?

As they climbed the hill past Adams Elementary School, she glanced over her shoulder. Peter stopped and looked down the slope, paying particular attention to the last intersection that they had passed.

"Did you see someone?" he asked.

"How would I know?"

"With professionals, you probably wouldn't."

"You have a lot of experience with it?"

"I used to be on a surveillance team."

"How does it work?" She was still glancing behind her as they walked. She needed something to give her confidence, to help her cut through what was real fear and what was imagined.

"We always learned with at least three people doing foot surveillance. A, B, and C. A is right behind the target, B farther back, and C on the opposite side of the street. They rotate, and at every intersection, A signals to the others which way the subject is going, and then B or C swaps in for A and on you go."

They were standing at the corner of Columbia and Eighteenth Street, the top of Adams Morgan, an intersection jammed with bikes and pedestrians and cars trying to work their way around them in the crosswalks.

"Can you do it with two?"

"If you need to, but it's harder."

She watched the crowds flow by, a messenger on a fixed-gear bike, a woman pushing a stroller, a woman in glasses with a laptop under her arm, making her way down to the coffee shop where all the work-from-home people camped out.

The fear had gone out of Rose's face, replaced by eagerness as she scanned the sidewalks.

"Show me how you do it," she said. She wanted to learn to tail. She wanted to be the hunter for a moment.

"You're sure?" Peter asked.

"Yes."

It made sense. The only way he had learned to pick up surveillance was by doing it himself.

Diagonally across the intersection from them, a man stood wearing a pair of blue over-the-ear headphones. He was over six feet and must have weighed at least two hundred and fifty pounds.

"How about that guy in headphones?" Peter said.

"The big one?"

"That's our rabbit." He was just a random civilian, but he was distinctive, a good way to learn.

"So how do we do it?" Rose asked.

"I'll start in B; you're A. Stay close but not closer than, say, fifty feet. When he turns at an intersection, signal to me which way he went, and then we'll switch." Peter let his hand fall naturally to his hip and then tapped it. "Left hand if he goes left, right hand if he goes right."

"Got it."

"Are you sure you want to do this?"

She didn't even look at him. Her eyes were fixed on the rabbit. "Isn't it too easy with the headphones?"

"It'll be a good way to start."

27

The man in headphones started up Columbia Road, and Rose took off behind him. Peter let her get ahead by half a block, and once she passed a taco shop, he took up the B position.

Normally, first-time trackers act strangely, showing their nerves. They keep their arms too still and walk with too much determination. But Rose moved with ease, blending in among the other pedestrians as they neared Sixteenth Street.

Peter sped up, closing the gap to get ready for a potential switch. He had lost sight of the rabbit, but that was fine.

Rose stood across the street, waiting between two mothers with strollers, her hand resting on her right thigh. Peter looked in that direction, up Sixteenth, nodded to her, and crossed over. She smiled but didn't hold eye contact for any longer than was strictly necessary.

This is what she wanted: some semblance of control, of familiarity with the dangerous world into which she had been thrust. She was enjoying herself, forgetting the grief and fear for a moment.

Peter kept his pace up, not so fast as to stand out, but close enough to keep eyes on the subject as the sidewalks grew more crowded. After another block, the man turned right down a side street to the east. Peter crossed and signaled, and Rose picked up the A spot once again.

There were more people here, outside the Columbia Heights Metro station and a three-story mall. It would be hard terrain even for an experienced tracker. Peter looked over the crowd: corner guys sitting on buckets, Salvadoran ladies selling fresh fruit, commuters and shoppers. When Rose glanced back, Peter held his hands in front of him and brought them closer together, indicating to Rose that she should close the gap. She got it and hurried on. Out of the corner of his eye, Peter saw the blue headphones disappear. The rabbit had taken them off.

Peter never let Rose out of his sight and watched her standing at the corner of Columbia and Fourteenth Street. Her natural cool was starting to fray as she scanned the streets around her. She had lost the rabbit. Peter crossed toward her.

"He took the headphones off," she said.

"You did really well."

Rose craned her neck around. She wasn't giving up. Peter had been trying to make it easy on her with the headphones. But focusing on an easily trackable object like that can be tricky if it disappears. He'd even heard of targets exploiting the phenomenon: wearing a red hat or a bright windbreaker to make the pursuers complacent, thinking that it would be an easy tail, and then losing them by ditching the object.

"It's tough here," he said and pointed to the crowd. "Maybe he told you where he was going, without you realizing it. Do you remember what he was wearing?"

Rose frowned, trying to recall. "Black jeans . . . no . . . dress pants. And a windbreaker or shell, light blue, maybe Patagonia."

At Quantico, instructors were always quizzing them. They would have somebody walk into class, hand the teacher an envelope, and leave. Teachers would then ask the auditorium full of relentlessly eager-to-please trainees what the person was wearing, what color his hair was, his eyes, whether he was wearing glasses.

The first few tries were mortifying. People would swear that it had been a white guy in a blue sweater wearing glasses, only to find they were 100 percent wrong. The fact was—and this made surveillance work so much easier for trackers—people walk the same ruts every day, with tunnel vision, blind to the world around them. By the end of his time as a G, those observations had become automatic, and Peter would silently record everyone who passed without even thinking of it.

Rose was right about the description, though they were black jeans. That sort of recall and observation was excellent for someone who wasn't trained.

"He had a tote bag too, right?" she said.

Peter nodded. "Did you see something folded up in there?"

"Yes." It was the bag that he'd put the headphones into. He thought there was a magazine or circular or *USA Today* sticking out.

"Reusable bags. Folded up inside that tote. Is there a fee for plastic bags when you shop here?"

"Five cents," Peter said. They could have been shopping bags.

Rose shook her head. "I would say he was going to the grocery store, but we walked right past one."

She studied the signs on the mall—Target, Best Buy, Marshalls.

"There's a Giant right around the corner," Peter said. It was on their side of the street.

"What if he lives around here? He threw something in the trash when we first saw him. So maybe he's hungry. He goes down to Adams Morgan to grab a quick bite, pizza or something, and then stops at the grocery store near his house to stock up."

"Sounds good to me," Peter said. Rose was already heading toward Giant. He followed her through the crowds and slipped in past the automatic doors behind her. He had always loved the rush of working a tail and could see it had hooked Rose, too.

She walked across the front of the store, checking down each row, not looking too out of the ordinary, as if she were searching for an item in an unfamiliar market.

At the far end, she hit produce and circled the edge of the store, past the dairy and the meats and the breads, but there was still no sign of him. She stopped at the rear of the store, near the bulk food bins.

"Did they look like bags to you?" Rose asked.

"I thought it was a magazine or circular at first."

"Maybe I'm just imagining things." She put her hands on her hips and suddenly looked downcast. "I mean, how do you lose track of an enormous dude in blue headphones with a baby face and a tote bag?"

Peter's eyes opened wide, but he fought the urge to look to his left. Rose did look, and her mouth fell open.

Headphones man was staring at them, a package of pork chops in his hand, and on his face a look that said *who the fuck are you people?*

Rose was already stepping backward and turning, her hand closing on Peter's wrist, drawing him down the aisle and away from the stunned man. The embarrassment had turned into punchiness by the time they reached produce.

"Burned, we're burned," Rose whispered, and Peter laughed along with her. Blue Headphones disappeared around the end of the aisle, and Peter kept an eye out. They walked to the far end of the section and peeked around to see their target heading for the self-checkout machines, still casting suspicious glances around the front of the store.

"Hang on a sec," Peter said. "He's checking out. We're fine. Good eye!"

Rose hugged him from the side. She looked up at him and laughed again, pulling away as she watched the man in headphones walk away through the windows at the front of the store.

Rose lifted a bunch of grapes and examined them. She twisted one off and popped it in her mouth.

Peter watched her out of the corners of his eyes. She twisted off another and held it out to him, but he declined. She looked at him curiously.

"What is it? These? I didn't have lunch. Relax; I'm going to pay for them." She glanced down at the fruit. "Are you worried about the one I ate, the weight?"

She took a few steps toward a produce display and asked a kid stocking apples, "Is it cool if I try a grape before I buy them?"

He shrugged. "I don't think anybody cares."

Rose turned to Peter, but he still wasn't satisfied, and the giddiness of their successful pursuit started to evaporate.

"Ready?" she asked, gesturing with her head toward the self-checkout. She put the grapes down on the scale of the register, then smiled at Peter. Her thumb was on the scale, adding weight.

"There you go," he said.

28

They exited onto Fourteenth Street and headed south. Rose offered the bunch of grapes to Peter, and he picked one off.

"You have a good read on people," he said as they turned onto Columbia Road.

"I used to work retail in LA, boutique-y stuff, perfume and jewelry. It's awful; half of it is profiling people and playing on their psychology, their needs."

"What do you do now?"

"Investor relations most recently, then I had a startup in LA. It's the same thing, but you're selling yourself, really."

Peter nodded, impressed. The people he knew who had stayed on in finance and successfully exited a startup now seemed to spend most of their time cultivating expensive hobbies.

"Not like that," she said. "It blew up in my face."

"What do they say? 'Fail quickly'?"

"Fail early, fail fast, fail often. That's mostly bullshit. But this wasn't an idea that needed shaking out. It would have worked."

"What was it?"

"Loans to small businesses. Streamline it and take the pain out of it. I had a deal all set, and when we went to close in New York one of my funders, my main guy, tried to have . . . investor relations with me." She raised an eyebrow.

"I see. And you—"

"Ultimately told him to fuck himself. After many, many subtler attempts. I was friends with his wife. The whole thing was awful. How did you get in the rescuing damsels business?"

"You rescued yourself, getting out of there and getting to a phone."

"I know. It was a joke."

"Oh." Peter took another grape. "Sure. I had a family background in law enforcement. It's pretty straightforward. You get to help people, stop bad guys. It's never really that simple, I know, but it's good work."

Rose was silent for a moment. They were now cruising down the sidewalk next to Meridian Hill Park.

"Straightforward, hmm? It's funny, the thing with the grapes back there. You don't seem uptight, but that really bothered you."

She narrowed her eyes slightly, appraising him in a way that Peter hated. He knew why it had bothered him, the little theft, and more than that the attitude of not caring or letting things slide. Sometimes he got sick of having to follow every bureaucratic rule to the letter, but he was still a stickler for basic honesty.

He knew it was crazy, how that kind of thing always made the muscles around his spine tighten up: casualness about cutting corners, about cheating. It was through those thousand small compromises that the agent working for his dad got away with treason for so long. They all seem so small until someone ends up dead.

"What's your angle?"

"Sorry?" Peter asked.

"Are you supposed to be here? You didn't want to get involved yesterday. Or couldn't."

"You asked me for help."

"Simple as that?"

"Yes." It wasn't so simple, of course. He was out on a limb no matter how carefully he played this. But when she asked for his help, he really had no choice, though he didn't feel like getting into the reasons why with her, or even examining them too closely himself.

Rose was shrewd, zeroing in on his weak points, sketching out his psychology. Peter began to wonder how much all of this was an act: her playing that she needed help in order to get him close, to draw out the answers she sought.

It made him wary, of course, but it only added to his curiosity about her.

"So, what can I look out for? For people following?" she asked, changing the subject. Maybe she had picked up on his reaction.

"It's hard to make out a good tail. The FBI will use twenty or thirty people for a proper job, with six trackers cycling through. Look out for people carrying packages or backpacks, because the pursuers will often have to switch out clothes. Forget about paying attention to hats and jackets, they're too easy to change, but shoes and pants and skirts are good cues. They need communications, but radios and talking into your wrist really stand out, so the best bet is something like the white earbuds that come with an iPhone. They have mics and are inconspicuous."

She stopped and looked down, thinking through something.

"Back at the corner," she said. "I thought I saw the man who was following me, across the street. He was a hundred yards behind us."

"What did he look like?" Peter said, not turning.

"Middle-aged, average height, brown hair, navy suit."

"Did anything in particular stand out?"

"No. That was what was so strange. He looked almost . . . generic."

"That could be eighty percent of the guys working in Washington."

"Which is why I think I'm seeing him everywhere?"

"It's a possibility. Once you start thinking about this stuff, you see threats all over the place. It's happened to me, too. Have you been sleeping?"

"Not really. Whenever I shut my eyes I am back . . . back there."

The house. The closet. He put his hand on her shoulder, and his eyes covered the street on both sides behind them.

"I don't see anyone."

She pursed her lips. "Thanks."

They continued talking about small things—details of tradecraft, the things she noticed while practicing surveillance—until they reached the hotel and crossed the lobby to the elevators. He walked her to her door, and she dipped her key card and cracked it open a few inches.

After one step inside, she paused.

"Are you okay by yourself?" he asked.

"I think so."

He wasn't sure when or if he would see her again, and

there was one question he wanted to ask. It had been troubling him the entire time.

"Rose?"

"Yes."

"Why do you trust me? Why didn't you want to talk to the other FBI people?"

She lifted her shoulders. "I don't know."

"Did your aunt and uncle give you anything? Or tell you anything else? Anything that might give someone a reason to be after you?"

"Just what I told you."

"Did you hear them talk about anything strange that night?"

She smirked and shook her head. "Take without giving."

"What?"

"You gave me this whole song and dance about how you can't talk about what happened, and now you're pumping me for information."

It was fair. He was in the dark as much as she was, and over the course of their time together, he had forgotten the rules he was normally so careful about.

"You're just like the others," she said. "Was this all to get me to confide in you?"

"Like who?"

She stepped farther inside and turned, one hand on the door.

"Thanks for coming out, Peter. It was kind of you. I'm going to get some sleep now, okay?"

There was an iciness to it, a dismissal.

"You sure you're okay?"

She nodded and shut the door.

29

Peter left. He walked six blocks before he turned around, went back to the hotel, and took the elevator to the third floor.

Ten minutes had passed, but as he knocked on the door, Rose answered quickly, as if she'd been expecting him.

"Hey," she said and brushed her hair back. "Listen. I might have overreacted there. I really appreciate the help. You want to come in? I was making some tea."

"Sure," Peter said. He looked up and down the hallway, and stepped in. What had brought him back, turned him around on the P Street sidewalk?

He looked almost . . . generic. The line had stayed with him, troubled him.

Rose smiled at Peter, shut the door behind them, and locked it.

"Huh," she said, then turned the handle and opened the door.

Peter watched. Normally opening the inside door handle pulls back the dead bolt with an electromagnetic *clunk*. But there was no sound. The lock was dead.

She looked at him, and he raised his finger, then leaned out and scanned the hotel hallway. Standing just inside the open door of her room, he tested the key card in the lock. Nothing. Anyone could have gotten in.

"What's happening?" she asked.

"The locks are down."

Before she could respond, a light at the end of the hallway went dark, then another. The rest blacked out in quick succession, closer and closer.

The overhead light in the room cut out, plunging them into darkness.

"God, Peter," she whispered. "The same thing happened that night."

He took her hand, already trembling, and brought her to his side. Time seemed to slow down, and every sound sharpened.

The fear made his legs feel heavy. Part of him wanted to freeze, but there was something else happening, a rush priming his muscles, driving him forward to close in on whoever was coming.

He was looking for a man. That's what had turned him around on the street and brought him back to Rose. When he exited the hotel ten minutes ago, Peter caught a figure at the edge of his vision.

It was what he *hadn't* noticed that had raised his suspicions. The man seemed to disappear into the background like a blank space moving through the city.

Peter tried the light switches just inside the door, but they were all dead. Rose took a step back into the room, but Peter didn't want to get cornered, so he led her the other way, into the dark hall, turning right toward the stairs.

His eyes hadn't adjusted, and he jammed his finger reaching for the wall, finding it closer than anticipated. He moved toward the faint red glow ahead, where the hallway turned. It was an exit sign, just out of view.

Cold, warm, cold: his fingertips ran over the cheap wallpaper and the steel hotel doors as they raced toward the exit. He kept his breath even despite the escalating tempo of his heartbeat—a wash in his ears and the hollow of his throat.

Scuff scuff—footsteps on the carpet. Someone else was here, was close. Without thinking, he stepped ahead of Rose and kept himself between her and the threat.

The first touch came just as he was able to make out the silhouette in red. A hard edge, maybe the side of a hand, slammed into his throat, and he gasped, a long croak, but he kept moving, driving himself toward the shadow. His hand brushed a man's arm, and Peter dropped his shoulder, pushed hard with his legs, and drove him into the wall. Peter stumbled away, gasping for air. On the wall to his right, he made out the T-shaped handle of the fire alarm, and he hauled it down.

"Rose," he tried to yell, but he could barely make a noise through his injured throat. The alarm enunciator let out a piercing beep, and a strobe flashed at the end of the hall. For an instant of white light, the scene was clear: the man had been knocked to the ground and raised himself up on one knee, his face down, out of view, as he pivoted toward the exit.

Peter's reflex was to rush him, the same powerful drive he'd run a thousand times on the court, to haul him into the light. But he checked himself. His first priority was to get Rose out of here. There could be more attackers coming.

He looked behind him and in the next flash saw her. By

the next strobe, the man was gone. Guests stuck their heads out of their doors, peering fearfully into the dark.

He ran to her, put his arm around her shoulders, and by the red glow of the exit sign, found the push bar on the door to the stairs. Emergency floodlights filled the stairwell, nearly blinding him as they sped down the concrete steps.

They ran across the lobby as the pain spread in his throat and his breath came in wheezes. A hallway near the restrooms led to a side entrance on Nineteenth Street. Peter stepped into the circle toward a taxi, his arm up. Cars honked and dove as their drivers slammed on their brakes. The cab flashed its lights and they raced to the side door.

He helped Rose in first, while he held the door and scanned the street, then climbed in after.

Someplace safe. "The White House," Peter croaked to the driver. "Seventeenth and G."

He looked at Peter with wide eyes. "Are you okay?"

"Just drive," Rose said. The cabbie nosed into the traffic toward Connecticut Avenue. They watched Dupont Circle shrink in the rearview as the first sirens—police and fire—lit up the streets to the north.

30

Peter, still barely able to speak, called ahead to Diane Farr. A Secret Service agent was waiting for them at the southwest entrance, out of sight of the news networks that were normally camped out near the North Lawn.

Peter recognized the agent, Daniel Akana, a burly man of Pacific Islands descent who, unlike many of the other agents, often carried a hint of a smile. But his face was grim as he rushed Peter and Rose inside.

Peter's throat felt like a crumpled drinking straw. His labored breaths were driving him to panic, but the swelling didn't seem to be getting any worse. Farr joined them in the West Wing corridor and marched them past rubbernecking staffers into the White House proper and a small medical clinic.

Peter lay on a table in an exam room. This office, just inside the mansion, attended to the first family's health and any emergencies that came up for staffers and visitors. While the on-call physician examined Peter's throat, Farr talked quietly with Rose and led her into the hallway.

The doctor—a navy surgeon—pocketed her penlight. "I'd like to get you to GW hospital, just in case," she said, as she handed Peter a bag of ice to drape over his throat.

"No," he whispered. "I'm good."

She checked her watch. "If that swelling's not down in a half hour, you're going," she said, then stepped out.

The cold pushed back the pain, and a bead of condensation ran down his neck. He stared at the tiles of the dropped ceiling and the cold white fluorescent lights, and his mind kept crashing back into that hotel hallway.

He wanted to remember the face from the strobing lights during the attack, anything specific. He found nothing. Rose hadn't been able to describe the man stalking them. Now Peter understood that was the attacker's gift.

Another Secret Service agent came in and took Peter's statement on what had happened, but the agent had no information about whether they had found the attacker from the hallway.

After the agent left, Peter waited for his heart to slow down. It never did. He checked the clock. Twenty minutes. He couldn't be sitting around here. His chest rose and fell, and his breath came with pain, but it was coming.

He sat up and gripped the table with his free hand. He was still jacked from the run-in and needed to move. That killer was out there. He stepped out of the exam room into the hall.

The doctor was talking with a nurse a few feet away. "Hold on," she said to Peter.

"I'm okay."

"You need to rest."

Over her shoulder, Peter saw Farr approach from the small reception area.

"Diane," Peter said. "What's going on?"

"Is he all right?" Farr asked the doctor.

"I can breathe," Peter said. "I'm fine."

The doctor looked from him to Farr and perhaps saw that something was happening that reached above her very estimable pay grade. The White House docs were used to their clients' agendas taking priority. She ran her fingers over his swollen windpipe and nodded to Farr.

"I'll keep an eye on him," Farr said. She led him toward the door, and the doctor gave Peter a stern look and pointed to the bag of ice in his hand.

"Where's Rose?" Peter asked, as he and Farr walked through the gallery toward the West Wing.

"She's fine. She's with Hawkins. A debrief. He's running the response to this."

Peter shook his head.

"Relax," Farr said. "It's not an interrogation. They're in the mess."

"You need a dragnet. The attacker shut down all the lights at the hotel, just like at the Campbells' house. It's the same killer. We need to find him."

"We have DC police and the FBI on it. This isn't the Wild West. You're not going to posse up and go looking."

She opened the door to her office, and they stepped in.

"Where was her security?" Peter asked.

"We had a patrol, a regular check."

"That woman trusted us, and we nearly got her killed."

Farr cocked her head and eyed Peter with the look of a patient parent. He was out of order.

"What were you doing there, Peter?"

"What? I was looking out for the witness."

"Why were you there?" She emphasized every word. Was she suspicious of him, even after he'd stopped the killer?

He felt the anger coming and closed his hand slightly, scythed his thumbnail into the side of his finger and found something soothing in that pain. He went on, choosing his words carefully.

"She called me. She needed help. Her security was gone and she thought she saw someone after her. She was right."

"Where did she get your number?"

"I gave her my card after the funeral, in case she needed help. I told her I would get her to the right people."

"Did you tell her anything about the case?"

"No. Not even what she already mentioned on the phone that night. We walked around. I showed her a little bit of how to pick up if someone was following her, something to make her feel better. You want to go after me, that's fine. But you should be asking why Rose was left wide-open for this man to come take her."

"That is an excellent question."

"What's going on, Diane? What is that emergency line for? Why is all of this eyes only?"

She shut her eyes and nodded along to the questions, as if acknowledging that they were fair.

"We should talk, Peter. You know when I first saw your file, I thought you were just a classic brownnose."

"Sorry?"

"Kiss-ass. Color inside the lines. Try to prove you're not your dad. Get the bureau to pat you on the head."

Peter's fist tightened. The ice ground together. "What is this?"

"But I always wondered if it was more than that. Maybe you were some kind of mission fanatic, trying to make up for what he did no matter what harm it would bring on yourself. God," she said, shaking her head in disbelief. "You rushed the attacker at the hotel?"

Peter's throat hurt with every pound of his pulse. This whole scene felt like he was watching it from above. What was she getting at?

"I'm not on a crusade to clear my father's name. I've never gone near that."

Farr sat behind her desk, dialed in the combination lock on her drawer, and pulled out a sheaf of papers.

"I don't think you are. I think you're trying to make up for the lives he lost by doing what you think is the right thing here. Is that it? Part of it?"

His jaw tightened. That was some deep, dark shit she was digging in, but in a way it was obvious. "Sure," he said, keeping his voice calm.

"How serious are you about that, Peter? Doing the right thing no matter what the cost?"

"What do you mean?"

"Let's take the most extreme example. What if, hypothetically speaking, you were investigating your own father back then. What if you came across evidence that conclusively showed he was involved in espionage? What would you do?"

"What the hell is this?" Peter growled, forgetting the pain in his throat for a moment. It came back, even stronger, and he shut his eyes.

"Everyone wants to do the right thing when it's easy," she said. "But how committed are you? Just answer the question. What would you do, against your own father?"

"Destroy him." Peter said it quietly. It was the truth. Was she testing him? Trying to find out if this was too personal?

If he was compromised by his past, running on anger or desperate to atone?

She sat with his response for a moment. "And this Rose Larkin thing. You maintained an interest in the case even after you were warned."

"Yes."

"Why?"

"Because she needed help, and she asked me."

"Would you do it again? What if it cost you your job?"

Peter looked at her. You can never get in trouble with the truth. That's what they always told him. This sure felt like trouble.

What if Rose called again? What if no one was there? Innocents. Unanswered calls. It was treacherous ground, a part of himself he had never really understood. He wouldn't lie.

"Yes," he said.

She looked at him coldly for a moment and then relaxed, as if satisfied.

"Good. I need a fanatic right now. You have no idea what we're up against." She looked at her desk phone, then at the door and the window. "Come on."

She stood, the papers in her hand.

"Where are we going?"

"Sit Room," she said and tapped her fingers on the pages. "It's time I read you in."

31

Farr led Peter down the hall. Extra Secret Service agents stood by the main West Wing entrances, carrying submachine guns. The whole place felt like it was on a war footing.

They entered the Sit Room and walked past the watch officers into the small breakout conference room, one of the most secure spots in the White House. She frosted the windows and shut the door. The hiss of white noise worked in the background.

He took the chair opposite her as she sat and ran her finger over the papers.

"We tell a lot of stories around here about the importance of speaking truth to power, of going after corruption even at the highest levels. I imagine you've seen enough to know that's all romanticized. You know what happens as often as not."

Peter nodded. "The powerful bury you."

"That's right."

Farr took the cover sheet off the papers. "This is hard for me because I need to ask you whether you want to be read in on a program before you can really understand what it's about. I'm telling you this now. As a young guy with a career ahead of you, you should just walk away."

"I'm not hunting promotions," he said. The whole scene felt wrong, sitting down here with the chief of staff like he was her confessor. "I get it."

"You don't," she said. "That's the problem. Before I can tell you anything, you need to sign this. If you ever talk about anything I share with you now or at any moment going forward, you'll go to prison for five to twenty years. You won't be able to defend yourself because nothing we talk about can be brought up in a courtroom in your defense. You talk, you go away. That's it."

Somehow, Peter knew that those papers were part of the reason Farr had brought him into the West Wing in the first place.

He lifted the pen. He kept his word. He didn't share secrets. He had nothing to be afraid of. And he wanted to know what the hell was going on.

He turned the papers around and signed twice on the last page. She retrieved them and sat back in her chair.

"Do you understand now why everything you heard on that phone was eyes only to me and Hawkins?"

"Not fully," he said. "Whatever Rose's aunt and uncle told her, and she told me—about the red ledger and OSPREY—is valuable enough to kill for. So you wanted to keep the circle small."

Farr nodded.

"Were the Campbells counterintelligence?" Peter asked.

"Yes. Retired. They worked for the CIA and then an FBI squad. They were investigating a cell of foreign intelligence officers . . . and their agents."

She didn't go on, simply watched him for a moment.

Agents—that meant the foreign spies' sources, the Americans they had under their control.

Farr was rattled. She wouldn't take precautions like these unless this was the worst-case scenario.

That emergency line went eyes only to her and Hawkins. There was only one reason she would silo the information like that, to avoid the normal, carefully mapped-out channels of the intelligence and national security agencies. It was the same reason you would use off-books personnel, like Henry and Paulette Campbell.

Peter leaned forward. "There's a threat from inside? Someone in the government?"

Farr stared at him. She looked like a woman in mourning. "Yes."

"Christ," Peter said. He ran his hand over the cheap veneer on the table. There was a traitor. He understood why she asked him about his father. It was happening again, but now Peter was at the center of it.

"So the Campbells reported straight to you to protect their information from a mole?" The word felt so strange as he said it. "They were trying to find out who it was?"

He wished he were more shocked, but the CIA had been shot through with leaks for its entire existence.

He glanced at the papers. "But still. Why report to *only* you and Hawkins? If the Campbells' investigation was codeword classified, the only people who know about it would be so senior . . ."

"That's correct," she said.

Peter looked down, trying to absorb it. Operations like these, known as special access programs, were limited to only the highest-ranking national security personnel. That meant Farr was worried about someone near the top of the intelligence world.

His mouth was as dry as paper. "That's why you put me on the desk. Because I'm a nobody. If it is an insider, there is no way I would owe them. No one would have bothered getting to me. I have no relationships with anyone with any clout. I couldn't have been compromised."

"That was part of it."

He shut his eyes. He knew the other part. His father. An older betrayal. His original sin. No one would be more motivated to go after this than Peter was. She could trust him.

"The Campbells worked Russia, right?" Peter asked. "Is that the hostile intelligence service here?"

She studied his reaction. "I know it hits close to home, but you can't let it be about revenge. Can you keep your head straight on this?"

He looked at the bag of ice, forgotten and half melted. A Russian operation had brought down his father. Someone just tried to break his neck. So yes, he had plenty of goddamn motivation. All he could picture was closing in on that man at the hotel and beating the life out of him. But Peter had a lifetime of practice checking himself, of hiding that anger.

"I'm good," he said and brought his shoulders back, projecting calm. "You don't have to worry. Can you tell me what the red ledger is?"

"We believe it documents the meetings between Russian intel and their source in the US government."

"It's enough to find the source?"

"We think so. Or else they wouldn't take such a risk to hunt it down."

"The Campbells had it?"

"They did, or were close, but now it's gone."

Peter glanced toward his desk and then leaned over the table. "The night they died, they said something was happening in six days. There's only two left."

He hadn't been able to stop thinking about that deadline, about the rumors circulating since the funeral that Russians had killed the Campbells. On those long nights on watch, he had been reading anything he could on the Kremlin's plans.

He swallowed and went on: "The Russian president and the foreign minister are going to be in DC in two days. Is that part of this?"

Russia was on the march against the US and its allies around the world. After murdering dozens within its borders, now it was killing dissidents with impunity in London. It had forces fighting within shooting distance of American soldiers in Syria.

Its president, Josef Vikhrov, a former KGB officer with a serpent's charm who had killed his way to the top, was stealthily massing troops along the border with Eastern Europe, disguising the movements as training exercises. Russia had used the same pretexts before they invaded Ukraine.

Something was happening, soon, and there were a dozen tinderboxes that could light up in an instant, in Washington and overseas.

"We don't know," Farr said.

Peter brought his hand down on the table. "It's in two days!"

"Watch yourself, Sutherland," she said in an icy tone.

"We are taking every precaution and throwing everything we have at this."

He raised his palms as a mea culpa before he went on. "What are they planning, Diane?"

"The answer's in that ledger. It will show us who's helping them and what they're plotting. With that, we can stop them."

"But they're killing everyone who knows about it."

"Yes," she said. "That's what the night action line is for. The Campbells operated with a great deal of independence, to protect their work. They didn't report every detail of their investigation to us. We are trying to find all of the sources they were talking to, who know about this, who might be at risk now. But the Campbells also gave them that number in case of emergency. If anyone comes after them, they'll call."

"Am I a target?"

"After tonight, it's possible." She squared up the papers. "That's it. If you're going to get yourself killed, I thought you should know why."

"What can I do?"

"Take Advil. Ice that neck. We have coverage on the emergency line tonight. Get some sleep for once in your fucking life."

"Where's Rose Larkin?" Peter asked.

"She's still in the mess. We're setting up a security detail for her, two agents I trust, around the clock. This won't happen again."

"I need to talk to her."

Farr leveled her eyes at him. "I'm glad you were there for her tonight, Peter, but that doesn't mean I'm not furious you went around me. I read you in because you deserve to know, and people are going to be asking a lot of questions and you need to understand the stakes. That means you need to be more careful, not less. You're not going to go around chasing bad guys. You're not trained."

"Rose would be dead if I wasn't there."

Farr sighed and looked at his neck, the growing blue-black bruise.

"You *are* probably the only person she trusts right now," Farr said. "Hawkins talked to her, but she seemed . . . cagey."

"You wouldn't be?"

"I am. I'm terrified if you want the truth. I'm an MBA. This isn't my world. There's an enemy inside, someone powerful, and I have no idea who they are and who else they've corrupted. This is all . . . it's too much."

She stood up. "Go talk to her," she said. "But everything she tells you comes straight back to me. Be careful, Peter. You need to watch yourself."

"I won't get out of line."

Farr cleared her throat and straightened up. She had let her fear show through for a moment, and now she covered it again.

She studied Peter. He was leaning forward, balls of his feet on the ground, ready to move. The fight was still with him.

"Has it even sunk in?" she asked. "What happened back there? I'm not worried about you getting in trouble with Hawkins. I'm worried about you getting killed." She forced a smile and a quiet laugh. "And I don't have time for the paperwork on that, okay?"

Farr pressed a button on the wall. The glass cleared, and the white noise cut off. She left, and Peter strode out after.

The other watch officers knew better than to ask, but Peter still felt eyes on him as he walked back into the basement corridor.

32

The White House Mess, the dining room for senior staff, stood directly across the hall. The basement was an odd place: left for M&Ms and all-night coffee, right for nuclear crisis. Farr headed upstairs, and Peter entered the mess. Rose was sitting with one of Farr's senior aides, a man named Julian, looking over some papers.

Peter pulled a glass from a rack near the galley and filled it with cold water. He took a sip, swallowing carefully, the movement sending a stab of pain along his throat.

Julian stood. He was forty, but seemed much younger, with a grad student air. A bow tie and suspenders Yalie, he went out of his way to say things like "whomsoever" and "It is I."

He dipped his head to Peter as he exited the mess, and Peter joined Rose at the table.

Her face was pale and drawn.

"Are you okay?" She reached out and put her hand on his forearm.

"A little banged up, but I'll be fine. You?"

She looked down at her hand. He could feel it trembling. She drew it back and covered it with her other hand.

"I don't know. They said they'd move me to another place. The Mayflower."

"That's good. They deal with a lot of diplomats there. It will have better security."

"Will you come with me?"

"Of course. We're going to find these people. You're safe."

She pressed her lips together, as if deciding whether to say something.

"What is it?"

It took her a moment to respond. "Nothing."

She was hiding something, but Peter didn't press her as she studied her hands. "They're probably ready," she said, then stood up. "Julian said they're bringing a car around."

As Peter led her out through the West Wing, he forced himself to slow down; he was striding through the hall. Farr was right. It hadn't sunk in. He was still going on reaction, adrenaline—*What next? What next?* And now there was a danger that chilled him as much as the killer he'd slammed into in the hallway. The threat was close, perhaps inside these walls.

As they turned toward the exit, Peter saw Hawkins at the far end of the hall. Their eyes met for an instant, but Hawkins just kept walking.

"Peter?"

He tensed. Rose was looking up at him, closer than he expected, and he realized he'd been staring, standing squared off, a warm flush working its way through his body, like a man wading into a fight.

"They're waiting," she said.

33

Peter walked Rose through the Mayflower lobby—all white and gold with coffered ceilings and marble floors—and kept thinking of his surveillance lessons, a string of exercises at Hogan's Alley. That was the tactical training center at the FBI Academy in Quantico, though the name was deceptive. It was a complete small town, with a post office, theater, and deli that really served sandwiches, a place where you couldn't walk more than twenty feet without a pistol flashing in your face or a robbery jumping off at the bank. The crack and hiss of gunfire was ever present, and every detail was engineered to keep you on guard and shred your nerves.

Now back in public, in another hotel after the first attack, he felt the same way: tweaked, paranoid, exhausted. Everyone from the concierge in his thin-lapelled suit to the tourist checking out in cargo shorts looked like a killer.

He knew enough to know better, to manage the fear. He couldn't imagine how Rose was handling it. They took the elevators up. One guard stood outside the elevators, and the other walked them toward the room, dipped the key card and opened the door. Peter went in first and checked the bathroom and closet, while Rose walked in behind him.

Her suitcase and laptop bag were waiting in the bedroom. The security team had already moved them over.

There was a large sitting area with a sofa, side chair, and television. The whole place was luxe, gray linen fabrics and marble tables and hammered-nail furniture. Peter walked with the guard back to the door and asked about their plans. They were on in two twelve-hour shifts, and would change over at eight A.M.

Peter thanked him and ignored the guy's double take as Peter went inside the suite and shut the door.

Rose sat down on the couch and Peter took the chair. The adrenaline was running out. His body felt like dead weight.

"There were cameras at the other hotel," Rose said. "Did they get a photo of him?"

"No."

"Is that normal?"

"It happens more often than you would expect. But they're looking into how they failed. That might point to who did it."

There were three cameras in the lobby and one at the far end of the hallway where he had been attacked. They all took a shot every six seconds but had gone out during the attack. Only the most powerful actors—intelligence services and militaries—had that kind of tech. This was a quiet war.

Rose looked at him and swallowed, her face pale. He had tried to soft-pedal the information, but she understood its gravity.

"A foreign intelligence service may have been involved," she said. "That's what they said when they interviewed me. Who?"

He leaned forward, elbows on his knees. "I will ask to clear more information for you. I can call right now."

She waved it away. "Not now. What does it matter? I don't want to know anything more about this. That's why they're trying to kill me."

Rose stared into space, black circles under her eyes, her blinks drawn out like a lizard's.

Her head dropped. "They're going to kill everyone who knows about this. Hunt us down."

He stood and put his hand on her shoulder.

She looked at him. "He saw you, Peter, that man from the hotel. You know everything I do. You think they're just going to let you go on with your life?"

"We have the FBI and Secret Service on this. You're safe."

She rested her face in her palms and rubbed her eyes. After a deep breath, she turned back to him, her gaze suddenly sharp.

"Do you trust those people we talked to?"

"Who?"

"At the White House. The people you work for."

"Why? What happened?"

"The night my aunt and uncle died, that man Hawkins took me aside and had me run through everything I had seen and heard. He told me not to tell anyone what I told you over the phone. The red ledger. OSPREY. He didn't want me to talk to the police or the other investigators. I think they were FBI. Why would he do that? Keep it to himself?"

Now that Peter knew that Hawkins and Farr were worried about a mole, it made sense why they would tell Rose not to tell anyone else. But it was making her suspicious of them.

"There could be a reason," he said. "If what your aunt

and uncle told you is very sensitive, they restrict it to certain people. Sometimes just a handful."

"Or he might want to keep it secret for his own reasons."

"Was that your read on him?"

"I didn't trust him. But trust isn't my strong suit."

Peter stepped away. *Cagey,* that's what Farr had said.

"Did you hold something back? Something your aunt and uncle told you?"

Rose avoided his eyes. He was careful with his distance. He didn't want to crowd or intimidate her, make this feel like an interrogation.

"Anything I tell you, you'll pass it on to them."

"I won't. But you should. Any piece of evidence could help find who killed them, could help stop this."

"You won't?"

"If you tell me in confidence, I won't."

"Swear?"

"I swear."

"That must mean something, coming from the grapes guy." She sat back and looked at the far corner of the room. "I heard my aunt and uncle talking, that night. They said something about a chemist, and a book . . . a binder."

"Do you think they meant the ledger?"

"I guess so. I overheard them as I came downstairs so I didn't catch it exactly. They were going back and forth on what they should say when they called in. It was like they were arguing about whether to tell the people you work for about the sources they had. Have you ever heard of a chemist mixed up in this?"

"No."

"They didn't put that in the message they had me give.

Why would they be worried about talking to the people they worked for, the people *you* work for? Maybe they didn't trust them?"

"That could be. But protecting the identity of sources is very common. You pass on the intel, but protect the source. Did they know any chemists?"

"No. I've been racking my brain ever since that night."

"If those details can help find who did this, you need to pass them on," Peter said.

"I don't know."

"They said whatever is going to happen would happen in six days. That's Sunday. You need to share those details, or let me. You could help stop whoever came after us."

She clasped her hands, brought them to her lips.

"Rose—"

"I trusted the people you work for, and someone tried to come into my room and kill me. I need time." Her voice was a plea. "If they didn't say it, why should I?"

She held up her hand. Tears were close, but she fought them back. She didn't trust Hawkins and Farr. He couldn't blame her for that. Farr had just told him that she didn't know who could be trusted as well, and only hours ago a killer had slipped through Rose's promised protection.

"Take your time," he said. "Don't worry about anything tonight. You're safe, and you've been through plenty for one day. Rose?"

"What?" she asked brusquely. She was on defense now, expecting more questions.

"No one should ever go through this. And the way you're handling it—you'd have made your aunt and uncle proud. You're tough. You're going to be fine."

"How are *you* handling this? He tried to crush your throat. Aren't you Mr. Nobody? Aren't you freaked out?"

"I am," he said, but kept thinking about her question. He'd been moving too fast to absorb everything, and now, as the night grew late, it was catching up with him. "These people after us just caught the attention of the most powerful office in the United States. We're going to be okay."

He didn't know if he was lying about the last bit. But he didn't mind that one lie. He needed to say it, to believe it himself tonight.

Rose had given him a lot, and she was coming around on sharing what she knew. The fear and shock of all this would be less overwhelming by daylight.

"Are you hungry?" he asked. "Do you need anything else?"

"I think I saw some tea in there." She started to get up from the couch, checking out the coffee maker on the dresser.

"Take it easy," he said and stepped toward the machine.

"Do they have anything without caffeine?"

"Here you go."

Peter dropped the tea bag in one of the coffee cups and ran the coffee maker with the basket empty. He turned around a minute later. Her eyes were shut, so he placed the cup on the coffee table in front of her and took the side chair.

After a few minutes, her leg jerked. He waited awhile longer. Her head listed over to one side. She had fallen asleep.

"Rose . . . Rose," he whispered. The last thing she needed was a surprise.

She sat up with a start and rubbed her cheek with the back of her hand as she looked around the room, then focused on him.

"You should get some sleep," he said.

"How long was I out?"

"Maybe five minutes."

She walked toward the bedroom, then turned back. "Do you have to go?"

"No."

She nodded, her hand on the doorframe. "Good."

The door closed, and the sound of running water filtered out. Twenty minutes later, she came out, wearing oversize gray sweatpants that said USC Football and a V-neck T-shirt.

Peter stood, keeping his hands at his sides and projecting more of a bodyguard feel, seeing everything and seeing nothing. This was her space, her guard was down, and it didn't feel right to be lounging in it unless she asked him to.

She glanced at the door. "Listen, I know that there are people, security outside, but I was wondering if you could stay. At least for a little while."

"I'm not going anywhere, Rose."

She gave him a half-embarrassed smile. He dipped his head slightly and smiled back. He could tell she hated asking for help, could tell she was still rattled. Her aunt and uncle—she said they were the only people she ever trusted. For her to ask this was no small thing.

"I didn't get a chance to say thank you, for . . . back at the hotel," she said.

"You're welcome. But you don't have to say anything. It's my job."

She said good night, stepped back into the room, and shut the door. A moment later her light went out. Peter was exhausted, but still restless. He stepped quietly across the carpet toward the window.

Light traffic ran down Connecticut Avenue. Looking southeast, he could just barely see the trees of Lafayette Square, north of the White House.

There was a traitor at the highest level, working with Russia, a crime that would be unimaginable if he hadn't lived through it when he was young. Hadn't he spent his whole life fighting toward a moment like this?

Farr had trusted him with the truth, a chance to fix the past. That's what had driven him so hard since the first phone call. But now, sitting here alone in the dark, all the fear he'd kept at bay surged back in. He could feel the dried sweat on his skin, with its faint ocean smell. He swallowed. His neck was raw and swollen.

They could have killed Peter at that hotel. And Rose was right, they weren't going to stop until everyone who knew about that ledger, including him, was dead.

Just let this go, a voice in his head said. *Walk away.* But that was the pain talking, the fatigue.

He watched a few people rush toward the bars near Dupont. He had lived by night for the last year, but he had never seen it, never even had a window. A light rain fell, and he lost track of time, watching the colors move, the street signs and headlights reflect in streaks along the roadway.

Peter's eyes drifted up Connecticut Avenue toward the heights of Georgetown, wreathed in fog. He could just make out the white towers, the red lights: the Russian embassy on Mount Alto. It was one of the highest hills in the city, with direct sight lines to the White House, the Pentagon, the Capitol, and the State Department.

The US had leased the land to the Soviets in the sixties. By the time anyone in government realized that they had just given up a perfect listening post to the USSR, it was too late. The Soviets could target American secrets at will, could snatch whatever they wanted out of the airwaves.

Peter had spent most of his life in the shadow of Russian intelligence, had studied it the way other kids collect sports stats. The US thought the Cold War was over, but for Russia it had never ended.

Once a global superpower, Russia now had an economy smaller than Italy's and Brazil's, ruined by naked political corruption and falling oil prices. It tried to mask its weaknesses with what weapons it had left: nuclear arms and espionage.

Former members of the secret services had fully captured its government. They were handpicked by President Vikhrov. It was a country run by spies with few natural borders and paranoia about foreign threats built into its DNA. Through its many political spasms, it always came back to autocracy and a need to attack, to kill or be killed. Peter grew up on *Looney Tunes* reruns and *Pokémon*, and his father cowboys and Indians, but the Russians grew up dressing up as spies and soldiers of foreign wars.

Vikhrov, who had held power for nearly twenty years, had seen the US bring down other long-serving autocrats who lived lives of impossible luxury and indulgence. He'd watched as Saddam Hussein was dragged from a hole in the desert and hanged in a ghoulish celebration. He'd seen

Qaddafi hauled through the streets, tortured and shot dead while he pleaded for his life.

In Vikhrov's mind, hitting back against the US was about reclaiming Russia's rightful role as a world power, but it was also a simple matter of survival for himself and his family. Russia had more spies working in Washington now than they did at the height of the Cold War.

Peter and Rose had met one asset tonight.

Peter knew about tracking targets, knew that it worked on an iceberg theory. If you find one adversary, there are three dozen others, hiding in plain sight, blending into the city as everyday Washingtonians.

They were out there, and they were taking risks like never before. Peter studied the street, every car and truck, every figure, using what he knew of surveillance to work backward, to see the seers.

They were hunting Rose now, hunting him. He crossed his arms and scanned the sidewalk. They would come in the dark, he knew.

And Peter would be there when they did.

34

Dimitri stepped across the fine sand of the equestrian arena. It was housed in a barn, gleaming aluminum with steel trusses, immaculate, and open to the night at both ends.

He had been summoned here by his superiors, and as he looked out over the black sky dense with stars, he wondered if this was where he was going to die. Had he drawn too much attention over the last week? Become a liability?

At the far end of the facility, a man crouched in an open stall, feeling along the ankle of a two-year-old chestnut colt.

He turned and stood as Dimitri approached, and waved him over. Eugene Balakin, former president of the Kamensk-Uralsky Metallurgical Works, owned a half dozen homes in New York, Los Angeles, and Washington, including this estate, his newest dacha. He wore a double-breasted suit with a dove-blue pinstripe and stepped through the hay in black suede loafers that to Dimitri's eyes looked a lot like bedroom slippers.

Balakin was spending too much time in the Emirates and the south of France and at Thoroughbred auctions in Ireland and Kentucky, trying to copy the peacock manners of Saudi princes and other oligarchs. He passed himself off pretty well for a miner's son and former FSB enforcer from Yekaterinburg. A member of the Russian president's inner circle, he was known as Vikhrov's Shovel because of a youth working the Ural coal seams and a talent for burying people.

He was one of the half dozen channels Dimitri used to stay in touch with his superiors. These moneymen and former security service officers like Balakin had better access to Vikhrov than the overweight spy chiefs at the DC embassy and one-tenth the scrutiny.

Dimitri had known Balakin for twenty years, but he'd been around long enough to know, too, that it was always a friend who killed you. As he scanned the dark barn interior, Dimitri wondered how, and even if, he might resist. He would fight back, he decided, probably more out of habit than anything else.

Dimitri examined the horse, the muscles working under a shimmering coat.

"Beautiful," he said, *prekrasna*. He rarely spoke Russian in the open, and his voice surprised him. It sounded like a stranger's.

"She's still finding her legs," Balakin replied, keeping the conversation in Russian. "Came over from the Gulf on Tuesday." Balakin took a step toward the heater that hung over the stall. "I would bring you inside, give you a proper welcome, but . . ."

Dimitri waved it away. Better out here, in the shadows.

"You should see these little old ladies," *babushkas,* he said, rolling the word around in his mouth, "coming by, asking for tours." Balakin pointed to the brick house on the hill behind them, a colonial masterpiece with three wings. "It passed down in Washington's family until a few years ago. They must think I'm going to trick it out like an Odessa brothel." He shrugged and laughed, as if maybe that weren't such a bad idea. "You had some trouble in the city?" he asked.

Dimitri stiffened. "I did. I take it that leadership is not happy."

Balakin mimed talking with his hand.

"Huff and puff, you know, but they wanted me to tell you to keep it up. They need everyone who knows about this operation handled. The Kremlin has full confidence in you, and the *rezident*"—Russia's top spy in Washington, who operated out of the embassy—"is in line, too, although you know what a pussy he is, just wants to make sure he can go to all the right parties."

Dimitri took a long breath of cold air. So this wasn't the end. He was already close to the edge, killing the Campbells, the attack at the hotel, moving too fast, too boldly. And still they wanted more.

"They know that could mean taking out senior people in the government?" he asked. "It could be a firestorm."

"They do. You have license. Whatever you need. We're close. This country is so strong it can't see its weakness, the fault lines, like cheap glass. Touch the right place and it shatters. We won't be humiliated by the West any longer. This is our stand."

"How many are there, here in Washington? How many like me?"

Dimitri and the other officers under deep cover worked in cells, some coordinated by the *rezident* and some taking orders straight from the Kremlin. They never knew each other's real names. But over the last months he had seen more and more new faces. Young men, bolder and more reckless than he.

Balakin smiled. "You just tell me how many you need."

He reached down and lifted a nylon case from behind the stall wall. "They sent this for you in the last pouch." He handed it over, then reached inside his jacket. He came out with a gold money clip and counted off a stack of sixty hundred-dollar bills, a small sliver from the wad of dollars and euros, and handed it to Dimitri.

Dimitri put the cash in his pocket and was about to open the case when his phone began to vibrate. He checked the screen. It was BEECH. "I should get going," he said.

"Of course," Balakin replied. "Happy hunting."

35

The rain pinged off the roof of Farr's sedan as she drove up Connecticut Avenue, heading for her condo. American University Radio had switched over to the BBC World Service. As they went on in their regional British dialects about the violent suppression of a miners' strike in Chad, she hit her limit of bad news for the day and switched the station. A woman named Delilah was taking calls on the soft rock station, her voice as warm and inviting as a clean comforter.

Linda Ronstadt started in over a slow bass run, singing "Blue Bayou," and it was cheesy, and it was perfect, and Farr turned it up.

A minute later her phone rang. She stabbed the knob on the radio, killing the song. The caller ID on her cell phone said Hawkins, and she answered.

"Go ahead."

"Are you at the office?" he asked.

"On my way home. What's up?"

"Do you have a detail with you?"

"No." The agent who usually worked her detail, Akana, was easygoing and usually left her to herself after she got home.

"I have something for you. We should talk."

They were talking of course, but *we should talk* had a special meaning in this case. They were both worried about the mole, about anyone finding out about the investigation. Phones were bad. The office was bad. He meant face-to-face where no one would be listening or watching.

"Fletcher's," she said.

Hawkins laughed. "Man, this is getting to you."

Fletcher's Cove was an inlet tucked in the woods along the Potomac, about twelve minutes out of town at this time of night. Beside it there was a gravel parking lot and a boat rental spot, all inside the C&O Canal park. This late you could count on it being empty.

"They took a shot at that girl in the middle of Dupont Circle. Yeah, it's getting to me. This is worth my time?" Farr asked.

"Guaranteed. I can be there in ten."

"Give me twenty-five."

"What for?"

She didn't answer and heard him laughing over the phone.

"Yes, I'm going to do a little SDR," she admitted. A surveillance detection route, a way to check for tails.

"Enjoy," he said. "I'll see you in twenty-five, by the water."

Twenty minutes later, she pulled off Canal Road and navigated the unpaved path to the parking lot. A white brick house where the lockkeepers had lived stood to her left. Even this close to DC, the spots along the canal felt like they were from an earlier time.

There were no lights in the lot. Hawkins's car was already there. She parked next to it, but it was empty. Her shoes crunched on the wet gravel, and the whole place smelled wild after the rain, like nitrogen-rich earth.

She crossed a footbridge over the canal with its murky black water.

"Hey." She jumped back and heard Hawkins laughing.

He raised his hands in front of him in a calming gesture. "Sorry, sorry. I thought you saw me."

Farr shook her head while she caught her breath. "No, I didn't see you. I nearly had a heart attack."

He was standing twenty feet down from the bridge, near the boathouse, and she walked toward him.

Both of Hawkins's hands were stuffed into the front pockets of his jacket. He brought the right out and extended it toward her, a phone cradled in his palm. He pressed the button on the side, and the bright display hurt her eyes after her time in the dark.

It was a photo of the interior of a garage or a storage unit. Brown and white cardboard legal boxes covered one wall, alongside a few nylon range bags for carrying weapons.

"It's the Campbells' storage unit. Out near Springfield."

"Under their name?"

"They used an LLC. 214AFG, LLC. The name appears to be just random numbers and letters."

"They didn't go in for cute stuff."

"No. But it wasn't too hard to find. They left some breadcrumbs in the encrypted communications drops they used to use at the bureau, and the combination."

"Insurance? Did they know someone was after them?"

"Seems like. Most of the stuff in there was deep-freeze,

old files on sources, all meticulous, but there was a shopping bag, too. Looked like it'd been dropped there in a hurry. There was a ledger inside."

"Red?"

He nodded. "We have it."

Dimitri turned off his headlights and parked on a quiet side street. All of these neighborhoods had paths that led down to the canal and the woods along the river.

Hawkins and Farr were meeting near the water, but he didn't want to telegraph his arrival. He had removed all the car's interior lights and replaced a relay in the fuse box. When he shut down the headlights, the vehicle was completely dark.

The motions were routine, but this was no ordinary crime. Everything was set. He had the go-ahead. In less than forty-eight hours, a plot years in the making would pay off. But only if he found that ledger.

Dimitri clamped a hand on the wheel. That fucking book. They had managed this whole operation so well, managed even to obscure the real cause of the Metro crash that killed twenty-one people.

And then the ledger showed up. The man behind it was a midlevel intelligence officer named Anton Novikoff, a kid really. He had made the arrangements for some of the early meetings between Dimitri and other Russian officers and BEECH, the source inside the US government. It turned out Novikoff had maintained a record documenting the real players behind the train attack and the outlines of the rest of the operation. He kept it in case his superiors tried to scapegoat him for the violence, pin it on the junior officer while the rest go free, a not uncommon tactic.

After all those people died on the Metro, Novikoff panicked. He didn't want to be blamed. He thought if he made a deal with the Americans, if he helped the Campbells' investigation find the mole, they could protect him from men like Dimitri. He was wrong.

Novikoff was a young man, thin and pale with red hair, weak-looking, but when Dimitri found him and questioned him, he held up for a surprisingly long time. He had a strange habit of growing quieter the more intense his pain became. Dimitri respected that and didn't make Novikoff suffer any more than necessary before he killed him. He had given the ledger to the Campbells, but now no one knew where it was.

If it went public, it would not only ruin the rest of this operation, it would blow back catastrophically on Russia, make the Kremlin an international outcast, and justify the most severe counterattack from the US.

Dimitri pulled a nylon case from under the seat and zipped it open. By long practice he could work these tools in the dark as easily as he could reach up and touch his nose.

He took two small cylinders from the snug foam lining of the case. The first was heavy, a black cylinder about the size of a roll of quarters, with two small metal nubs projecting from the end. The other was a matte aluminum rectangle that looked like a particularly rugged butane lighter.

He slipped both items into his left pocket, stepped out of the car, and eased the door shut, then started through the woods.

He moved quickly through the dark, though the terrain was unfamiliar. It would've looked odd, if anyone were able to see him: a man in his midfifties, moving effortlessly through the scrub, vaulting over downed trees, and gliding through the woods as silently as fog.

Ahead of him, all was black, but that was fine. He knew where they would be.

36

Farr handed the phone back to Hawkins. He was standing with the glow from the nearest light behind him, leaving him in silhouette.

"Where is it now?" she asked.

"Still in the storage unit. I want to be careful about chain of custody. I didn't want to do anything solo. You can check my notes."

He handed her a folded sheet of paper. It was an ingrained FBI habit to write up notes after every meeting or lead, and share them soon after: a way to document an investigation and back up any potential future testimony.

"Good."

"Though I doubt any of this will ever end up in a courtroom," Hawkins said. "Did you tell anyone else what I was working on?"

"No. And who else knows about this?"

"No one. The book listed a series of dates, records of meetings and phone calls. The Russians have a senior source inside the US intelligence community."

"You're certain?"

"Absolutely. Codename BEECH."

"We have the name?" she said. "That's unbelievable. How high up?"

"He must have serious access. He's valuable enough that the Russians killed the Campbells with no stealth in order to protect BEECH's identity. We've never seen them take such an aggressive risk on US soil. And there is something strange, too. The ledger makes several references to a date last fall. It's the night of that Metro crash."

"What do you make of it?"

"I don't know. If the Russians were involved in that somehow . . ." Hawkins lowered his voice. "Diane. Do you know anything else? Do you have any sense of who BEECH is?"

She shivered; maybe it was the cold. "No. But if we have times, dates, and places, we can probably narrow it down until there's only one left. We'll find him."

"Yes, we will."

Farr wheeled around, thought she heard something in the woods to her right.

"What is it?" Hawkins asked.

"Nothing."

Dimitri heard the slightest click coming from the radio in his pocket, short bursts of whispering static, the sound of someone on the other end opening the channel briefly but saying nothing.

Long short short long. Long short short long. It was the kill order.

Dimitri picked his way through the trees above the

canal, taking care to remain in the shadows. The meeting was over, and Dimitri watched his target approach the car. He darted to the passenger side, staying low, keeping the car between himself and the mark. The car beeped, and the doors clunked open: the keyless entry. It was unlocked.

As the figure came up the driver's side, Dimitri circled behind. Hawkins opened the door with his left hand, and as he stepped in, Dimitri touched the black cylinder to his left temple. Ten thousand volts entered his brain, and Hawkins began to list to the side like a falling statue, every muscle in his body in spasm.

Dimitri was ready, his hip close to Hawkins's, to better bear the weight as he hugged his right arm around Hawkins's chest, and stepped back, laying the two-hundred-and-twenty-pound man on his back. The eyes had a hint of nystagmus—twitching left and right, a sign of extreme fear. The man could still see and understand everything, but could not move or react.

Dimitri watched another car pull away at the far end of the lot. He wanted to question Hawkins, but he didn't have time, not here, not with a man this senior who would raise attention as soon as he went missing.

Dimitri brought out the silver rectangle and held it over the man's open right eye. With his left thumb and forefinger, Dimitri held the lids open while he placed three drops onto the sclera, near the tear duct, and then repeated the same process for the left eye. He brought his fingers down, closing both lids at once, and counted. One one thousand, two one thousand . . . up to five.

It was done. He squatted low near Hawkins's head, then dragged him into the trunk of his own vehicle. Dimitri held his gloved hand to Hawkins's carotid, and felt the pulse grow faint, beat by beat, like the bass thumping in a car driving off.

He picked up the keys from the ground, stepped into the car through the still-open driver's door, and started the car. His own heart was beating strong. He glanced at himself in the rearview as a very different drug flooded his body. It was the rush of knowing death, risking his own and causing another's, a chance every time, still a thrill after all these decades.

He waited until he was five miles away, on a two-lane winding through the horse farms of McLean, and then lifted his radio to his lips.

"It's done," he said.

A woman answered: "You were supposed to wait until I was gone."

He could hear the tremble in her voice. Diane Farr was terrified, and rightly so. She had given him the kill order: *long short short long,* sent from the radio in her pocket.

"I made a judgment call," Dimitri said. But the truth was, if there was going to be killing on American soil on her orders, he wanted her close to it.

"What happened?" he said.

"He had my codename," Farr said. "He was close. He knew about the train crash."

"Did he find the ledger?"

A pause. "No."

37

Farr felt her pulse pumping in her hands as though the steering wheel itself were beating. Her mind was still in that parking lot, replaying the scene second by second: Who had seen her? Would any cameras have picked her up? What did she touch? Hawkins had said that he told no one where he was going, but what if he was lying?

She was fine, she told herself, but that did little to put the fears to rest. She had been briefed on a half dozen counterintelligence investigations. She knew how sloppy they were in reality, how riven by turf battles between headquarters, the spy hunters in the Washington Field Office, and local FBI. The most notorious traitors had been taken down, not by some bolt of investigative genius or a stray strand of DNA, but because of leaks from the other side, or because their own complacency and arrogance led them to be caught red-handed.

But those rationalizations did little to stop the vinegar sweat running down her ribs or the hot flush of blood in her cheeks.

The road curved gently. Only once she entered the turn, and her body was pulled to the side, and the wheels screeched, threatening to let go, did she notice that she was going twenty miles an hour over the speed limit.

Farr pressed the brakes, took a deep breath, and did everything she could to calm her heart.

The atlas lay open on the passenger seat. She found the road in the index, narrowed it down by the grid numbers. McDowell Road appeared on her left, and she turned, craning her eyes to see the numbers on the auto shops and little aluminum-sided houses.

She wasn't using her GPS or her phone. There could be no trace of Farr being here. Good tradecraft meant going back in time, to paper maps and not knowing where the fuck you were. Acid climbed in her throat. For half the drive, she thought she would be sick and had taken the lid off her travel mug just in case.

Her headlights flashed off the numbers on a mailbox ahead—13220. She slowed the car down and looked to her right: a dual bay garage, both rolling doors down, stood next to a lot covered with gravel and broken-up asphalt that might once, decades ago, have been a gas station.

Three hundred yards down, she parked on the other side of the street and took another look at Hawkins's notes. She pulled on a pair of nitrile gloves, the type doctors use for exams, and a shower cap, and walked back to the garage.

She came up around the side of the building, sticking to the shadows. On the rolling door was a burly Sargent and Greenleaf padlock, the same kind she'd seen on military sites.

28–9–45: the combination from Hawkins's notes. Farr prayed they were right. Having to put a car jack under this door and tear it open would not help with her stealth. The dial turned freely, and after the last number she pressed on the latch and the lock let go with a satisfying click.

She reached down and hauled the door up a few feet, then crouched and went inside. It was exactly as Hawkins had described. She brought the door down behind her. In the perfect dark, the room felt like a crypt.

Her last word to Dimitri stuck with her: "No."

Had she hesitated, or otherwise tipped him off that she was lying? This was his world, of deceit and killing. And she was being so careful tonight, because she was afraid of getting caught, of course, but that paled in comparison to what Dimitri might do to her. She couldn't shake the feeling that he had followed her somehow, that he was outside or here in the dark with her.

Farr clicked her flashlight, and an electric whiteness filled the room. In her mind, she expected to see Dimitri, or Hawkins, with his eyes bugging, tongue black, and skin cadaver-yellow.

The unit was neat, with boxes carefully stacked in rows. She scanned the labels and saw they were old files.

She stopped and listened, sure she heard something, but it was just her imagination.

The shopping bag lay in plain sight, and she pulled back the crinkling plastic to find a plain red ledger. It wasn't the blood-red leather-bound tome that she had imagined, but an inexpensive notebook an office drone would use to keep his expenses straight.

The pages flipped under her fingers, until she came to a list of dates and places. It read like an arborist's field notes: ELM, ASPEN, OAK. They had used species of American trees for codenames on this operation. She was everywhere: BEECH.

It was odd to see all the meetings laid out, the dates and places. It looked so deliberate, like evidence, like a conspiracy, and each one brought back a moment in her mind: a beautifully prepared dinner of duck and homemade brown bread at a farmhouse in the Czech Republic, with grandkids running around in the yard catching fireflies; a lunch, sitting at a table overlooking the Ruhr valley, with glasses of prosecco, and an old economics professor, now a billionaire mining oligarch, telling stories of his first business, smuggling Levi's on trains from Dresden.

It didn't feel like treason.

Farr guessed that was the point, to lure her into the trap with something sweet, one small step at a time, so slowly that she never appreciated the full gravity of what she was doing until the snare closed around her.

Then the train crashed. Though it looked like an accident, Farr knew it was an attack. There were dead bodies in the Metro, and she realized what kind of people she was dealing with. Everything since that moment had been an exquisite hell.

Her intentions didn't matter. She had helped a foreign government with a plot on US soil and now they owned her. That was always how they did it, a handful of tiny infractions, luring you over the line, and then brutalizing you with the truth of what you've done once you had gone too far to turn back.

That was the essence of her odd marriage to Dimitri. Both she and the Russians needed to make sure that everyone who knew about this book was dead.

Another murder tonight. The first had been so remote, like something you would read about in the newspaper. With the Campbells, the killing had moved closer. Farr knew them. She got the call when they were attacked. She went to see the aftermath. Now Hawkins. While they talked, she had ordered his death; it was as simple as pressing the button on her radio: *long short short long*. She'd been there while he was executed. A vision filled her mind of her own fingers crushing his windpipe. Death was coming closer and closer.

Her radio clicked on and off, on and off: Dimitri. She faced the door, and her whole body tensed as she lifted the handset.

"Where are you?" she asked.

"Better you don't know."

"What happened to the other car?"

"Everything is taken care of," he said. "Relax."

"I'm retracing his steps, to make sure no one knew where he was going."

"Helpful. He didn't find the book?"

It was in her hand. "No."

She was blind in that garage, but for a moment Farr was certain that he was outside, that he could smell the deceit coming off her even over the radio, that with every step, every breath, she gave herself away.

But this book was her weapon against him and against everyone. It documented the whole plot, the attack.

For years the Russians had constrained themselves to mostly economic and scientific espionage. Even the long-running illegals program that was uncovered in 2010 hadn't done any real damage to the US. Everyone assumed it was the last vestiges of the KGB—all the wise ones had already cashed out to the private sector—doing operations for operations' sake, just to feel like they were still spies.

But this evidence demonstrated Russian active measures at their most extreme; it was a road map to war. If she needed it to, the ledger would give her enough leverage to save herself from Dimitri, because if it went public, the US would have no choice but to strike back at Russia.

"Did he tell you anything else?" she asked. "To help us find it?"

"No."

"Is he . . ."

"Yes."

"So we're okay."

"No. The Larkin girl knows more than she's letting on."

Farr suspected the same thing. Rose was acting strangely in interviews, wary, withholding. Perhaps her aunt and uncle had told her something else, maybe mentioned other witnesses who had helped with their investigation.

"I have that under control," Farr said. "Stay away from her. The FBI and DC police have a dragnet over downtown because of your performance at the hotel. She trusts Peter Sutherland, and Sutherland trusts me. I'll talk to her tomorrow and find out what she knows."

"And if she knows too much."

Farr's voice broke as she said it: "She's yours."

38

Peter sat by the window in the hotel room and watched the first light filter through low clouds, the sky going from black to gray as dawn approached.

It was exactly a year ago that he survived the Metro crash.

He remembered the day perfectly. He was coming from an interview for a promotion at FBI headquarters, but he already knew they would shoot him down. He'd seen it in their faces. That was before Farr gave him his chance.

He was still working surveillance then, and by habit took a seat at the end of the Metro car with his back to the wall. It gave him a view of every exit and every passenger.

A veteran in a Korean War ball cap hid his confusion from his wife as he puzzled over the Metro map.

A young woman feigned interest as her older colleague, boss most likely, held forth with his brilliant opinions about the election and the front-runner's big speech tonight.

The train filled up at Metro Center, so he stood in the aisle and pressed his back against the door that led to the next car. He was always so good about the rules then, spoken and unspoken, even little civilities like giving up his seat for someone who might need it more or the safety notices and No Eating and Drinking signs beside the train door.

A woman carrying a Bethesda Public Library tote bag looked to the empty seat, and to Peter, and the corner of her mouth ticked up. He half expected to catch a line in return like, "Oh no, do I look old enough that people are offering me seats?"

Before she could say anything, a woman in her early twenties darted between them and planted herself in it, somehow managing the entire maneuver without looking up from her phone.

The older woman's eyes met Peter's and they both laughed. It was such a normal evening.

Then the train jerked back, a sudden slowing, and went dark for a moment, lit only by the lights of the tunnel as they strobed by. The woman with the tote bag stumbled forward. He caught her arm and steadied her.

Peter leaned forward to balance as the train accelerated and the lights came back on. The others went back to their phones, but Peter kept watching, listening, absorbing every detail.

The rhythm of the wheels on the tracks—*tha-dun, tha-dun, tha-dun*—picked up, and the tunnel lights flashed by faster and faster. The flimsy pages of the *Express* shook in the commuters' hands. Something was wrong. They had too much speed.

Another jolt shook the car. The woman beside Peter put her foot out to catch herself and let out a small cry of surprise. There was a mood of general annoyance: rolled eyes and shaking heads, just another day on the Metro.

Peter held the pole, with its oily sheen, and took a step

to his right to peer out the window. Tunnel lights shot by, punctuated by the odd emergency alcove or blue glow of a safety phone. They were going even faster.

Ahead, the lead car turned into view as it started down the long curve in the tunnel. It leaned hard to the left, and one of the wheels threw off a shower of sparks.

Peter was used to blending in, working against his size, keeping a low profile in surveillance and in general, so it surprised him how easily the feeling of command came to him. He stood to his full height and took a step forward, looking eye to eye at the other passengers.

His voice filled the car: "Everyone sit down! Hold on to something!"

They looked at him, some stunned, and then sat and gripped the handrails. The man who'd been going on about politics earlier took a step toward him, as if to object.

The scream of metal on concrete filled the car, and that man, suddenly afraid, dropped back into his seat. Peter turned and watched through the window as the lead car of their train tilted off the track.

"Hold on!" Peter yelled, then grabbed the pole overhead and set his shoulder against the wall of the train.

Peter knew the crash was coming for them, each car driving into the next, chaos racing back along the train like a shock wave.

As they entered the turn, their car jumped and tilted on its side. Seatmates pressed together and slid into the windows. Those in the center struggled to stay upright, but the sudden deceleration ripped the poles from their hands and threw them against the walls.

Peter's fingers slipped off the metal. He slammed into the

door, slid up the wall, and hit the ceiling as the train car rolled, sending him past upside-down advertisements.

It happened in less than a second but passed with a dreamlike slowness as gravity seemed to go mad, with riders sprawled along the ceiling and the tops of windows, and some wrapped around the metal poles like hanging laundry.

The lights died. Screams and grunts filled the car. Peter lost all sense of orientation. He was in midair and then slammed into the wall. His head snapped against the aluminum.

Smoke stung his eyes as he came to. His balance was off and it felt like a knitting needle had been driven through his temple.

He crawled low through broken glass, coughing. He couldn't get the taste out of his mouth and throat—the chemical tang of burning plastic and paint.

In the faint glow of the tunnel's emergency lights, he could see shadows inside the train, some moving, some still. The car tilted far over on its side, sixty degrees off vertical. He picked his way back, walking along the wall, hand on the floor or the tops of the seats to steady himself.

The woman with the tote bag crouched by the exit, blood smeared on her cheek. She scratched at the seam between the doors, driving her fingers into the thin crack and pulling. The smoke thickened. Sweat dripped into Peter's eyes. The fire was getting closer.

They wouldn't get anywhere. There was a release beside the door, but a plastic section of wall had been knocked loose and was covering the handle.

Peter had to get to it to open those doors. He stepped toward them. "The handle," he said. "I need—"

"We're all trying to get out," barked the man Peter had

figured for a boss. Peter didn't have time to argue. He moved the man to the side with one hand on his shoulder as easily as pulling a drape. In the same motion, he brought his foot forward and drove it through the plastic panel, shattering it. He reached in and twisted the door release handle.

Peter crouched and hauled the left door open, driving with his legs. The man watched, stunned for a moment, and then he and the woman joined in.

They opened it as far as it would go, shoving it back through the warped metal. It was only two or three feet wide, and with the angle of the train car on its side it looked like a half-open cellar door, but it was enough.

The passengers moved toward the exit, helping the injured, using their cell phones as flashlights. The metal walls were hot to the touch now, and black smoke billowed in, choking with every breath.

Peter helped a young woman out the door and heard a voice behind him. He walked back and found the man in the Korean War hat on the ground, his leg wrecked, his wife struggling to help him to his feet.

He brought the man's arm across his shoulders, eased him up, and walked him to the door, following his wife. Peter half carried him out the door. The vet gritted his teeth against the pain as they landed on the track bed.

Peter stooped under the wreckage, helping the older man along in slow steps—he must have weighed nearly as much as Peter—and they climbed onto the catwalk along the tunnel wall.

The heat stabbed into his back. It felt like his clothes were melting onto his skin. After a minute, the fumes grew so thick that he couldn't see, could only feel that hand in his, the arm tugging against his neck as the man limped beside him, panting from the exertion.

There were cries behind him, coming from deep in the tunnel, audible even over the crackling static of the fires. He took a breath of smoke. His head went light, and he stumbled slightly to the side, his hip banging into the guardrail.

He shut his mouth, stilled his lungs, and went on. Thin beams of light crossed through the murk, and ahead there was a glow like a cloudy dawn: Farragut North. The man slumped down. Peter pressed his legs into the floor and did all he could to keep the man standing.

A face mask appeared out of the black, suddenly close. A DC firefighter stepped in and took the man's other arm. They went on, the last forty feet of the catwalk, and then onto the platform. Another first responder rushed in and took Peter's spot beside the man. Peter heard screams from the tunnel and turned.

"You can't go back in there!" a firefighter yelled to him and grabbed for his shoulder. Peter pulled away and started back, five steps before his vision wavered. He stumbled and they dragged him out of the smoke. It was thicker now, smothering like a pillow over the face.

Someone led him to the stairs. His mind clouded by the fumes, he trudged up the dead escalator with the others: mothers and fathers and daughters and sons, tourists and feds, painted in ash and blood.

39

Pale sunlight angled in through the drapes. Peter touched the tips of his fingers to a white line just above his hairline. The crash had left him with a grade-one concussion and that scar. It only showed when he had a fresh haircut.

Like the rest of Washington after the accident, he'd been on high alert, eager to help find out what sent that train off its tracks and cost so many lives.

Metro and the National Transportation Safety Board called in an outside investigator to avoid any conflicts of interest, and the conclusion came back months later. Parasitic oscillations had developed in the automatic train controls, a result of trying to marry a state-of-the-art computer system to aging wires and failing infrastructure. It was an accident.

A door whispered open, and Rose tiptoed into the sitting room, circling toward his chair.

"Morning," he said.

She jumped back and put her hand to her chest. "Sorry, you startled me a bit. I thought you were asleep."

He stood. It was just after dawn. She was wearing a pair of jeans and a sweater.

"You spent all night in that chair?"

"I moved around a little." He was used to spending nights awake, on watch, sometimes two in a row. Last night had been relatively cushy by his standards. "How did you sleep?"

She made a doubtful face for a moment, wondering, he guessed, if it was a resentful dig at her. It wasn't. She seemed to pick up on that and looked at him warmly.

"Really well, thank you. Do you want some coffee or anything?"

Peter checked his phone. Six thirty A.M. The optics on this were bad, he knew. He would talk to Farr before she heard from someone else that he'd spent the night in the hotel room of a witness.

"I'm good, thanks," he said. "I'm going to step outside for a phone call."

"Okay."

He left the room and started walking toward the sitting area at the end of the hall. His phone buzzed in his hand. It was a White House number.

"Sutherland," he said when he answered it.

"How's it going, Romeo?" It was Farr.

"I—"

"Relax. I know you're not that stupid. You're both in the room?"

"She is. I stepped into the hallway." The security team must have told her that he spent the night.

"Good. Sit tight. I need to talk with Rose. I'll be there in five."

It took three. She probably had been driving by on her way to work. Peter hung out at the chairs near the elevators, because he wanted to catch her on her way in. The elevator arrived with a ding, and Farr stepped out, holding a tray with two coffees in it. She looked exhausted.

"Walk with me, Peter," she said, glancing at her phone. "I don't have much time. I need to run some more questions past her."

"Before you go in."

She pocketed her cell. "Yes."

"She's scared. She doesn't know why Hawkins told her not to talk to the police or other FBI."

Farr's face turned grim. "Did you tell her our concerns about someone inside?" she asked in a low voice. "Why this is siloed?"

"No. I wouldn't. But I would like to tell her something, at least in the broadest outline, to help explain it. It would make her understand why this case is being handled so oddly and put her at ease."

"And make her more likely to work with us."

"It could help." Peter chose his words carefully, trying to concentrate despite the lack of sleep. He was careful not to reveal that Rose knew more than she was letting on. But she had important information to share—what she had heard the Campbells discussing that night and the mention of a chemist—information that might help stop the killers.

"You give her the broadest possible take," Farr said. "That we are keeping this buttoned up because not everyone can be trusted with secrets like this. Nothing about the specifics."

"Sure."

"Is she ready?"

"I'll tell her you're here. She's still a little shaken up."

"I get it," Farr said. "I wouldn't be in a trusting mood either if somebody tried to kill me while I thought I was under protection."

Peter knocked on the door. Rose let him in and looked into the hallway. Farr smiled at her but stayed outside.

Rose closed the door behind her and Peter, and dropped her voice to a whisper. "What is she doing here?"

"She just showed up. She's overseeing this personally. She wants to ask you a few questions to help find out who's behind this."

"I know who she is. I read the paper. Did you tell her? About the other things I heard?"

"No. But you should. I can't get into the details with you, but the reason that Hawkins told you to talk only to him is because not a lot of people can be trusted with this information. It's being tightly held."

"They don't trust the people they work with?"

"I didn't say that."

"The FBI? The police? The White House? They're scared of someone inside there? Jesus Christ, Peter."

"It's a common practice to compartment these things."

"How long have you known her?"

"Eight years. I met her when I was in college."

"She seems . . . I don't know. I like her."

Four knocks came at the door. Rose took two deep breaths, then nodded yes. She straightened out the arms of her sweater while Peter opened the door.

Farr stepped in. After a few pleasantries about how Rose

was doing, Farr lifted her eyebrows to Peter, who caught the message.

"I'm going to step out."

Rose nodded and he left the two of them alone in the room.

40

Farr's wrist ached from holding the tray of coffees for so long. She had grabbed them on her way back from her grandfather's old house in the Palisades, where she had locked the ledger in the gun vault upstairs. The property was currently empty, and she controlled it through a family trust that made it difficult to trace it to her.

She set the coffees down on the table and pointed to the couch, as if asking permission to sit. This was the closest thing this girl had to a home now, and she'd been attacked in a room just like this one, so Farr would tread carefully.

Farr needed Rose at ease, willing to talk, because if she knew anything more about her aunt and uncle and what had led them to the red ledger, Farr would have to give her up to Dimitri Sokolov.

"I picked up an extra," Farr said, and lifted a cup from the tray. Rose took it, along with a creamer.

It was such a simple thing: a gift, but even the smallest gift could create a sense of indebtedness. Farr wanted the truth above all, and she wanted the truth to be that this girl knew nothing. Because even as she sipped her coffee and smiled and kept up the chitchat, warming Rose up, the thought of what she might have to do made her stomach writhe.

Please, Rose, please—I know you're smart, but don't be too smart about this. For your sake. But even when they talked of nothing of substance—how Rose was settling in, whether she needed anything else—there was a sharpness to the young woman. She seemed to be studying Farr, quick glances to her shoes, her purse, her nails, appraising her like a veteran salesperson, or an investigator.

Rose's eyes lingered on Farr's nails. What was she looking at? Farr's breathing picked up. She couldn't push away the feeling that Rose somehow knew that she had spent the night sneaking around. But that was just nerves. *Get ahold of yourself, Diane.*

There was an instant's reflection before Rose spoke, a careful weighing of the words. Farr could tell there was something she was holding back.

Farr couldn't have that. There wasn't room for doubt on this. She put her coffee down and leaned forward, eye to eye with Rose.

"Rose. I know this is difficult. But I need to ask you. Is there anything your aunt and uncle told you that night? Anything you saw or heard that might help us find out who was behind this?"

Rose put the coffee down and looked up, trying to recall. "They were distracted as we drove home, I remember noticing that. Dinner was normal. They were worn out from traveling. We just told old stories, stupid stuff from growing up. Then I went to bed. I woke up because of the smoke alarm."

Rose picked at the plastic lid of the coffee cup with her

thumb and continued. "I went downstairs, and they gave me the number, and told me what to tell Peter about the ledger and OSPREY. And they told me to go. They said to trust them, that they would explain everything later." Her voice wavered with emotion, but she pressed on. "That was the last time I saw them."

Rose took a deep breath and shut her eyes. Farr nodded along through all this, letting Rose find her voice, build momentum. She let the silence work on Rose for a while, but she wasn't giving anything else up.

"And that was all? They didn't tell you anything else? You didn't see anything else? Hear them talking about anything?"

Rose looked down and to the left, then shook her head. "No."

Farr's phone vibrated in her pocket. She silenced it and glanced down. One text message: "Where are you? Meeting in the Oval in 10."

She stood and thanked Rose.

"Of course," the young woman said.

Farr's face relaxed into a smile. "You take care of yourself, all right? We're all very impressed with how you're handling this. It's not easy. Let me know if you need anything at all. We will do everything necessary to make sure you're safe."

She took out a business card and wrote out her direct line on the back.

"Thank you," Rose said, her eyes signaling gratitude perfectly as she took the card, holding it like it was a fragile object. The girl was good.

Farr turned and left. What she wanted to do was sit Peter down and sound him out on anything the girl might have told him, but all she had time for was a quick heads-up as she passed him in the hall. "Can you be in my office at five P.M.?"

"Absolutely," Peter said. "What else do you need?"

"Nothing." She looked at the dark circles under his eyes. "You need to sleep, Peter, please. Get out of here. I'll see you at five."

She kept walking. It wasn't until the elevator door closed that Farr could let her composure drop. She held her hand against the wall to steady herself and shut her eyes as her head fell forward and her throat worked.

Rose had failed the test.

Down and to the left. The girl kept glancing toward the side of her dominant hand. It was a sign of creative thinking, of deception. It wasn't proof enough on its own, but everything about Rose's performance—too innocent, too earnest, hiding away calculations and layers of intelligence—led Farr to the same conclusion. The girl was holding back, and she was good at it. Maybe it was that Rose just wanted to play dumb so that everyone—friend or foe—would leave her the hell alone. Or maybe she didn't trust Farr. Suspected her. Whatever it was, Rose was holding her own secrets, and that couldn't stand.

Farr had to call Dimitri. Rose belonged to him now.

41

When Peter entered Rose's room, she avoided his eyes.

"You all right?" he asked.

"Yes."

"What is it?"

"I didn't tell her."

"About what you heard? The chemist?"

"Yes."

"Did you lie to her about it?"

Rose nodded, and Peter let out a long breath. "Why?"

"I don't know," she said. "I don't want more people coming after me."

"You're already in danger, Rose, and she can help. What your aunt and uncle told you could help."

Rose pressed her lips together.

"You don't trust her," Peter said.

"I don't trust anyone, especially not now. She seemed nervous, sick almost. There was something off."

Peter dragged his hand back through his hair. "It's bad enough I didn't tell her this morning."

"Did she ask?"

"No. Not directly. But this isn't some semantic game. If

I'm withholding, I might as well be lying to her face. Where I work, that world runs on integrity. It's not like out there, where everybody cheats on their taxes a little bit, pads their résumé, twists the truth to get ahead. The slightest hint of deception, even the appearance of it, and I'm out on the street."

"I understand."

She couldn't. She didn't know the story, why he had to be twice as careful as anyone else.

He stepped closer to her. "Forget about me. She can help you find who did this to your aunt and uncle, who came after us last night. You're putting your life—and the lives of others—at risk by withholding information."

"You're going to tell her."

Peter could justify that easily, even though he had promised he wouldn't. He was here to protect her, not make her happy or make her like him. The fear was paralyzing her, and he couldn't let it take him, too.

But she had been right about someone following her, and the security on her yesterday hadn't been enough. He could see her side, and he didn't break his word easily. Integrity cut both ways.

Dual allegiances, to his word and his job. Hiding things. This was dangerous terrain.

"I won't. But take some time with it and tell them. Don't worry about how it will look, changing your story. They'll understand the pressure you're under; they'll be glad for the truth. I'm going to go home and get some sleep. There will be a guard outside the elevators." He opened the door. "I'm meeting with Farr at five."

If she didn't help, he might have to.

She reached out and touched the back of his hand. "Thank you."

"You're welcome. Do the right thing here, Rose."

He stepped away, and she stood in the doorway and watched him go.

42

After he made it home, Peter slept for only a few hours. The sun crawled under his blackout shades, and his throat ached with every breath. The rush of traffic and rumble of garbage trucks filled his apartment. He had earplugs and the white noise machine, but the sounds weren't what was keeping him up. He was used to them by now. It was figuring out what he was going to do next.

If he was withholding, freelancing, he might be starting down that same road that his father had taken.

The decision should be simple. He just met this woman, so why wouldn't he simply go to his bosses and tell them everything he knew?

He touched his fingers to his bruised throat. Maybe it was because he'd seen death come for her twice and had come to respect her fear, her wariness.

He couldn't let anyone else get hurt. He thought of those people on the Metro, the ones he couldn't save. He still heard their voices crying for help from the tunnels, not every day, not anymore, but close to it.

He sat on the edge of the bed and reached for his phone. Too tired to think clearly, he needed to get out of his own head. As he thought through everyone he could possibly confide in, he realized perhaps he had built this honest life up too well. There wasn't a single person he felt comfortable even talking to about this kind of question. Everyone would tell him to follow the rules and silently note that maybe it had been a mistake to trust Sutherland after all.

Leah, his ex, had always been his confidante, his escape, but now she was gone. He scrolled through his contacts, saw the name, and was dialing before he even thought about it: his godfather, Greg.

He answered on the fourth ring: "Peter. Hey. Nice surprise. How are you?"

"Good. You?"

"I'm fine, actually not far from DC." The wind hissed in the background.

"Is that right?"

"Fort Washington. I'm at the marina. Working on *Joust*, if you can believe that."

"What?" It was the boat Peter's father had owned when Peter was a kid.

"I'm fixing it up. Long story. Listen, I can't hear you too well. It's pretty windy here. Is everything okay?"

"Yeah. I was wondering if you want to meet up."

"Absolutely. Sorry for all the phone tag," Greg said, though Peter knew it was mostly his fault. "I know your nights have been crazy. Maybe lunch next week?"

"Could I swing by the marina?" Peter asked.

Greg's tone changed, as if he could tell this was more pressing than a family catch-up. "I'm here all morning." He said something else, but Peter could barely hear it with the wind. "Fort Washington Marina. If there's someone at the guard booth, just tell them you're here for *Joust*."

"Will do."

43

An hour later, as Peter cruised along the Potomac, the river wide here and surrounded by woods, he was glad to be gone from the city. The last year had felt like one long endless day, switching back and forth between his blacked-out apartment and the blacked-out ground floor of the West Wing. The sun, cutting in shafts through high clouds, dazzled him. He wore a button-down and a loose tie. Together they covered most of the bruise on his neck. His jacket lay on the passenger seat.

There was no security guard, and the gate was open. Peter rolled across the gritty lot until he saw it, floating in a slip on the last dock: a C&C 30, white with blue bottom paint and a red stripe just under the gunwale. It looked like most of the other boats had been hauled out for the season.

He started walking toward it. The whine of an orbital sander cut off, and his godfather stood on the deck, wearing an old flannel shirt stained with paint, and pulled off his mask. Greg moved to the stern and stepped onto the dock.

Greg wrapped his arms around Peter and looked him up and down. He smiled but then something happened to the smile, a flicker of unease. Peter could guess. He got it a lot: he looked just like his father.

"It's good to see you, Peter."

"You too."

A silence passed, both of them wanting to say more but not sure what, just looking at each other warmly while the waves splashed against the pilings beneath them.

Greg cleaned his glasses on the sleeve of his shirt. His sandy hair blew in the wind, as tousled as Peter remembered it. A few grays mixed in near the temples, but he still appeared much younger than his years.

He usually had a kind look that made him seem like he had just been pleasantly surprised, and he often seemed to be in his own world. That aloofness tended to fascinate people, women especially, though he had never settled down with anyone. He was good-looking, but shy, awkward around new people, always neat in his appearance. Even his work shirt was tucked in. Peter's father had told him that Greg had suffered from a stutter when he was a kid.

Peter watched the water lap against the bottom paint. How many hours had he spent with a sanding block, scraping away on the hull in the winters? His father thought it would build character, which now seemed like a dark joke. Peter found out in middle school that the keel was lead, and his dad gave him a half smile. "You do fine on your tests."

Greg was still looking at him. There was something parental about it, proud, some awe that the helpless little kid he'd known was now out in the world.

"It had been up on blocks for years," Greg said. "I gutted the electrical, put a new mast in, and redid about half of the fiberglass. Go on." He cocked his head toward the boat.

Peter stepped across the black-green water, put one foot

on the rail, and dropped into the cockpit, the fiberglass flexing under his feet.

He hadn't been on that boat for fourteen years. He and his mother and father and Greg would go out on the bay, with a few sodas and beers and two eighteen-inch deli sandwiches in a red Igloo cooler, and reach back and forth until the sun set.

There was always some disaster: the engine would die, or the boat would run hard aground and the whole family would have to hang out over the water on one side while his dad gunned the engine and shouted, "Farther out! Three—two—one! Lean!" Finally they would tilt it far enough to free the keel, or simply wait for the tide to rise and save them.

Greg reached into the cabin, then tossed something to Peter. He snatched it out of the air. A can of Orange Sunkist.

Peter laughed. It had been his favorite. "Where did you find this?"

"They have it up at the machine by the port office. Always reminds me of you."

Peter tapped the top of the can and cracked it. Greg watched him and raised an eyebrow. It was a beer drinker's move that Peter had picked up during college.

He'd seen Greg only a few times since he left for school. In his godfather's mind, he was probably still the gangly teenager who lived in sweats and fell asleep at his laptop, wearing huge headphones and watching old Jordan videos.

They talked for a bit about what Greg was up to while Peter sipped the soda. He was a civil engineer, a soil and drainage specialist on large-scale infrastructure projects. They traded a few of their favorite maritime disaster stories, and then Peter paused, and ran his hand over the worn leather of the wheel.

"So what's going on?" Greg asked.

Peter looked at him.

"Or did you come out here just to catch up? That's fine."

Greg had always been able to tell what was on his mind. "No. I'm jammed up on something. At work."

"Have you talked to the people at work about it?"

"Some. I thought I could use another perspective, and where I work . . . it's a small world."

"I know."

"You know what I'm doing now?"

"I heard."

Peter had fallen out of touch with almost everyone he knew growing up, Greg included. Part of it was leaving behind anything that had to do with his father, even the people he loved. Greg had been the hardest. He'd looked out for Peter after his mom died, and then slowly over the years they'd drifted apart, Peter's fault mainly.

Part of it was that he was worried Greg would talk him out of working for the bureau. Peter's father's death had hit Greg hard. He'd never been quite the same, withdrew even more.

"You sure you can talk about this?" Greg asked.

"Nothing classified," Peter said. What was he thinking? He shouldn't be talking about this to anyone, but he had no one else he could confide in.

Peter followed Greg's eyes to his own hand, to his thumbnail dragging along the side of his finger. He hadn't even noticed he was doing it. Greg looked up to Peter's face, suddenly wary.

"I'll give you the basic contours," Peter said. "What if you had to choose between keeping your word to someone and doing what your bosses tell you?"

"Is that all there is to it?"

"Let's say, to get the job done, you had to do it in a way your bosses might not like?"

Greg rested his hand on the winch and gave it a turn, the ratchets chattering inside.

"You do the right thing and follow the rules," Greg said. "And then one day you start to wonder if those are two different things."

Peter considered that for a moment.

"You know your dad used to do that . . . the thing with your hand. His was more of a fist."

"Really?" Peter thought he would have remembered that.

"He would get frustrated easily, with the way things were done, would always want to step in and fix it himself. It's not necessarily a bad thing. But I've always wondered if that's how he started out down the wrong path, thinking he was doing the right thing. The road to hell . . ." He closed his eyes, fought back some emotion.

"Is it true?" Peter asked after a moment. "What they say about him?"

"No one will ever know for sure. Your dad used to ask questions like this, Peter. The fact that you came to me makes me think that maybe you've already decided. That's why you're not talking to your peers."

"I have to be extra cautious at work, because of everything that happened."

"Sure." Greg chewed the inside of his lip and looked over the water. "Be careful thinking you've got it all figured out, that you can handle it. That's what happened to your dad. You've always been pretty good about following the rules, Peter."

He nodded.

"That's not just for them, your bosses, whoever. It's for you. It protects you."

From their suspicions? Or from himself? Did he have whatever fault it was that ultimately ruined his dad? Greg was too kind to spell it out, but the suggestion was there.

"Do whatever they say, Peter. And maybe you won't have to choose. Maybe there's some way to be honest with yourself and them. But don't take the rules into your own hands."

Peter let the words sink in.

"Thanks."

"That's all I got. Maybe you came here hoping for something different, but . . ."

"No. That's what I needed to hear."

Peter finished the drink. He had to meet with Diane Farr soon. He had been lucky this morning that she hadn't asked him outright if Rose knew anything else. There was no way he could keep his word to Rose without deceiving Farr.

"I've seen this go badly. Be careful, Peter."

"I will."

They stood in silence for a moment. The halyards slapped the mast in the cold breeze. It sounded like church bells.

"Have you had lunch?" Greg asked.

"I'm okay."

"You need to go?" He must have picked up on Peter's body language.

"I'm sorry to be so abrupt with all this, but I should probably get back."

Greg raised his hands. "I understand." He took a step toward the railing and hugged Peter around the shoulders. Peter climbed over and hopped onto the dock.

There was an awkward silence, as if Greg didn't want to pry and Peter didn't want to drag him into this.

"Thank you," Peter said. "I mean it."

"Any time. You sure you're all right?"

His godfather was looking at him closely now. Peter wondered if he'd noticed the tinge of blue bruise on Peter's throat, poking above his collar.

"Yeah."

Greg couldn't hide his concern, but he didn't speak to it. There was a kind of trust there. "I'm here if you need anything," he said. "Keep your head down, okay?"

"I will."

44

Five minutes after Peter left the marina, he was merging onto the highway, his eyes darting between a braking car ahead and one coming up fast in his rearview. His cell started to ring. He entered the lane and reached for the phone.

"Sutherland, where are you?" It was Farr.

"On the road. Near National Harbor."

An annoyed sigh came from her end. "I thought I told you to get some sleep. I need you at my office. Come straight here. This whole fucking thing is getting out of hand."

"What's up?"

"I'll explain it to you when you get here."

The line went dead. He kept on past Bolling Air Force Base and over the Anacostia into DC, and then crossed the Mall, going up Seventeenth Street to the White House. He pulled into a parking garage on G Street that had a special rate for West Wing staff.

He had just walked through the gate to the White House, when his phone rang again.

"Rose Larkin," the screen said.

He answered it. "Rose. Are you okay?"

"I'm fine." The words were clipped.

"Are you at the hotel?"

She hesitated. "You didn't tell anyone what I told you, right?"

"No. What's up? Where are you, Rose?"

No answer.

"Rose. You're making me nervous here. What's going on?"

"If I told you where I am, would you promise not to tell them?"

"I can't lie for you, Rose."

"I just need time. I don't have anyone else."

"Where are you? You need to get back to the hotel where you'll be safe."

"It's not safe there."

"What are you talking about?"

"I left."

"What about the guards?"

"They followed me."

"They're supposed to."

"Not where I could see them. They were far back. If you're trying to protect someone, wouldn't you stay close?"

There were reasons you would stay back: if you didn't want the target to know you're following them, but that would be surveillance, not protection.

"What am I, bait?" she asked.

God, what if she was right? That was another reason for a long tail, if you wanted to see where the target would go or who would come for them.

But perhaps she was grasping at shadows. He thought that showing her the basics of surveillance would give her confidence, but it might have made her more paranoid.

"Rose. There's a lot going on, and you have every right

to be concerned. But you have to let me help you. Where are you?"

No answer.

"Fine. It's just me and I won't tell anyone. Where are you?"

"Swear?"

"I swear."

"I'm on the Metro. I found something, Peter."

Metro. The word sent a chill through him. "Where are you going?"

"Tenleytown."

"Rose, wait. You shouldn't be out on your own."

"I have to go." She whispered it, as if there was someone nearby trying to listen in. "I'm fine. You know where to find me."

"Hold on—"

The call clicked off, and he turned to see two uniformed officers of the Secret Service ten feet away. A marine guard stood under the West Wing awning, as one did whenever the president was working.

This was not a good place to be acting suspiciously and shouting into a phone about threats.

He dialed her back twice, but each time it went straight to voicemail. Half of those Metro tunnels were dead spots.

Now he knew what had pushed up his meeting with Farr and set her on edge.

He went inside and found her in her office. She dismissed the aide she was talking to. Peter stepped in and she gestured for him to shut the door.

"Your girl pulled a runner," she said.

"Where was the guard?"

"Rose did an out and back in the lobby bar. Multiple exits. Where do you think a girl like that would've picked up surveillance smarts?"

Peter nodded. Fair enough.

"Do you know where she is, Peter?"

He took a deep breath in. He had been weighing this decision for hours. Time was up. He would have to lie, break his word to Rose, or directly refuse to obey his superior.

"Yes."

"Where?"

"She was panicked. The only way I could get her to tell me where she was going was to give her my word I wouldn't tell anyone else."

"So where is she?"

Peter didn't answer.

"Are you telling me that you're willing to throw your entire career for some promise to a woman you didn't even know last week?"

"It was the only way I could find out where she was. She's in danger. I did what I needed to do. I'm the only one she trusts, and if she doesn't trust me we lose our best chance of her helping us find these killers. So let me go get her and talk some sense into her and bring her in safely."

Farr stood up and walked around the desk. She stopped a foot from Peter, her eyes fixed on his.

"I understand that," she said in a steely voice. "Now tell me where she is."

"I can't."

Rose had been right before, about being followed, and doubting her had nearly cost her life. She needed his help.

In the end, all Peter had to guide him was his word. He

was ready to walk. Working for the FBI, this whole crusade to prove himself had been a bad idea from the start, and now, exhausted beyond caring, he had flat-out told his boss no. It felt good after all these years of deference. It felt like power, and Farr was stunned.

She let out a whisper of a laugh and shook her head.

"I guess the girl is smarter than I thought. No one stands their ground like that. And I imagine that's why she trusts you, and why we have at least one person in the entire bureau who knows where she is. Now get the fuck out of my sight."

Peter cocked his head, wondering if he was being fired.

"Get her before someone else does. I'm glad she's your problem and not mine. We can cover the emergency line until you get back."

"Thanks," he said. He turned on his heel and started walking away before she could change her mind.

"Don't thank me yet," she said, and he paused by the door. "There will be consequences for this. Find her and bring her straight back here. That's it. You step out of line and you're done."

45

Tenleytown. Peter knew where Rose was going. That was the closest stop to the crime scene: her aunt and uncle's house in Spring Valley. He tried her cell again, but there was still no answer. The Saturday traffic wasn't too bad as he took Twenty-Second Street to get around Dupont Circle and then turned onto Massachusetts Avenue.

The clock and the driving absorbed his attention, and as he forced his way into a right-hand turn lane, someone honked. He looked back and ignored them, but farther back he saw a familiar car. It was a black Mercedes sedan and Peter took a mental snapshot: well-maintained, tires gleaming, Maryland plates. Traffic stacked up and the intervening cars blocked the Mercedes's tag before he had a chance to remember it.

It wasn't surprising that he thought he'd seen it before. The attack at the hotel had left him paranoid, seeing stalkers on every corner, tails with every car, imagining the whole hidden machine of Russian espionage in the capital aimed at him. It reminded him of how his dad used to joke about the John Birch Society types, seeing Commies everywhere, looking under the bed every night. It was a joke that didn't age well.

But that Mercedes had his old surveillance instincts tingling. He slowed and watched as the other cars passed him, but it never did, just stayed patiently three cars back. He felt the first flush of adrenaline.

As Peter entered the leafy neighborhoods of upper Georgetown, he took a few turns out of his way, and caught another glimpse of it, a block and a half back.

They were hunting him.

Without using a signal, he pulled into the driveway of an office complex and parked in one of the spots. After six seconds, the Mercedes passed. There was no slowing, no driver craning his neck to see Peter. The man behind the wheel was either innocent or professional enough not to play follow-the-leader into a lot with no exit.

Peter drove off, picked his way back to Massachusetts, and had gone another mile when he caught sight of what looked like the same car on a side street, paralleling him. It was too far to be sure, but he wasn't taking any chances.

He stopped at a red light with a Delayed Green sign. The cars across from him waiting to turn left would get the signal soon enough. He watched the first one, studying the reflection of its brake lights on the car behind it.

As soon as their pale red glow disappeared, he gassed it across the intersection. The acceleration pinned him to his seat.

The other drivers would think that he was just some idiot who didn't realize he had a delayed green, but the move would buy him distance from any tails.

He turned right into a tight alley and kept it at twenty-five, whipping past garage doors, then turned again on a narrow connector and cut across the next side street.

He forced himself to ease his grip on the wheel. Four more turns and he was back on his way. His eyes constantly cut to his mirrors. He saw no one following, no Mercedes.

Ten minutes later, he pulled up to the Campbells' house and stepped out of the car. A police crime scene sticker sealed off the front door. The sun disappeared behind the hills to the west, and the trees overhead were turning into black shadows. The blinds were down, but a light was on inside.

Peter's hands crept forward, and his chest felt heavier with every breath. This was where it all started, the site of the murders.

He walked up to the front door and knocked three times, hard. The light went out. Whoever was inside was watching him now, and he stepped back a dozen paces so the streetlight could catch his face.

He hoped it was Rose in there.

The garage door started up with a mechanical grind, and Peter flinched back. The figure standing inside was backlit, but as the door drew up he could tell from the stance and the stature: it was Rose.

He walked toward her slowly.

"Are you by yourself?" she asked.

"Yes."

"You didn't tell them?"

"No. What are you doing here, Rose? This is a crime scene."

"You don't have to tell me that. Come inside before someone sees you." She stepped back into the garage. As she turned Peter saw that she was carrying an aluminum bat.

The garage smelled like smoke, but underneath that was

a familiar scent of cardboard and damp wood and motor oil. It enveloped him, and for an instant he was back in his parents' garage mixing oil in with the gas for the hedge trimmer. This was such a normal, unremarkable home. He had heard it all, but it was still hard to believe what had happened here.

Rose closed the garage door and they entered the house. There was no crime scene tape or hanging plastic or markers on the inside. It looked like the forensic techs had finished with the site, but it was still not a good place to be hanging around.

"We shouldn't be here, Rose. You should come in."

"Maybe there's something here," she said. "That night, my aunt and uncle were talking about a book or a binder."

"The red ledger? But it wouldn't still be here, Rose."

She leaned the bat against the wall in the family room and crouched down. She took out a book on the lowest shelf, riffled through the pages, and put it back, then searched another. Peter looked up and down the shelves.

"It must be more than that," Rose said. "There must be something I know that can be helpful. Why else would someone want to kill me to shut me up? Why else would the people you work for be so desperate to find out what I know?"

"The shooters had access to the site. And then the FBI. If there was something here they would have found it."

She opened another book. Peter looked to his left and saw the bloodstains spread out on the floor, two of them, now dried into black flakes. The patterns suggested a head shot on the left: single source, high-volume bleeding. A slower death on the right.

He rolled his shoulders back and looked away. They needed to go. There was the evidence to consider. Peter had seen killers walk free on technicalities—contaminated crime scenes, clouded chains of custody. But it also wasn't right that she should have to see the blood and brain matter, and someone might have followed him or her here.

As she paged through another book, moving like a machine, he wondered if the shock had her now.

She lifted what looked to be an engineering manual in a blue plastic cover: *Information Technology Management.*

"Rose."

"A book, a binder."

"They wouldn't have kept it here," he said. "That's one of the first things you learn about keeping a cover. You always keep your two lives separate."

"They weren't themselves that night. They seemed . . . hunted. Maybe they didn't have time to get rid of it. Maybe they hid it here."

Peter looked over the shelves. There were hundreds of books: paperback mysteries, spiral-bound songbooks, beautiful first editions in black leather with gold-stamped titles. It would take an FBI team with X-rays a week or so to go through them all properly.

Peter looked out the window. "It's not safe here."

She stood and turned to face him. Her eyes dropped to the bloodstains, and she shut them tight, trying not to cry.

"Okay."

Peter put his arm around her and gently led her toward the door to the garage.

The cold and the lingering smoke inside the garage hit them. Peter pressed the door opener.

As they stepped onto the driveway, Peter wished he had a gun, something to defend themselves.

Rose entered the code to close the door, and they walked to Peter's car and climbed in.

He pulled out, eyes on the rearview, looking for the Mercedes. After a minute, he hit the brakes and stopped in the middle of the tree-lined street.

"What is it?" Rose said. "Are you okay?"

Peter turned to her. "You heard them say a book or a binder?"

"Yes."

"Could it have been one word, a bookbinder? A person? They talked about a chemist, too."

"I couldn't find anyone they knew who was a chemist."

"Maybe they were talking about two occupations, chemist and bookbinder. I know it's old-fashioned, but they had those bound volumes that made me think of it."

"Some of those were gifts. From a friend of theirs. She was an antiques dealer, I think."

"Rare books?"

"I don't know. I just remember talking about it with them when I was a kid. I used to hole up there and read: Jules Verne, *Alice in Wonderland*."

Stay out of this. Leave it to your superiors. Peter, more than anyone, knew the rules, knew exactly what he should do: keep driving straight. Bring her back to the West Wing.

He palmed the wheel around and headed back to the house.

46

Peter took a last scan of the street, then he and Rose walked into the house through the garage. She went to the shelves in the living room and eased out one of the volumes.

It was *Alice's Adventures in Wonderland*, and she leafed through the thick linen pages. Illustrations flipped by: a shocked Hatter, slipping off his shoes, and the Queen of Hearts with her impossibly fat face, shouting, "Off with her head!"

On the title page, in a perfect cursive, there was an inscription.

> *"How do you know I'm mad?" said Alice.*
> *"You must be," said the Cat, "or you wouldn't have*
>   *come here."*
> *Welcome to Washington, loves.*
> *Emily*

"Emily, is that the antiques dealer?" Peter asked.

"Yes. She gave them this."

"But not recently?"

"No. I used to read it when I was a girl."

Rose felt along the spine, searching for hidden objects.

"Did she give them other antiques? Or was it mostly books?"

"I don't remember anything but books," Rose said.

"Did you meet her? Do you know her last name?"

"Maybe at a barbecue, but I don't think I could identify her. I couldn't have been much more than fourteen. But how many bookbinders could there be?"

A creak came from upstairs. Peter froze and listened for a moment, but it was just the house settling.

He knew they were close to something. It felt like standing at the edge of a great height.

Peter took out his phone, and searched Google Maps for "bookbinding" near DC and then "book restoration." There were only five hits.

A quick scan of the images attached to each listing showed that two of them were in strip malls, one in Frederick and one near Annandale. Those two seemed to focus more on binding and printing dissertations, not antique books and rare volumes.

He tried a few more, until he saw a listing with a phone number and an address but no website: ELK Conservation.

"That could match her initials," Rose said.

The address was in a residential area, and he clicked on it. The Street View brought up a photo of a stately two-story Georgian home outside of Alexandria with a long sweeping lawn and an iron fence.

He showed it to Rose.

"That's hers?" she asked.

"Yes. How do you buy a house like that with a business that doesn't seem to exist as much more than a phone number?"

He copied the telephone number, then went to a website called Whitepages.com. It had an option to do a reverse phone lookup, but that only gave him a company name: ELK Conservation, Inc. That was probably enough, though.

He pulled up the website for the Virginia State Corporation Commission and tapped in the name of the company. Corporations usually listed an officer as a point of contact. The search results came up: Emily L. Krysanova, Owner. She had the same address from the Google search results.

"Emily Krysanova, does that sound familiar?" he asked.

"No, but that doesn't mean it isn't her."

Peter typed "Emily Krysanova Alexandria" into Google and clicked on the Images tab. Dozens of faces stared back at him, profile photos of women young and old, many from Russia, among a clutter of random images: a woman on a bicycle, a chess match.

On the second page, there was a shot of three women and one man in *Washington Life,* the local society magazine. It was typical fund-raiser fare: centerpiece flowers climbed to the ceiling around a crowd of very well-put-together people smiling stiffly into the camera. They looked like they were spending a lot of money to have very little fun. The woman on the left, according to the photo caption, was Emily Krysanova.

He tilted the phone back to Rose.

"Do you recognize her?"

She studied it for a moment, then looked to him. "That's her."

He downloaded the photo and spent a few more minutes searching LinkedIn or Yelp or Facebook, for any trace of a public life or online presence, but Krysanova was mostly absent from the web.

"So we have a bookbinder named Emily," Rose said.

"And that business is a decent cover."

"For?"

"Forgery. Flaps and seals. Espionage tradecraft."

Peter felt warm despite the chill in the house. He rocked his weight from foot to foot. They'd found another witness, someone who Rose's aunt and uncle seemed to be keeping from their superiors. She might be in danger. They needed to move.

"She might have answers," Peter said.

Rose's face turned up at that with an expectant look.

"Not us. I've had enough Hardy Boys for one day."

"What are you going to do?"

"Call this in to my boss, and then get you someplace safe."

"But you said you wouldn't tell them."

"I said I wouldn't tell them that you knew more than you were letting on. I said I wouldn't tell them where you are. But this"—he pointed to the book that Krysanova had inscribed—"is a lead in a double homicide investigation and a counterintelligence operation that is about eight levels over my head. I may have already torpedoed my career. That's fine. But this evidence is different. I sit on that, and I'm obstructing justice. I sit on that and I'm breaking another oath. Someone is killing the people who know about this, and if she's involved, she needs more protection than I know how to handle."

"And me?"

"I can try to find a way to keep you out of this. You can

go back to Los Angeles. But we need your help to go after the people who killed your aunt and uncle. It's your choice, but I have to call this in."

He lifted his phone.

Rose didn't object.

Peter tried Farr's cell phone. It rang six times, and after a clicking noise, a voice came on, a man's. It was Farr's aide.

"Diane Farr's office."

"Julian, it's Peter. Is she in?"

"I'm afraid not. I can pass a message on to her."

He looked at Rose. "Have her call me as soon as she can." He read out his cell number.

"I will. And what is this about?"

"Just have her call me. She'll know. And this is for her only, okay? I know some material goes to her and Hawkins."

"You didn't hear about Hawkins?"

"What?"

"He didn't come to work today, missed the morning roundup, didn't give so much as a word. Have you talked to him?"

"No. Is he sick? Where is he?"

"No one knows. Let us know if you hear anything at all."

"I will."

Peter hung up and brought the phone down to his side.

Had the attackers gone after Hawkins, too? If they did, that meant no one was safe. Peter needed to find Krysanova before anything happened to her.

"We should get out of here," he said.

Rose nodded. They walked back through the garage to the car, and Rose paused by the passenger door. "I'm not going back to that hotel."

"You don't have to."

"What if someone is ahead of us?" Rose asked. "What if someone comes for her?"

"Then you should be as far away from that as possible. I'll find you someplace safe to stay," he said.

Rose leveled her eyes at him. She wanted to know what was happening as much as he did.

"If I did find a spot for you," he asked, "would you still go looking for Krysanova?"

She hesitated for a moment. Was she calculating? Thinking through a lie that would let her get away, get to the source?

"I have to know who killed them," Rose said. "What are you going to do? Lock me up somewhere?"

At least she hadn't lied to him. "No."

"Are we going?"

Peter ran his thumb over the sawtooth bumps of his car key.

You've already gone too far. Don't take this into your own hands.

Farr had told him directly. Bring Rose back to her. Nothing more. He knew the rules, knew exactly what to do, knew the risk. That's why he'd always been so careful, that fear—the same fear holding him back right now—that once he crossed a line he wouldn't be able to stop.

But all those thoughts seemed so far away, like an argument in another room. He couldn't let anyone else get hurt. All he could see was Rose standing there over the last of her aunt's and uncle's lives dried on the floor. All he could hear were those voices calling out through the smoke on the Metro.

"We'll drive by. See if she's there. Make sure nothing is happening."

They climbed in, and Peter turned the key. The engine thrummed to life, and he could feel his heartbeat, each pump a dull ache in his bruised throat. No one was going to die on his watch.

47

Peter's eyes flicked back and forth between the road and the mirrors while they drove. He occasionally pulled a quick out and back in a neighborhood to sweep for any tails. He saw no sign.

At the edge of Alexandria, they drove down a highway crowded with commercial developments and apartment buildings, then turned onto a side street. It left the strip malls behind and turned into a curving road with large houses set back, nearly out of sight behind hedges and fences. Peter checked the numbers on the mailboxes.

"That's her house," Rose said. "You passed it."

It was intentional. Peter peered at it out of the corners of his eyes. "We'll park around the side." He didn't want to draw attention.

"Did you see something?"

"The back window. I'm not certain. But it looked like someone standing in the dark."

"One person?"

"There could have been more out of sight. It was a quick look."

He turned right down a lane that led around the side of

the property. The bows of trees arching overhead blocked out the last light.

They stepped out, and Peter eased his door shut. Rose followed suit. He locked the car with the key, not the fob, to avoid any beeping or flashing of lights. As his eyes adjusted, he could pick up the shape of the branches overhead and old wooden telephone poles standing out against the sky.

Peter led them back to the road, and they moved along the fence line until the property came back into view through the trees.

"Hang back here," he said and nodded to a spot near the corner where the bushes would give Rose some cover from the road. He noticed his senses focusing, the night sounds of frogs and crickets growing clearer. He missed the action, the hunt.

"I'm going to take a look," he said and handed her the keys. "If anything happens, just run. Go to the car and go to the police."

"I can go with you."

"I'll be right there," he said and pointed to the driveway entrance. He wanted a better look at that window. "I'll check it out first."

She nodded, and he slipped away along the fence. He rounded the mailbox and stepped across the driveway until he could get a view of the side of the house. There was one light glowing, which might have been left on to make the house look inhabited, but there were no newspapers or circulars piled up, and even with all the trees, the old Jaguar out front was clean of leaves.

Something whispered across the grass behind him, and even as he turned, startled, the voice spoke: "Stop and extend your hands to the side. If they come near your body I will shoot you."

Peter's breath caught and he let it out slowly, mouth tight, as he turned around and brought his hands up.

A woman stood in the moonlight, the pistol held in front of her in a confident isosceles stance. She had silver hair, and fine features, and wore a belted tweed coat.

A hunting coat.

Her voice told volumes: a patrician British accent with a hint of Russian left over in the extra breath around the vowels. This was Emily Krysanova.

"I'm not armed," Peter said. "I'm not here to hurt you. I work for the FBI, and I'm trying to find out who killed Henry and Paulette Campbell."

Krysanova ignored his words. "With your left hand," she said, "take the lapel of your suit jacket and lift it away from your body, first the right side and then the left, so I can see your waist and under your arms."

Peter lifted the fabric away.

"With your left hand raise your jacket by the back of the collar and then turn."

He tugged it up, feeling like a scarecrow twisting in the wind. "Can I show you my credentials?"

"That would prove nothing."

Spoken like a true forger. She took three steps closer and raised the pistol, aiming at his face.

"Hold on—"

She didn't respond, just studied him, and then whipped to the left where another figure approached out of the darkness.

It was Rose.

"Emily. My name is Rose Larkin. Henry and Paulette Campbell were my aunt and uncle. Do you remember me?"

The gun tracked back and forth between Rose and Peter. He bent his knees and shifted his weight onto the balls of his feet. No. Rushing Krysanova would be suicide. She had left enough distance between them to give herself time to target and shoot.

"Arms out, come three steps closer," Krysanova said.

Rose complied, and even with the gun aimed at Rose's head, Krysanova showed a hint of a smile. Her aim returned to Peter, but her words went to Rose: "You look lovely, child."

"I brought him," Rose said. "He's helping us."

"This isn't your world, Rose. How can you trust him?"

"He's with the FBI."

"So?"

"My aunt and uncle gave me a number to call. People they trusted. He answered."

"The emergency line?"

"Yes. He was on the other end."

Krysanova called to Peter, "What are the codes? For night action?"

"What's the number?" Peter asked.

Krysanova chuckled. "You're worried about my bona fides?" She repeated back the digits. "Your turn."

"Pen. Clock. Door. Fire," Peter said.

She lowered the gun. "Christ. Why didn't you use the signal when you first showed up?" She searched the street. "And where's your car?"

"Around the corner," Peter said.

Krysanova shook her head, annoyed. "You nearly got yourself killed. Come inside. It's not safe out here."

They entered through the foyer, and Krysanova took a last look outside, the gun hanging in her hand by her right thigh, and then closed the door behind them. It was a beautiful mansion, with marble floors and paneled walls. A curved staircase wrapped around the entry and led to the second and third floors. To their right was a library lined with old volumes.

Large arched windows filled one wall of a formal sitting room ahead, and standing in front of one was a white bust of a classical figure, maybe Diana or Hippolyta, the shoulders just above the sill.

That was the figure Peter had seen standing in the dark when he first drove by.

The place had a hip, rich, eclectic vibe that Peter didn't see all that often around Washington: abstract expressionists on the wall alongside contemporary large-format photography, a long wooden table surrounded by Philippe Starck chairs, and high on one wall, the horned skull of a steer. It looked like a modern gallery.

"Phones," Krysanova mouthed, and after a look back and forth between them, Peter and Rose produced their cells. Krysanova pried the back off Peter's Android model and pulled out the battery, then frowned at Rose's iPhone before she led them down the long central corridor of the main floor and turned right into the kitchen.

She opened the freezer door and placed both handsets and the battery inside on top of a box of phyllo dough.

She relaxed slightly now that the phones were out of the way.

"Did you see anyone outside?" she asked. "Did anyone follow you?"

"We're clear."

"Good," she said, and turned to Rose. "I'm so sorry about your aunt and uncle, dear." The sadness touched her slate-blue eyes. It looked so natural there.

"Thank you," Rose said. "Do you have any idea what's happening?"

Krysanova nodded soberly, like she had expected this. "We should talk downstairs."

She pulled her car keys off the counter and opened the door near the rear of the kitchen: a broom closet. Krysanova stepped inside and gave them a little flick of her head as if to say *come on*.

Peter and Rose exchanged a skeptical glance and crowded in the closet doorway. Krysanova passed her keys over a junction box on the wall above the light switch. A hollow *thock* came from the rear wall, which Krysanova pressed. The wall swung to the side. Lights glowed from beneath them, where a steep set of stairs led into a basement.

Peter and Rose craned their heads to look down, and Krysanova descended the steps without a word as if this were the most normal thing in the world.

48

Peter was the last one down. He paused on the final step and looked around the basement.

Halogen lights shined down from overhead. They followed Krysanova into a workshop dominated at one end by two long, well-worn workbenches. Their surfaces were crowded with a neat array of razor knives, glues, and spray bottles. The farther bench had a Mac desktop computer connected to two thirty-inch monitors and a light box for color correction. A door to one side had a heavy black shade drawn across it: a darkroom, Peter guessed.

On the wall, a flat-screen TV showed the feed from four surveillance cameras on a grid.

This was a forgery shop, and Krysanova clearly some kind of intelligence player. She had greeted them with a drawn pistol. Peter shouldn't be here, he knew, but this woman had the answers they needed. He was careful. He could handle himself, keep from getting played, from aiding the enemy.

He wasn't his father, he told himself, but he couldn't hold off a dark thought: *Not yet.*

To the right was a small sitting area. An old stereo receiver hooked up to a pair of speakers and a record player sat on an antique table. Vinyl albums filled the bookshelf to the left. There were two chairs and a matching sofa, in green upholstery with a carved wood frame. It was ornate, old-school, Soviet grandeur with a touch of kitsch.

"Nostalgia," she said. "I can't get away with it upstairs. Do you want anything? Tea? Water? A drink?"

"I'm fine," Rose said. Peter held up his hand to say the same.

"I'm surprised that you're part of this, Rose," Krysanova said.

"I was there, the night my aunt and uncle died," Rose said. "Now whoever took them is after me."

Krysanova took a deep breath. Obviously, by allowing them in here, she wasn't trying to conceal that she was involved in covert work or that she knew something about all this. She didn't even seem surprised that Peter and Rose had found her, nor did she ask how they did, which seemed odd to Peter.

"It's Russia," Krysanova said. "I don't know the name of the man who killed them, but he is SVR"—Russian foreign intelligence, comparable to the CIA—"although an attack like that would have to get approval from the Kremlin, from the very top, Vikhrov himself."

"But why were they killed?" Rose asked.

"They had something very dangerous."

Rose ran her thumb along her curled index finger, and Peter could tell she was hesitating, not sure what to say about her aunt's and uncle's last words, and about the ledger.

"You're worried about giving me more than you're taking," Krysanova said. Sadness touched her eyes. "You would have been a good intelligence officer. Your aunt and uncle were so proud of you, Rose." She sat in a chair and laid the gun on the end table to her right. "Please," she said and indicated the couch.

Rose sat, and Peter, after a moment's hesitation, followed suit.

"Do you remember me, Rose?"

"Yes. From their house. You would come by on the weekends."

"I'm surprised. You were so young. That was a hard time for me. I was often out all night. Ugly work. Sometimes I would go straight there in the morning, and you would be watching cartoons or reading. It was nice to see love like they had, or you, with those round cheeks, saying whatever was on your mind. They never had children. The work was too dangerous. They were always afraid that somehow, they would get dragged in."

She closed her eyes and shook her head. It pained her to see Rose drawn into this.

"Do you work for the Russians?" Rose asked.

"I did."

"What did you do?"

"What didn't I do for my country?" She laughed, a bitter sound. Peter sat, keenly aware of how she watched him. He kept his bearing straight, forced any reaction or tells from his face. She didn't have to say it outright. He knew. Here he was, trading with a Russian spy.

Peter studied the way she carried herself. She was perhaps sixty, still beautiful, and there was something practiced about her manner, the way she put them at ease with a faint smile and looked directly in their eyes. She seemed like a very good actor. The Russians had always relied heavily on sex and coercion in espionage. They had whole schools dedicated to training women for the work.

"Bookbinding," Peter said. "Did you work on documents?"

"You can say it. A forger. It doesn't bother me. That has been my specialty for the last twenty years or so. I picked this up later in life. You have to adapt. Before that my job was to make Americans trust me no matter what it took, to lower their guard, to compromise them."

"And who do you work for now?" Rose asked.

"My loyalty is to money these days. Ultimately everyone's is, I found, especially my old employers'. They looted my country. Scavengers, this dictator we have now chief among them. Practically pulled the wires from the walls of headquarters to sell for scrap. Imagine if someone turned the nation you loved into one big *mafiya*. Murdered anyone who stood in their way, for greed alone."

She paused and purged the anger from her voice. "It's nice to dispense with the facades. I work for myself, for this." She held her hands up, pointing to the mansion over their heads. "It's all so much simpler that way. No illusions."

"You were a source for my aunt and uncle?"

"I helped them track Russian espionage activity in the US for many years. They were the best counterintelligence officers America has ever produced."

"You said they had something dangerous."

"Yes. I know you may not want to tell me anything they shared with you but let me guess. They talked about something red."

Peter watched Rose, impressed how well she hid any reaction. "Yes," she said.

Krysanova shut her eyes and kneaded her temple. "That fucking book. I helped them find it. There was an illegal—a Russian officer working without any kind of diplomatic cover—named Anton Novikoff. He was a go-between, moved money around, kept the accounts, acted as a courier. I can't remember what his cover name was, something ridiculous like Tom Grant. His English was perfect, though. He could sell it."

"Was he a chemist?"

"Yes. That was Anton's cover. He had been trained in it. God, he could bore you senseless with that stuff. He was maybe this tall"—she held her hand up in the low five-foot range—"red hair and very pale, and just lived for tango. You put him out on that dance floor and he might as well have been six feet tall, Sean Connery in his prime. He was a cutout used to facilitate meetings between high-level SVR officers and a source inside the US government. It turns out he was keeping a record of all those meetings. In a ledger."

"Like for expenses?" Peter asked.

"Yes. I imagine it's what he had handy."

"And just paper and pencil?"

"That's the only way to keep a secret these days, darling. Person-to-person, and pen and pad. If it's recorded digitally, anywhere, Russian intelligence can get to it. They can get inside anything."

"Does it identify the source?" he said.

"Only by a codename. BEECH."

Rose leaned forward. "He gave the ledger to my aunt and uncle."

Krysanova nodded slowly. "I put them in touch. Anton was terrified when he found out what he was working on."

"What was it?" Rose asked.

"He came to understand that his superiors were planning an attack. That's why he came to me."

"The Russians are going to attack the United States?"

"It wouldn't be the Russians, of course. It would be blamed on someone else, a likely suspect, Chechens or Saudis, and there would be no way to trace it to the Kremlin. The attackers themselves might not even know. That's how these things go. You meet somebody who claims to be Israeli or Saudi and in the end you have no idea who you're working for or what you're doing. That's the Russian way, to cloud the truth until nothing can be trusted. *Maskirovka,* the masquerade. It's maddening. It's why I left. And now they're poisoning the world with it through all these little screens we're addicted to."

"What kind of attack?" Peter asked.

"I don't know."

"And now whoever killed them has the ledger?" he said.

"Perhaps. It's a curse. Once Anton realized what he was involved in, he thought he could protect himself by keeping a record of the meetings, in case they tried to pin it on him, to cut out the cutout. The Kremlin didn't like that. When you're involved in an operation that sensitive, you know that it is just as dangerous for you as it is for the target. If anyone found out or was able to trace the plot back to Russia, retaliation would be justified by the US. It would be catastrophic. Wars have been waged over less."

"It doesn't say what the actual operation is?" Peter asked.

"Not as I understand it, but he didn't share everything

with me, especially near the end. He didn't want to make me a target, too. It's names and dates and places for these clandestine meetings. As far as evidence goes, that can be as powerful as a photo or a recording. Those can be forged. But these were senior officials. Most of their travel is publicly known. With the information in that ledger, even just a copy of it, you could track down who from the US and Russia was in each place. Each entry narrows the circle, until it's around their necks. And he was terrified these last few weeks. Maybe he found something more. He was good at stealing information, brave, even when he was spying against his own superiors. Whatever he discovered, BEECH and the Russians will do what they need to find it and keep it secret. Extreme measures, but I can understand why they would stick their neck out now."

Peter thought he knew the answer: the deadline. "Why now?"

"That was why Anton panicked. Whatever this is building to. It happens tomorrow."

"The Russian president will be in DC," Peter said.

"Yes, and the foreign minister is already here."

"What's going to happen?" he asked.

"Everyone who could tell us the answer to that question is dead."

"Anton Novikoff?"

Krysanova closed her eyes for an instant. "He's on a cold storage shelf at the Atlanta medical examiner's office. The official story was that it was a hit and run. But they killed him."

Peter gritted his teeth but held back the emotion, even as the images of his father's fatal crash flashed through his mind: the left hand hanging out of the broken window, perfect in the midst of all that destruction, as if he were just holding it out to enjoy the drive on a summer's day. Both men had gotten caught up in Russia's games. Peter's father died from desperation, but Anton Novikoff's death, like those of Henry and Paulette Campbell, was straight murder.

There was only one saving grace in all this. The killers were taking an extraordinary risk to find that book and eliminate anyone who knew about it, drawing attention to themselves on the eve of the deadline. They wouldn't do that unless the information in the ledger threatened everything they had planned. If Peter could find that book, maybe he could stop whatever was coming.

"Where's the ledger now?" he asked.

"I don't know," Krysanova said. "Anton was going to give it to the Campbells."

Rose leaned forward, her palms on her knees. "Did Anton Novikoff ever use the codename OSPREY?"

"Not that I know of. But I don't know what name he used with your aunt and uncle. Was that one of their sources?"

"Yes," Rose said. "Who else knows about this? Is there anywhere else we can go?"

"Anton had one contact I know of, a last resort."

"Who?"

"I just have a codename. GIDEON. Anton met with him looking for help, a way to outplay the Russians. He was going to use him as a backup if things didn't work out with your aunt and uncle. He talked about GIDEON like he was a legend, a spy who had played all sides against each other for decades and somehow survived. He's dangerous. Anton only went to him because he was desperate."

"How would you find him?" Rose's fingers tightened, squeezing her legs. She was hooked, Peter could see, wanted to go deeper into this world.

"GIDEON has a signal that can be used to set up a meeting. Anton gave it to me." Krysanova rose, picked up the gun, and walked to a filing cabinet. She rested the pistol on top and dialed in the combination. After a moment of leafing through the folders, she pulled out a single sheet.

"There is a fire hydrant on the National Mall, in front of the carousel. To ask for a meeting, you put a mark on it. I have the notes on the meeting site and the protocol here. He's very careful."

She shut the drawer and held up the paper. "I was waiting to contact him, until I understood more about what was happening."

"We need to talk to him," Rose said. "Whoever is killing these people, they're after me, too."

"I have the same concern." Krysanova looked at the gun. "It's why I'm taking precautions."

Her eyes went back to the camera feeds.

"I thought I saw someone following me. That's why I called."

"Called?" Peter said.

But Krysanova wasn't paying attention to him. On the screen, a sedan had pulled up on the road in front of the property.

"Yes, I called the number Henry Campbell had given me. The emergency number. The night action line. Henry said it went to people they trusted. That I could use it if I ever felt I was in danger. That was an hour ago. I thought they sent you," she said, looking to Peter.

"That's not why we're here," he said, walking toward her, looking at the screen.

Rose stood up beside him. "I overheard my aunt and uncle talking about a bookbinder the night they died. We traced it back to you. We don't know anything about a call."

Krysanova picked up the gun and walked to the steps. Peter and Rose followed her upstairs to the kitchen. Pausing by the dining table, she put down the page of meeting notes and wrapped both hands around the grip of her gun. She crossed to the living room window, in the dark, and peered out beside the blinds.

Lights pulsed on the street, the high beams of the car. Three short, one long, and two short. The driver repeated the pattern three times. Krysanova let out a long breath and relaxed, lowering the gun.

"It's fine. When I called the emergency line, that's the signal they said they would use to let me know it's safe. I'm expecting them."

She walked to the front door, standing in the dark foyer. "Stay there. They're only expecting one person. I don't want to spook them."

"Wait," Peter said. "Who did you talk to?"

"A young man. Very polished. Maybe a Midwestern accent."

That must have been Julian, the aide, working the day shift.

"He put me through to Diane Farr," Krysanova added. "She said she'd send someone to bring me in." She turned on the foyer lights. "I'll explain that you're—"

The glass panes to the left of the door shattered into the room and tinkled across the marble. Krysanova took a long backward step but then her body went rigid. The bullet, entering above her right brow, took the upper right quarter of her head off in a long jet through the foyer. Peter heard bone skittering across the marble floor. He grabbed Rose's arm before the body hit the ground and hauled her away from the light.

49

None of it felt real. Peter's mind went back to Hogan's Alley at Quantico, heart pounding as they ran the same active shooter drill for the fifth time. He didn't need to remember anything from the training. His muscles moved almost on their own.

With Rose covered behind the wall, he killed the light and shot forward in a low crouch toward the gun. He felt along the cold floor until his fingers touched the back of Krysanova's hand and then the frame of the nine-millimeter. He took the pistol and turned.

She was dead. There was no doubt, but still, even with the gunman closing in outside, Peter had to force himself to leave her and move back to cover.

Rose pressed her back against the wall, hands held together in front of her chest, shaking, breathing fast.

"We need to run," he said. "The back."

She nodded and took a long breath. "Okay."

He took her hand, and they ran through the dining room and into the kitchen. Peter stopped and opened the freezer door, while Rose stood by the table. He slid his hand onto the switch to keep the freezer light off and took their phones and his battery.

They moved on through the rear hall into a mudroom, hit the back door, and went outside. Peter scanned the yard. It was too dark to see much more than the black outlines of trees between them and the side lane where they had parked.

A few lights from the street cast the faintest glow along the side of the house, so he circled in the other direction, away from the house. He went to the left over the trim grass lawn and then the branches and leaves of the woods, Rose at his side. Peter slowed, looking back, raising the gun. Was that the shooter?

A flashlight shot toward them, a blue-white electric shaft as bright as day. It covered the side yard in great arcs, and then tracked toward them. It was too far for Peter to shoot, and firing the gun would only give him away.

Rose looked over her shoulder as the light swept toward her, then lunged behind a tree as it flooded around her. Peter was twenty feet from her now. The light cut back his way, and he threw himself behind another tree. The light hit it, and the beam, cut in half by a long shadow, lit up the leaves and grass on either side of him.

It reflected enough ambient light that he could see Rose hiding, pressing against the bark of the other tree, looking at him with dread. He raised his hand as if to say *hold*.

His body was in revolt: cold sweat on his hands, blood pumping loudly in his skull. He had never faced fear like this, but pressure he knew, knew how to control it, calm his heart, steady his hands. He could turn it, use it to fight, to win.

The light passed between them, over the spot where Rose was hiding, then stopped just beyond her, between her and the car. The shooter was moving now. The light grew brighter and bounced slightly as he walked. It edged back and fixed on the tree where Rose stood.

He would find her soon. Peter crept around, trying to get a glimpse of the gunman. He was still too far away to hit with a pistol. The shot that had killed Krysanova was long and accurate, which meant there was a rifle coming. Peter wouldn't stand a chance.

Rose lifted her hands slightly, desperate to know what to do. Peter raised the gun. He tapped it, so Rose could see, and held up three fingers, pointed to her and then to the edge of the woods: *I shoot, you run.*

They were on top of a low rise. If she ran downhill toward the car she would find more cover. He just needed to get that light away from her. The shooter was moving to her side now, and Rose sidestepped to stay in the shadows. She was breathing way too fast, and Peter hoped she wouldn't freeze up. He raised three fingers on his left hand and nodded, and after a moment she nodded back.

He straightened the three fingers on his left and readied the gun with his right. *Three.*

Two. She got low, ready to sprint.

One.

He leaned out slightly and fired two shots. The flare from the barrel of Peter's gun lit the woods red. The man, nearly sixty yards out, didn't retreat; his light fixed on Peter, who took cover, pressing his back against the tree as the rifle rounds came. The afterimage of his own shots still burned blue in his vision.

Crack. The whole tree shuddered against his back as the rifle round buried deep into the wood. His body tensed, but he held still. They sounded too faint. Maybe the shooter was using a suppressor on the gun, or maybe it was a strange trick of perception from all the adrenaline, like tunnel vision.

Crack. Another round. The bullet hissed and the side of the tree blew out in a cloud of splintered wood. A third shot, on the other side, tore off more bark. The shooter was slow, methodical, precise. That meant fixed attention. That meant Rose had a chance.

The light came closer. Peter knew that if he stuck so much as a finger past the edge of the tree, it would be gone. Pistol against rifle, coming from cover—shooting back was suicide, even without fear jacking him up. He could see his breath in the cold night, but still a drop of sweat ran down his back, and an awful smell of terror rose off his body.

He wanted to hear the engine, wanted Rose to get the hell out of there—but part of him didn't. He didn't want to be left alone here to die.

He could see telephone poles sticking up at the edge of the woods. One of them had a black cylinder in silhouette near the top: a transformer.

He needed to draw away the shooter's attention, the way his first shot had for Rose. If he could get that transformer to blow, he would have his distraction.

Peter raised the gun, focused on the front sight, and lined it up on the transformer. He pulled the trigger and the gun jumped in his hand.

Nothing happened to the transformer. Had he missed?

The rifle fired again, and the tree boomed against Peter's back. He aimed his gun and took three more shots at the transformer.

The tree shook again. The shooter was coming around fast, and there would be no place to hide. Peter could hear the footsteps now, rushing over the leaves. It was going to come down to this, face-to-face. And a thought tried to take over his mind, impossible to conceive and yet so real: he was going to die.

He took a long breath in and let it out, and felt the gun, the checkered grip against his palm, let the present fill his mind and keep that fear at bay. Turning slightly, still close to the tree, he brought the pistol to a high carry, ready to shoot.

Then lightning exploded down the hill, a white arc shooting across the power line, flashing the whole night blue with a boom he felt in his chest. The transformer had finally blown.

Peter ran, angling slightly so that the shooter would have to lead him, making the shot harder. Another bang, and a tree exploded to his left and something stabbed above his collarbone. He groaned in pain and clapped his left hand over it, but kept going.

He vaulted over a fallen tree and sprinted down the hill, legs like pistons. The light searched for him, but the gunman must have lost sight of him over the rise. Peter wheeled toward the lane, then heard an engine growling behind him: his car, lights off, racing toward him.

Rose was at the wheel. He grabbed the door handle while the car was still moving and threw himself into the passenger seat. "Go! Go! Go!"

She punched it. The rear tires screamed and then caught, and the car shot down the road. Rose kept up the speed around a curve, holding steady even as the tires squealed and drifted.

Peter felt his collar. He was breathing fine, but his fingers came back smeared with blood. He wiped it on his pants before Rose could see it, then sank back in his seat.

50

"Are we clear?" Rose asked.

Peter checked the mirrors again. "Yes. Good driving."

"LA standard," she said, hugging the wheel, her face as white as printer paper. He'd navigated them on local roads to 395 North, and now they were speeding along the interstate.

"Where do I go?"

"Exit up there." He pointed to the left, toward a seemingly endless limestone facade.

"The Pentagon?"

"Pull in the south lot. It should be open. It's the safest place I can think of."

She turned onto Rotary Road, and then crawled through the empty lots surrounded by Jersey barriers. Guard booths stood between them and the Metro entrance.

"There." He pointed to a spot halfway across the parking area.

Rose pulled into the space and put the car in park. She held the wheel with both hands and let her head fall forward.

Peter put his hand on her back. "Are you sure you're okay?"

"Yes. I didn't get hurt, but I feel a little sick."

"You want some air? Walk around?"

"I'll be fine." She looked at her hands, opened and closed them. "I can't stop shaking, but—Jesus, Peter! Your neck."

He touched the fabric at his neck, then looked at his fingers. Less blood now. It stung like venom but he was so relieved to be alive he didn't care.

"It doesn't feel too bad."

Rose hissed as she helped him open his collar and looked at the wound. Peter checked the glove box and pulled out a pack of tissues, then dabbed along the cut. It burned but he could move his head fine. He pulled out a fresh tissue and pressed it down on his neck. "It'll be all right," he said.

She rested one hand on the wheel. "Back at the house . . . was she . . . dead?"

"Yes."

Rose shut her eyes. "God. Do you believe what she said? About calling Farr? Do you think Farr sent that car to kill her?"

Peter fought to stay calm, to order his thoughts. Krysanova called the emergency line and talked to Farr. Farr definitely sent that car. The driver used the safe signal that Farr provided. And whoever was in that car killed Krysanova.

He turned to Rose. "She must have."

She held the back of her hand to her mouth and looked out the window.

Peter sat back. A wave of nausea ran through him. Now he finally understood why every call on that line went eyes only to Farr and Hawkins.

"She's using the emergency line to find anyone who knows about what's really happening," he said. "Your aunt and uncle gave that number to the people who were helping them find the truth."

"And so she killed them? She had my aunt and uncle murdered?"

It was hard to conceive, but Peter had seen it before, the scandal that took down his father, betrayal at the highest level.

"I think so," he said. His stomach tightened. He had played a part in Farr's crimes. He remembered all those endless hours, remembered the first time the emergency line had rung, months ago, remembered the urgency in the caller's voice. Was that another source? Another witness? He had delivered that person straight to Farr. Was that caller dead now, too?

"What could Farr possibly be protecting that would be worth doing something like that?" Rose asked.

"She's protecting herself, by keeping it secret. And you heard Krysanova. The scale of this thing. It's insane."

She didn't say anything, and he thought maybe this was too much for her to take at once: getting shot at, getting hit with this news.

"Rose, listen—" he said gently.

But she cut him off. "Krysanova said that whatever happens will happen tomorrow."

She didn't want consoling. She wanted answers.

"That's the same deadline my aunt and uncle gave me the night they died," she said. "We have to move. We have to find out what all this builds up to."

She rocked slightly, thinking, trying to marshal all that fear and adrenaline and find a way forward.

"OSPREY," she said. "You think that was the codename

they used for Anton Novikoff, the guy who made the ledger?"

"That matches up with everything we know."

"But that means the best witness on all this is dead. Jesus." She turned and faced him. "We should go to the police."

"We would sound insane. And I don't know how long we'd last once Farr figures out what we know."

"Did whoever killed Krysanova see us?"

Peter played the events back in his mind. The foyer. The woods. The flashlight. The last desperate sprint. "No. The light never hit me or my face directly, and he might not have seen you at all."

"But when I ran?"

"He was firing at the tree. It's not certain, but he might not know that there were two of us."

"How do you know it's a he?"

"I don't."

"GIDEON," Rose said, suddenly remembering. She pulled a piece of paper from her pocket and unfolded it: Krysanova's notes. "I took this from the dining table."

Peter looked over the paper. As Krysanova had said, it was a meeting protocol: instructions on how she could signal that she wanted to connect with GIDEON—by leaving a mark on a fire hydrant on the National Mall—as well as the meeting site itself, deep in Rock Creek Park.

"We have to find GIDEON," Rose said. "He's the only other source we know about. He might know what's happening or be able to help us stop it."

He looked at the paper. The person requesting a meeting was supposed to scratch the paint on top of the hydrant, where the word "open" appeared in forged letters above an arrow. The signal was a vertical scratch through the O in "open."

He looked at the times listed on the paper. If they left the mark tonight, it would set up a meeting the next morning.

"Even if we do use this signal, even if we wanted to get deeper into this, the meeting wouldn't be until tomorrow morning at seven."

"But you said we can't go to the police or the people you work for," she said. "Isn't GIDEON our only option?"

"Krysanova also wasn't sure if she could trust him, said he was ruthless. We almost died back there, Rose, and I don't think we should crash a meet-up with some underworld figure we know nothing about."

"Let's signal, at least. We're running out of time."

Rose was desperate. He was too, but he wasn't ready to give himself up to that world—of secret meetings and deals with potential enemies of the US.

"Not yet."

"So what are we going to do?"

Peter watched a plane cross the sky on its final approach to Reagan National. "First, get you someplace safe."

"Me?"

"I have work tonight," he said. "Farr sent me to find you. If I don't report back, that will raise suspicions."

"You're going straight to the woman who just tried to have us killed?"

"Yes. She must have communicated with the shooter somehow. If I could find a trace, a phone log, anything concrete, I could blow the whistle, take it to the inspector general for intelligence."

"She's the chief of staff. Won't she find out?"

"There's a way around her. There has to be. Is there anywhere you can stay, someplace that wouldn't be obvious? A place where the FBI wouldn't look?"

Her head fell back against the seat. "The FBI is after me?"

"As a witness, yes. But they're not going to find you."

"I don't have anybody like that I can call. Can they get information from hotels?"

"Yes. All your credit card transactions. A hotwatch, they call it. They don't even need a warrant."

"Maybe if I pay cash at a hotel? Can you even look up something like that?" Rose took out her phone. "'Hotels that take cash DC'?"

"There can't be many, and that would be the first place I would look for you."

"Airbnb," she said. The blue glow of her phone lit her face. "My company's account."

"Is it linked to a credit card in your name?"

"No. Our HR guy set up the account."

Peter brightened. "That should work. As long as it's not tied to your Social Security number."

Rose held the phone out to him, and he studied the map of available rentals. "There," he said and clicked on a room for rent for the night near U Street in Washington. "It's right around the corner from the Third District headquarters of the DC police." He returned to the listings page, scanned the map again, and pointed at the phone. "And here's an embassy, which means there might be some Secret Service nearby, too. That will make it harder for anyone to try anything there."

She took the phone and tapped the screen.

"Booked?" Peter asked.

"It says instant, yeah."

A knuckle rapped on the window, and both of them jerked back in their seats. It was the Pentagon Police. Rose looked at Peter nervously, and then, as if flipping a switch, composed her face into a mask of calm, turned, and rolled down the window.

They couldn't see the cop with the light in their eyes.

"You can't be in here without a permit."

He turned the beam to Peter, who tried to offer him a pleasant, harmless look, but it felt off, twitchy. Surely some leftover panic was showing.

Peter glanced down, and saw the blood on the tissue in the cupholder.

"What are you doing here?"

Peter turned slightly, but not enough to bring the cut into view. "Is the memorial open?" he asked. There was a September 11 memorial near the Pentagon. It was the best excuse he could think up.

The light went straight into Peter's eyes, and the officer didn't respond for a moment.

"You're looking for the memorial?" Another pause.

The cop's boots ground against the asphalt, and his right hand drifted toward his duty belt, his pistol.

He hooked a thumb inside the leather.

"You need to park at Pentagon City Mall and walk back. It's about five minutes. Go out. Left then right. You can't miss it."

"Thank you," Rose said. She smiled as the officer stepped back, then she put it in drive and rolled toward the exit.

51

The Airbnb rental was in a house on an odd block of Florida Avenue just north of U Street, and it faced a high retaining wall. Florida Avenue was the old boundary road of the city of Washington inside the larger, ten-mile-square District of Columbia. The city grew until they became one and the same.

The house was a red stone Romanesque, the door tucked back in a dark archway. Rose wanted to drop off Peter at the West Wing, but he had insisted on taking her here. She knocked on the door while Peter stood behind her, scanning the street.

Cleaned up, the cut on his neck wasn't too bad, maybe an inch long. It could have used a butterfly bandage, but it had stopped bleeding. He had changed into a spare button-down he kept in the car.

The door opened, and a black woman in her fifties or sixties appeared in the frame. "Mary?" she said to Rose.

"Yes," Rose replied. "Carolyn?"

"That's right."

Rose introduced Peter as "Chris" and Carolyn invited them in.

Watercolors filled the walls. There were several paintings

of Meridian Hill Park—it was just down the street—in winter and summer, with the statue of Joan of Arc standing at the top of the long cascading fountain.

"Did you do these?" Rose asked.

"Yes."

"They're lovely."

"Thank you." Carolyn led them down the hall to a first-floor bedroom that might have been a converted study. The furniture was spare but seemed well cared for: an upholstered chair beside a desk, a queen bed, and a bookshelf stuffed with paperbacks and a few romantic comedy DVDs.

"Here's your key," Carolyn said. "Do you need any help getting around the neighborhood?"

"No, I'll be fine."

"Okay," she said and seemed to be measuring them for potential trouble.

"There's coffee, and help yourself to eggs and toast or anything in the fridge in the morning—"

Something clattered down the stairs, and a high-pitched yapping filled the house. Two terriers, Peter thought they were schnauzers but wasn't quite sure, came sprinting down the hall.

"Oh, the girls are up."

The dogs hopped up on their hind legs, sniffing madly at Peter and Rose until one broke off and ran to the front window to bark at a car passing by.

Out of sight of Carolyn, Peter lifted his thumb to Rose. Crazy dogs would be good to have around, and he liked that Rose's room was close to a back door so she could slip out easily.

"I'll let you two get settled," Carolyn said.

"Thank you," Peter said. "This is a beautiful home. I'll be heading out for a bit. Visiting a friend."

"Coming back late?"

"No," Peter said. "If he and I go out, I'll stay with him. I wouldn't want to wake anyone up."

The woman eyed him. She had been acting a little more suspicious once they reached the room. Maybe she noticed that they had no luggage.

"Yes, well," she said. "That would be for the best. I usually go to bed around eleven."

"Of course."

Carolyn smiled, uneasily, but she let it pass and after chatting for another minute, she retreated to the living room.

"Are you sure about this?" Rose asked.

"Yes. If someone else calls the line, I need to be there. Maybe I can find out more about what's happening. And there might be some trace of who Farr talked to, something I can use for proof. There's not a lot of time. I have to try. Are you okay here?"

Rose nodded.

"If anybody comes to that door who you don't know, or she doesn't know, don't answer it," he said. "Don't even talk back. Just go out the back to the police station."

"And you'll have your cell."

"It won't work in the Sit Room, but there's still the emergency number. Do you remember it?"

Rose repeated the digits. "I can't forget anything from that night."

Peter lifted his chin slightly. "The cut. You can't see anything, can you?"

"No. It's under your collar."

He shook his hands out, like he used to when getting ready for a game. "I should get going."

Rose stepped in and pulled him close. The move took him by surprise, and as he held her he felt oddly calm in the midst of all these threats.

"It's going to be all right," he said.

"You don't know that." She was trying to keep from crying. "But thanks."

Slowly, she eased her grasp, and again he was astonished that a civilian who had seen three people killed could hold it together as well as she was now.

He was surprised *he* was holding it together, but the madness and danger seemed to shrink back, and he felt like he was watching himself from outside his body, as if it weren't real.

Peter was at the center of something he didn't understand, and yet part of it was so simple and obvious, despite the sweat and the panic and the fear. There was something coming, and he had to stop it. The anger had him now. This was the same betrayal that had destroyed his family.

There was no question; he was going straight at Diane Farr.

52

Dimitri Sokolov checked his phone, then looked on idly as a man with a contractor's trash bag slumped over his shoulder opened the trunk of a black BMW.

The cleanup at Krysanova's house in Alexandria had been fast, the scene ugly, but all was done in time.

To take care of the last details they had parked here, west of Alexandria, in the shadow of the freight tracks and the Beltway.

The man hefted the bag into the trunk and slammed it shut.

He looked to Dimitri, who nodded. The man climbed in the car and took off as a CSX double-decker thundered past.

Dimitri waited for the noise to subside and lifted his phone.

"What's happening?" Farr asked as soon as she picked up.

"The woman who called for help. I took care of it."

"She's . . ." He could hear Farr's breath picking up, growing shallow.

"That's right," Dimitri said. "Where are you?"

"Parking. At work."

"Can anyone hear you?"

"No."

"The woman, Krysanova, she wasn't alone."

"Did you . . . take care of the other person?"

"No. He escaped. I believe I wounded him."

"Who was it?" she asked, her voice pained, creaking like someone with strep throat. Her fear was getting the best of her.

"I don't know," Dimitri said. "I'll handle it."

"The police?"

"They won't find anything. Her house is clean." He paused. "And she didn't have the ledger."

"Damn it!" Farr said.

Dimitri caught the slightest hesitation before her response. Was she hiding something from him? Or was it simply her nerves?

"No one on your end has learned anything about where it might be?" Dimitri asked.

"No."

"Good. We are watching another witness who might have been working with the Campbells. Katie Chen."

"I remember her—she was part of the Metro crash investigation," Farr said. "But I don't think you need to do anything. We kept her from looking too closely into the real cause."

"Still, she's a complication. And we don't have time for any more complications. We need all the witnesses gone, and there is only one day left. Where are Peter Sutherland and Rose Larkin?"

"The girl slipped away from her security detail. Peter went to find her. He'll tell me where she is."

"Find him now, and Rose. Tell me where they are, and I'll take care of it. We need this all cleaned up by tomorrow night."

"Both of them?" Farr asked. "Peter could be useful. If any of this gets out, we can place the blame on him, for the deaths, the train crash, all of it. People are already suspicious of him because of his father."

"We can do that just as easily if he's gone."

She didn't answer. He heard those fast, shallow breaths.

"Are you there?" Dimitri asked.

"Yes. I'm . . . it's so many people who are going to . . ."

All the killing was getting to her. This wasn't her world.

"It's just a few more," Dimitri said. "We're in far enough that we can't stop. If anyone who knows goes public, if that ledger gets out—"

"I know."

"Tomorrow night. President Vikhrov and President Travers will both be here. It will happen and then all of this will be over. One more day, and you'll be free."

No answer. She was panicking.

"Where do you go, Diane, when you have time off? When all this is finished? Take a deep breath and picture it."

He waited for a moment, then continued. "This will all be over, and you'll be there, and none of it will have ever happened. One more day."

A deep breath. "I'm okay."

"Don't go into the West Wing if you can't keep yourself under control."

"I'm fine."

"Tell me if anyone else calls the emergency line. We need all of the Campbells' witnesses."

"I will. I need to go."

She disconnected. Something was off with her, Dimitri thought, more than the nerves. Was she holding back something? Did she know where the ledger was? Did she already have it?

He pinched the bridge of his nose and sat back against the hood of his Accord. He would need to find out, might need to take care of her as well at some point. But not tonight. Too many others needed his attention now.

He opened the trunk and from a first aid kit pulled out a bottle of hydrogen peroxide. He'd already washed his hands, but this would take care of the last traces of blood. Unlike bleach, it destroyed DNA.

He hummed quietly as he rubbed his palms together and felt the peroxide bubble and burn.

You are the sunshine of my life . . .

That song had stayed with him for the last week. He hadn't thought about it in ages, until he heard it during the surveillance of the Campbells' house, the night they died.

It had been one of his wife's favorites. At their summer house, she would tune into the Western propaganda stations broadcasting rock and roll into the USSR and try to break him out of his strictly classical tastes.

They would lie on the deep pile carpet and listen for hours. As he remembered her singing along quietly, her head on his chest, he smiled and dug the last trace of red out from under his nails.

He checked his knife—clean—slid it back in his sheath, and slammed shut the trunk. He needed to get moving. It was going to be a long night.

53

Peter entered the West Wing and walked down the hall toward Farr's office. He had left his car in the garage on G Street, with Krysanova's gun locked in the glove box.

The office was quiet, though there was always a handful of staffers working on the weekend.

Peter looked at the closed door of the Oval Office. Travers would want to know what was happening, if Peter could get to him. But Peter would sound like a madman if he charged in now. He needed proof.

The door to Farr's suite was closed. He walked back down the hall.

"Bear, are you working tonight?" Peter turned to find the uniformed Secret Service officer who worked the main entrance.

Office chitchat was the last thing Peter felt like doing now, but he needed to keep up a veneer of normalcy.

"You bet. What could be more fun than a twelve-hour shift on a Saturday night, right?" he said. That seemed to do it. The guard smiled.

"Have you seen Diane?" Peter asked.

"She went out a little while ago."

"Thanks," Peter said and checked the clock.

He went around the corner, swiped his ID in the door to Farr's suite, and stepped inside.

She had directed the killer to Krysanova's house. Every action leaves a trace. They taught him that at Quantico. Dirt carried from a crime scene in the seam of a sneaker, a cell phone tower ping, a chemical trace in the clothes.

Farr wasn't trained in countersurveillance. She would make mistakes. Peter needed something to connect her to the crime.

As he passed between the assistants' desks, he thought through the timeline. Krysanova's call to the emergency line had gone to Julian, then Farr. Did she take the call here? Or was she out? And how did she communicate her order to the gunman?

The door to her office was open. He stepped inside, past the fireplace and long conference table on one side of the room, and approached her desk.

Sneaking into offices, stealing information: he had spent his whole life recoiling from these crimes, but now, despite the fear of being caught, the sweat beading on his skin, they brought him a strange thrill. He felt switched-on, hyperaware of every sound.

He took his cell phone out and shot a video of the gray LCD display as he scrolled through the call log on her desk phone. Almost all of the numbers he recognized: 202-456 and 202-395 lines were internal White House communications. None from area code 571, for Alexandria. She hadn't taken the call here. There was no chance she called the shooter from her office, of course, but now at least he had a record of everyone she talked to. He doubted she was in this alone. Was Hawkins part of it, too?

Her filing cabinets were protected by a combination dial. He tried the drawers on her desk. Only one opened without a key, but all it held was a tidy collection of pens, legal pads, and rubber bands.

Peter eased the drawer shut and stepped away from her desk, then came back to it and crouched. A charger with cables coming out of its three USB ports was plugged in to a wall outlet. There was a cable for Farr's personal iPhone and a micro-USB for the official encrypted Blackberry he'd seen her use. But what was the third cable for? Was there another phone?

"Evening." The words were muffled, distant, but it sounded like Farr, maybe talking to the guard at reception. He moved quickly out of her office, but checked himself. He couldn't be seen sprinting if she came into the suite.

The door to the hall was open a crack. He was halfway past the assistants' desks when he heard Farr's voice just outside, talking to Julian. They passed by.

The door didn't move. Peter waited. He could make out only a few words of their conversation.

Ten seconds, twenty. He couldn't see anything through the crack. Had they moved on?

He wanted to check the phone log downstairs in the Sit Room, and if Farr was going to find him, better that he be sitting at his desk like a good soldier. He took three deep breaths, cleared the tension from his face, and exited into the hallway.

They were gone. He took the long way around and trotted down the stairs to the Sit Room.

You're walking too fast, he thought, slowing his steps. He kept his phone in his pocket and switched it to airplane mode so that the sensors in the secure area wouldn't pick up any emissions.

He greeted the other watch officers quickly, went to his workstation, and sat down. Calls with foreign heads of state were all recorded, but this line, as far as he knew, wasn't.

There was a log, however, that might show if the call had come to this phone before Farr picked it up. He took his cell out again, and, keeping it hidden close to his chest, took a video of the call log. There it was, on the night action line, a 571 number. It was Krysanova's home line. He recognized it from when he had looked up her business to find her address.

He noted the time. He could put together a sequence. It wasn't much on its own, but that was how you build investigations, how you take someone down: fact by fact. What he wanted was camera footage from Krysanova's house that showed the shooter using the signal and a recording of Farr giving Krysanova that same signal.

That left him to look for communication between Farr and the man who had hit the house. Peter wondered if he could get any details from the other staffers, who might have seen her take the call or duck out to give the order. There were plenty of cameras around this place. If he could find an authority to look into it, they might be able to piece it together.

His desk phone rang. A red light pulsed above the display, which flashed the active extension: 2461. It was the emergency line.

A cold feeling ran through him. He checked the incoming number and lifted the phone.

"Go ahead," he said.

"H-hello?" the caller said in a tentative voice. At the same time, Peter heard the door to the Sit Room swing open.

"Yes. Do you have a code?"

Farr walked in.

"Pen. Clock. Door. Fire," the caller said.

"Who is this?"

"I thought you were supposed to connect me to someone."

"I'm here to help."

"The Campbells gave me this number."

"They're gone."

"Someone killed them?" Her voice was faint with fear.

"Yes. Where are you?"

Farr rounded the corner, and Peter stepped against the wall of his cubicle, keeping his body between the phone and her.

"In Rockville. I'm worried people are following me."

He craned his neck and saw that she was coming for him. His job was to pass calls on. There wasn't a good reason for him to be on one of these lines, and now was definitely not a good time to be drawing attention to himself by acting out of the ordinary. But he couldn't leave a source twisting in the wind, and he sure as hell wasn't going to pass this woman on to Farr. He wanted to hit the white noise, but that would raise her suspicion.

"What's your name?"

"Katie Chen."

"Okay, Katie. Go to the police. Can you use your phone to find a station nearby? If you tell me where it is, I'll come to you."

"What's happening?"

"Did you work with the Campbells?"

"Yes." She was panicking. Each rapid breath came across like static on the line. "They wanted to know if the Russians, if they could get to our infrastructure. If they could control it. If anyone else from the government had talked to me. Had pressured me."

"Can you slow down for me, Katie? Control *what*? Pressured you about *what*?"

"Is that what this is about? The accident?" she said between halting breaths. "It wasn't an accident."

"Katie. Tell me where you are."

"Oh God. I—"

The phone went dead.

"Hello? Are you there?" Desperation tinged Peter's voice. Another life was at stake on the end of the line, but Peter was careful not to let his words rise above a normal speaking tone.

Farr was watching him, walking closer. He should get off the phone, but he couldn't leave Chen out there.

"Hello?"

No answer.

"Hello?"

She was gone. Farr waited to his left, leaning against the pillar. She held a manila folder in her right hand and tapped it against her open left palm as if she were trying to cut off her fingers.

Peter replaced the phone in its cradle and hit clear on the call log with his knuckle at the same time.

"Is everything okay?" Farr asked. Peter tried to think. Maybe he could say he was calling over to the CIA for a quick question about one of his research jobs, but that would be too easy to disprove.

"I think so. The voice—it was all static. I couldn't even make out who they were. I thought maybe they said NSA."

The NSA was about five times larger than the CIA and much more opaque. Still, as an excuse it was only slightly better than "wrong number."

"That is odd. I'll have the switchboard check it out."

She stared at the phone for a moment.

"No log?"

Peter checked again. "No."

"Huh." She frowned. Peter felt his shirt, damp with sweat, bunch under his arms.

"How did it go with Rose?"

"We were supposed to meet at the Starbucks in Tenleytown, but she didn't show. She must have spooked. I tried to call you but couldn't get through."

After all the years of honesty, of hewing to the truth like a superstition, it surprised him how easily the deception came, how natural it felt.

"I had to run out," Farr said.

Out. So maybe there was an in-person meeting, or she left the office to make contact with the shooter or a go-between.

"Do you think she'll come around?" Farr asked.

"I don't know."

"Jesus. Her and Hawkins."

"Hawkins?"

"Julian said he told you."

"Right," Peter said. "What's happening? Is he okay?"

"This is strictly between us, understood?"

"Understood."

"He's gone without a trace. No signs of violence or duress. Not a word."

"Like he fled?"

Farr nodded slowly.

"What the hell is going on?" he asked.

"I don't know but run everything through me now."

God. Peter had wondered if Hawkins and Farr were both part of this plot. Maybe Hawkins had run, but Peter felt a wave of nausea as he realized the other possibility: Hawkins had come close to the truth about Farr and she had him taken out, too. Was that why she volunteered that he fled? Was it a way to draw suspicion away from herself?

He took her in: the no-bullshit demeanor, the lips slightly pursed, the air of absolute competence. This was the woman who never failed to make him smile with her dark humor, the woman who had given him his chance. How was she capable of this?

"Are you okay, Peter?"

Had he let the suspicion show? "A little run-down from last night, but it's fine."

"No. Your neck."

He touched his throat, the bruise from the attack in the hotel. "It's not so bad."

"Not there." She tapped the side of her neck to indicate what she meant.

Peter reached up to the same spot on his own and felt the slightest dampness. He looked at his reflection in the glass partition: a drop of blood, no bigger than a dime, had soaked into the collar of his shirt.

"Shaving," Peter said. "Rushing out the door."

Farr let it drop, but she was still looking at him. She went on naturally, even brightened a bit. "I'm going to be here all night with this Hawkins thing. I'll have Julian come in a little early tomorrow. You can head out."

"I don't mind."

"You can't help me by dying on your feet, Peter. Go home. Get some rest. I have people out looking for Rose. She'll be okay."

Did she know about the injury? Put together that he was at Krysanova's? The shooter could have noticed his hand going to his neck as he ran.

Here he was, with the enemy among the foundations of the White House, both knowing what was going on, and both of them lying through their teeth.

Still, some part of Peter couldn't believe it. It was easier to think that he was delusional than to accept the facts he had seen and heard.

Treason. But why? It didn't matter. He knew it was true. He had seen those headlights flash and seen Krysanova's life torn away.

Farr couldn't do anything to him here. What was her plan? To follow him to Rose? To follow him to any other targets or evidence he had uncovered? To simply get him far enough away from the White House that he too could be made to disappear?

A sit-in wasn't going to help matters, and he needed to move. He thought of the call from Katie Chen: another witness out there, desperate. Maybe she had an answer. Some kind of attack was coming, and Peter would use any room to maneuver. Surely there was someone in authority who would listen, who would at least consider what Peter had learned.

But Farr must have known that, too. Maybe the shooter would take him as soon as he was outside these gates.

Peter looked at the clocks. He knew what he had to do.

"I'll wrap up here," Peter said.

"Good." Farr brought the folder to her side. She walked over to the Sit Room director's desk, and they began talking.

Was she watching him? That was fine. Peter reached under the file drawer on the left-hand side of his desk and grabbed his gym bag. He kept it low, so that Farr couldn't see it over the desks as he exited the Sit Room, went upstairs, and then stepped outside into the Rose Garden.

It was game time.

54

Once Peter was clear of the colonnade, he dialed the number that Katie Chen had used, but there was no answer. Then he called Rose.

"Peter, are you okay?"

"Everything's fine. I found someone else who's involved in this, a witness. Katie Chen. Have you ever heard that name?"

"No. But that's great. Where is she?"

"Rockville. She's in trouble. She called the emergency line. She said that she worked with your aunt and uncle, that she knew about their investigation and maybe what the Russians are up to."

"Well, what is it?" Her voice was tense, breathless.

"I don't know. She was cut off. Here's the number she used." He read out the digits. "Can you call her? You can use the night action code to prove you're legit."

"Tell her to stay away from Farr?"

"Yes. She has to get someplace safe. We need to find out what her role in this is and what she knows."

Perry, the former body man, was walking at the other edge of the lawn. He saw Peter and gave him a nod.

"I'm on it," Rose said. "Did you see Farr?"

"I did."

"How is she? Does she suspect you know what's going on?"

That drop of blood. That forced smile.

"I think so."

"Peter." Rose's voice was insistent. "Get out of there."

The clock was ticking. There wasn't enough time for a formal request to an inspector general, even if anyone would believe him, even if he could manage it without Farr's knowledge.

"Not yet. There's someone here I need to talk to."

That was one of the benefits of having a killer after you, Peter guessed. It meant you didn't give a damn about the White House rules.

55

A chill wind blew from the Potomac, and Peter looked to the windows of the Oval. They were dark. The president was probably in the residence, getting ready for the game. Peter could catch him on his way out, cut him off.

He crossed the garden and waited to ambush President Travers.

He saw the shadows move, the door opening from the White House, and stepped under the colonnade, eyes ahead, as if he didn't know the president was coming his way, flanked by two Secret Service agents.

"Peter," Travers said and looked at the bag. "Are you playing tonight?"

"Sir. I was going to check with Perry, see if you needed an extra man."

"Double or nothing?" Travers said with a smile and moved closer. The agents, as always, trailed silently a dozen feet behind them. Peter's opener hadn't drawn any attention.

"The Cavs game last night got me fired up," Peter said.

"I know," Travers replied. "Those last two minutes. Unbelievable."

Peter stepped beside the president. Some basketball

chat was always welcome. He was inside the bubble that normally protected Travers.

Farr, as chief of staff, could easily hear about anything suspicious in her West Wing. He didn't know how this would go, and it was a violation of every standard of working in the White House, but that didn't matter now.

"Mr. President," Peter said quietly as they walked.

Maybe Peter's tone gave it away. Or maybe it was the floodlights lighting up the ugly blue bruise on Peter's throat, but Travers caught on that something was wrong.

"Is everything all right, Peter?"

Peter glanced at the lead Secret Service agent, Daniel Akana, the barrel-chested veteran he knew from the West Wing. He was one of the supervisors. Travers edged closer.

They were crossing toward the court, where the other players were gathered under the sodium lights. They were still out of earshot, but Peter didn't have much time.

"Sir," Peter said. "I wouldn't bring this to you unless it was a matter of security and there was no other choice."

"What are you talking about?"

"You know that there is concern about a penetration by a foreign intelligence service at a high level."

Travers looked from one side to the other. "Peter. Not in the open. There are proper channels for this kind of thing."

"And if my concern were with the channel itself?"

The other players were watching them from a distance now.

The president looked dumbfounded. "Who are we talking about here?"

Peter wanted to pull him aside and tell him the whole

story, from beginning to end, to shout that an attack was coming and people were going to die. That he had a goddamned traitor in his house.

Bruised, with a trace of blood on his collar, Peter knew what he looked like: a lunatic. But he needed to move slowly, let the facts speak for themselves, or else he would end up in a Secret Service interrogation room or involuntarily committed at St. Elizabeths.

"Diane Farr. I don't know if you're aware that I handle communications about the investigation. It's eyes-only to her, but information came in that made it seem that she was involved in the penetration, a suspect herself. I'm concerned that sources might be in danger, and frankly I wasn't sure who else to go to. I wouldn't come to you unless it was a clear and immediate threat."

The Sit Room was one of the few places where a junior employee could suddenly be called on for advice by the president with no filter between them. Words like this from a man who sat in that room meant something.

The president didn't respond. The wind pushed a few leaves past them. Perry started walking toward them from the court. "What's going on?" he asked.

Agent Akana didn't like this odd sidebar. He edged toward Peter and the president.

Here we go, Peter thought, wondering whether he'd be better off in St. Elizabeths or jail.

Travers took another look at Peter's neck. He took the agents aside, and Akana spoke to him briefly. Then Travers came back to Peter.

"We can't talk about this here," he said. "I'll have Secret Service take you someplace safe, put security on anyone who might be at risk. Everything comes across Farr's desk, but I can find someone who can handle this."

"Thank you, sir."

"Thank you," he said and eyed Perry approaching. "Now I know you're not a politician, but could you sell it to the guys?" He put on a smile.

Peter nodded and turned as Perry arrived, basketball under his arm and with another player strolling up behind him. "Are you playing tonight, Peter?" he said and gave him an easy underhand pass.

Peter caught it, and palmed it, then handed it to Travers.

"I'd love to, but my neck is a little jacked up. I should probably head home."

He walked back along the fence toward the pool house, scanning the long shadows cast by the court floodlights. He looked at the chief of staff's office and saw the light was on.

Akana came up beside him as he walked and spoke into his ear. "Southwest gate. There will be a car."

Peter nodded and checked his phone for a message from Rose, but she hadn't called back. An unmarked Dodge Charger idled in the parking lot for senior staff, at the edge of the driveway to the southwest gate.

As he moved closer, he saw a Secret Service agent sitting in the driver's seat, his window down. He had a hard, professional look despite his baby face.

"Peter Sutherland?"

"Yes."

"Credentials."

He handed over his lanyard, and after a quick inspection of the ID and his face, the agent nodded his head toward the passenger seat. Peter walked around the car and climbed in. "Where are we going?"

"North Capitol Annex. It's a secure site. Akana will meet us there."

The agent gave Peter another look, up and down, measuring him as if he couldn't figure out why he merited this kind of attention.

They turned out of the gate, and Peter watched the White House disappear in the rearview.

56

The city rolled by outside Peter's window. The glass towers of the unions and the lobbying shops on Sixteenth Street gave way to churches and embassies as they moved out of downtown. They turned right north of Columbia Heights, into a neighborhood that Peter didn't know well. Small row houses passed by and suddenly there was park on all sides, and signs for the Old Soldiers' Home.

Through a guarded gate, in a flash of white, he saw an old brick house on a hill. President Lincoln's Cottage. He had heard of this place but had never visited: Lincoln's summer home during the Civil War, where he drafted the Emancipation Proclamation. Now it was nestled on the grounds of the Old Soldiers' Home, a retirement village for veterans, surrounded by cemeteries and parks.

They emerged on the other side, on Hawaii Avenue, and pulled up in front of a midcentury red brick house with a flat roof. It looked like a small municipal building with its square windows edged in aluminum, but it seemed to be a residence. It was set on a large lot, cut off from its neighbors by busy four-lane streets.

The intelligence and national security agencies had lots of these secret spots around the capital. Across from the Russian embassy in Glover Park there was a famous surveillance post, a normal-looking home except for the cameras planted behind every window and the FBI crews within.

The agent led Peter up the stoop and keyed in a code on the door lock. A small black dome camera hung, barely visible, in a corner above the door.

They stepped inside. The place had the feeling of a little-used vacation condo: cheap matching furniture from a catalog, old carpet, a stale smell from disuse and windows that never opened.

A safe house.

"Do you need anything?" the agent asked.

"I'm fine. Sorry, I didn't catch your name," Peter said.

"Collins. Justin Collins. Are you all set here?"

Peter looked into the kitchen. "Is someone coming to meet me?"

"That's what I'm told."

"All right, thanks."

Collins held up his keys and moved toward the door. "I'm going to do a lap around the block, check things out."

"Sure," Peter said.

Collins nodded, stepped out, and shut the door. As tired as he was, Peter was too restless to sit, so he wandered the house, peering out the first-floor windows beside the drawn blinds.

There were three small bedrooms upstairs, each furnished with a twin bed, bedside table, and lamp. The only sign that anyone had ever stayed here were a few paperbacks—Sidney Sheldon and Michael Crichton and Ron Chernow.

Peter checked his phone again: no word from Rose.

He watched the street, but there was no sign of Collins. He dialed Rose's number, but his phone never rang, it just showed the connecting screen. Something was wrong with the signal.

He walked downstairs and turned the knob on the front door. But when he pushed and pulled the door wouldn't budge. There was a dead bolt, but no twist knob to draw it back on his side, just a hole for a key he didn't have.

He crossed the house to the rear door in the kitchen. He seized the knob and wrenched it, but that got him nowhere. Another dead bolt.

He was locked in.

57

This was no safe house. This was a prison. Peter started back to the living room.

The lights cut out.

Now he understood: a car had brought him here and left him to cut any trace to the White House, to hand him over to the killers. Interrogation or execution: he wondered which would come next.

There was no time to think about that. He had to move. His phone showed no signal, and the light from its display would serve as a beacon, marking him out as a target. They would want surprise, so he guessed the back door would come first. He slipped into the kitchen, feeling along the wall to find his way. He tried to look out the window, but it was too dark to make out any clear figures on the grounds.

The faintest whisper of metal on metal came from the rear door: the lock turning. He stood between the stove and the hinge side of the door. His fingers touched the cold sheet metal of the stove—a cheap white box like the one in his apartment. He slid his hand across until he felt one of the grates and pried it up. He couldn't remember if there had been anything sitting on top of the range. One sound could get him killed.

He raised the grate gently, the bright rasp of metal on enamel just barely audible as the door eased open.

The attacker moved in, no more than twelve inches away on the other side of the door. Peter kept his mouth open wide enough that his breath wouldn't make a noise and lifted the grate up. It felt reassuringly heavy in his hand.

He hoped his eyes would adjust enough to get a clear look, but the darkness was almost total. He listened and felt the floor flex through the soles of his shoes as the man came closer.

Kill the lights. The attackers had done it before, the night they took the Campbells. The man was moving surely. He probably had some kind of night optics. As soon as he was around that door, he would take a full scan of the room and Peter would be done.

The door pulled away from his shoulder, and Peter brought the grate down edge first like an ax through the dark. It swung through the air, touching nothing, and then it hit. It was later than he expected, but a solid blow.

A man grunted and took a heavy step back, but he didn't fall. Peter felt the door and pivoted around it. He ran for the outside as a suppressed round snapped behind him and a red light flared. A bullet slit the air near his head and he kept on, across the wooden deck.

Streetlights filtered through the trees, strong enough here that he could make out the silhouette of a man behind him, just as a flashlight beam flicked on ahead of him, blinding him: another attacker.

Peter was moving fast and already close enough to drop his shoulder and charge, catching the man ahead in the breastbone and knocking him against the deck railing. Wood splintered and nails squealed as the man made a strangled sound. Peter wanted to run, but he caught a glint of light near the man's right hand: a pistol.

He grabbed that hand and twisted it back as the man struggled to bring the gun around to point the muzzle at Peter's ribs. Peter didn't have enough leverage on the man's wrist, but if he let go to try for a better grip on the gun, the man would have his chance to shoot.

They stood in a desperate embrace. Peter waited for a shot from behind, from the man he had attacked in the kitchen. He didn't know why it hadn't come yet; maybe he had dazed that man more than he thought.

Peter bent his knees and then drove forward with everything he had. The railing let go with a crack like close lightning, and they fell back. The drop seemed to last for seconds, until Peter landed half on the man as he thudded against the ground on his back.

Peter felt the gunman's ribs break against his chest and heard a louder snap, like a dry stick cracking.

The man's arm went limp, and when Peter looked at his eyes, they looked blankly up and to the right. He made no noise, no struggle, and when Peter put his hand to the ground beside him, he felt something warm.

A black pool grew out from the back of his head, shining in the streetlights.

Dead.

No time to think. Move. Peter scanned for the gun, saw no sign of it. It must have tumbled away as they went over the railing. He wanted that pistol. He wanted to close on the other man in the kitchen. Rage coursed through his veins like fire, but he heard steps on the deck and knew another gun was coming behind him. He had to get away.

He pushed himself up to his feet and sprinted flat out, fists pumping through the air. He leaped high enough to catch the chain-link fence at the rear of the yard near his waist and threw himself forward, over it, pointing his head toward the ground. He clawed his fingers through the links on the far side and swung his legs down, landing on his feet on the grass.

He darted across the street and along the brick sidewalk. A light flashed from the yard he had just left, sweeping down the street toward him.

Headlights filled the road. A Metro bus was approaching. The lighted sign above the windshield read Not in Service. The bus would cross between him and the house in a moment. There was a chance he would have time to run in front of it, but he doubted it. And even if it did stop, there was nothing to keep the men chasing him from killing him and the driver.

The pursuer's flashlight fixed on Peter as he ran down the street. He was lit up, exposed, an easy shot. But then the bus passed on the road between him and the attackers, cutting off the light. He had a moment's darkness, a moment hidden from their view.

He cut right, toward a black fence, and hauled himself over. The top of a picket dragged across his ribs.

He took off through a graveyard and watched as the flashlight scanned down the street, then turned toward the tombstones and mausoleums. He ducked against the iron bars of a crypt, felt the cool air embrace him as the light passed over, and ran on.

From the worn stones, Peter could tell it was a centuries-old graveyard. He picked his way through the shadows and jumped back. A woman reached out with one hand as if begging for mercy, her face a green-white ruin of weathered copper. A statue.

He saw a stand of hedges on a low rise and ran for them. Inside was a small clearing, with a high-backed stone pew circling one edge. It offered cover from most sides.

Lights flashed along the branches and marble. It was some kind of shrine, with another sculpture—the cemetery was full of these figures—a woman wearing a shroud, looking at him impassively, the fingers of her right hand held lightly to her face.

The attackers searched near where he had first entered, then seemed to move on.

He waited a moment longer, his lungs burning and his palms damp with sweat, then leaned against a crypt wall and let his head fall back.

The president was part of this. There was nowhere he and Rose would be safe.

The understanding weighed on him like wet clothes on a drowning man.

He saw those blank eyes again, heard the skull crack. He had just killed someone. The knowledge seemed to grow, from a thought to a feeling, a numbness running down his spine and through his limbs.

A minute passed, maybe two. Light played down the street. There were other parks, other places to hide in this oddly quiet hilltop neighborhood. He could only hope that they had lost him as he ran through the landscaped hills toward the far side of the churchyard.

58

Dimitri stepped into the backyard of the safe house and shut the gate behind him. Peter Sutherland had escaped, for now. Dimitri crouched next to the body, surveying the broken railing of the deck and the pool of blood soaking into the earth.

The dead man couldn't have been more than twenty-five. He was backup. They had worked together a few times before, and he'd been the second through the door when they hit the Campbells' house. Dimitri didn't know much more about him except that he was a paratrooper and had a son back home. He never liked to lose a soldier, but at least this boy had died fighting.

He looked over the caved-in skull with fascination and, despite it all, a hint of admiration. Farr had told him that Peter was a Boy Scout, easily handled, but she had clearly underestimated him. Dimitri had tangled with him in that hotel hallway. He remembered Peter's eyes under the strobing lights of the fire alarm, and he recognized a brother, a killer.

This was going to be more interesting than he thought. But he wouldn't have to wait long to see Peter again. Dimitri had a good idea where Peter was going: to Rose.

She was somewhere near U Street. They would have the exact location soon, by tracking her cell phone.

Dimitri lifted the encrypted phone and called Balakin.

"I need more men," he told his handler. "I need watch teams. I need hitters."

He didn't care if he had to call out every illegal in Washington, flood the city. Rose and Peter weren't going to get away.

59

Peter crept through the alleys between the row houses until he reached Sixteenth Street, where he hailed a cab. After he gave the address on Florida Avenue, the driver resumed his phone call, laughing and going on in a language Peter couldn't understand.

Peter was glad to be left alone, to find a moment of rest on the vinyl seat.

They rolled down Sixteenth toward U Street and the house where he had left Rose. The high walls of Meridian Hill Park climbed to their left. Red and blue lights flashed, reflecting on the buildings as they neared Florida.

"Stop," Peter said.

The man was barely paying attention, and Peter leaned forward and grabbed his shoulder. "Stop here!"

The driver looked back with an indignant stare. Peter held out a twenty, more than enough for the fare, and stepped out. This was DC and around the corner from a police and fire station, so flashers were normal, but somehow he already knew that the emergency was at the house where Rose was staying. Had the killers already been here?

Peter's lungs felt like they were balling up in his chest.

There was a dead body at the safe house on Hawaii

Avenue, with his fingerprints all over it. The police were the last thing he needed, but he had to make sure Rose was okay. He put his head down and walked on the opposite side of the street. The lights grew brighter. At the house, the front door was open, and the woman who owned it was talking to two uniformed DC police officers.

There was no ambulance he could see, but that didn't mean Rose was safe. He didn't slow or break his stride as he passed the house. If she'd seen them coming, if she had done what he said, she would have run. There was no one in the back of the patrol cars, no sign of an EMT inside the house.

If there had been an attack or murder here, there would be a lot more than two cop cars and a casual interview on the stoop. The police were looking for Rose. They had found her here. That meant someone had conducted a credit card search or a trace on her phone or his: a serious dragnet. He had told Rose that if anyone she didn't recognize showed up at the Airbnb rental, she should go to the police, but now he knew she wouldn't even be safe at the station.

He reached the end of the block and turned, and started back the other way on W Street, toward the Third District headquarters. Crossing under a pale yellow streetlight, he could see the other man's blood caked on the back of his hand.

A cruiser rolled by. Peter stuffed his hand into his pocket and walked toward the station, a two-story building on a dark street with a parking garage in the back. Two officers approached, talking: a woman carrying a duffel bag and a man with his thumbs hooked inside his body armor. They went silent as Peter walked by. He kept his eyes ahead.

If Rose was in the station, he needed to get to her before

Farr could. He reached the corner, and as he neared a high hedge, a hand closed on his shoulder. He seized it and turned to see Rose's frightened eyes.

He dropped her hand and exhaled as relief surged through him. "Are you all right?"

"Yes." She lowered her voice. "The police showed up and I ran. I didn't think I should go to the station, but I knew you would come here."

She looked at his hand, at the blood. "What happened to you?"

"It's not mine. Let's go."

She nodded and stayed close by his side as they walked south to U Street, and then west, blending in among the crowds bouncing between the bars and restaurants.

"How much cash do you have?" he asked.

"Twenty-five."

"I've got eighty, but we should get some more."

"What's happening?"

"They're coming for us. I think Farr might have help."

Rose looked down for a moment, in shock. It was sinking in: they were running from the police now, fugitives.

She was tough; it didn't slow her down for more than a second. "There's a Wells Fargo," she said and pointed across the street.

They ran over through a break in traffic, and Peter dipped his card in the ATM. They needed money before they tried to disappear. Farr might be tracking their cards, but she must have already known they were in the neighborhood. He would risk it before getting out of here.

"Please try again," the screen read.

He tried his credit card from another bank.

"Please try again."

"Here," Rose said, holding hers out.

He dipped the card in. Same message.

Peter's eyes went to the security camera, then down. He took Rose's arm and led her away. As they walked toward Fourteenth Street, he stripped the back off his phone and pulled out the battery. Rose's eyes opened wide, and he held out his hand for her phone.

The battery didn't come out. He kept walking, looking into trash cans as he went. He stopped in front of a McDonald's and reached into the trash. Among the empty soda cups and water bottles, there was a paper plate with a piece of foil on it—discarded from somebody's jumbo slice, the local drunk food specialty. He pulled out the foil and wrapped her phone in it.

"Seriously?"

He nodded and searched the street for a cab. Rose looked over her shoulder, rocking slightly, the panic growing.

"Peter, this is . . . what's happening?" she asked.

He held her shoulders gently and looked her in the eye. "Rose. You did great at the house. We will get through this."

"Okay. Okay. What now?"

They needed to get away from their last location, and they needed their own vehicle. Anything they would likely have keys to would be known to the authorities soon enough, but they didn't have enough money to come up with something else. He would start by getting back to his own car in the parking garage.

He waited for an independent cab to appear. A Toyota Avalon with Selam Cab Co. stickers on the side approached, and Peter stepped out into the street and flagged it down. He and Rose climbed in. Peter wanted the least tech-forward transportation he could find.

"Eighteenth and G," he said. A block from the White House.

60

Rose and Peter stepped out of the cab in front of the garage in Foggy Bottom where Peter had left his car. The ornate facades of the old State, War, and Navy building loomed to the east, just next to the White House. This was too close, but he needed his car.

Late on Saturday there wouldn't be many people around. Peter walked with Rose past the garage gatehouse and down the narrow pedestrian path along the concrete wall.

Three floors down, they reached his row. He held his hand back, to signal Rose to stop. He usually took the Metro to work, so didn't expect anyone to anticipate that his car would be here.

An exhaust fan whirred to life behind him, and Peter spun toward it, hands up.

"What is it?" she whispered.

"Nothing." He was on edge, looking for a threat in every shadow. "I'll go ahead in case they're sitting on the car. Give me two minutes. I'll tap the horn when I'm good."

"Okay."

He left her by the elevators and walked along the row toward his Ford. There was a thick pillar ahead, and he hung back. Something was off. He scanned the windows of the parked cars, and then caught it in a reflection: a shadow moving behind a pillar.

He didn't walk to his car. He stole to the right, hugged the wall, and circled around the column.

Brian, his friend from the National Security Council, stood there, his cell phone in his hand, and a pair of Lexus keys in the other. As Peter's shadow covered him, his eyes opened wide like a startled deer's. Had it only been five days since they were hanging out at the happy hour at Tonic? It felt like a month.

"Hey, Brian." He kept his tone calm, as if they were running into each other in the West Wing hallway, but Brian's whole body stiffened.

"Peter."

"Were you hiding?"

"No, I . . ." Brian seemed to search for a good excuse and came up with nothing.

"If you were," Peter said, "you'd want to be more careful about your reflections." He pointed to the window where he had caught sight of Brian.

Brian smiled weakly. "The things you don't learn sitting at a desk."

Brian was an analyst. They wouldn't have sent him to stake out Peter's car. Peter looked down the aisle and saw a Lexus SUV with a Bethany Beach sticker on the rear window. Brian was just going to his car, and he must have caught sight of Peter or Peter's car and been about to call it in.

That meant someone, maybe Farr, must have told everyone Peter worked with that he was a threat. Everyone would be looking for him.

Peter considered the cell phone. "Why were you hiding?" he asked.

Brian's breathing picked up and Peter moved a little closer. He was conscious of his size and usually careful not to intimidate. But now he stood up straight, shoulders back, the mere fact of him a six-foot-six physical threat.

"What did they tell you about me, Brian?"

The other man didn't respond, and Peter moved closer still, looking down at him now.

"Just that they're looking for you. You'd mishandled classified information. People are saying maybe you had something to do with these deaths."

"And . . ."

"That was it." Brian squeezed against the wall. "What are you going to do . . ." he trailed off, though it was clear where he was going: *to me.* Maybe it sounded too pathetic.

"Who were you going to call?" Peter asked.

"Diane Farr."

It surprised Peter, how quickly he could go in their eyes from colleague to criminal, but they had never really trusted him. His father's history had always colored his own. And now he could see a certain smugness behind the fear: of prejudice confirmed.

"I'd like to borrow your cell phone," Peter said. Peter needed time. He couldn't let Brian make the call.

Brian found some backbone and straightened up against the wall. Peter feinted at him, barely an inch at the shoulders, but fast, and any fight went out of the other man as he cowered back. They already thought he was a killer—and they were right, he guessed—he might as well take advantage.

Peter reached down, eye to eye with Brian, and took the phone from his hand. There was no signal in the garage. He couldn't have called it in yet. Peter walked backward to his car and beeped the keyless entry.

"It's not me, Brian. You won't believe me, but that's the truth."

He stepped in and backed the car out, then tapped the horn as he raced toward the elevators.

He slowed, and Rose threw open the door and jumped in before he even came to a full stop.

"What was that?"

"Friend from work." The car's tires chirped slightly as he raced up the spiraling route out of the garage and handed Rose his wallet. "Could you pull thirteen bucks out of there?"

He gave his ticket and the exact change at the booth, and pulled onto the street.

"Peter. You're bleeding."

His ribs. He knew. Just a scrape from the fence. He needed a place to stop, to think. He needed rest. He had some ideas.

61

Peter drove down Nineteenth Street. It was the first time they had a moment to breathe, to talk without fear of someone else close by.

"What is happening?" she asked.

"You're going to think I've lost my mind."

"You can tell me," she said.

"The president plays basketball with a few of his staffers, and sometimes I'm in the games."

Rose's eyes narrowed. "You talked to *Travers*?"

"There wasn't a lot of time. I had to try. I felt him out, about whether I could raise suspicions about Farr. He was receptive. He told me he'd get me someplace safe, find someone I could talk to who would be outside of her influence. An agent, I thought he was Secret Service but maybe he wasn't, took me to a house near the Old Soldiers' Home."

He stopped for a crew of GW students in the crosswalk.

"It was a setup. They came for me."

"Who?"

"The same killers. The lights cut out, just like at the hotel."

"Are you saying the president . . ."

"He must be. She's his chief of staff. She's an extension of him at this point. I should have known. As if she'd be trying to pull something on this scale by herself."

Peter drove on. As the Lincoln Memorial rose to their right, Rose pointed down the National Mall.

"GIDEON," she said. "We can leave the signal tonight for a meeting, like in Krysanova's notes. The carousel, it's right down there."

"We don't know who he is or who he works for."

"We're going to have everyone looking for us," Rose said. "We need help."

Peter cut into the left lane and turned onto Constitution.

"If we signal him tonight, when do we meet?" Rose said.

He checked the clock. "If it works, seven o'clock tomorrow morning in Rock Creek Park."

Rose watched the trees and tourists whip by as Peter crossed the Mall heading south on Fourteenth Street.

"Here," she said, and he turned left down a one-way street. The red sandstone Castle of the Smithsonian rose to their right.

"That's it," Rose said, pointing to the blue and yellow circus top of the old carousel, closed for the night. "Slow down."

He pulled over in front of a row of parked cars, his front tires in the crosswalk. A green hydrant stood twelve feet from them. "You remember how to leave the signal?"

"A vertical scratch through the O," she said, her fingers on the door handle.

"I'll look out."

Rose stepped onto the curb, with her keys in her hand, and walked across the wide path.

She barely broke stride as she brushed by the hydrant, then walked six feet past it. After a moment to admire the strange Gothic towers of the Castle, she came back.

"Got it," she said.

Peter glanced at the hydrant as he pulled out. No one would pay a scratch any mind, just wear and tear, unless they were looking for it.

"Nicely done."

He headed for the Fourteenth Street Bridge, passing the Tidal Basin and the Jefferson Memorial, then followed the exit toward the George Washington Memorial Parkway South, and Alexandria. As he drove, he noticed that Rose was studying his hand.

"Where did all the blood come from, Peter?"

He stared ahead at the road, thinking of the sickening crack of that man's skull against the ground. He didn't answer.

"Did you get through to the woman who called on the emergency line?" he asked. "Chen?"

Rose watched him for a long moment and let her question drop.

"No," Rose said. "I looked up everything about her that I could find. She works at Heller and Wolff. She's an intellectual property, IT, and corporate security specialist. Does that mean anything to you?"

"Heller and Wolff is a massive law firm. They do a lot of government work."

He told Rose about everything Chen had said on the phone: Russians going after infrastructure, an accident that wasn't an accident.

The answer was there, he knew, but it wouldn't come. He

was too tired or tweaked to put it together. Still, Chen was their best hope.

A cop car appeared behind an overpass: a speed trap. Peter and Rose both sat back, rigid, eyes ahead as Peter watched the car recede in the mirrors.

Rose swallowed. "Is he coming?"

"No," Peter said.

Rose lowered her head. "Everyone is after us."

"We have to assume so." Peter had spent years watching, closing in on criminals. Now he was the target. His hand shook and he gripped the wheel harder.

As they neared Alexandria, he turned down a street that looked straight out of the fifties: bungalows and streets with no curbs or sidewalks.

Ahead in the fog, he saw what he wanted: wire wheels sticking out from under a car cover. There were no lights on in the house. He parked, then unlocked and opened the glove box. Krysanova's pistol was sitting on top of his registration. He reached past it and took out the Leatherman multi-tool he kept in the car.

He picked this neighborhood because on the back-streets there were older houses and older residents, Sunday drivers. Cars would sometimes park here, too, for the short subway ride to Reagan National airport, to beat the long-term parking fees. It was a good spot to find clean plates that wouldn't be missed for a few days.

"Are you going to steal a car?"

"I'm not a thief," he said, surprised by the sharpness in his voice. Then he looked down at the tool in his hand. He knew all of this from chasing thieves. A car, plates. Either way he was still stealing. At this point he didn't know who he was or what he was capable of.

"Just the plates."

He stepped out of his car and walked around to the front of the other car, raised the cover, and removed the two Phillips head screws holding the plate on. Rose got out of Peter's car and walked behind the covered car, returning a minute later with the rear plate in her hand and her keys dangling from her fingers. She must have used the tip of a key on the screws.

They swapped the plates between the two cars, mounting Peter's on the vehicle under the cover.

"Won't that let them know who to look for, if they can ID our plates?"

"Yes. But it'll buy us time. I've worked cases like this before. People sometimes don't notice until the registration expires or they get a ticket. How often do you check your own plates?"

He started his car and drove south through Alexandria.

"Are you sure you're okay?" She was looking at his shirt, the bloodstain on his ribs.

"It's fine," he said. "Cuts and bruises."

"Is there anyone we can go to, anyone who would believe us?"

"Not without proof. We need to find Chen. She's the last witness we know of. We need to get to her before they do."

A pair of Golden Arches rose through the fog ahead on the right, and Peter pulled off the highway and into the parking lot.

"Here?" Rose asked.

"They usually have a pay phone, and free Wi-Fi." Only the drive-through was open. Inside the chairs were flipped upside down on the tables.

Peter took the SIM card out of his phone and put the battery back in place, then powered it up. This way it would act like a Wi-Fi-connected tablet and be harder to trace. He wouldn't get calls, but he could check his voicemail over Wi-Fi by using an app on his phone. After the phone turned on, he glanced at the app, but there were no new messages.

He lifted the center console of his car and pulled out a handful of quarters. He and Rose went over to the pay phone. He handed her his cell and asked her to check the local news sites for any mention of the attack on Hawaii Avenue, or any sign that the police had issued an alert with their descriptions. He lifted the pay phone and dialed the number Katie Chen had called from.

It rang five times, and then a low voice came on the line. "Hello." It was a man's voice: officious, busy, and slightly pissed. In the background Peter heard sirens, and the crunchy voices of radio communications. Cops at a crime scene. He put his hand on the cold metal side of the pay phone, to steady himself.

"Yes. I was trying to reach Katie Chen."

"Who is this?"

They would want to know who was calling and would want more answers than he could give. He had a suspicion of what had happened to Chen, but if he just played along as a friend they wouldn't tell him what he needed to know.

"This is Officer Cruz with the Arlington County Police

Department," Peter said. "We have a warrant out for Ms. Chen for failure to appear."

"I wouldn't hold your breath. What was the charge?"

"Speeding violation." He didn't want to throw off the investigation, but it was the only way he would get a straight answer.

"She's dead."

Peter kept the emotion out of his voice.

"Since when?"

"Maybe an hour. Mugging. Did she have any other warrants?"

"No."

The detective, a man named Swinson, gave Peter his information and told him to call if anything else came up.

Peter hung up the phone, and Rose looked at him expectantly.

"They killed her," he said in a flat tone. His eyes went to the ground, the weeds coming up through the cracked asphalt.

"What?"

"That was the police. They had her phone."

They were closing in, killing everyone. He and Rose were the last ones.

"How did she die?"

"A mugging. That's what the cop said. But they murdered her."

Rose looked across the lot, eyes unfocused, her breath coming in jags. "What are we going to do, Peter? Where can we go?"

Standing in this lot, the smell of fry grease in the air, he felt the same cold desperation, but his was shot through with rage. He wanted at these people. He felt like he would blow if he didn't move, didn't smash a window or tear that goddamn phone from the wall. He drove his nail into his knuckle, felt the stab of pain. He needed to think clearly.

He reached out for Rose's arm, to calm her down. He knew where they could go.

Before he could speak, his phone buzzed in her hand.

Rose looked at the screen. "It says there's a new voicemail," she said. "Someone named Leah."

She handed him the phone and he played back the message.

"Peter, it's me." His ex-fiancée. He shut his eyes. God it felt good to hear her voice. "I know we haven't talked in a while, but can you call me back? I'm worried about you."

He lowered the phone.

"Who was it?" Rose asked.

"A friend." He lifted the pay phone. How did Leah know about this? Had someone threatened her? She was in New York. How could they have possibly gotten to her this fast?

Leah picked up on the third ring, a wary edge to her voice. "Hello?"

"It's me. Are you okay?"

"Yes. Thank God. What about you? Are you in some kind of trouble?"

"I'm fine. This is all a misunderstanding. Did someone talk to you?"

"Someone from your office called and asked if I'd seen you or heard from you."

"Who?"

"I don't know. They said they were from the White House."

"What did you tell them?"

"That I hadn't. Where are you, Peter? Do you need help?"

He needed money. A place to sleep. A different car. *Where are you, Peter? Do you need help?*

"Who talked to you, Leah? Do you remember his name?"

"Let me help you. Where are you?"

"You're in New York?"

"Yes, but I want to help."

It was the second time she had asked for his location. Why that detail? She was so far away.

"Peter, please—"

He hung up but held the handset for a moment while he looked at the ground. She was helping them track him down.

Five years together. He thought back to the moment he put the engagement ring on her finger during a cloudy Big Sur sunset, remembered getting caught in a downpour on the trail back down the mountain, Leah laughing, not caring at all.

And now she thought he was a traitor.

Rose moved closer to him. "Are you okay?"

"Yes," Peter said. He let his hand drop and killed that memory. Sentimentality wasn't going to get him out of this.

"Who was that?"

"Nobody. We should go."

62

Washington looked so small in the distance as they crossed the Potomac on the Wilson Bridge, entering Maryland.

"They're watching your apartment?" Rose asked.

"I have to assume." His mind went back to the last summer with his father: the day agents came to the house with a warrant, and he and his mother sat at the kitchen table while the FBI searched the house.

"That phone call was from my ex."

"Girlfriend?"

"Fiancée. Long story. It sounded like someone called her and tried to get her to help find me. They're covering all their bases. Do you have everything you need? Medications? We have to go to ground."

"My stuff's back at the hotel, but I'll be fine."

Peter was surprised again at how comfortable she seemed to be with running, how adaptable. Her eyes went back to his hand, the blood like rust around his fingernails.

"I killed a man," he said. "I didn't mean to but I did. He was going to shoot me and I tackled him and his head hit the ground."

She swallowed and looked straight ahead for a moment. "Are you okay?"

The rush of running, of escaping had tapered down and he was feeling almost human.

"I'm fine." He let out a breath, a disbelieving sigh. "I don't feel anything."

"Shock."

"Maybe."

He knew that wasn't it. The threat had come, and he had done what needed to be done. He had never killed someone. He had never really even hurt anyone. Hanging out after practice, when other kids would start to mess with him, he would always tie up, grapple, or walk away rather than fight. He was so much bigger, he never worried about winning; he worried about hurting the other kid.

But everything that had happened at that house, and back at the hotel, had come so easily, so naturally. He was good at it. Surviving, maybe killing. There were parts of him he had always kept in check, always bounded by the rules. Now he was scared what he might find as he crossed those lines.

He had no idea who GIDEON was, but if a veteran like Emily Krysanova was afraid of him, he was formidable. Peter wanted to do this the honest way, hated having to deal with someone like that.

But he had no other choice. The Russian president would be here in less than twenty-four hours. The deadline was tomorrow. They were out of time.

If the signal they left for GIDEON worked, it was eight hours until the meeting with him in the park, and they needed a place to lay low. Peter could take them to *Joust*, his godfather's boat. There was nothing to connect him to it. It would be safe for the night. He drove along the Potomac toward Fort Washington and saw the lights of a 7-Eleven ahead.

Peter picked up toothpaste and toothbrushes, two prewrapped sandwiches, instant coffee, and bananas. He found Rose in an aisle near a small section of soup cans. She took two off the shelf.

"Great," Peter said. "There's a stove on the boat."

He pulled a prepaid cell phone off a shelf and looked over their haul, tabulating the total and then thinking through how much cash was left. The cab rides had been expensive, and once they ran out of money they were done. While Rose was looking the other way, he put his can back on the shelf, went to the counter, and checked out.

Fifteen minutes later, they were at the marina. It was little more than a row of docks and a long parking lot with a bar and crab shack now closed for the winter. Peter had never seen a guard there. Old watch-key boxes hung at the end of each dock, but there was rust on the chains. Even if someone came along, two people on a sailboat with no signs of forced entry was easily explainable.

After Rose got out of the car, Peter took the pistol from the glove box and slid the magazine out in his hand. There were small holes to check how many rounds remained: eleven.

He replaced the magazine, chambered a round, slipped the gun in his belt, and untucked his shirt over it.

He led Rose down the dock and pulled the stern line to bring *Joust* up close. The tide was low, and Rose stepped down to put one foot onto the railing, then hopped onto the fiberglass seats of the cockpit. Peter handed down the bag from 7-Eleven and came aboard.

A combination lock secured the companionway that led into the cabin. He dialed in the numbers. The wheel turned with difficulty, but when he pushed in the brass shackle, it popped back out, open. They'd had the same combination since he was ten.

He lifted out the piece of wood that covered the companionway. The motions were automatic and brought back memories of summer afternoons.

Peter didn't think of them much anymore; all the joy was now cut through with the doubts about what had been going through his father's mind when he stared out over the river.

A faint smell of brine and mildew rose up.

"The yachting life," Peter said as he clambered down the steep steps into the cabin.

"I'll take it," Rose replied.

She followed behind him while he switched on the batteries and hit the overhead light. It came on with a reluctant fluorescent buzz. He sat down and put his head back, relaxed for the first time in fifty hours. He shut his eyes, and three inches of foam cushion over marine plywood felt like a bed at the Four Seasons.

He was crashing, exhausted. There was a pop and the smell of sulfur hit his nose. Rose was at the stove, a match between her fingers.

"The pump is down there," Peter said, leaning forward. "It's an alcohol stove."

"I've done some time in trailers. You take it easy."

The smell of tomato sauce filled the cabin, and for the first time, it seemed, Peter could feel the pain of his encounters. His ribs were screaming. As he tugged his shirt away from his skin, the pain spiked. He gritted his teeth and let the shirt fall back. He would deal with that later.

Rose came over to the table with two plastic bowls full of SpaghettiOs—she'd split the can—and two of the sandwiches.

"You should have all the soup," he said, looking at one of the bowls, and slid onto the bench at the table. "I'm okay."

"You need to eat."

She took a bite, and he tried a spoonful. Salty mushy nothingness, with a beef flavor mixed in.

"Holy shit that's good."

"Right?" she said, the corner of her mouth ticking up. "I grew up on this stuff."

He opened one of the sandwiches and bit off a corner. It was chicken salad, more mush, but he was grateful for it.

Peter sat back. "How are you holding up?"

Rose thought for a moment. "I'm just going with it. Everything has been so upside down since that night at my aunt and uncle's house. I guess I got used to it, or numb. And growing up was . . . rough sometimes. My mom and I did our share of running around . . ." She shifted on her seat like she didn't want to talk about it. "I've been through a lot. I'll be all right."

Peter nodded and a moment of easy silence passed. "I know you will," he said.

After he scraped the last bits of soup from his bowl, he took his and Rose's dishes back to the sink.

"Jesus, Peter."

He turned his head. "Huh?"

"You're bleeding."

He nodded slowly, like somebody acknowledging

that the dog needed to be taken out, but not wanting to do anything about it. Rose pulled a first aid kit from the navigation station, and then dampened a bundle of paper towels at the sink.

"Here," she said and sat on the long bench, with the kit on her lap. Peter joined her. The cut was high, halfway up his ribs.

"Take that off," Rose said, eyeing his shirt.

"This was your plan all along?"

"What?"

"Just trying to get my clothes off?"

She let out an incredulous laugh. "Try flirting with me when you're not covered in blood, okay?"

He took the pistol out of his waistband and laid it on the table, then pulled his shirt off, fast, and hissed from the sting. It was a black bruise with a two-inch-long cut at the center, not deep but also not clean. Rose wiped away the dried blood, and then, without a word, cleared the other man's blood from his hands. For that part she avoided his eyes.

She dabbed Neosporin on his ribs and then laid a wide bandage over it.

Peter watched her, and when she was done she turned her face up. His body was wrecked, and the fear pressed in on him like damp DC heat, but still he found himself smiling at her.

She smiled back and leaned against the cushion. As she rested her head, her eyes eased shut. It looked like all the life had drained out of her. A gust of air pushed in through the open hatch, and the hairs stood up on Peter's skin. Rose crossed her arms over her chest and fought back a shiver.

"Here," he said. He pulled a faded blanket down from the shelf behind him and draped it over her.

Peter sat, and for the first time since he'd been jumped at Rose's hotel he tried to rest, to put aside for a moment the endless calculation of what to do next and how to survive.

The adrenaline had run out. Now they were left with the facts: he had been betrayed by everyone he had once trusted and the only thing he had ever believed in. They were alone, broke, and cold.

"Are we safe here?" she asked.

The truth was that nowhere was safe. "We just need a few hours to get some sleep."

"But what now? They killed everyone."

"GIDEON." Throwing in with a spy. Becoming everything Peter had spent his life trying to avoid. "We'll talk to GIDEON."

She shook her head slightly, and her face was grave. GIDEON was a slender reed. But it was all they had.

"You should try to sleep," he said and looked to the forward cabin.

"Not by myself."

He took her by the hand.

At the front of the boat there was a V-berth, a low-ceilinged space lined with cushions that doubled as a bed. He helped her up. On the narrow shelves on the wall were old nylon and knit-cotton blankets, the same ones his mom and dad would bundle him under when they did overnights at Mattawoman Creek. He pushed aside his old life preserver and took down both blankets.

"I'll be right back. I'm going to lock up."

She nodded and pushed back into the berth. Peter cleaned

the dishes quickly, shut the companionway and padlocked it from the inside. He came back to the sleeping area, put the gun on the shelf that ran along the side, and raised himself onto the platform. Rose was already lying down.

He lay beside her on his good side, and she pressed against him, laying her head on his chest, wrapping her arm around his waist.

"Are we going to be okay?"

He had told her he wouldn't lie to her, and he wouldn't.

"I won't let anyone hurt you."

She didn't say anything for a moment, then he felt her chest hitching as she cried in silence. He held her tight, and she grabbed his shoulder, pulled his face toward hers, and kissed him, brought him in desperately.

He felt her tears cold against his cheeks, although by now she had stopped crying. There was no intimation of sex to any of it, just closeness, a closeness like he'd never felt, as if they had known each other for decades, had built a quiet love over years.

He put his arm around her, her head resting on his shoulder, and ran his hand over her hair.

They stayed like that for a long time. Her breaths became slow and even. She was out.

As tired as he was, real sleep never came, just hours of Rose's chest rising and falling against his as the boat creaked along the pilings.

He knew the threat was closing in and waited for the light to come.

63

The dawn was a faint glow through the fiberglass hatch overhead.

"Rose," he whispered, and she answered him in a clear voice, as if she was already awake.

"Yes?"

"It's time to go."

She kissed him again and put her hand to the side of his face, took him in warmly. "You're a good guy, Peter."

He was starting to have his doubts. She made it sound like high praise, like she hadn't known such a thing existed.

They went into the main cabin, and Peter started a kettle of water and opened the companionway six inches. Rose looked over a few snapshots that were tucked into the nav station, leaned in toward a photo of Peter, maybe ten years old, fishing with his godfather and his dad.

The instant coffee was bitter, but the caffeine and the sunlight made him feel a hundred times better than he had last night.

They climbed out of the cabin and sat in the cockpit. The warmth of the enamel mug seeped into his hands.

Wisps of fog floated toward them over the river. The water was a blanket of silver.

"Why are you doing this, Peter?"

He cocked his head. "Doing what?"

"Why did you trust me? Why didn't you tell your bosses where I was? It was your job. You went against them."

"You were right."

"I still don't get why."

He watched the waves lap against the breakwater.

"I looked you up when I was at the Airbnb," she said. "You were in that train crash last year."

"You read the thing in the *Post*?"

"'Rescue on Train 2561.'"

"That article." Peter shook his head. "They didn't spend a lot of time talking about all the people who died after I got out."

"You did everything you could."

"It wasn't enough."

"I read about your dad, Peter."

He took a long breath in. This was always the worst moment. When do you tell somebody who you are? How do you talk to them after they find out?

"Is it true? Was he a spy?"

He looked at her, looked for the distrust. Even Leah, his fiancée, had flashed it at times. But Rose showed no sign.

Peter saw them again: all the embassy sources working for American intelligence whose identities were leaked to the Russians during his father's scandal.

Most were executed quietly, but one couple—a man and a woman—was taken on the street after they returned to Russia. Maybe to make an example of them.

Kremlin thugs shot them on the steps of their apartment

building. Their kids found them lying across the stoop, keys in hand and groceries spilled out in the snow.

The next day, Peter made his confirmation. His dad stood with him up on that altar, swearing before God to live a faithful life. In the middle of all that.

"I don't know," Peter said. "He died before he could tell anyone, before anything was proven."

That was a hard summer. News trucks camped out on their street. Photographers stuck their cameras in the windows if he and his mother tried to get some sunlight. Peter read the news, knew the rumors. He couldn't stand to be in the same room as his dad, couldn't stand to talk to him, couldn't sit across the table from him and listen to him chew.

"He called me the night he died," Peter said. "I think he wanted my help."

Peter dragged his nail along the side of his finger, caught himself, and stopped. He was pushing back against the memory, not wanting to relive it again.

Rose saw the gesture but looked up quickly. "What did he say?"

"I was out. Things were tough at home when all that was happening, tense. My mom went to stay at her sister's. I would sneak out and go play ball. Free throws, practice drives, whatever. I'd spend hours at this playground that was through the woods behind my house.

"When I got home, he wasn't there. But there was a message waiting on the cordless phone. It was so strange. My father called his own house and left a message for me. His voice was breaking. He said he was proud of me, and he loved me." Peter stared at the water. "That was it."

"The last time you heard from him?"

"Yes. I listened to it twice, and then my mom came home and told me he was gone." Peter shook his head slowly. "It was a car crash. He'd been drinking. No one ever figured out if it was deliberate or not."

They sat close, and she laid her palm on his thigh. The intimacy felt like the most natural thing in the world.

"Do you think he wanted to say something?"

"Maybe he wanted to confess. Or deny it. Or just ask for help. I put a decent face on it, but I think he must have known that all those suspicions, they were getting to me, too. I didn't trust him."

"Peter."

He nodded slowly. He knew what was coming.

"Peter, you can't take what happened to him on yourself."

"I know. I've tried. For years."

"So when I called for your help . . ."

"That's right." He took a deep breath. He couldn't let it go unanswered, couldn't walk away no matter what it cost him.

He didn't know what was driving him: that call from his dad, those voices on the Metro crying out in pain, the lives that were lost because of his father's scandal.

He'd spent his whole life thinking that if he just played by the rules he'd be okay. He could make up for his father's sins. Honesty would save him. The truth would save him. And that had brought him here: a hunted man, to all the world a traitor just like his father.

Peter drained his mug. The only thing that mattered was that they get through this.

"Running," he said. "It doesn't seem to faze you."

Rose leaned back and thought about it.

"Growing up, we were always running from the landlord, or some boyfriend of my mom's, or someone she'd ripped off. She wasn't even at Henry and Paulette's funeral. She had some excuse, something about her passport."

"Where is she?"

"Belize, I think. Some guy with a boat." She laughed. "I hope it's a nicer boat. I don't even know if she can come back to the States. I heard her on the phone once talking about back taxes, warrants. I guess, growing up like that, I should have learned your lesson. Just be honest. But that's not what happened. Forget the rules. Forget the truth. You do what you have to do to survive."

The words hung in the air. Peter did what he needed to do last night. He killed a man, and he expected that knowledge to come at him like a hangover: a sick feeling of pain and remorse. It didn't.

He'd been so careful for so many years, doing everything right, following every rule. He knew part of the reason why: he was afraid of what would happen if he strayed, afraid of finding out that he was his father's son, an all-American face wrapped around something ruthless, dark, and lethal. And now he took that inheritance as a gift. He needed to survive.

"I'll give that a try," Peter said.

"We could run."

Peter shook his head.

"No. They're afraid of something, scared enough to kill, to risk everything. We get that truth, and we go straight at them."

"Will that work?" she asked. "Won't they lock us up, or pin it on us, or kill us?"

"They'll try. They're going to try either way. Our only option is to make a lot of noise on the way. But you should go, Rose. If they come after me, they could get you as an accessory. You should say I coerced you, that you had no idea what I was up to."

She tipped her coffee cup back and emptied it, then let it hang from her finger while she looked across the river.

"No. I owe them this. I'm not going to let them die for nothing. I don't want to talk about what could happen. I don't want to think about it."

Rose stood. "Let's go."

64

On the way back into DC, they stopped at a 7-Eleven and picked up a second prepaid cell phone. Peter was now down to twelve dollars and the change in his car. He was going into the meeting with GIDEON alone at first, to make sure it was safe, and needed a way to communicate with Rose.

Rose powered up the phone as they passed the National Arboretum and the crumbling kilns of the old brickworks beside it.

Peter pulled up to a red light. A Metropolitan Police Department cruiser stopped in an oncoming lane, fifty feet away. Peter pressed back in his seat as he saw the cop look in his direction. Did they have a description of his car? Find the stolen plates?

"You see him?" Rose whispered.

Peter nodded. The light turned green, and he eased the gas down and drove on, watching the patrol car disappear in his side-view mirror. It stopped at the next intersection, just barely visible, but Peter saw it make a U-turn, following him now.

Rose's eyes were on her mirror. "Is he coming for us?"

"I don't know," Peter said. He looked ahead to the next

intersection, saw a box truck in the right-hand turn lane, and accelerated toward it. The cop was two long city blocks back.

"Hang on to the handle," Peter said and gripped the wheel. He waited for the truck to swing wide to make the turn, pulled ahead of it, then cut it off and took the right turn himself. The truck shielded him from the view of the patrol car.

He drove on the side streets and cut back under the elevated train tracks where a red light stopped him. The tracks overhead formed a kind of low tunnel. He could see a few bedrolls stashed behind the support beams.

"Is he gone?" Rose asked.

"I think so." A train rolled above them and the grind and creak of the rails swallowed up his words. He remembered the screaming wheels of the Metro on the day of the crash, felt the heat at his back, the fumes in his throat, the voices echoing from the tunnel.

"Peter," Rose said, but he could barely hear her. A horn blared behind him. The light was green. He pulled out.

The Metro. That was the answer. He looked to Rose.

"The firm where Chen worked, Heller and Wolff, I know why that name jumped out at me. They investigated the Metro crash."

"*Your* crash?"

"Yes." Peter drove on, ready for a cop car to come speeding up at any moment, sirens blaring.

He turned the wheel to the right and drove into a parking lot with a Safeway and a Golden Corral, then pulled up outside a Starbucks.

"Shouldn't we keep going?"

"Yes, but I need to see something." He turned his phone and connected to the Starbucks Wi-Fi.

It took a moment of searching, eyes darting back and forth between the phone and the street, to find the final report on the Metro crash. Chen's name was on one of the last pages.

He handed Rose the phone and sped out of the parking lot.

"Chen was on the team that investigated the crash," he said. "The agencies farmed it out to her law firm. She did the computer forensics."

"But doesn't this say the crash came from neglect? Bad maintenance and worn-out equipment?" she said.

"That's bullshit. When I talked to Chen on the emergency line, she said the Campbells were asking her about infrastructure, and how it could be controlled. Or hacked. She said that there was an accident that wasn't an accident. What if it's the train crash? What if the Russians sabotaged the Metro? They could have done it with a cyberattack, could have broken into the system."

"Why would they kill innocent people?"

"The crash was a month before the election, the night of a big foreign policy speech by Travers's opponent. She used to be the head of Homeland Security. That rally was supposed to make her look tough, like a real commander in chief. What if in the middle of it, the Metro gets wrecked by a cyberattack?"

Rose considered it. "She looks weak, it hurts her in the polls, Travers pulls ahead. That happened in the first few days, I remember, until it started to look more like an accident. Besides, the train crash wasn't what really hurt her right before the election, it was the fund-raising stuff. The financial scandals." She shook her head. "I don't know, Peter. And do you really think that Travers would let all those people on the train die just to make Gibson look bad?"

Peter palmed the wheel through a right turn. "No. But that system is a mess. Maybe they didn't mean for it to be that bad. We know Farr is working with the Russians. Let's say they plan a cyberattack, nothing lethal, just a show of force, to embarrass Gibson and help Travers win the election."

"Do they have that capability?"

"Absolutely. They could stop the trains, shut out the lights, cause panic, whatever. They could cover their tracks, make it look like an accident or even make it look like another country was behind the attack: North Korea, Iran."

Rose leaned forward in her seat. "And their show of force spirals out of control?"

"Right. They didn't mean for it to get that bad, but the Metro is falling apart. The conductors can barely keep those trains from bursting into flames as it is. On that system, any kind of cyberattack could quickly cascade into a disaster."

"And then the investigation finds no foul play."

"The Russians would have had to hide their role from the start, and if his campaign were involved somehow, Travers would have to help cover up what really happened. The investigation didn't really get going until he was in office."

"Chen said she was pressured. Did she say by who?"

"No. But it must have been Farr or someone else in the

administration, keeping her away from the true cause of the crash. She was suspicious, and somehow your aunt and uncle found her or she found them."

Rose looked down. "And if Travers was elected after being complicit in that attack—"

"The Russians would own him, a sitting US president."

"They had to make sure he won. Remember all those scandals that came out about his opponent's inner circle in the final weeks of the election?"

"It was a lot of good reporting but it could have been seeded by the Russians. *Kompromat* they call it— compromising material, dirt. They could have gotten it through hacking. They made sure she lost."

"But the deadline is today. If the attack already happened, what is this all building up to?"

"Vikhrov is on his way from New York. The foreign minister is already here. What if they're going to meet with Travers? They could ask him to pay them back for handing him the election, to give them something they want."

Peter thought of those Russian troops massing along Europe's border.

"But what are the Russians after?" Rose asked.

"I don't know. The US has kept Russia's military in check in Eastern Europe and in Syria. Maybe tonight Travers stands down and lets them attack, take what they want. The train crash could have been just the beginning of the violence."

Rose chewed on her thumbnail and looked out the window. "This is fucking crazy."

"I agree. But it's the first time any of this makes sense. The red ledger must have contained proof of the arrangement.

That's why they need it gone and everyone who knows about it dead."

"By tonight."

"If it went public, it would blow up their deal."

Peter looked at the clock and pressed the pedal down. He needed to make that meeting with GIDEON.

Rose held her palm to her forehead and took a deep breath. "We don't have enough time."

"We have to try. We'll talk to GIDEON. Krysanova and Novikoff thought he could help expose all this, maybe help find that ledger. Maybe he knows the truth. Maybe he has some evidence. Maybe he can point us to people who do. We'll see what he has to offer."

"And how do you know he won't try to kill us, too?"

Peter glanced at the rearview.

"I don't."

65

The notes that Rose had retrieved from Emily Krysanova's house laid out all the details of the meeting site. To find it, Peter drove deep into Rock Creek Park, a 1,750-acre expanse of woods, creeks, and boulders that cut the District almost in half. Hidden within it there were homeless encampments and mostly forgotten ruins of forts from the Civil War.

They cruised along Beach Drive, past Peirce Mill, a nineteenth-century stone landmark. Peter's whole body tensed as they went by the US Park Police headquarters, then crossed the creek.

Storms had raised the waters and they rushed and splashed over the rocks. The sounds of the city disappeared. He parked near a picnic site with a stone grill, and then he and Rose looked over the notes from Krysanova.

They stepped out of the car, and Peter pointed down a horse trail. They started walking, and after ten minutes turned off the bridle path and climbed a steep hill away from the creek. In a quarter mile, they reached the crest, and Peter picked his way through the underbrush.

Peter focused on every sound and movement between the trees, watching for someone following, someone closing in.

He looked down into a small streambed below, marked

by a little-used trail. A fallen tree bridged the stream, and beside it there was a manhole cover. It looked odd in the middle of the woods, some part of the city's drainage.

"Is this it?" Rose asked.

Peter studied the path and then looked back at the notes. "There," he said and pointed to the downed tree.

It was still forty minutes until the meeting. They weren't sure if the signal they had left on the fire hydrant had worked, or if GIDEON would show.

Peter wanted to be early in any case, to see if it was an ambush. He knew about surveillance, but spycraft was alien to him. He could be walking into a trap.

"What now?"

The higher ground gave him the vantage he wanted: a clear look through the leafless trees to the meeting site.

"I'll go down," he said. "You hang here, in case it's a setup or something goes wrong. They have no idea who I am. I don't know how they'll react."

"If I see something off, I'll call you."

"I'll put it on vibrate. He might be armed. That's to be expected. Call if there's something coming I can't see. People moving behind me, something like that."

He handed her his keys. "And if anything goes wrong, run."

"Peter. Are you sure about this?"

"I am."

Farr and the Russians had something to do with that train crash. They murdered those people. And he would do what he needed to get back at them.

He embraced her, then started picking his way toward the stream. The morning sun was filtering into the valley.

Dew hung from the tree branches and soaked the hem of his pants. The stream was running quickly, rushing through rocks, and as he moved closer, he realized he wouldn't be able to hear someone coming.

66

The trail wasn't much more than a line of dirt covered with rotting leaves. He stopped just beside the manhole cover.

Scanning the high hill to his left, he didn't see any sign of Rose, but on a second pass he caught her profile behind a tree. If he hadn't known she was there, he never would have found her.

The waiting and empty time were far worse for his nerves than any action. He was walking unannounced into a game he didn't understand, threatening the secrecy of someone he knew only by a codename, who lived and died by secrets.

Krysanova's gun was tucked into the back of his belt. He hated carrying it unholstered, but he had no safer option.

He tried to see everything, hear everything at once. But he was on low ground, unfamiliar terrain, at the mercy of the other party.

The bright sound of a bell made him reach for the pistol by reflex. But there was no one there. He took his fingers off the gun's grip. It rang again, under his feet, from a drift of leaves piled around the exposed roots of a pine tree.

Peter took a step toward it and brushed away the leaves. His fingers ran across something smooth: a phone under plastic. He thought for a moment that it might be an explosive device, but if it were he would already be gone. He pulled out a ziplock bag with a cheap-looking mobile phone inside, took the handset out, and answered the call.

"Hello?"

"Who are you?" It was a woman's voice, American English with a faint Slavic accent. Peter turned slowly, scanning the trees. He was almost certain he was being watched, but there was no sign.

"My name is Peter Sutherland. Emily Krysanova sent me. I came to meet GIDEON. Is that you?"

"Are you alone?"

"Yes."

He heard only a disappointed sigh. "Don't lie to me, Peter. I have her here."

He looked to the trees where Rose had been hiding. "Don't you dare—"

"She's fine. Lovely thing. That doesn't mean she isn't dangerous. Doesn't seem particularly bothered by the pistol pointing at her. What did you do to Emily Krysanova?"

"We went to her for help, the night she was killed. We had nothing to do with her death. She told us about this meeting. We want to stop whoever killed her. Are you GIDEON?"

A pause. "Talk, talk, talk," she said. "What do you think you're doing?"

"We want the ledger. We have information to trade."

There was no answer, just rustling over the open phone line and then a muffled voice speaking a language he couldn't understand.

After a minute, Peter broke in. "Come down here and talk."

The woman came back, sounding annoyed. "Listen. This isn't a fucking game. And you have no idea what you're doing. Don't bluff. Don't posture. Do what I say, and you two might survive."

Peter felt a surge of anger, but she was right.

"First, put the gun on the ground." She must have watched him reach for it.

"And then start walking up that trail," the woman continued. "In about four hundred meters, you'll see a path to the right. Take it and walk till you see the piles of stones."

"I need to know she's okay."

Rose spoke in the background: "I'm good, Peter. It's okay."

"Satisfied?" the woman asked. "Now put down the gun before things get savage, would you?"

Peter laid it on the dirt. He had no other choice. He started up the path.

"I'm walking."

"I know."

The call ended.

67

Peter hiked farther up the stream valley. After five minutes, he could see no sign of other trails or the city. He had heard of cases where it took the police years to find a body back here. Now he understood why.

He could barely make out the path. The gnarled roots of a chestnut oak hung over it. At points, he had to bushwhack through the tangled underbrush.

He crossed the stream on a thick downed branch. Thirty feet up on the far side, the path turned right down another stream cut, this one shallower. A face of granite boulders lined one side. He could pick out grooves and tool marks. Twenty feet in, the ground flattened into a surprisingly wide area, and neat rows of stacked stones ran to his left. Vines twined through the piles, and green lichen filled the details of the stones. He looked more closely and saw they were broken-up chunks of fine masonry, columns and decorative stonework.

It was an old quarry. Footsteps echoed to his right. Peter turned and turned again once he realized that the sound was reflecting off the stones. Rose came up the trail. Ten feet behind her, a woman followed, holding a handgun by her side.

Rose seemed calm. Her eyes met Peter's and she gave him the faintest smile, a look of reassurance.

The woman had Rose stop on the trail and walked past her to Peter. She patted him down without a word and took back the cell phone that had been buried and the prepaid phone that Peter carried.

"GIDEON?" Peter asked. The woman flicked her head up the path, behind Peter. He turned.

A man stood between the stacked stones. It was his godfather.

68

Greg stood half shadowed by one of the stone piles, wearing a suit but no tie. He looked like the godfather Peter had always known, handsome and kind, but any trace of the shy stammerer was gone.

He held a SIG pistol in his left hand. Peter's mind rebelled, but he forced himself to think through it. How could this be the same man who Peter had just gone to for advice, on the same boat where he had slept last night?

"What is this, Peter?"

Peter tilted his head to one side, stunned. "*You* are asking *me* what this is? Who are you?"

"I think you know by now. Why are you looking for me?"

"I'm looking for a spy who can help me understand why a woman named Krysanova was murdered in front of me, and why people are trying to kill me now. I'm looking for help, for someone named GIDEON. Instead I find you. Someone I trusted like a father—" Peter cut himself off, shaking his head. He hadn't trusted his father. "Holding a gun on me."

"You're FBI, Peter. I have to be careful. People start dying and then you come looking for me. You're sneaking up on a meeting site that was shared only with two contacts, using signals that only they knew. Both of them have been murdered. I have to ask what's going on."

"Krysanova gave me the instructions on how to signal you. She got them from a man named Anton Novikoff. We are all on the same side in this. I'm here because I have no one else to turn to. You think this is some kind of counterintelligence sting?"

"I can't afford to make mistakes. I work for myself, Peter. I don't have diplomatic immunity. I'm not protected by any embassy. If I misstep, I end up in prison or dead."

In prison. Dead. Peter's eyes were on his godfather but all he could picture was a slideshow of bodies, all the sources that had been exposed and murdered because of the leaks in his father's department. He'd never understood how his dad got dragged into espionage. And here was Greg, exposed at last. Now the past began to make sense.

His face felt hot. How strange: the black eye of that gun should have terrified him, but somehow it only set him off, primed his muscles, made him want to charge.

His thumbnail drove into the knuckle of his middle finger, by habit. The woman had walked back the way she had come and was now standing past Rose, gun ready, covering both her and Peter.

He needed calm, needed something to bring him back to center, needed to breathe. But he forced his hand to relax. He didn't want to stop this. He didn't want control, not anymore.

Greg placed the gun in an inside-the-waistband holster on his left hip. Peter approached him, between the two rows of carved granite. Greg's face twisted into something pained and sweet, like it hurt him to show it, but he was glad at last to have the truth out. He raised his hands to the side, a gesture of surrender, as if to say *I'm sorry*, and leaned forward.

He might have been expecting an embrace. Peter drove his fist into his godfather's stomach with a short, efficient upward blow. A strangled gasp filled the quarry, and then Greg went silent, the wind knocked out of him, diaphragm in spasm.

The woman raised the pistol and aimed it squarely at Peter.

69

Peter ignored her and watched his godfather's face redden. Greg put one hand on the stone and waved the other in the air, calling off the woman.

He couldn't shoot his godson. Even in GIDEON, Peter could see a shadow of Greg, a decent man.

Peter crouched face-to-face with Greg. It was reckless, but his thoughts were coming too fast, his heart pounding too hard to care. Greg was the traitor, and now everything made sense.

"You were the one who dragged my father into this shit. You killed him."

Greg straightened up and took a few shallow breaths, his eyes clamped shut.

"How did it work?" Peter asked. "Did you turn him? Did you steal those secrets from him and then let him take the fall?"

"Peter, that's not it. You don't understand."

Peter stood up.

"Don't make me do something I don't want to do here," Greg said.

Could Greg really shoot him?

"We can help each other," Greg went on. "I know what

you're after. The red ledger. I can help you find it. I know who's killing all these sources. I know who's hunting you. I can help you stop them."

Was that how it started with Peter's father? A favor? Something that Greg used, like the tip of a pry bar, to turn him. These promises, how many of them were lies, a way for Greg to exploit Peter's desperation?

"You worked at the White House," Greg said. "Did you find out who the Russians have inside?" Greg studied him. "Yes. That's why you're here. If we work together, I can get you out of this."

"No," Peter said.

"They're going to kill you."

Peter looked down the path, then back to Greg. "I'm not going to help you."

Peter turned and started walking away. Rose approached him, while thirty feet down the path, the woman brought her gun forward to a low ready. She was good with it. Her movements all seemed as natural as breathing.

Rose met him on the path, her face full of fear. She took him by the wrist. Peter stopped and glared at her.

"What are you doing?"

"There has to be another way." His chest rose and fell, the anger pumping through him. They were halfway between the woman and GIDEON on a trail hemmed in by rock.

"Peter, please," Rose said, measuring her words. "Think about it. He can help protect us, get the proof we need."

"That's the man who turned my father."

Rose looked back at Greg, her eyes narrow. "What the hell is happening, Peter? He was in one of the photos on the boat with you."

"He was my godfather. He lied to me my whole life. He was the one who dragged my father into this world."

"GIDEON?"

"Yes."

She took his other hand and pleaded in a whisper, "I know this is hard, but we need his help."

"Do you know what you're asking me to do?" It meant following in his father's path, becoming everything he'd spent his life running from. "He destroyed my family."

She let his hands go and moved closer, then stood on her toes, and brought her mouth near his ear.

"Do you think they'll let us go now that we know who he is? Do you think we can survive without help? Everyone is after us. There is no way out."

He looked at the walls of the quarry. It was a good place for an execution. He glanced to Greg. Peter had no idea what cruelties lay behind that face he knew so well.

Rose stayed close, but now there was indignation in her voice. "You're not the only one who's lost someone. You want to let those fears run your life forever? You want to die to prove a point?"

He looked to his left, where the woman stood ready with the pistol. She seemed calm, but Peter could see the veins in her neck standing out. She was primed, waiting for an order or provocation. Greg approached from the other direction and then stopped, twenty feet off. He probably knew that any words from him would only set Peter off.

"There are worse things," Peter said to Rose.

"And what about me? And what about what we know? And stopping the people behind all this?" Peter shut his eyes and took three long breaths. A bird called. The last leaves rustled in the wind.

"You're not your dad," Rose said. "You're not going to turn into him if you break some rules. You have a good heart. Trust it."

He would rather die. But he wasn't in this alone. He faced his godfather.

"I want that ledger."

Greg nodded. "I wish there was another way, Peter, but it's time you learned the game."

70

Greg looked down the path—maybe they were too exposed—and then gestured with his head back toward the stones.

Peter started walking deeper into the quarry. "Who are you?"

"I'm the man you know," Greg said. "Real name. Real birthdate. Real Social Security card."

"And who do you work for?"

"For myself."

"People don't spy for themselves. This all needs to start making sense, or I'm out." Greg knew that Peter was inside the White House. He wanted information. That gave Peter some leverage.

"Do you work for the Kremlin?" Peter asked.

"I did. I started with them without even realizing it. It was before you were born. I was on a fellowship, working for the West German government in Bonn. I did a lot for the antinuclear movement, too. We were trying to build bridges between the two sides. A friend introduced me to some students from Leningrad. This was the time of *perestroika* and *glasnost,* reformists. We all hoped we could help the USSR become a democracy, welcome them to the West, help their economy along. I gave them some articles on engineering. It seemed totally harmless."

"They weren't students," Peter said.

"No. But that's how they work. Once you do anything, even the smallest thing for the other side, they hold that over you, they leverage you into something bigger, and something bigger still. You believe in an ideal at the beginning, or maybe it's all rationalization, who can really tell? I told myself I was helping the USSR keep up, to make sure that the US wouldn't upset the Cold War nuclear balance. I was trying to stop a war, stop the bomb. As I got in deeper, it was about helping Russia become a real democracy, enter the community of nations. Soon enough you run out of lies to tell yourself. In the end Russian intelligence owned me, and I didn't want to be owned."

Peter wasn't sure how much he could trust any of this. "So how did you get out from under them?"

"I did some work for the French, and they helped take care of the Russian threat. And ever since then it's been making a deal here, a deal there. Robbing Peter to pay Paul, trying to keep all this shit from touching my real life. You do what you have to do."

That Peter understood. "And now you're freelance?"

"Yes. It's a certain role. I'm neutral, Switzerland."

"Everyone trusts you?"

"Everyone distrusts me equally, which is as good as it gets."

He reached his hand out to Rose. "I'm Greg. I'm sorry we couldn't meet under better circumstances."

She shook his hand. "Rose."

"And this is Ileana."

The woman with the gun dipped her head in mock courtesy.

"Don't let her fool you. She's a sweetheart."

"Where's the ledger?" Peter asked.

Greg smiled and appraised Peter, like a man who had finally heard an interesting offer.

"How much do you know?" he asked.

Peter hesitated. He didn't want to offer up any details to Greg, not without getting something back in return.

"Krysanova sent you to me," Greg said. "She was on my side. She knew I was the only way out of this."

Peter and Rose glanced at each other.

"I know you don't want to give anything away," Greg said. "How's this? A high-level mole in the administration working with Russia, and a list of meetings and secret plans recorded in a red ledger by a go-between named Anton Novikoff that would reveal who it is. Henry and Paulette Campbell got it, and then they were killed." He dipped his head toward Rose. "I'm so sorry. Truly."

"How did you know who I am?" she asked.

"It's my business."

"Did you know them?"

"By reputation. Mutual acquaintances. I spent twelve years playing cat and mouse with them. They were the best." His lips drew tight. "What happened to them, it was vile, cowardly work. Even in this world, there are rules, and their murder violated every one of them."

"Who did it?" she asked.

"The same man who killed Krysanova."

Greg watched Rose, watched the anger steel her. "You saw him?" he asked her.

"No. But I was there that night," she said.

Peter remembered that blank of a man in the hotel hallway. "We've been attacked twice, at Krysanova's and the night before, but we never saw his face."

"I can't believe you survived," Greg said. "His name is Dimitri Sokolov. They used to call him *steklo,* glass. People look right through him as if he's not there. He's a breathing nightmare and should have been put down years ago. The Russians have been assassinating their enemies overseas for a decade, and now Dimitri is off his leash here. He's stalking both of you. Now that you know about the ledger, he won't stop until you're dead."

"Does he have it?" Peter asked.

Greg thought for a moment. "No. He's still on the hunt. He needs that ledger. The Campbells had it at one point. Do you know who was running their investigation on the political side? Who they were reporting to? I know about Farr and Hawkins. Was there anyone else who might have been able to find out where it is?"

"Those were the only two," Peter said. "I know Farr is working with the Russians but I'm not sure about Hawkins."

Greg grimaced slightly. "Hawkins is dead. We think Dimitri killed him, too."

Peter felt cold all of a sudden. A senior advisor to the president, murdered. Jesus, no one was safe.

"Which leaves Farr," Greg said. "I think we found your mole."

"She killed Hawkins?" Peter looked down for an instant. "Did he find out about the book? And what, Farr had him killed to avoid being exposed?"

"As I understand it."

"Then where is the ledger?" Peter asked.

"If the FBI had it, or the Russians, I would know."

"How?"

"I have my own sources. The FBI searched a storage unit that belonged to the Campbells but found nothing."

"Then Diane Farr took it," Peter said.

"That's where this all points."

Rose turned to Peter. "But why would Dimitri still be looking for the ledger if she has it?"

Greg answered her. "They're working together, but his loyalties are to Russia. Both the Kremlin and Farr want that book for their own reasons. I believe she took it without telling Dimitri. Do you know how powerful that ledger is?"

"It's proof that the Russians rigged the election," Peter said. "They crashed that Metro train. They killed twenty-one people."

A proud smile spread on Greg's face. "That's it, Peter. You—"

"Don't," Peter said. The last thing he wanted to hear was that he was a natural spy. All he had going into this were theories and suspicions, but now based on Greg's reaction he knew it was the truth.

"Dimitri wants it for Russia," Greg said. "So they are the only ones who have proof of treason at the highest levels. They have a compromised president under their sway."

"And Farr wants it destroyed?" Rose asked. "To cover up her role? Protect the president?"

"Possibly," Greg said. "Or she wants it to protect herself. If it implicates the president or whoever else was involved, it could give her leverage, make sure she doesn't take the fall."

Peter looked over the carved stones. One part of all this still bothered him.

"I was on the train that crashed. Why would they pick me to be part of the investigation?"

"They kept you in the dark on what you were doing?"

"Yes. I just handled an emergency line."

Peter thought back to that strange interview with Farr in the Situation Room. She made it sound like she had plucked him for this because no one was more motivated, but now he understood: it was because everyone was already suspicious of him.

Peter tapped the side of his fist against a broken piece of granite. "I was the perfect scapegoat. My father's son."

"If she needed someone to take the fall," Greg said, "she could even frame you as being involved with the crash somehow."

"Jesus," Peter said. He had seen the look on Brian's face in the parking garage. Farr was already making him out as a killer.

Ileana spoke up in a language that sounded Russian but wasn't quite. Greg listened, and when she had finished, he admonished her: "Fine, but let's keep it in English, okay? That's not helping."

Ileana returned an impish smile, lifted her phone, and walked to the far end of the row of stones.

"Was that Ukrainian?" Peter asked.

"Belarusian. We've been looking at Farr for a while, patterns of life, possible hides. We've been looking at everyone involved in this."

"Do you know where she put the ledger?"

"No, but we might be able to find out. Come on."

Greg had done everything right to get Peter to trust him, but he wasn't ready to go along with him just yet. He needed to think, to buy time. He rested his hand on the stones and looked more closely at a carving.

Greg stepped beside him. "They're from the renovation of the Capitol in the fifties. They dumped them here."

"I thought the columns were in the arboretum." There was a beautiful display, thirteen columns set in a field, like a Greek ruin.

"The best are. The broken ones they dumped in a couple of spots in the park." He ran his finger over a carved leaf. "These were commissioned when they rebuilt the Capitol in the 1820s, after the British burned it. Different times, different allies."

Peter let the point go. "Krysanova said that there was a clock on this."

"Tonight," Greg said. "President Vikhrov will be at the Kennedy Center, a joint production with the Washington Ballet and the Mariinsky. But before that Travers will meet Vikhrov at his hotel, the Hay-Adams. He's in the Presidential Suite. It won't be publicized, and they will work out a deal."

"And Russia uses the ledger as leverage for what? How do you pay someone back for handing you the presidency?"

Greg ran a knuckle along his cheek and said nothing.

"Travers keeps the US at bay while Russia takes a slice out of Europe?" Peter asked.

Greg narrowed his eyes at Peter, a mix of suspicion and amusement. "You don't disappoint. Who told you that?"

"It's my business," Peter said. It was another guess confirmed.

"They could go straight in and seize the Baltics," Greg said. "For a start. The Russian troops are ready on the border."

"They can't just invade."

"No. But there are massive ethnic Russian populations in those countries, Estonia and Latvia. There is a playbook for this kind of thing. A provocation. Assassinate a pro-Russian politician, a bullet or a bomb, and Russia sends in undercover troops to protect its people, install a puppet leader."

"Like what they did in Ukraine, but bolder," Peter said. "Will they move tonight?"

"Impossible to say. But Vikhrov, even after all his Botox and PR consultants, is still the same man who blew up apartment buildings, killing his own citizens, and blamed it on terrorists to consolidate power. Everything is in place. Once he has his deal, the violence could begin any second. They want back everything the Soviet Union lost, and more. Greater Russia. Piece by piece. It's a centuries-old dream. That's why they won't let you live to see tonight, Peter. They won't let anyone stand in the way. I can help you. Come on."

Ileana shouted from the other side of the quarry, again in Belarusian. Greg yelled back, then shook his head. "Don't mind her."

"What did she say?"

"She's working on getting the last of Farr's financial records, anything that can help us find where she might be hiding the book."

Peter checked Greg's watch. "There's no time. We need to go after it now."

"Then let's go," Greg said and gestured down the path. Peter remained to the side and held his hand out for his godfather to go first. He wasn't going to show the other man his back.

71

They walked back to the path and Greg turned right, away from the direction Peter and Rose had come. The trail climbed up, toward Connecticut Avenue and Chevy Chase.

"My car's the other way," Peter said.

"The police are looking for it. We'll take care of it for you."

Small favors, Peter thought. *That's how it starts.*

"And the gun I left?" he asked.

Ileana patted her pocket. The others waited on the path ahead, and Rose gave Peter an impatient stare. He went on, following behind the other two with Rose. A few minutes later they stepped out of the woods onto a side street and climbed into a black Chevy Tahoe parked around the corner. A short drive took them into the underground garage of an apartment building on Wisconsin Avenue.

They parked and took the elevator to the twelfth floor, where Greg led them to an apartment at the end of the hall. It reminded Peter of a long-term-stay hotel: decent, generic furniture, bland art—landscapes and muted contemporary pieces—and no shred of any personal traces, like photos or clothes. It was another safe house, and as Ileana shut and locked the door behind him, it felt about as safe as the last one.

"We've been working on this since Anton Novikoff first contacted me," Greg said, opening the combination lock on a filing cabinet.

"This is what we have on Diane Farr." Greg dropped a stack of files on the kitchen table beside an open laptop.

Peter leaned over the table and looked through them. They were background: financial records, patterns of movement.

"We're looking for people she might have trusted with the ledger or places she might be keeping it," Greg said.

"She wouldn't hide it at her apartment?" Rose asked.

"Not likely given the level of care we've seen or the scrutiny she's under."

"How long have you been focused on her?" Peter said.

"We've been looking at everyone."

Peter's and Rose's eyes met. Were there files on them in there, too?

"Known associates?" Peter asked.

"Here." Greg tapped a folder. Peter sat and leafed through it, while Rose took a chair beside him. He had done these kinds of rundowns dozens of times, though usually special agents were the ones organizing the hunt and handing out assignments to Gs like Peter.

"Can I use this?" Peter asked, pointing at the laptop on the table.

"Sure." Greg punched in the password for a guest account.

"If she did want to use that ledger as insurance against

being killed, I don't know who she could have trusted it to," Peter said. "It's too valuable."

"There are ways, but I agree," Greg said. "I think she kept it herself."

"Any other properties?"

"Not in her name, but we did a search on any corporations . . ." He looked around the table, then slid a folder across to Peter. "Here it is."

Greg rested his hands on the table. "You work with Farr," he said. "Did you see anything that might help us find it? Hawkins disappeared the night before last. We think that's when she must have gotten the ledger."

That was the night Peter stayed with Rose at the Mayflower. He thought back to the following morning: the dark circles under Farr's eyes, the tray of coffees, her staring at her phone as she walked down the hall. He was always watching, always silently filing away every detail. He played the scene back in his mind. He had something. That's what Greg was hoping for, to draw information out of him not through coercion but kindness.

His godfather looked down at him, and smiled, waiting, but Ileana came over a moment later, with a phone in her hand and an urgent look on her face. She said something quietly in Belarusian. Greg excused himself, and they stepped into the bedroom, speaking quietly.

Peter started looking through the files. This was the game: he needed his godfather's help, but could he take from Greg without giving himself up in return?

"What are you looking for?" Rose asked Peter in a whisper.

"Hiding sites."

Peter scanned the lists of bank accounts, investments, and corporate holdings. There were a few obvious candidates: a safe-deposit box, a storage unit, payments to a jewelry store, where safeguarding of valuables was often offered.

He pointed them out to Rose.

Diane Farr was careful, untrusting. He doubted she would give the book to someone else. He played back the moments he saw her that night and the next morning. Something had happened. Something shook her. She had come early enough to the hotel that he doubted she could have made it to a bank or jeweler, which left the storage unit.

He went on to the real property, something she owned, something she could access with no one seeing. That made more sense. There was the condo, but that was too obvious.

Greg had pulled records on everything. Peter liked the looks of a family trust called Brook Lane. Attached to the incorporation papers were tax documents and refinancing agreements for a property in the Palisades, an affluent section of DC that hung down on the steep hills of the Potomac in the northwest of the city.

"Family trust," he said to Rose, and turned the sheets toward her. "It's a good way to protect the house from lawsuits and bankruptcies. A lot of this would have been hard to find, and no one should have access to these financial records."

Rose pulled the computer toward her and opened a private tab in the browser, then punched in the address. She found it on Google Maps and went to the Street View: it was a run-down mansion, half-hidden by trees.

"Is it hers?"

"Not technically," Peter said. "She's the executor for someone named Ellen Farr. Original owner was Graeme Farr. The taxes are a mess. It's probably why it's empty. It's all tied up."

"It doesn't look very secure."

Peter checked the time stamp on the image and leafed through copies of permits. "That's three years old. It's been totally redone."

Rose was typing something into the computer. She turned the screen to Peter.

"Her grandfather owned it. Look." Peter followed her finger to the page. Graeme Farr was a director at Christie's, the auction house's Washington representative. He dealt in antique guns and timepieces.

"Wouldn't the house have a vault or safe?" Rose whispered.

Peter nodded. "Look up Davenport Coffee."

"What's that?"

"It's where Farr brought the coffees from that morning."

"How do you know?"

"The logo on the cup."

She showed him a coffee shop on a map. It was three-quarters of a mile from the Palisades house.

"How did you remember?"

"It's just practice. This was my job. You hang on to every detail."

Rose looked down, then turned to him.

"When I saw Farr that morning, I picked up something," she said. "It was a really faint odor, maybe varnish or paint. I thought maybe she'd redone her nails."

"Or she'd been to a newly renovated house."

Rose nodded, stiffening as Greg came out from the bedroom.

"All good?" he asked, then looked down at a stack of paper.

"Sure." Peter opened more tabs on the web browser and began looking up all the other candidates where Farr might be hiding the ledger. He wanted to cover his tracks as much as possible in case Greg was still able to access the browser history.

Greg approached and stood over Peter. He closed his hand on Peter's shoulder.

"You found something?"

Peter tapped the papers. "It's hard to say. This is great information. There are a lot of places in here she could have put it."

"You used to track people," Greg said. "Where do you think it is?"

"It could be any of them."

Peter glanced to Greg's holstered pistol. Ileana stood six feet behind him, her hands held loosely in front of her at her waist, an easy draw for her gun.

Greg grinned. "You have something, don't you?"

Peter took a long, measured breath and studied the papers, thinking of the best way out of this, perhaps by throwing Greg off the trail.

"That's fine," Greg said, as his hand slipped from Peter's shoulder. "You don't want to tell me."

He paced around the table and looked across at Peter and Rose.

"There's a safe-deposit box—" Peter started to say.

"Peter, listen. I'm not trying to shake you down for

information. And I'm not going to use you to get the book myself. You came to me for help. I gave it to you. You have something, great. I want to help you, but if you don't trust me, I understand. Let me know what I can do, and I will stay out of your way."

"Why would you do that?"

"I'm still your godfather, Peter. I want to see you make it out of this safely. You have just about every law enforcement agency in the capital hunting you down: DC cops, FBI, Secret Service. But the Russians are the ones you should worry about. They want your scalp. Let me help you."

Killing with kindness. That's what Farr had done, what the president had done. Peter trusted no one. He had something, a plan or the outlines of one. It meant putting himself right in front of the people who most wanted to kill him. It meant using their treachery against them.

"You'll let us go?" he asked.

"If that's what you need."

Peter sat back. "We need cars, two of them, and my gun back, and our phones."

"That's no problem," Greg said and nodded to Ileana. "And get him a clean gun, the SIG."

Ileana handed them their prepaid phones, then stepped over to a locked cabinet and dialed it open. There were a half dozen plastic storage boxes stacked neatly on one shelf. She took out a small range bag, unzipped it, and removed a holstered SIG pistol, a modern polymer version with no hammer. She handed the gun, along with four magazines, to Greg. He placed them on the table next to Peter.

"Peter, you can't kill your way out of this."

"It's a precaution."

Greg went into the shelves and came back with a smartphone. He checked something on the screen, then passed it over.

"Blackphone," Greg said. "You ever use one?"

Peter nodded. "We had them in evidence a couple of times." They were built from the ground up to be encrypted and untraceable.

"If you need anything, you can use that to reach me securely. My contact info and public key are already in there."

Greg opened his wallet and counted out a slim stack of small bills, maybe six hundred dollars, then handed them over to Peter. He hesitated. It felt like being bought.

Rose took the money and pocketed it. "Thank you."

Peter took out the pistol and did a quick function check, trying not to let the shake in his fingers show.

Greg studied him as he reholstered the weapon. "Don't go after them on your own, Peter. I know you're angry, but you have to be careful."

Peter slipped the gun into his waistband. "So what do you want in exchange?"

"Nothing," Greg said.

"Something for nothing?"

"Yes. You're family."

There would be a price, Peter knew it. "Is that how you started Dad down this road?"

Greg's mouth tightened. "It's not like that, Peter. Let me help you. Where are you going?"

"I appreciate all this, but the rest I do on my own."

"This is big. You'll need help. You need me"—Greg tapped his finger on the Blackphone—"you call. I'm there."

Peter picked it up and slipped it in his pocket.

"So that's it?" Greg asked.

"That's it."

Greg dipped his head, and Ileana shut and locked the cabinet.

Peter walked back to the elevators, and they all went down together. The black Tahoe was parked against the far wall, and as they came near, the lights flashed on a Volkswagen Jetta that Ileana had just unlocked. The keys dangled from her fingers, and Peter pointed to Rose. Ileana tossed them to Rose, who walked over to the Jetta and opened the driver's door.

Peter needed to go over the next steps with Rose, but not here. As he turned, he nearly bumped into Ileana, who had silently come up behind him.

"I like that girl. This all seems so natural to her." She smiled. "Like she's been doing it for years."

She put the Tahoe key in Peter's palm, her fingers slow on his skin, and walked away.

Greg had been talking to Rose by the Jetta door, leaning in close, but then he came over to Peter.

"You sure about this?" he asked Peter.

"I am," Peter said, then thought for a moment. "You always warned me off working for the FBI. Were you worried I would come for you? Find out who you were?"

"No. I was worried you'd make it. I never wanted to have to bring you into this."

"So much for that," Peter said. He walked by Greg, tapping him lightly on the shoulder with his knuckles. "Thanks for this."

"Any time."

Peter met Rose by the Jetta.

"What are we doing?" Rose asked.

"Follow me out of here. I'll pull in someplace where we can talk."

"Sure."

She climbed in, and Peter returned to the Tahoe and started it up.

72

Peter stripped the battery from the Blackphone as soon as he pulled out of the garage, in case Greg could follow its location. He drove north to Tenleytown, looking for tails behind Rose's Jetta in the rearview, and led her into the parking lot at Fort Reno Park.

The highest spot in DC, it was also the site of the only Civil War battle that happened in the District. A fort and sandstone castle stood behind high fences, their red brick crenellated towers looming oddly over the baseball diamonds and low-rise apartment buildings.

Rose pulled her car around in a circle next to his, driver's window to driver's window.

Peter couldn't help but laugh.

"What?"

"That's a cop move. Pull into the space."

Peter had to make sure that Greg hadn't put GPS trackers on the cars. Greg understood that Peter and Rose knew more than they were letting on. Maybe he let them go in order to follow them, hoping they would lead him to the ledger.

Peter had planted a lot of beacons when he worked surveillance. It took him fifteen minutes to sweep both cars.

They were clean. He slid the carpet back over the spare tire in the Jetta's trunk.

"You should lay low," he said.

"Not happening. What's your plan?"

"I'm going to that house in the Palisades."

Rose looked around the park. "You think Greg will try to take the ledger for himself?"

"Yes. That was all too easy. But I should be able to tell if he's following us."

"He seemed genuine."

"He's a professional liar."

"Then why would he have let you go do this on your own?"

Peter watched the trees bend in the wind.

"Because he wants to turn me. To own me. You have to do that slowly, so slowly the victim doesn't see what's happening. He knows he can't coerce me—"

"But maybe he can seduce you?"

"Right. He thinks we can't handle this, that we'll have to go to him for help."

"Can we?"

"We'll see."

"What can I do?"

"I want you to park near the White House and look out for Farr. I think there's a way to force her to react, to lead us to the ledger. I want you to try to follow her if she moves. She drives a blue Audi A6. It'll be the only one parked inside the White House fence. Try to follow her, see where she's going. If she's coming here, she'll probably head through Georgetown. See if you can tell if she's traveling alone, or if there are other people and cars with her. I think she'll be by herself. I don't know who else she would trust with it. But that will determine everything."

"You're going after her?"

"I am," Peter said, pulling the key to the Tahoe from his pocket.

He didn't care what happened to him. He'd felt fear earlier, turning his stomach, but now he knew what he needed to do, and that fear changed into something else. It was a focused high, like his best days on the court, and he found himself savoring it as it drew him into the dark.

"But if the ledger is there," Rose said. "It must be locked up."

"Farr will let me in."

"In what world would she do that?"

Peter scanned the street and looked back to Rose. "If she thinks I already stole it."

73

Forty-five minutes later, Peter put the Tahoe in park, grabbed an ax and a backpack from the passenger seat, and stepped onto the quiet street.

Dead leaves piled against the curb. The woods sloped down to the Potomac. This was the Palisades, and Farr's grandfather's house was right down the street.

He had stopped at a little hardware store on the way out of Tenleytown. It was a mom-and-pop place with prices written on the items in magic marker. Searching its crammed aisles, he didn't know if he'd find what he needed in a store inside the city, but there it was: a thirty-six-inch ax with an ash handle.

During his time as a G, he'd seen some smart thieves at work, guys who left no trace. One crew would swap out a car key for a dummy after a test drive, return to the dealership at night, and drive away as easy as that.

For this, Peter didn't want easy. He didn't want surreptitious. He wanted forced entry, as big and brutal and destructive as possible. Being seen was the whole point of this gambit.

He held the ax under the blade as he moved toward the back of the house.

It was Federal style with high peaked roofs, so perfect he could tell it was uninhabited. There were no drapes on the windows, no hose on the spigot in the back, no mat at the back door.

Adrenaline primed his body. His heart thundered in his chest as he strode toward the back door.

Through the window, across the dining area, he could see a wireless camera. That was good. There was no other security in plain view, and if there was an alarm, he would know soon enough. Let them come.

He let the ax slip through his fingers and caught it at the end of the handle as he climbed the back steps. He tightened both hands around the ash handle and hauled it back, over his head, then whipped the heavy blade forward. The steel hissed through the air.

He called up the anger he'd spent half a lifetime hiding, let the rage against Farr and the other killers flow through him, pulling with all the strength he had.

Peter was done with their rules. Enough with the Boy Scout shit.

The ax entered the door where he wanted it, just above the brass handle, and the blow shook his body. He hoped to take out the lock face and maybe the dead bolt cylinder in one go. But the door split along the panels, and he ripped out the strike plate and twenty-four inches of frame with it.

He entered a breakfast area. The camera was straight ahead. He walked toward it and then passed into the foyer. A job-site smell hung in the air—paint and hardwood varnish—and his footsteps echoed back against the bare walls.

There was another camera in this front room, aimed at the front door. He tapped the ax against its cord. The blade slid through the wires, and the green LED at its base died.

The front door had magnetic switches that would trip an alarm if it were opened. The alarm panel should be here, too, in an easy-to-access spot for someone coming home, but there was nothing on the wall. He opened the closet door. The panel was on his left, going off, which was what he wanted.

The cameras looked like a separate system. They were IP cameras, hooked up wirelessly to the internet so that someone with a smartphone or computer connection could log in and view them from anywhere. Farr could be watching right now. The panel let out a piercing beep, over and over, but Peter ignored it.

He wasn't worried about the police. Even if the system was hooked up to a dispatcher, they would call the homeowner first, and Peter assumed that Farr would want as few people as possible involved if she kept her secrets here. Even if the police came, the quickest response would be five minutes, and that was enough time.

The empty house made for an easy search. He climbed the steps as they curved in a grand spiral around the foyer and went room to room at the top, on the third floor. There was a library to his left, maybe an office. The safe could be in there. At the end of the hall, an open door led to the master suite: a bedroom with a sitting area on the right.

Another camera sat on a windowsill, pointed toward the side of the room. That was an odd location. As he moved closer, he saw that it was aimed at a walk-in closet in the master suite. He'd found it.

Peter stepped inside. The walk-in was ten by fifteen feet, a dressing room really, with full-length mirrors and built-in shelves and drawers. There was a vault door to his right, painted beige to match the room, with a safe dial and lever near its center.

He put his bag down next to it, then walked back toward the camera in the bedroom. A light swing of the ax shattered it into pieces, and Peter knew the last thing Farr would see was him standing over her secret.

He had no robot dialer or high-powered drill. He couldn't crack a safe if he had all the time in the world. Holding the blade of the ax in his hand, he cut at the hard plastic of the dial, marring it to leave signs of manipulation. Then he turned the ax around and drove the handle through the plaster beside the safe, punching holes beside the hinges and dead center, in line with the dial and lever.

He stepped back, satisfied, then shouldered his bag, picked up the ax, and walked out. The alarm wailed and filled the house.

On the ground floor, Peter paused just outside the rear door and glanced up at the last camera. He had known it was there. He'd left it intact, because he wanted to be seen, and he wanted to be seen leaving.

He'd done his job, and the last image he left her was of his ax swinging toward the camera. The housing shattered, and plastic rained down on the hardwood floor.

He left through the rear door that he had smashed, holding the ax close by his hip. He strode out to the car and put the ax on the floor in the back.

Every instinct told him to flee. The police could be here soon, and Farr's killers, and perhaps Greg and Ileana, too, though he had done everything he could to evade them and check for tails. They still might have found a way to stab him in the back and try to take the ledger for themselves.

Sticking around was insane, which was why he needed to do it, to remain here in the eye of the storm, the last place anyone would expect to find him.

He walked to the woods at the edge of the backyard. He had a decent view of the street both coming and going, and a hard thirty-second run to his car if he needed to escape.

Most important, hiding here was his best chance to come up unseen behind anyone who came into the house.

His hand drifted toward the gun. The anger burned in his chest like strong liquor. He didn't know what he was capable of anymore, how far he would have to go in there. He didn't know if he would make it out, but that didn't matter anymore.

He needed to get the evidence before more people died to keep it secret. He needed to stop Farr and the other traitors from selling out the US.

Five deep breaths brought his pulse down slightly. He ran his hands down the sides of his legs to dry his palms, then picked up one of the prepaid phones and called Rose.

"Everything okay?" she asked.

"Yeah, you?"

"I'm fine," she said. "I'm watching the lot now. Her car is there."

"Call me if you see her move and try to see if any other cars go with her."

"And follow?"

"Stay eight cars back. Do what you can. But no closer, and if you see anything out of the ordinary, pull off. I only need to know if she's coming this way, and if she has protection. And Rose, please, don't come near this house."

Rose had the address, and they had already covered the basics. It was much safer to follow someone if you had a sense where they might be going.

"What about your protection?"

He felt the weight of the gun hanging from his belt.

"I'm good."

"Okay . . . wait. Her car is moving. I'll call you back."

"Be careful."

"I will."

Peter pocketed his phone and stood in the shadows. A car hummed down the street. His attention snapped to it. Every rustle and breath of wind set him on edge.

The call from Rose came ten minutes later.

"She's coming toward you, on MacArthur."

"Good. Alone?"

"As far as I can tell."

"Let me know if she heads somewhere else and don't get too close to the house. If she does come straight here, I want you to stop on MacArthur, at the entrance to the neighborhood. Keep your eyes out for anyone who's backing her up. This won't take long."

"I want to be there."

"It's better this way. It's better one of us stays back."

"But . . ."

"Please, Rose."

She needed to live to tell the story. She needed to live.

"Rose?"

"Okay. Good luck."

"Thanks."

He rested his hand on the grip of his gun. Farr was coming.

74

Farr's Audi rolled down the street and parked near the front of the house. A moment later, she crossed through the side gate and followed the walk into the backyard.

She scanned the windows, and Peter saw that she too carried a pistol, drawn and held ready. She had a high, confident grip, with her finger extended along the frame. She knew what she was doing. She looked along the tree line, looked straight at where he stood half-hidden by a plane tree. He pressed against the peeling bark.

The wind caught the back door to the house and slammed it shut. It sounded like a thunderclap in the middle of the quiet afternoon. He'd destroyed the lock and latch, and the door swung freely.

Farr turned, her back to him now. She aimed the pistol at the door. She relaxed and lowered the gun as she approached the rear door, then stepped inside.

Peter drew his gun and double-checked that the safety was off, then slipped through the trees toward the house. He knew where she was going, and the high windows would offer a vantage on the deck. He didn't have much time to get to the door without being seen.

He cut toward the hedges, moving in a fast walk until he

was twelve feet out from the deck, and then there was no choice but an open sprint to the back door.

He pressed against the wall beside that rear door. The wind had left it open six inches. A last deep breath, and then he shouldered it open and stepped inside, following his pistol as he swept the ground floor.

No sign of her. He crossed to the steps, treading lightly on the balls of his feet. After all the uneasy anticipation outside, now a strange exhilaration took hold of him. Whatever would happen would happen. At least he could get on with it, could give into the manic energy pumping through his veins and move.

How long does it take to open a safe? How long would it take her to realize that the theft hadn't occurred? That it was about to happen now?

He hit the third floor: hallway clear, then he heard a soft rushing sound from inside the master suite: *click-whirr, click-whirr*. She was turning the dial. She was occupied, and both of her hands would be full in a second.

He checked the light: it came from within the room. If he stepped in the doorway there would be no shadow, no hint. He passed into the open doorframe and saw her on one knee in the walk-in closet, peering at the safe dial and closing in on the last number with trembling fingers.

Her gun was holstered. She grabbed the safe lever with her left hand and drew back the bolts. The heavy door opened with a faint groan from the hinges. Peter exploited the noise and her distraction to close the distance to the entry of the walk-in.

As she stepped inside the vault, he stopped just outside

the closet. He could hear her breath let go: a sigh of relief. A red ledger lay on top of a rack of jewelry shelves. She grabbed it. Peter stepped closer and raised his pistol. Farr froze.

"Don't," Peter said. "Hands to the side."

She held the ledger in her left hand, while her right hung down by her thigh, eight inches from her gun.

"Peter? What in Christ's name are you doing?"

"I'm not fucking around, Diane. Put your hands out."

She turned slowly to face him.

"You're confused. You're in over your head. This is a mistake. Put that down and we'll talk."

"Hands."

"Someone's using you, Peter. Who have you been talking to? You know what happens when people start making their own rules."

He knew it. He'd lived it. He didn't care. He was in this with open eyes.

"This isn't you, Peter. Is it the girl?"

She stepped toward him. She seemed more confident now, as if the initial shock had faded, as if she knew he would be the obedient subordinate he had always been. The distance between them closed, between her face and the gun, and her hand inched toward her holster.

Peter turned slightly, raising his left hand toward her. He put space between her and his SIG, held it closer in, near his chest.

"Stop."

Another step. She was bold now, forcing the issue, confident that Peter wouldn't, couldn't kill her. He sidestepped back, and she raised the hand that was holding

the ledger, palm toward him, a calming gesture. She had
seen him retreat, and she would exploit it.

"Don't make me, Diane."

His finger slipped from the frame to the trigger, and her
hand went to the grip of her gun.

The crack of a nine-millimeter round split the air.

75

Peter's hand was steady on his gun. It hadn't moved. He hadn't fired. Farr stepped back, shocked, and held her arms out to the side.

Rose stood in the bedroom behind him, another SIG drawn and aimed straight at Farr's head. A wisp of smoke escaped the barrel. The muscles in Rose's forearms stood out. She was gripping the gun tightly, and there was the faintest shake in her fingers.

A wash of plaster dust lay on the ground between them. Rose had shot up, as a warning, but her next shot was lined up true.

She was liable to fire again just from the tension, but Peter's first priority was Farr. The surprise of the gunshot had thrown her, and Peter rushed toward her, knocking her hand away from her holster, and then snatching the gun out of it, drawing it smoothly from the Kydex sheath.

He pivoted back on the hardwood, out of the line of Rose's fire. He flicked the safety on Farr's gun and tucked it into the back of his belt.

He seized the ledger from Farr's hand, then took a step back, standing in the entry to the closet.

"Rose. I've got her. You can take your finger off the trigger now. Put it on the side of the gun."

He glanced back. The muscles in her forearms tensed. She could shoot without even meaning to.

"She killed them," Rose said, her voice an odd, emotionless monotone.

"I have the ledger, Rose. We won. We just need to get out of here."

"She killed them."

"Rose. There's a right way to do this. Don't give them what they want."

She stared at Farr.

"Tell me the truth," Rose said. "Why did you do it?"

"You're both deranged. Just put that down before you get us all killed."

Rose's lips tightened into a flat line.

"Rose," Peter said.

Her hands closed on the grip like she was wringing out a rag.

Engines gunned in the street.

Farr smiled.

Peter knew in an instant: they were inside a noose. "We've got to get the fuck out of here."

Rose's eyes darted from the front side of the gun to Peter: an uncertain look.

"You're traitors now," Farr said. "The only way out of this is through me. You need to make a deal." She pointed at the ledger.

Rose lowered the gun and took three steps toward Farr, who looked ready to devour her.

"We'll take our chances," Rose said. Her hand shot out

with startling speed to shove Farr. She stumbled into the vault and threw her arm back for support. Rose hauled the door closed and threw the lever.

Farr pounded on the door and screamed as Rose put her hand on the safe dial, then glanced to Peter for confirmation. He nodded, and she spun it.

Someone would come looking for Farr, and she could call out the combination to them, but this would buy time. Peter dipped his head toward the door and took the lead, gun out, as he ran down the stairs.

An SUV slammed to a stop in front of the house, rocking on its springs, and Peter and Rose tore toward the back door. Peter threw it open and they ran across the patio to the hedges in the side yard: decent cover until they hit the trees. Over the hill to the right, sirens screamed in the distance: police or FBI. Rose and Peter cut through the woods back to Peter's car.

There was no one he could see on that street, but the sirens multiplied and moved closer. He threw the driver's door open and swung himself into the seat, while Rose took the passenger seat. Peter handed her the ledger.

His instinct was to stomp the gas, but he brought the car up to thirty-five miles an hour, then kept it steady as Rose watched the road behind them. He didn't want to draw attention.

Rose looked down into the back seat. "What's up with the ax?"

"Long story," he said. He saw police flashers ahead and turned, looking for a clear way out of the neighborhood. "Where did you get the gun?"

"Greg gave it to me when we picked up the cars, just in case."

Peter pulled up to a stop sign and saw a black BMW M5 fly past them, fifty miles per hour on the side street.

The passenger had a trim beard and black-bead eyes. That was no cop. Peter looked down to see that Rose had the ledger on her lap and was snapping photos with one of the cell phones.

"I'm sending these to myself, so we have a record no matter what happens."

Peter turned around a corner, and then heard the whoop of sirens ahead, near the entrance to the parkway he had been planning on taking. He palmed the wheel around and went down a leafy road.

"Can you find another way out—" The prepaid phone started ringing in his pocket. He raised it to his ear as he turned again.

"Peter? Are you okay?" It was Greg.

"I'm a little busy right now."

"I know."

"Did you send these people?"

"No. I'm nowhere near you, but we can listen in on police radio traffic, and some FBI counterintel, and get a sense of where they are. They're swarming the Palisades. Farr's grandfather's house—that was it, wasn't it? How did you know?"

Peter didn't answer.

"Doesn't matter," Greg said. "You've got to get out of there."

Peter looked to Rose, who nodded her head: *Listen to him.* Peter wondered if this was all some game to get him to hand over the evidence. How could Rose, who had no experience, be so cool in the midst of this madness? He had worried that she would fire that gun by accident, but she handled it like a pro.

"Peter?" Greg asked.

"Who else is after us besides the police?"

"It's former Russian military intel, the GRU, in the lead. They're blood drinkers. But they've called up every illegal they have in the city. It's an army coming for you, Peter. You need to come in."

"The police have me blocked in this neighborhood. I can't get out."

"Where are you?"

The roar of the M5's engine came from a block over.

"Potomac and Galena."

"Head northwest on Potomac."

"I saw cops that way."

He heard cross talk, Ileana's voice.

"They're gone," Greg said. "They were moving. But they'll have that buttoned up in a second. They're sending out everyone. They'll have roadblocks up. You need to go."

Peter whipped the car around.

"You alone?" Greg asked.

"I have Rose."

"The ledger?"

"It's safe. How did you get this number?"

"When Ileana took your phone in Rock Creek, she checked it. I needed to be able to reach you. The Blackphone was dead."

Peter still didn't trust Greg, but he needed to get out of here. He could figure the rest out later.

"So how do we do this?" he asked.

"You might be a little young to remember *Pac-Man*. Give Rose the phone. You need to drive."

"And your blood drinkers?"

"We can't get their comms or location. You have to keep a lookout."

Peter handed the phone to Rose. She concentrated as she talked to Greg. "We're going north. Okay. Okay." She used her free hand to point the way, toward the road where he had heard the sirens.

He could be driving straight into the arms of the police. There was no way they would believe his story. They would hand him straight over to Farr. He took the risk. At the intersection ahead, there was no one.

Rose pointed right—opposite from the direction he had expected—and he turned onto a wooded two-lane road. She flagged him left into another neighborhood, and he cut down the street.

Sirens came bleating a minute later. He came out of that development beside a small shopping center on a four-lane road, and Rose updated Greg on their location.

"South?" Peter asked.

She shook her head no. "They have the car description."

"Where are we supposed to go?"

"He can bring us in."

Peter clenched his jaw as she pointed him down another side street.

"We have no choice," she said. "They're going to have helicopters up in a few minutes. We need his help."

Peter already owed Greg, and now he would owe him

everything. He leaned forward and looked up at the cloud-streaked sky, searching for helicopters.

"Show me where."

76

Greg stood on the sidewalk outside DC General Hospital and pulled on his cigarette. This was the meeting site that he had given Peter and Rose. Ileana was keeping a lookout on the west side.

The hospital had been abandoned years ago and was now surrounded by a chain-link fence. A host of community health service and other municipal buildings adjacent to it still seemed to be in operation, though their parking lots were empty on this weekend afternoon.

He didn't have great lines of sight to see if anyone was approaching, but they were the best he could manage.

Peter and Rose were late. He lifted his phone and tried Ileana. It rang six times, seven, while he muttered, "Come on, come on."

She didn't answer. "Where are you?" he said under his breath, then took another drag. He didn't smoke, but it was good cover for waiting around without looking suspicious. He wanted to walk over to check on her but had to be here when Peter and Rose arrived.

He let out a clouded breath and brought his shoulders back, trying to relax. The cigarette hand lowered naturally to his side. He let the smoke fall and seized the grip of his gun.

"Don't turn." The voice came from behind him before he could pull his pistol from the holster. "Hands out."

Greg didn't react.

"I'm not the police. I'm happy to kill you."

He held his hands out to the side and looked over his shoulder as Dimitri Sokolov circled him, the gun held in close.

"How are you, Dimitri?"

"Busy as ever. You?"

"It hasn't been too bad recently. How's Carolina?" Dimitri's wife.

"She passed."

"I'm sorry to hear that."

"Thank you. It was for the best. She had been sick for a long time." He paused for a moment. "I know that Peter Sutherland is on his way. I need you to signal to him that it's safe to meet."

"And what will you do?"

"I don't want to kill him or the girl. I need the book back."

"You don't *want* to kill them."

"I'll do everything I can. It will happen one way or the other. If you put your face on it, make him think it's safe, make it as smooth as possible, I'll do what I can to avoid it."

Greg pressed his lips together and looked at the sidewalk.

"I know you're close to him, Greg. I know you want that book as badly as I do. If you help me here, we will read you in on it. The people I work for will forget everything that's happened before between you and them. You know how valuable that is. Ileana will be fine. You will be fine."

"It's family."

"He's not your family. I know this is hard. I appreciate that. But I know you've done this kind of thing before. And worse. It's the job."

Greg didn't answer.

"I respect that," Dimitri said and lifted the gun. "Close your eyes."

Greg shut them and took a long breath in through his nose. Dimitri aimed. Greg's eyes snapped open, staring down the bore of the pistol.

"Wait."

"Is that a yes?"

Greg nodded.

"I need to hear it," Dimitri said.

"Yes. I'll do it."

77

RFK Stadium towered to their left as Peter drove down Twenty-Second Street. A desolate-looking building filled the horizon ahead. "That's DC General Hospital," Peter said. To the right the National Guard Armory, a vaulted gray fortress, hemmed them in.

"Straight ahead," she said.

They both spoke in low tones as they scanned the streets. This was a grim corner of DC, home to the jail and the old Congressional Cemetery.

"Where is Greg?" Peter asked.

"He said he'd be on the far side. He wanted us to park out of sight and walk."

Peter pulled over.

Rose had the ledger open on her lap. "It's all here. Every meeting, every location, every date. Dresden, Prague. This must be Farr; she used the name BEECH."

Peter looked at Novikoff's notes, a mix of English and Russian. "It was her and people from the GRU, the SVR, the First Building—that means the president himself," Peter said. "It's Vikhrov's headquarters in the Kremlin, the old Senate building."

She pointed to a date, circled in black.

"That's the night of the Metro crash," he said, studying the Cyrillic writing. He saw a rough schematic map of the Metro, with the Operations Control Center at the center of a web of lines and computer hostnames. He checked the date of the entry: a month before the derailment.

"Jesus," he said. "Those are operational plans."

Rose turned more pages. Peter saw the name Gibson, Travers's opponent in the general election, and a word he knew even in Russian: *kompromat*. Dirt. The kind that tanked Gibson's campaign in the final stretches of the race.

Dates and times. Names and places. If FBI counter-intelligence got their hands on that book, they'd be able to run the whole plot down, discover everyone involved, find out who crashed the Metro, who threw the election.

Rose flipped through the ledger. The last two pages in the book were scrawled with notes: they looked like dates and names to follow up on, and quick entries to be put in order later, and then, at the bottom: "Who is OSPREY?"

Rose looked at Peter. "But that's Novikoff's handwriting."

Peter studied the page. "He's not OSPREY."

"Then OSPREY might be alive. The original source."

Peter's eyed widened, and he looked to Rose. They had the ledger. Maybe the Campbells' source was still out there. He was almost afraid to hope this would all work out, that he would jinx it somehow.

He watched a cop car drive through the intersection, the officer inside looking their way behind his wraparound shades.

"We don't have a lot of time," Peter said.

"Greg is around the corner."

"We're just going to hand it over to him?"

"He'll help us get the truth out."

"You trust him?" he asked.

"He saved us."

"He wanted that book. Now he'll get it."

"We need to go, Peter."

He watched her for a long moment, taken again by her calm through all this. Maybe that looked like suspicion.

"What?"

He wouldn't lie to her. "This seems so natural to you."

"What are you saying, Peter?"

"You've never done anything like this before?"

"I've been through some awful shit. I learned to put my head down and get through it. You think I'm hiding something?"

She shook her head and looked out the window.

"Are you?" Peter asked.

"What? A spy? Working with Greg somehow? You asshole." She grimaced, as if holding back the anger. That was fine. He could take it. If they were about to go against the sitting US president with the help of a foreign agent, he wanted all the cards on the table.

"No," she said. "I'm terrified and doing my best to keep it together and find a way out. This is how I work. I get cold. I get through it. And you . . ."

She looked out the window again, censoring herself.

"Go ahead."

"You were on that emergency line the whole time. Other people called, didn't they?"

She stared at him.

"They asked for your help," she said, "and you served them up to their killers."

He remembered the one other night when the phone on his desk had rung, the controlled panic on the line as the man recited the code. Could Peter have known? Could he have seen something if he weren't blindly following the rules?

"Your hands aren't clean," she said.

"You're right."

It was true, and he deserved that. She wiped her fingers under her eye, pushing away tears, then dried her hand on her pants.

He'd had to ask, to know, because once that book went out, there was no turning back.

"I'll go," Peter said. "You stay here with the book." If it was a trap, he wanted to be the one caught.

"Fine."

"Listen, Rose . . ."

"Let's just get through this, okay?"

"Give me ten minutes. I'll call if it's going to take longer than that. And if you don't hear from me, something went wrong. Just go. Send what's in that ledger to everyone: the papers, the inspectors general, the intel committees."

"I've got it."

"You okay?"

She checked her phone. "It's time."

Rose gave him a strained half smile. It was enough for now. The pressure and lack of sleep were getting to both of them. He didn't fault her for anger, for a sense of betrayal after seeing the people she loved murdered by those they trusted, by the people Peter worked for. There would be time to make it right, he hoped, but not now.

He stepped out of the car and started walking toward the hospital. His godfather was waiting.

78

Peter came around the corner. Parked cars lined both sides of the street. This was the spot, but Greg was nowhere to be seen. The gun still hung on Peter's hip. He pulled his shirt back, over the holster, for an easier draw.

After walking another fifty feet, he saw movement and wheeled to his right. It was Greg. He came out from behind one of the buildings near the hospital and moved at an angle toward the cars. There was no sign of Ileana.

Even with his doubts, Peter felt a surge of relief when he saw the familiar face. Greg would know how to get away, how to get this information out.

That meant a lifetime of running, of hiding. Peter pushed the thought away. He had enough to worry about in the present.

Peter smiled as his eyes met Greg's. As he came closer, Greg paused. His eyes narrowed and his mouth tightened, an expression of pain deeper than any Peter had ever seen on his godfather's face. Greg shut his eyes and then shook his head left to right twice, barely moving an inch, just enough to be seen.

Not safe.

Peter froze and drew, but even as he brought the gun

forward with both hands, two shots rang out and echoed down the street. Peter couldn't tell where they had come from. Greg's shoulder twisted back as if shoved by an unseen hand and a cloud of red glistened in the air behind him. He took a staggering step back and then fell, grunting in pain on the ground.

Greg had shaken his head to warn Peter off, sacrificed his life for his godson's. Peter knew what he should do: *Run.*

Peter scanned the street. He couldn't leave Greg here to die. He sprinted to the edge of the parked cars and ran along them in a low crouch.

Sirens were moving in. Greg groaned, but the sounds were faint, with no breath behind them. Peter stopped twenty feet from where Greg lay on the sidewalk and peered around the car that gave him cover. He expected a bullet any second, but there was no sign of any shooter.

Greg's half-lidded eyes met his, and Peter mouthed, "How many? Where?"

Greg shook his head. He didn't know. He was still alive, his hand pressed to his sternum. It was a chest wound, maybe the lungs or heart. Blood pooled on the sidewalk beneath him, a red-black mirror.

Crouching, Peter leaned out from behind the car. No fire came, and he ventured farther. Nothing. He ran toward Greg.

Once in the open, he swept the surroundings with his gun. It was clear. He dropped to one knee beside Greg and tore open his shirt. Two holes. One bubbling. Peter covered the wound with his palm, trying for a seal.

"It was Dimitri. Where's Rose?" Greg gasped.

"Here," Peter said and brought Greg's hand up to the

hole in his chest, helping him cover it. Peter needed to find something to use as an airtight bandage.

"I shouldn't have doubted you," Peter said. This man had offered up his life to protect Peter.

Greg shook his head, and his shoulders rose, just barely, a gesture of resignation.

When Peter learned that Greg was a spy, he assumed that his godfather was the one who had lured his father into that life. But what if it was the other way around?

"It was true." Peter's voice was a shocked whisper. "Everything they said about my dad. He was guilty. *He* turned *you*."

"Let it go, Peter," he mouthed. "It doesn't matter. I'm done. Get Rose. Get out."

His lips kept moving but no words came, and all Peter could see were the whites of his eyes.

Peter glanced over his shoulder. He could see figures at the end of the street and hear the sirens coming behind them. He ran his fingers into the hollow of Greg's throat but felt no pulse.

The police would be here any second. He could hear the sirens. They could do more for Greg than Peter possibly could, and the shooter might be going for Rose now.

He ran toward the low fence on the other side of the courtyard, vaulted over it, and cut across the grounds, straight to where Rose was parked.

He called her as he raced around a trailer in the shadow of the main hospital building. The phone rang, and he continued toward the street where Rose was waiting. A prerecorded voice came on the line: "The subscriber you are trying to reach is not available. Please leave a message."

His car was there. He jumped a concrete barrier at the edge of the lot. Even from across the street he could see something wasn't right. The passenger door was open. He raised the gun and closed in, but she was gone.

All that remained was a streak of blood on the curb.

79

Peter searched the street in both directions. Another promise broken. Another call unanswered. And now they had the ledger. It was all for nothing. Or worse. He had done the job as well as any traitor: handed them all the evidence that they would need to bend the president to their will.

Two days without sleep. His godfather's blood on his hands. He was running on adrenaline and fumes, and that bright stain on the curb nearly broke him.

He stepped into the car.

Watch. Listen. Follow. That had been his job for years. He found people, and he would find Rose. Where would you go if you were them? Away from the city, from the authorities.

Based on the sirens, the police were closing in from the west. Driving his car put a target on him, but he didn't care. He had to get her. She was alive. He had to believe that.

A block north, he saw a white Ford Explorer turning right. Low on the rear bumper, there was a smear of red. He had taught her about tails: how to hide, how to be found. Rose was calling.

He took off after the Explorer. The weekend traffic was relatively light, so he stayed far back. The SUV turned and took the bridge over the Anacostia River, heading for the high-crime neighborhoods in the far southeast of the District. He followed past the swamps and brown braids of the river's tributaries. If they kept going, the traffic would get lighter soon and make it harder for him to hold the tail without being seen.

The SUV cut right and exited the highway at the next intersection. The traffic light turned yellow. Peter gunned it up the shoulder, but the right-turning cars blocked him. The SUV disappeared behind a shopping center.

He leaned on his horn, but by the time he made it through the light, the Explorer was gone. He followed the road and after a half mile came to a four-way stop.

He cursed under his breath and pounded the steering wheel with his palm. He'd lost them. To his right were single-family houses. Good privacy. He started to turn that way and then saw the street sign a block ahead.

Burnham Road. He had seen that name in the ledger. It was one of the few meet-up sites that wasn't in the usual diplomatic sphere of luxury hotels and restaurants and affluent enclaves. He drove on.

Ahead, backing onto the highway and the train tracks, there was a warehouse cut from the fifties. It had powder-blue paint and glass tiles and the broken remnants of a neon sign advertising some long-gone family department store.

Peter didn't slow as he drove past and, looking to his left, caught the Explorer parked near the loading docks in the rear.

Why would Dimitri reuse an address from the ledger? A quick changeup to get away from the police, to rally more of his killers by his side? Peter didn't know much about abductions, but based on a few stories from the veterans at the field office, he knew things only got worse with every move: more isolated, more secure, harder to escape.

The doors were locked, surely, and Peter had to assume that Dimitri had picked up on the tail and was waiting for him.

Perhaps the blood was a trail, breadcrumbs to lure him here, so that Dimitri could take out everyone who knew the details of the ledger.

He would be waiting, ready to spring on Peter, surprise him. So Peter had to do him one better. He leaned back against the headrest and jerked his seat belt, setting the ratchet tight against his chest, then pushed the accelerator to the floor.

The engine roared and revved up with so much torque that Peter had to fight the wheel back to center as he shot up the driveway, toward the chain stretched across the entrance. It tore at the plastic fenders of his car, then let go with a squeal and a snap. The speedometer climbed—twenty-five, thirty—as Peter pointed the car at the windows of the old showroom, hands low on the wheel to let the airbag do its thing. Suddenly all he could see were glass tiles. He shut his eyes as the crash came.

His head snapped forward, straining his neck. The jolt ran up his forearms like an electric shock, but it wasn't as bad as he expected. The airbag didn't blow, and in the chaos of shattering glass and screaming rubber, he slammed on the brakes and braced for a sudden deceleration.

He stopped thirty feet inside the empty showroom. Insulation and dropped-ceiling tiles hung down in front of the blown window. From inside the dark and dust-swirled space, the hole the car had punched in the wall—with gray clouds streaking a brilliant blue sky beyond it—didn't look real.

The car was still rocking on its springs as Peter climbed out, drew his gun, and circled to the trunk in a low crouch.

His hands were shaking. He had the manic energy that comes after a fall or crash where you might say you're okay but be walking on a broken leg. He scanned the darker recesses of the showroom: offices and shelves and hallways leading farther back into the warehouse.

He caught a reflection in one of the office windows: a man coming around a partition, squinting against the kicked-up dust. Peter readied his gun and aimed where the man would come out. Behind the man, Peter could make out dark hair and a woman in an odd posture: shoulders back like she was stretching. It was Rose, her arms bound behind her back.

The man stopped, and Peter centered the front sight of his pistol on the partition. He would go no closer. Peter eased the trigger back, and the gun bucked in his hands. A second shot. A third. Fourth. The blast reverberated through the empty space.

"Rose! Run!" Peter yelled.

He heard fast footsteps and then saw Rose take off, deeper into the warehouse, with the man following after.

80

Peter chased them, glass crunching and sliding under his shoes. The whiplash in his neck mellowed into an even throb. Offices passed on his left, and he entered a long central hallway. At the far end, there was a padlocked rolling door, probably a loading dock. He checked the doors as he went: each gave onto a high-ceilinged storeroom dominated by twelve-foot-high steel shelves. Some were cut up into smaller spaces, and some led deeper into the building. It was a warren. From somewhere in there he heard rattling: handcuff links.

Stay alive. Get the truth out.

But he didn't care about the truth anymore. He didn't particularly care about staying alive. In the end, he was back at the start. Rose was in there somewhere, hunted and terrified. This time he wasn't on the other end of the phone. He was here with her, with a gun.

He pursued the noise and darted through the open door, remembering what the agents had taught him at the practice ranges in Boston.

Doors are good places to get killed. Get through and get your corner.

Running to the right, he could just barely make out the

sound of more footsteps. He took cover behind a wide set of metal shelves, then leaned out, to the right, offering the smallest target possible, not much more than the gun and a quarter of his face. He saw nothing and then repeated the same move to the left.

The back of the room lit up brilliant white, and then lightning struck his hand and his face. Pain arced up his arm.

He went back to cover and checked his hand: a wound ran from the base of his index finger toward the wrist. Blood pooled and he wiped it away: cuts, not a bullet hole. With the blood, they looked worse than they were. Peter's hand burned, but he could still move it.

The polymer frame of the gun was smashed and cracked like a cheap lighter in a parking lot. It had caught the bullet. His cuts must have been from frag. The barrel tilted left, off-center. He tried racking the slide, to check the action, but it moved only a quarter of an inch and jammed. Useless.

"No!" It was Rose's voice. There was pain in it, panic. Peter ducked low and inched toward the door. He could hear her struggling, closer to the opposite corner now. Peter reached up and hit the lights.

The room went black.

"Ungh!" Rose was still fighting back. Her voice was a beacon. Peter stood. In the sudden dark, they would all be blind. He needed something to draw Dimitri's attention as Peter moved on him. The shelves were massive and would take a moment to fall if he could tip one over. He could use the distraction to get closer to Dimitri and jump him.

He bent at his knees and hips, set his shoulder against

the shelf, and pushed hard, straining. It lifted, slowly, and teetered on the edge of balance. He drove his legs into the ground and tipped the shelf the last inch. It began to fall.

Tracing the wall with his hand as his eyes adjusted, Peter ran toward the corner ahead. That put him at one end of a long row, with Rose and Dimitri at the other end. He could hear Rose's voice and went toward it. He hit something hard with his hip. A low metal thud. *Shit*. He'd given himself away.

It didn't matter. Something crashed to his right: the shelf he had tipped over, slamming down. The boom of steel on cement was like a cannon blast in all that dark, that silence.

Peter ran blind down the row. A muzzle flash lit the scene before him: Dimitri aimed his pistol where the shelf had fallen. With his nondominant hand, he held Rose's wrists high up behind her back, wrenching her shoulders. He was looking the wrong way, the gun off Rose now. He'd given Peter an opening.

Whatever had been on the shelf was still crashing and rolling over the floor. The noise covered the sound of Peter's footsteps as he sprinted through the shadows. At the last instant, the gun swung his way, but he was already in too close, charging Dimitri. His shoulder connected with the man's ribs, and he grunted as they both slammed into the concrete wall.

"Run, Rose! The door!"

The way he had come: it was a slant of light at the other end of the storeroom, a clear exit.

"Peter!"

His fingers touched the cement floor, then a man's eye and lips, then an arm. He seized the wrist. Another gunshot exploded, the barrel inches from his face. He could hear nothing but a piercing, high-pitched drone.

"He's got the gun," Peter yelled. "Get out! I've got him."

He didn't have Dimitri, but he would tell her whatever he must to get her out of here. A shadow moved across the light from the door: Rose getting to safety. Peter found Dimitri's other hand and choked up on both wrists. He felt breath in his ear and then caught the bitter chemical smell of burnt propellant: the barrel near his mouth. He dropped to his side as the heat and light of another shot flared in his face.

It missed, but the blast and pressure made the room spin. He thought he might vomit, but he held on and brought both his hands to the grip of the gun, the cuts singing with pain as he wrested it away from Dimitri's fingers. Peter turned the pistol around and got a decent grip with his right hand even as Dimitri fought for the gun. He knew from the sounds of ragged breath where the other man's head was.

His finger reached inside the trigger guard as he tore Dimitri's other hand away. He had the shot.

Cold pain flared along his thigh, and his knee dropped to the floor. A slash from a knife. The gun pulled from his grip, and the blade came again, across his shoulder. He was on one knee now and felt Dimitri pulling away from him, in control of the gun.

81

Peter swung the side of his hand through empty air, then back, and caught Dimitri in the jaw. The gun fired over his head, and in the red flare it was clear who was in control.

Dimitri held the pistol in front of him, slightly dazed from the blow, but still managing the weapon expertly. Peter took a stumbling step forward and then right, toward a faint line of light ahead along the back wall. The light spilled through a steel sliding door. Peter shouldered it open and slipped through. Dimitri was right behind him, moving with unsteady steps, but Peter didn't run. The gun was already coming his way as he drove the door shut. He heard a muted crunch and a scream.

Dimitri was partway through, his left hand crushed in the door, his right still holding the pistol. Peter took off. In the rear of the space, there was a pair of swinging doors that led to what he took for an employee break room. The light was good there, and he ran inside. The rush of air from the door set a Styrofoam cup rolling down the hall.

A steel door with a push bar led outside. Escape. He listened and caught no sound of Dimitri. Had he lost Peter? Gone back for Rose? Had Peter pushed him toward the easier target? He pressed open the door. Sunlight warmed his face. He squinted, could smell the grass.

Run. The instinct was so strong.

He stopped on the threshold and turned back the way he'd come. "I'm right here!" he yelled. His voice reflected back from all those empty halls. He kept the fear out of it as best he could, and its strength surprised him. "Come on!"

A low laugh answered him.

"That's sweet, Peter. Are you trying to buy time? Trade yourself for her?" The voice was closer than he anticipated. "It doesn't matter which of you dies first."

Peter stepped outside and limped across the cracked pavement of the side lot. High fences ran to his left and right. He couldn't get back to the car by going around the building. Twenty feet ahead, there was a dumpster and a panel truck stripped almost to the frame, sitting on its bare wheels. They would offer some protection.

He made it to the dumpster before the first shot came. The air hissed and dirt kicked up ahead of him. Dimitri was outside. At least Peter could lure him away. At the edge of the lot, a hill choked with weeds and gnarled trees ran down to the railroad tracks. The steep grade would give him cover, and the fence on one side was rusted and half-collapsed, offering an escape.

He might be able to work his way around back to his car if he made it down there, to find Rose and get out. He stumbled through the underbrush. The thorns tore at his face and pulled at the cuts on his hand and the slash on his leg.

Brown-orange water pooled at the bottom of the hill, a creek choked with leaves and plastic bags and dead branches. He splashed through the mud sucking at his shoes and then stumbled along the gravel beside the train tracks.

The fence ended twenty feet ahead of him. If he stuck by the tracks, he could make it around. Blood pumped out of the cut in his leg with every step. The pain was fire pushing toward his heart, but he could manage it. The muscle was beginning to spasm, his whole quad tightening up, quitting. He could barely drag his foot through the stones.

An overpass ahead brought the highway over the tracks and this little stream valley. It was dark underneath, like a tunnel, and the sounds of traffic echoed back.

Peter stepped toward it, but something was off. He stopped, and the gravel crunched behind him. He turned to see Dimitri, twenty feet away and closing, the gun out in his right hand. His left was a mangle of bone and skin and blood. Anger twisted the man's face into something animal.

What does a hand mean to a killer? What had he lost? Why hadn't he already shot Peter?

"Right there is fine," Dimitri said.

Peter held his hands to the side. At least he'd bought Rose time. She could tell the story.

82

He waited for the shot, but nothing happened, and Dimitri could probably read his face, the anticipation giving way to surprise.

"If I wanted you dead, you'd be dead," he said. Now Peter understood: Dimitri didn't have the ledger.

He needed Peter.

The Russian stepped closer. It was eerie to see him up close at last, with his bland fatherly face.

"You're good at this work, Peter. All the lies and sordid shit we do." He glanced at his hand. "I guess that's why you were so careful for so long. We'll find her. We'll find it. Maybe it made you feel better for a little, playing the hero," Dimitri went on. "But you can see how pointless it is, can't you?"

A train horn sounded, echoing along the tracks through the underpass.

"This is how the world works. Coercion and violence. Dealmaking. Wading through this shit." He jerked his head toward the stream. "You've already chosen. Thrown your lot in with Greg. The whole world is a gray area, Peter. You can save her. Just help me out and stop lying to yourself with this do-gooder garbage."

"I don't know where it is."

"Every asset the *rezident* has is coming after you, Peter. I'm merciful compared to some of these men. I can get it out of you through pain, or we can work together. But believe me that we will get it out of you one way or another."

The stones began to move, the faintest tremble. The train was coming. Peter stepped onto the gravel beside the tracks.

Dimitri shook his head. "That's not the way out, Peter. I knew your father. It's true. He was one of ours. I guess you know that by now. I guess you see it in yourself. You've probably always known it. He tried to lie to himself about who he was. It tore him apart. That's the coward's way."

The ground quaked. Peter could feel the hum in the rails and hear the long cry of the train's horn.

Dimitri was right. Peter didn't know if getting the word out would change anything. This whole thing was so fucked from the beginning. But Peter wouldn't trade for his own life, and he wouldn't give up any information through whatever tortures Dimitri had in mind.

Peter took a dragging step through the gravel. If he was going to die, it wouldn't be under that train. He was going for that gun, fifteen feet off, aimed straight at his heart. It was just a different kind of suicide, but at least he would go down fighting.

The train entered the underpass: the chug of the engine a sudden roar. How far was it, he guessed, two hundred feet? A hundred?

Pop.

The train was so loud he barely heard the noise: something shattering to his left. The sound drew Dimitri's attention away.

Peter didn't hesitate. He did what he had done so many times, practiced endlessly on the hard courts, drove forward to close the space between him and his goal. Pain surged up his side, flooded out from his shoulder and up his neck, but Peter was flying. He was already inside Dimitri's reach before the other man broke his attention away from the new threat.

Peter knocked the gun away with his good hand, lowered slightly, and drove his shoulder into Dimitri's chest. The Russian stumbled back. The train horn blared. The steel wheels locked and screamed along the track. It felt like they were at the center of an exploding bomb. Peter caught himself, right leg forward, and gave a last hard shove with his right hand to Dimitri's shoulder.

The other man's arms wheeled back as he fought for balance. He came down hard on his side, across the tracks, and his head whipped against a rail.

Peter stepped back, and Dimitri raised himself on one hand in the instant before the train hit. Peter leaned away from the booming streak of silver, fighting the wind that slipped alongside the train as it pulled him in, his eyes closed to slits against the flying debris.

His hair blew forward, and he stepped down the gravel to the mud. The high-pitched whine of the brakes pierced the air. He looked back and saw a foot in a sock sticking out over the track. As the train passed and slowed, Peter stepped closer. Dimitri's jacket lay torn nearly in half beside a railroad tie, and Peter saw keys glinting in the dirt beside it. One of Dimitri's shoes had been knocked into the brown grass, fifty feet away. The body was destroyed.

Peter picked up the keys and started up the hill, limping

as fast as he could as blood trailed down his knee and calf. To his left, he saw the remnants of a shattered beer bottle. That must have been what distracted Dimitri.

And he knew who threw it. Above him, framed by two maples, stood Rose, her hands still cuffed.

83

"Where is he?" Rose called as she came down the hill.

"Dead. On the tracks."

She crossed through the trees toward him. "Jesus, Peter."

His pants and shirt were both soaked with blood, but seeing her, the feeling of just being alive still, flooded him with such relief that he forgot about the pain.

"I'm okay . . . I'll be okay."

With Dimitri's keys, he undid the cuffs, then squeezed her to him and kissed her temple.

She led him around the building, and he spotted Dimitri's Explorer.

"Are you okay? The blood on the curb, the car."

"It's nothing," she said as they reached the vehicle. "I fell and skinned my palm when they came for me. I'll drive."

He handed her the keys and climbed in the passenger side of the Explorer.

"Your leg," she said.

He pressed his hand down on the wound and winced against the burn. "It's fine for now."

Helicopter blades chugged in the distance. They had to go. Rose started the SUV and hit the gas. The tires spun out on the broken-up asphalt as they shot toward the exit of the warehouse lot.

"You need a doctor."

"I'm all right." Peter's eyes were on the mirror as he helped her navigate the back roads. The sounds of police sirens grew louder and louder, and then began to drop away.

"The ledger?"

"I hid it," she said.

"Near the armory?"

"Yes. I saw them coming. I didn't have much time. It's next to one of the parking lots. I can show you."

He opened his eyes wide, fighting against a wave of lightheadedness. They passed an industrial park and, on the other side, a lot full of sand and gravel.

"I think we're clear," he said. "There."

He pointed to an overpass for the highway, and Rose pulled under it. It would hide them from any aerial surveillance.

"Peter. Stay with me."

He pressed his hand down on his thigh and felt the warmth as the blood dripped over his fingers. He knew it wasn't an artery, and already it seemed to be slowing, but that didn't make it any less scary. He thought he might be sick.

"What do you need?" she asked.

"A compress."

He looked in the console, while Rose checked the back seats, and brought up a roll of duct tape.

"That'll work. I've got some clotting going with the pants, so just wrap around it tight." He turned on his side slightly, and she started in with the tape. Peter ground his teeth together as he heard it come *scritching* off the roll. The cut was on fire.

"Is that good?"

"Yeah," he said. She put on a tight six-inch-wide band.

"Your arm."

She went around the slash three times, moving with the calm efficiency of a medic.

He put his hand on his leg. The pressure was excruciating, but he was glad for it. Rose sat back, shut her eyes, and laid her hand on his.

"We're not done," she said.

He remembered Greg's words about the blood drinkers, Dimitri's warning that the *rezident* had given the command for its whole shadow army in DC to hunt him down. They played by mob rules, and would torture and kill without a thought.

"No," he said. "If the police don't get us, Farr and the Russians will."

He prayed that if they were caught, it be by the police, but that was no guarantee against disappearing, against being handed over to the conspirators.

"I could rest here forever," she said.

"I know. I know." He put his other hand on hers. "This will be over soon."

"One way or another."

"We're going to make it."

She smiled. "You're awfully confident for a guy held together with duct tape."

84

They switched seats, Peter limping around the car, and he drove them back across the river. He could handle the automatic vehicle with one arm and one leg, and Rose, who knew exactly where the book was, would grab it.

The DC police had blocked off some of the roads around the hospital. As he approached the armory, Peter wondered if Dimitri's men were hovering nearby, too.

Rose leaned forward in the passenger seat as Peter rolled slowly down the street.

"There it is," she said, pointing to a low cinder-block wall. Behind it was a blue construction dumpster.

Peter pulled to a stop, and Rose stepped out between two parked cars. She walked calmly, without the telltale swivel neck of someone afraid they were being watched. She leaned over the wall and reached into the gap between it and the dumpster. She kept walking—the whole movement was smooth—with whatever she'd retrieved hidden on the far side of her body.

Peter drove down the street about twenty feet, keeping pace with her, and she stepped out between the cars and climbed in. He pulled away as her door slammed shut. The ledger lay on her lap, a bit of dirt on the top of the spine but otherwise perfect.

"Thank God. Nice work."

"What now?" she asked.

Peter had been so fixated on getting the book, he hadn't gotten much further. They had only hours until the deadline. He checked the rearview, then hit the gas and cut down a narrow one-way between two buildings. He turned left at the end and then made a right turn after a rolling stop at the next intersection.

"What is it?" she asked.

"Black BMW."

"Was Dimitri working with other people?"

"Yes. We've got to get someplace safe." If you saw one, that meant there were fifty hiding.

He took them south, avoiding the highways. "Can you turn on the radio?"

"You want music?" she asked, surprised.

"Traffic and news."

She pulled up an AM traffic and talk station. The reporter finished up a piece on the federal budget and then started talking about road closures around the Kennedy Center because of security around the ballet.

"What are you thinking?"

"They might be watching the arteries out of town. And if we want to get that ledger in the right hands, we need to stay close to home—"

A new segment started on the radio: "There are two dead in Southeast Washington, in two separate incidents, and the police are on the lookout for two suspects—a white man and white woman in their late twenties. They were last seen driving a black Chevy Tahoe. Police caution not to approach and that anyone with information should call 911.”

“God. How long until they find us?” Rose asked.

They had left the Tahoe at the warehouse, but he didn’t know how much time that would buy them. The police would be out in force. “I don’t know.”

He drove past the harbor, into East Potomac Park, a long island squeezed between the Tidal Basin and Washington Channel on one side, and the Potomac on the other.

He pulled over, and could see the Bureau of Engraving and Printing buildings across the channel and the Washington Monument rising behind them. A police helicopter banked high overhead.

“Do you want to run?” she asked.

He thought for a moment. “You can’t run from the government. You can’t run from the SVR, the GRU, everyone from Russian intel. But we have a weapon. We have leverage.” He looked at the ledger.

“Get the truth out?”

“I don’t know if we have time. I don’t know if anyone will believe us. They’ll be looking for that move, going to the press. They might kill us first.”

He leaned over the wheel, looking for the helicopter. “But we can use the threat of making it public. There must be some way to play one side against the other.”

Rose shook her head. “You don’t want to play their game, Peter.”

He didn’t. Blackmail, hiding the truth: it made him sick. He’d run from it his whole life, run from his father’s choice. But if it was the only way to keep Rose alive . . . he didn’t know. Get the truth out—it sounded so simple, so right, but was it naive to think it would be that easy?

"We put this out there, we have targets on our backs," he said. "We might not live long enough to even see it go public."

Dimitri had been right. Peter had already crossed the line. He was part of this world now.

"You know the kind of power we have, with this?" he said. "The administration, the Russians. We're in control. You were right, Rose. That black-and-white stuff is a luxury. You do what you have to do to survive."

Rose touched her knuckle to her lips and looked out the window. Now she didn't seem so sure. "Are you saying that because you believe it, or because you're worried about me?"

Peter didn't answer. A helicopter came back over the Potomac. President Vikhrov and Travers were meeting tonight. Peter remembered Greg's words. They would make a deal, then the violence could start any second: a provocation, a prelude to war, a bullet or a bomb. Peter and Rose were running out of time.

"We have to move," he said.

Peter pulled out. They talked as he drove. The police would have a dragnet out for them, and the Russians would figure out he had Dimitri's car if they hadn't already. Every vehicle was a threat, every corner capture. There was no time, no escape, and no good options. But in the end, they knew what they needed to do.

Peter stopped the SUV and lifted the Blackphone. He looked across the Tidal Basin. A cold wind rippled the water. He watched the flag waving above the White House as he dialed a number he knew all too well.

202-456-2461. It was the extension he'd stood by for all those long nights. The emergency line. But now he was on the other end.

"Go ahead."

"Pen. Clock. Door. Fire. Give me Diane Farr."

"Thank you."

There was the sound of an exchange opening, of the call transferring, and then a single ring.

"Yes?" It was Farr.

"You know who this is?" Peter asked.

"I do."

"I want to deal."

85

Farr didn't respond. Peter thought the call had disconnected. Her voice came back, different now, its tone shifting like it was going through a synthesizer.

"Don't try to record this. It won't work."

"I don't need anything else on you, BEECH." He let it linger. It was her codename from the ledger and all the threat he needed.

"Welcome to the game. You get a little bit of power, and everyone's out to get you. That's DC. So what do you want?"

"These killers off my back."

"That's going to be hard, Peter. We think they're former GRU. Russian military intel. Not as well-known as the KGB or the SVR, but they're actually a lot worse, none of this Queensberry rules, gentleman spy shit. They've called out the savages. They're not happy about the ledger."

"I gathered."

"I'm not happy either. You locked me in my own fucking safe."

"It sounds like that worked out okay."

"These people after you are less forgiving. I might be able to stall them, but unless you come in, and I can guarantee that you and this information are under control, everyone you know and love is in danger. I'm talking about that girl. I'm talking about your ex in New York. I'm talking about men who learned savagery firsthand in the Soviet-Afghan War and would think nothing of killing a young woman."

"What the hell happened to you, Diane?"

She didn't respond.

"You can buy me time?" he asked.

"Just enough to come in. The two sides meet tonight, seven P.M. We need to finish this deal and put all this shit behind us. If you don't come in by then, it's hunting season . . . Peter?"

"I heard you." That was in three hours.

"So we'll deal," she said. "The ledger for your safety, for Rose's safety, and none of this ever happened."

"I'll deal. Just keep these murderers away from me, or it all goes public."

"Where can I find you?"

"I'll find you."

"Seven P.M."

He hung up.

86

The hands on the clock of the Old Post Office building hung straight down: six thirty P.M. Rose had pulled over on Constitution Avenue across from the Ellipse, the park just south of the White House grounds.

In the passenger seat, Peter wore a cheap pair of Dockers and a polo that Rose had bought at Rite Aid.

He checked the Blackphone one last time, scanning the news, looking for tremors of what was to come. What did Russia have planned that would be worth so much risk, so much death here in the capital?

He was used to the intelligence resources of the Sit Room, with its all-seeing eyes around the world, but now he settled for scanning the BBC and regional press. The warnings were there: unrest in the former Russian enclaves of northern Europe, the Baltic states; shoving matches in parliaments; violence in the streets; ethnic Russians claiming abuse at the hands of the Western-aligned politicians and national police; a shaky video of a woman with blood running down her cheek, her hand clamped to her face.

The Russians would trigger this kind of unrest themselves, bomb a building if they had to, anything for a pretext to invade. The Russian border with Europe was boiling over, ready for a final provocation.

Peter scanned the photos and videos for the special operations soldiers—the *Spetsnaz* in olive plainclothes with no insignia—who would silently infiltrate territories in advance of the main attack. In Ukraine they called them the little green men. He saw none, but that didn't mean they weren't there.

The stories he was reading seemed so small, minor scuffles in some forgotten corner of the map, but that was how world wars began: an assassination in Sarajevo, a radio station stormed on the German-Polish border.

He'd watched the troops building for months, the columns of trucks and armored personnel carriers pressing against the frontier like high water against a dam.

The United States was the only thing that could keep them in check, and now the president was in their pocket.

Peter put the phone down. He'd cleaned up his arm as well as he could without a shower. Three butterfly bandages and a line of Krazy Glue held the cut on his thigh closed. A bit of red had seeped through, but not enough to attract attention. It didn't matter. It was a short walk.

"Are you sure about this?" Rose asked.

He put his hand on the door handle. "Yes."

Rose leaned over and put her palm to his cheek. She studied his face for a moment, like she was trying to fix it in her memory, and then kissed him. She shut her eyes tight, trying to keep from crying, then pulled back an inch and rested her forehead against his.

"I . . ."

"Me too," he said.

She sat back, and Peter opened the door.

"I'll see you in a few."

She nodded and forced a smile.

Peter walked to the northern end of the Ellipse and faced the White House. The flag trailed gently to the east. Even now, after all this, the sight still moved him.

He knew the truth. His father had betrayed his country. He'd broken the same oath that Peter had sworn, to protect and defend the Constitution from all enemies, foreign and domestic.

If he didn't act, more people would die. The men and women behind the murders would go unpunished, would profit from the killings. This was a sin like his father's, only a thousand times worse: an election stolen, a democracy subverted, a puppet on the throne. They had bought the White House and paid in blood. This was his chance, at last, to atone.

He had a plan. It meant handing himself over to the killers. He knew he might not make it out of this. He was okay with that. Some things were worth it.

He thought of that last phone call from his dad. Peter could forgive his father for giving up his life. There were times when that made sense. But Peter could never forgive him for dying for nothing.

He lifted his phone and called the emergency line. The same answer, the same voice. It wasn't Julian; it was just another wide-eyed yes-man glad to have a seat at the White House. Like he had been.

"Pen. Clock. Door. Fire."

After a moment Farr came on with that whispering synthetic voice.

"You're out of time. Where are you?"

He looked straight at one surveillance camera and then another.

"Outside. Top of the Ellipse."

"You're *here*?"

"Let's talk."

87

How strange it was to stand like a tourist in the heart of monumental Washington, waiting, minute by minute, at least ten, until he almost grew accustomed to his jackhammer heartbeat.

A black SUV rolled in from the right, shielding him from the view of the White House. The windows were all mirrors in the night, and Akana, the Secret Service agent, stepped out, utterly calm as he surveyed the Ellipse.

He stood beside the vehicle like a chauffeur as Peter climbed in. Akana took the seat beside him and shut the door. Once they started moving, Akana reached over and searched Peter. He must have noticed the wounds, the way Peter gritted his teeth against the pain. Satisfied, it seemed, that Peter bore no weapons or recording devices, he sat back.

"The girl? The ledger?"

"I had to make assurances, in case I disappear."

Akana didn't respond, as if he had expected as much. The clock in the SUV's dash had been blacked out. They drove in silence, and through the tinted windows, Peter tried to follow their route.

After ten minutes, they pulled up to a gatehouse, and waited as a twelve-foot-high black barrier rolled back.

Peter was expecting something industrial or prisonlike, gray concrete and steel, but inside the fence, there were brick homes with porches. They looked like old officers' quarters. The SUV pulled behind another brick building, a one-story compound that reminded him of a sixties high school.

Akana guided Peter out with one hand on his good arm. The agent and another man walked him inside the building and down a long corridor lit by fluorescent bulbs. His shoes squeaked against the linoleum floor. The adrenaline amplified every sound, every sense.

After a right turn and then a left, Akana opened the door to a conference room with no windows and ushered Peter in. The other guard stayed in the hall.

At the front of the room were a pull-down screen and an overhead projector on a cart. Akana pointed to a chair at the conference table, and Peter sat.

Rectangles of unfaded paint on the pale green walls testified to old photos or portraits that had been stripped. The whole place looked like it had been untouched since the Vietnam War. It was all Peter could do to remember that he had the power at this moment, because he already felt like he had been disappeared, forgotten to time.

He had the ledger, and Farr needed it. That was the only thing keeping him alive.

The clock on the wall read 6:56.

Peter could see it all unfolding: the doors to the penthouse at the Hay-Adams opening on silent hinges, and Travers walking inside as Secret Service and their Russian counterparts sealed off the corridor.

The hushed opulence of the Presidential Suite. The

windows looking down on the White House. The tight diplomatic smiles as Vikhrov extended his hand. The two men alone, the truth forever hidden from history. How much would Travers give away? What was the presidency worth? How many more would die when he betrayed his country with a handshake?

Peter saw the troops again, waiting at the border, guns in hand, ready to take the parliaments, the town halls, the police stations, to haul those people back under the Kremlin's grip in a first strike at Europe.

The second hand ticked by. He had done what he needed, made his last desperate move, and now he could only wait for the storm to come.

88

Rose kept the SUV going just above the speed limit. She studied the cars behind her in the rearview, their windshields like mirrors in the night. Every few seconds she would reach down with her left hand and touch the ledger in the door pocket, feel the cheap tape along its spine.

The Blackphone rested in the cupholder. God she hoped this worked. She was safe, and the book, their only leverage, was safe. And Peter . . . he was in their hands.

She felt so alone. She glanced back at a black sedan, three cars behind her. She saw killers everywhere.

Headlights flashed across the road ahead, and a gray car shot out from the side street, and stopped, angled across both lanes.

Rose stood on the brake. Her seat belt locked and dug into her chest as her car pitched forward. She turned the wheel hard to the left but nothing happened. She was at the mercy of the skid.

Trees filled Rose's window, spinning past like vertigo, and the SUV shuddered off the side of the road, tearing through the grass of the shoulder. Rose's head slammed back as it came to a stop, but she was already moving, throwing open the door, ledger in hand as she jumped onto the weedy shoulder and took off.

A gun rose to her left, aimed straight at her, absorbed all of her attention like it was floating in space.

A blur flew at her from the right, as a man crashed into her, clamped his arms around her. He lifted her off her feet, her head thrown back as the book slipped from her fingers and fell on the street, its pages turning in the wind.

89

Four minutes until the deadline. It felt like surrender to ask the first question, to seem needy, so Peter simply waited, counting out full breaths and glad, for a moment at least, to rest his pained body. He knew it wouldn't last.

Two minutes later, Akana checked his phone and walked outside. He came back in a moment with Farr behind him. She walked in and grabbed a seat as if this were just a normal Tuesday morning staff meeting.

"So where is it, Peter? I assume you have copies, probably digital. It's a whole mess we have to clean up, and if we can't get our arms around this thing, everyone dies, so don't think this is chess or some kind of game. Just tell me where it is."

Peter smiled. After all that anticipation and dread, the actual moment came as a relief. He was building himself up, faking it in a way, but that confidence was addictive, its own drug. The smile unsettled her, broke through her boss act. And that was good. She wasn't a superior; she wasn't even on his level. She was a traitor.

"I need assurances," Peter said, "some guarantee that we'll be protected from your people and from whoever Dimitri was working for and with."

She let out a desperate, edgy laugh. "You want me to put it in the *Congressional Record*? Maybe have a Rose Garden press conference with these Kremlin knife artists who are out to kill you? How the fuck is that going to work?"

"I don't know." He checked the clock. "But you should figure it out. Or else everything goes out."

"Really, you want to play games? Your dad didn't care what happened to the people he loved. I have a feeling you do."

Peter tensed, fighting back the reaction. He leaned forward and spoke in an icy whisper.

"If we don't work this out," he said, "you're in prison for treason. Congress recognizes that train attack for what it was, an act of war. Or the Kremlin murders us all before we get to that. So what do you have for me, Diane? You said you wanted to deal, let's deal. Time's up."

She sat back in her chair, shaking her head with a hint of a smile. He'd seen it before, a certain Washington type; they bulldozed everyone in front of them. The fearful got in line, and those who shoved back got respect.

Farr tapped a finger on the table and appraised him.

"I always knew you were a treacherous motherfucker underneath it all. Maybe that's why I thought we could work together."

Peter shrugged.

"Your father was good. They never would have caught him, except he had a conscience. He was a bad traitor, because he couldn't convince himself he was a hero."

"You can't rattle me, Diane."

"It's a compliment. Welcome aboard, Peter. I'm glad you're done lying to yourself."

He had a feeling that her sudden amity and good faith was all smoke, a way to put him at ease, to work him by building a rapport as the best interrogators do. As soon as she had what she wanted, she would do her best to kill him.

That was fine, because both she and Peter were playing with hidden cards.

"I need to make some calls," she said. "And how can I verify that you don't have extra copies hidden away, that you won't turn around and stab me in the back?"

"You control every door and every piece of paper to the most powerful office on earth. I can verify, and if there's anything you don't like, at any point, kill me. It won't be hard."

She slid her chair back and stood. "It's harder than I thought."

Farr turned and walked out. Akana stared at Peter, who felt sweat drip along his spine.

It was seven o'clock.

Peter waited. A few minutes later, Akana took out his phone and looked at the screen. He had a good poker face, but Peter could tell that something was off. The phone buzzed in his hand, and he stabbed at the screen with his finger, silencing it for an instant, but it quickly began to ring again.

He went to the door, and as soon as he opened it, the echo of a pair of woman's shoes, clacking fast along the linoleum, broke the silence like a metronome. It grew louder and louder.

"What the fuck is this? Is he still in there?" Farr shouted from the hall.

"Of course. What's happening?"

But Akana didn't get an answer. Farr shoved the door open. The knob slammed into the cinder-block wall.

She held her phone up like a murder weapon.

"What is this?"

Peter leaned back and placed his hands on the table. She stalked around it and stood over him, while Akana shut the door and unholstered his sidearm, a black SIG.

Peter didn't bite. Time was on his side. Time was his weapon. This whole charade had been a bid to buy more of it.

"I just had the *Washington Post* call," Farr said as she slammed her hand on the table, "asking about a red ledger."

90

Peter was surprised that it was only one reporter, but maybe Farr was withholding. He and Rose had used the Blackphone to send images of the most important passages from the ledger, along with a summary of everything they had learned and suggestions on how to corroborate it, to the *Wall Street Journal*, CNN, Fox News, the *New York Times*, and the *Washington Post*, along with half a dozen inspectors general in the intelligence community, and the Department of Justice, as well as senior staff on the losing Gibson campaign.

"Sounds bad," Peter said and eased back in his chair.

She backhanded him with the closed fist that held the phone, then bent forward and put her face two inches from his. Her lips drew back, trembling, baring her clenched teeth.

The blow brought little more than a dull ache. So many other things hurt on his body that it barely registered. Peter rose from his chair slowly, then pushed it back and towered over her.

"Another suicide," she said, unfazed, and looked at him with disgust. "You think a tip from a nobody can change anything, a digital photo of a few random handwritten notes in some book by a dead Russian that no one's ever heard of? You think that's insurance? You're both going to die."

The anger softened into pity. "Peter, Peter, Peter. It didn't have to be this way."

Did he think sending out the evidence would save his life or Rose's? He hoped so but wasn't sure. The idea of two people with no clout taking down the White House seemed far-fetched. Woodward and Bernstein were good reporters, but people forget that it took the Supreme Court, the DOJ, FBI, and Congress to bring down Nixon. That was bureaucratic civil war. This was David and Goliath.

So much had been hidden already, so many unimaginable crimes committed. He didn't know what to believe anymore. He liked to think that in the end the truth would out, and justice would be served. But that sounded hopelessly naive in the face of all he knew.

He and Rose had talked it through as they drove and prepared to send those emails from the Blackphone.

He had been ready to make a deal, to play the game. Maybe Farr and Dimitri were right. All those things he had believed in for his whole life—about following the truth, about doing the right thing—just kept everyone else in line while the powerful did whatever they wanted.

He remembered Rose's words to him on the boat that morning. She had shown him that sometimes you have to forget about black and white and do whatever it takes to survive. That was the real world.

After he'd told her that in the car, she looked at him squarely. "No," she said. "I think you're right. I think you've always been right. I'm done with all that."

It might cost them their lives, but they had no idea if they would survive either way.

"Do it," she'd said, and he hit send.

The evidence had gone out. But they needed time for it to filter through all the gatekeepers, time to paint that proof across as many desks as they could, so that Farr couldn't erase it. So Peter had played along with what Farr wanted to believe, that he, like everyone else in DC, thought the truth was up for negotiation. Everyone looked out for himself. Everyone wanted a deal.

What a fucking town, where the last thing anyone suspects, where the trickiest thing you can do, is tell the straight story.

"It doesn't matter," Farr said. "No one will believe you."

They could cover it up, Peter knew. Who would believe it? But he was tired of playing their game. If he was going out, he'd go out on his terms. His dad had died for nothing. He didn't mind dying for something. Even if they had him, maybe he had won enough time for Rose to get away.

"We could have done so much," Farr said. She shut her eyes, pained, like she was already remembering him, like he was already dead.

She looked at Akana and nodded her head.

Farr left, and the door slammed shut behind her. Akana stood with his back to the door and drew his pistol.

91

Akana trained the gun on Peter's head, both hands tight around the grip. Peter looked straight at the barrel and clenched his jaw, steeling himself.

The growl of engines filtered into the room, cars or trucks pulling up outside. Akana kept the gun on Peter with one hand and checked his phone with the other.

He stood for a moment, his eyes fixed on Peter's along the gun sights. A step to the side, and he opened the door and exited. Peter heard the key rattle in the knob and the dead bolt slide, locking him in.

There was silence for a minute and then the sounds of more cars. Peter went to the door. There was no twist knob for the dead bolt on this side, only the slot for a key. He scanned the room for something he could pry the door with or use as a weapon.

He went to the projector. Maybe a shard of glass would work. He was looking for something to muffle the noise of shattering the lens when the sound of footsteps filtered through the door.

It was loud and getting louder. He could barely use his right arm, but he fumbled the lens out and threw it on the ground. It shattered, and pieces slid along the floor. As he crouched to grab one, the door flew open. The latch plate for the lock tore out of the doorframe, and two men in dark suits crossed through the door and went to corners of the room, covering Peter with their pistols.

He raised his hands.

The man on the right aimed his gun at Peter's head, while the other closed in and patted Peter down.

He pivoted back and nodded to the first gunman. Peter recognized both of them: Secret Service. God, how many people were in on this? Or were they simply following orders?

"We're good," one called into the hallway.

A figure stepped through the doorway, flanked by two more agents.

Peter's breath caught.

It was the president. He carried a red ledger in his left hand.

92

Even before travers said a word, Peter understood: they had gotten to Rose. Travers had the ledger, the original evidence. What had they done to her?

It felt like all the blood drained out of Peter's body, like he was puddling there on the floor. He put his hand to the wall to keep from falling.

Travers walked farther into the room and kicked one of the shards of glass, sending the jagged fang spinning to his left. He looked down at it, then picked it up and examined it.

Peter took a step toward him, and the second agent raised his pistol. Peter ignored them. His whole body drew tight, the muscles straining, like a set trap. He was losing control.

"What did you do to her?"

"Peter, I'm here to help." Travers put the glass down on the table.

"Is she alive?"

"Peter, please. Stay calm. For your sake."

"Where is she?" he growled.

"She's fine. She's here."

He spoke briefly with one of the agents, who clearly

didn't seem to think what the president was saying was a good idea but relented.

"Peter, you've been through a lot, and you have a right to be angry and not trust a word I say, but I am on your side in this."

"You want me to play along? Is that the deal? Some kind of trade?"

Nothing about it made sense. Why would the president be anywhere near this thing? The right move was to insulate himself.

"No," Travers said and stepped aside.

Rose came through the door.

"Peter!" She was untouched, walking on her own, her hands free.

"Are you okay?" he asked.

"I'm fine." She took a step toward him and then stopped. She was alive, but now the president had both of them and the ledger.

"What do you want?" Peter asked Travers.

"The same thing you do, Peter. I want to get to the truth behind all of this." He moved closer to the table. "I need the room," he said to the agents.

They hesitated, and one agent came up to the president and spoke into his ear.

"Fine," Travers said.

The lead man sent the other agents out and shut the door, then posted up at the head of the table. Travers put his hands on the back of a chair. His face was grave as he looked from Rose to Peter.

"I don't know if you'll believe any of this, but it's the truth," he said. "I knew your aunt and uncle, Rose. They were good people. I was there at the start of their investigation, but when I talked with them I used another name."

Peter took a step closer and put his hand on the table. He knew what was coming.

"I'm OSPREY."

93

Peter weighed the truth of it—Travers as the original source, as an ally—while he studied the president: the black hair with the gray at the temples, the easy posture of a former athlete, the eyes never wavering from his own.

Even after everything he'd been through, Peter found himself wanting to believe Travers, which was dangerous.

"First, I want you to know that both of you are out of harm's way," Travers said.

Peter glanced to the agent with the gun at the head of the table.

"You came to me before, Peter, with your doubts. And I understand why you might not trust me now. Farr wasn't alone in this. Others worked with her."

"The Secret Service agent, Akana."

"Yes. Everything Diane did with the Russians she did without my knowledge. Akana was working with her, and I suspect there were others. They were trying to keep this from me. Akana saw when you came to me at the basketball game. I didn't know he was part of this. He interceded, tried to make you disappear."

"He tried to kill me."

Travers swallowed, pained. "The safe house on North

Capitol? I had no part in that. It was their last-ditch attempt to keep it from me. I've had suspicions that something was wrong for a long time, but I didn't know who was behind it. I've been looking for you, for both of you, desperately since last night. I want to help."

"What do you want in exchange?" Peter asked.

"Nothing."

Travers took a chair out and sat, then held his hands out toward the table, inviting them to do the same. He moved like a humbled man, but his power still seemed to fill the room, charge the air like static electricity. Rose edged around the table toward Peter, wary of the agent's gun.

Her hand brushed against his, and he took it. He wanted to hold her, protect her with his body, but he didn't want to set off the agent. He and Rose both seemed to understand they needed to keep their guard up, to stay calm, in command.

She took a chair to his left, leaving one empty between them, and Peter sat, facing the president across the table.

"You know I'm an outsider here," Travers said. "I think you've seen enough of the White House to understand that the presidency is the most powerful office in the world, but in a way it's a prison."

It was true. Travers couldn't take a walk around the block. He couldn't even open his windows.

"Farr had a lot of power. Every meeting, every piece of paper. Everyone I wanted to see except for my family, it all went through her. Everything coming to me was against escalation with Russia in Eastern Europe, said that it would only embolden the pro-Russian forces, provoke the Kremlin. I didn't know why everything pointed in the direction of accommodating Russia. I didn't know it was Farr. But I've suspected there was someone disloyal in my house for a long time."

"Is it true about the train crash?" Peter asked. "The interference in the election?"

"So far everything you've put out there checks out, and we will run it all down. We're going to get you someplace safe while we do."

Peter pressed his palms to the table. That hadn't worked out well last time.

"You have every reason to be wary. That's why I'm here. That's why I have a twenty-four-agent detail from the Secret Service, and official cars. This is a public matter now. This"—he put his hand on the ledger—"is with Ashford and Berson and McLintock right now." The CIA and FBI directors, and the attorney general. "I would like you to talk with them as soon as possible."

"Has it been translated yet?"

"Yes. The Russia desk at the NSC is already working on it. It shows more than a dozen meetings Farr took, and who she took them with, along with planning notes for the Metro attack. It should be enough to attribute it all to the Russian services and ID the entities behind the election interference. We will run everything down to the last detail. This isn't going away. I won't let it."

"And the meeting at the Hay-Adams?"

The president hesitated, seeming surprised that Peter knew about a potential deal.

"It's off," Travers said. "Farr had been pushing me to work with the Kremlin, avoid confrontation at all costs. They counted on me being malleable. Maybe they would have tried to put leverage on me to go along. It doesn't matter now. I sent the secretary of state in my place with a simple message: no deals. Russia makes one move in Europe and we fight back. And if Vikhrov doesn't get his troops off the border in forty-eight hours, we'll ram a NATO armored column down his throat."

Travers looked at Peter's hand, his arm.

"You need a doctor."

Peter glanced down at his fingers. "I do," he said coldly.

"You don't believe me?" Travers asked.

"I don't know."

"Maybe I'm trying to get ahead of the scandal, now that it's public?"

"That would be the smart move."

"It's fair. Why would I open up a matter that would destroy me?"

"Yes."

"You know I wasn't supposed to be president. My family wasn't happy about it. It's a circus. But there was a lot of momentum building. I wasn't supposed to win the primary, and I sure wasn't supposed to win the general. It felt like an experiment, to see how far they could bring a candidate with no pull, no real political experience. People liked me because I was new, an outsider. I hadn't had time to make enemies. I overheard a fund-raiser joking about it once: they called me a 'host body.' A face for the poster. During the campaign and even more so now, I was in a bubble.

"Everything you say gets tested by the pollsters. Every piece of paper and conversation gets filtered through someone's interest. Everyone thinks the president is the most powerful person in the world, because you're so

428

visible. You get all of the flak, but so little real power. You can make some changes if everything lines up perfectly, but for the most part you're the rope in a tug-of-war between Washington lifers and the special interests that own them.

"I knew that going in. I was humble. I would learn as much as I could and try to make the right calls. During the election, some things didn't add up. The story kept changing on that train crash—I know you were there, you remember. And then everything broke my way, every bit of bad news for the other candidate, all those scandals that took apart her team.

"I know things get ugly during a campaign. I asked around. I knew that there would be some hardball, and I was fine with it. But I needed to know. And everyone I asked and everyone I talked to told me the same thing: we had nothing to do with all of those scandals coming to light. Just got lucky.

"What I can't stand for is people lying to me. And every single one of those people on my team all said the same thing. 'We don't know anything about these leaks.' It didn't add up.

"Now I'm in office, I'm getting white papers and memos and briefings. I'm dealing with the full spectrum of risks for the US and the world. I know that I was placed here and I know that someone's hiding something from me. I don't know who or what to believe. Do you know what it's like to benefit from something you can't trust?"

"I do." Peter had spent years going over his favorite memories of childhood, searching out the taint of his father's corruption. That trip to the Outer Banks, where he bodysurfed his first wave, was that because his father had gotten a payout from the SVR? Was it blood money?

"I guess you know that I don't like people to take it easy on me, and I don't like to be patronized," Travers said.

Peter had seen that much on the basketball court. Letting him win, faking it—you'd be barred for life.

"There were policies, like this Russian accommodation they were working on, that I didn't like. I needed to find out who was being straight with me."

He turned to Rose.

"Did you know anything about your aunt and uncle's work?"

"Only secondhand, after they died," Rose said. "They were FBI, counterintelligence."

"They were some of the bravest, most dedicated people that have ever served this country. I wanted to know what had really happened during the election. I wanted to know whose interests I was serving. I didn't have any real evidence. It wasn't the kind of thing you'd bring to the FBI to investigate, to open an official file. What if I was wrong?

"You are read in on a lot of secrets after you take the oath, and I learned about two cases your aunt and uncle had handled. I knew that they were discreet and fair and relentless and owed nothing to anyone. When I talked to them, they confirmed that they had heard rumors, just rumors at that point, of foreign influence. So I asked for their help in an unofficial capacity. I wanted to know what happened."

"The original source," Rose said. "OSPREY."

"Yes. I told them everything I knew and everything that concerned me."

"You sicced investigators on yourself?" Peter asked.

"I did. I wanted them to run with it. No one around me was giving me the straight story. I didn't want to interfere. So I handed it off to them, and told them to go to Hawkins and Farr if they needed anything. She was my closest confidante outside of my family, and Hawkins's reputation was impeccable."

"She took over the investigation so that she could stamp out any evidence of what she did," Rose said.

"So it seems."

"And, with respect," Peter added, "how can we be sure you're not co-opting this now, putting yourself on the right side?"

"Right now, you can't. But this job isn't worth selling my soul. It's humbling, you know. The responsibility, the nuclear codes and attack plans, the people you meet who put their faith in you, the letters you read every night. I knew it would be hard, but I never knew I'd be so disappointed by the people who I thought would help me—Congress, my own party. They're only loyal to their donors.

"You have to go on, to do the best you can, smiling while a dozen cameras shine and snap in your face, and three dozen reporters bark questions at you. You have to watch every word, to play a role, because a single mistake could crash the Dow or trigger an international crisis. There are days you want to say to hell with it, to blow the whole thing up and bring the temple down on your head. But that's just acting out. Because this job, this responsibility, is the greatest honor in the world. So you smile and do your best, put up with all the bullshit and try to do what good you can. Except for this—"

He stabbed his finger down on the ledger. "Your aunt and uncle were good people," he said to Rose. "They didn't deserve this. And I'm culpable. I started them in on this, and now I'm going to finish it. This is treason. This is murder. This is worth crashing the whole fucking thing down on my head and taking everyone with me. So don't trust a word I'm saying. Watch what I do."

He stood. "Are you ready?"

"Where are we going?" Peter asked.

"To tell their story."

94

Five black SUVs had parked in a circle around the entrance to the building, and Peter counted at least twenty agents covering them with M4 rifles as they were hustled out to one of the vehicles. The door was four inches thick. Peter and Rose took the bench seat opposite Travers.

They drove to the West Wing and entered through the southwest gate. The president marched them straight to the medical office, where the same navy captain from the other night cleaned and stitched Peter's wounds.

After making sure they were up for it, Travers took them down the hall, but Peter stopped outside the press secretary's suite. On the TV over the assistant's desk, CNN played.

A correspondent stood outside the West Wing—about four hundred feet away from where Peter was now—and talked about a string of suspicious deaths over the last forty-eight hours in Washington, DC, and reports, so far unconfirmed, that a foreign intelligence service was suspected to have a role.

"Our sources indicate that this may be part of a multiyear operation against the United States, including interference in last year's election."

Peter turned to Travers. He had sent the evidence himself,

but it was still surreal to see secrets that people had died for broadcast on the nightly news.

"It's all starting," he said.

Travers nodded and held his hand out to the side. They went down to the Situation Room's iconic command center, where the FBI director and the attorney general joined them in person, and the CIA director by videoconference.

This was going to be a long night, the first of many. The ledger had already made the rounds. Slowly, point by point, Peter and Rose laid out the contours of the story as the most powerful men in Washington listened and quizzed them, looking increasingly grim as they realized the scale of what they were dealing with.

There were questions, of course, there would be years of questions, of testimony, of depositions. It was the FBI director who finally asked: "When's the last time you two slept? Or ate something?"

Peter had to think about that. They called it for the night.

As they all exited the Situation Room, Peter finally let himself believe, for a moment, that he and Rose would make it out of this.

They had shared what they knew at the highest level and been seen in the White House with Travers even after they made it public. That would serve as insurance against them disappearing, but Travers wanted to reassure them further.

He put them up at Blair House, a brick mansion on Lafayette Square, across Pennsylvania Avenue from the White House, where visiting dignitaries often stay, and the president, by tradition, spends the night before inauguration.

It was an odd space, constructed from four nineteenth-century town houses that looked separate and distinct from the outside, while inside they had been unified into one large guesthouse, essentially the president's own luxury hotel. The kitchen sent up pasta primavera and brownies—the old Kennedy recipe.

Peter stayed in the shower for what felt like twenty minutes, letting the water wash away the blood and grime, and two days of fear and sweat. He came out clean, his skin flushed from the heat. Rose had a room next door, but as he passed it, he saw it was empty and then caught a glimpse of her through the door to his room.

He stepped inside and found her stretched out under the comforter.

"This bed," she said, eyes closed, palms to the ceiling.

Peter climbed in next to her. Any bed would have felt like a cloud after what he'd been through, but this was even better than he had imagined.

"Are we safe?"

"Yes," Peter said. "It's over. The hard part at least."

Rose let out a long sigh of relief. After a moment, she said, "God, this place is weird."

Peter laughed. The house made him feel like he was sleeping in a museum display: everyday life in the American colonies. Rose muttered something. Her eyes were already closed.

"What was that?"

"I'm stealing that mug."

She'd brought it in and left it on the nightstand. It was a standard White House guest mug, blue with a satisfying heft and the presidential seal.

"Go for it."

She didn't respond. She was already out. Peter pulled the sheets and blankets up to her chin. He lay down, and she rolled closer and draped her arm over him. Peter closed his eyes, and sleep came in an instant.

95

Peter walked Rose across the street to the West Wing the next morning. There had been a message waiting for them at breakfast. The president wanted to see them. They used the visitors' entrance, and as the marine guard pulled open the door, Travers was waiting for them in reception.

There were a few pleasantries about how their night was at Blair House, but the president's presence was the real point. This wouldn't be hidden away. He escorted them down the hallway, and as he walked out Peter saw the newspapers folded neatly on the side table. There was a two-column headline at the top of the *New York Times*: "Intelligence Agencies Investigate Russian Operation Against the US."

The *Post* had a package on the story, covering a quarter of the front page. They were already starting to corroborate the ledger.

Travers led Peter and Rose past the offices of the senior personnel and into the Oval.

It was another formal museum room, with the Resolute desk facing down a pair of sofas. Physically, it was less impressive than the room Peter had read about in all those histories. But as he stepped across the deep blue carpet, he felt like he was on a stage before thousands.

Travers gestured to one of the sofas, and Peter and Rose sat.

"How are you holding up?" he asked.

Rose looked to Peter, then Travers. "We're fine, Mr. President."

"Good. It's hard to convey how overwhelming a full press from the media and Congress will be once this really gets going," he said. "You should be prepared. You'll need a lawyer. The White House counsel suggested a few names. They're all attorneys at different firms."

"Defense?"

"No. More of a guide. They specialize in crisis communications and ushering people through confirmations. They can keep the press at bay and help you deal with this kind of scrutiny. Of course, feel free to reach out to others and get referrals on your own. This is going to be a three-ring circus once the full scale of it comes out, and a lot of people will use anything they can about your past and your family to destroy you."

Peter remembered the TV lights shining through his childhood bedroom, the correspondents doing stand-ups on the sidewalk at the height of his father's scandal: day after day inside with the blinds drawn, eating take-out and mercy casseroles from the folks at church.

"I've been through it before."

Travers nodded, his lips pressed together.

"Where is Farr? And Akana?" Peter asked.

"We have them both in custody. Investigating and prosecuting all of this will be a long process, but I guarantee we will see it through, no matter where it leads. I brought you here to express my gratitude more formally for what you've done. You both risked your lives. Peter, I know the challenges you faced, for years, and I am grateful we had you standing watch. And Rose, you and your family have sacrificed more than anyone could ever ask. The foundations of who we are as a democracy were under threat, and we couldn't have stopped it without you. So personally, and on behalf of the country, thank you."

Peter dipped his head solemnly and let the silence linger for a moment.

"If anything comes up," Travers said, "anything, you can reach me directly, here." He took a slip of paper from the side of the table and wrote out a number. "Day or night." With the last word, his eyes went to Peter.

"Are you asking us to keep you informed?" Rose asked.

"No. I will stay out of your way, unless you need help. There will be a special prosecutor, grand juries, congressional panels. I ask only one thing: hold nothing back. Give us hell."

Rose smiled and took the paper.

"Absolutely," Peter said.

96

Peter and Rose rented a place in the Shenandoah Valley, just outside Sperryville, to get away from the madness in DC as the scandal broke.

It was a two-bedroom cottage set among the horse farms and hollows, and the FBI set up security for them as witnesses. Even in the depths of winter, Peter ran the hills and ridges every day, for hours sometimes. He had missed the sun, missed daylight.

He and Rose did a lot of cooking and listening to music, and they would go upstairs and wear each other out in that delirious way of new love, or in the living room, or on the upstairs deck if they caught a warm day, hidden from view behind a white-planked railing.

It reminded Rose, she told him, of what her aunt and uncle had together, how they managed to keep it burning for decades, even on that last night. Some part of it was simply the pleasure of reveling in life, of a new chapter, after so much had been lost.

It felt easy and natural, the same way each one of them could pick up when the other wanted time to be alone, to think through the gravity of what they had survived and what lay ahead.

They both knew that their lives, every hard thing in their pasts, were being scoured and paraded across cable news. Peter had wrapped the cord around the TV and put it in the shed. The house was mostly quiet, except when they brought out Rose's aunt and uncle's records and set to work prepping dinner on the kitchen counter looking out at the woods, a bottle of wine open on the island. There was one album, he noticed, that Rose would never play, that she always flicked past quickly in the crates.

They were at the center of the storm, but the distance and quiet helped them weather it. Peter and Rose went back and forth to DC often, and sometimes they would take the Campbells' old Mercedes, now pushing 240,000 miles and mechanically perfect. Henry had left it to Rose in the will. They would hide out in a hotel between grand jury testimony and interviews with the special prosecutor.

Counterintelligence investigations are some of the longest and most complex cases handled by the FBI. This one just kept expanding.

At its center was Farr, who after a lifetime of being other people's deputy or chief of staff, and running the show with little of the credit, began to imagine herself a kingmaker. Travers's campaign was an experiment of sorts. No one thought he would win, so she felt there would be little harm in taking all the help she could get, even from donors, investors, and lobbyists with foreign ties. Some of them were on the Kremlin's payroll.

Farr thought the train attack was supposed to be nothing more than a demonstration of force, to embarrass Travers's opponent in the election. She and her backers seemed to think it would be little more than a prank, or dirty trick, halting the trains during one rush hour, and she even rationalized that it would draw much-needed attention to cybersecurity. They didn't account for how the Metro was always one mistake away from a fatal disaster.

After the crash, the Russians owned Farr. There was no way she would cross them and implicate herself in the murder of Americans. Some speculated that the Russians had crashed the train on purpose, in order to get that kind of leverage on her, but it was never proven.

Russian intelligence began eliminating anyone who could have exposed the truth, and Farr tried to tell herself at the beginning that the first deaths, however convenient, were accidents. As Dimitri Sokolov killed more witnesses, there was no way Farr could deny that she was complicit in murder. By then she was all in, afraid for her own life if she didn't go along.

She played that card in her defense, but the investigators ultimately nailed down her part in the murder of Hawkins, and of Rose's aunt and uncle.

For now, she was at the US Penitentiary in Hazelton, West Virginia. "Relieved, actually," Peter's lawyer pointed out.

Peter saw her only once, on an icy January morning outside the District Court in downtown DC, as federal marshals ushered her to a waiting SUV. She wore a long dove-gray coat over a bulletproof vest. Their eyes met for an instant as a marshal guided her into the back seat.

She betrayed the Kremlin's thugs, and prison was one of the few places she was safe. She would be there for life, depending on how the final charges came down. If she ever did see the sun again, she would have to live knowing that around every corner, behind every door, a Russian bullet might be waiting.

What Travers had told Peter—that he had first reached out to Rose's aunt and uncle, and had no part in Farr's plot—stood up.

Plans swirled in the House to impeach him, though he had dropped hints throughout the whole affair that he was only staying in office long enough to make sure everyone involved was held accountable.

His political opponents went after him for having stolen the presidency. His own party paid him lip service but had their knives out because he had brought the whole thing to light. Sworn enemies on both sides of the aisle were united in their disdain for the man who had put out the truth.

Washington hated Travers, but as he pushed for more sunlight on the scandal, his standing with the public and his poll numbers went higher and higher.

He called a Rose Garden press conference in early spring. There were rumors he would hand out pardons or kick off his reelection campaign. Instead he announced that he would not run again.

He hadn't been involved, but he still benefited from Farr's crimes, and the country deserved a clean start. That was the final proof that Travers had rooted out every element of the scandal, not in order to save himself politically, but because it was the right thing to do. The indictments had all been handed out. The investigation was in good hands. He would finish his term and step down, the work complete.

97

It was Peter's last day at the White House. He and Rose had finished most of their interviews and testimony. Their part in all this was nearly over. Their lease in the Shenandoah was up.

He had to sign a stack of papers to formally end his job on the watch. He went through them in the Sit Room, took a last look at his old desk and phone, swapped his badge out for a visitor sticker, and left.

At the top of the stairs, he was crossing toward the north exit when he saw a young man, maybe twenty-five or twenty-six, standing and looking down at a slip of paper. He seemed lost.

Peter gave a friendly nod as he passed.

"Excuse me?" the man asked.

"Yes?" Peter said.

"I was looking for the deputy national security advisor's office."

Peter had already noticed the spit and polish on the black Oxfords, the white shirt, navy suit, and perfect half-Windsor tie knot. It was either his first day or his first time at the White House for a meeting, and the guy had that shine. He could have been Peter a little over a year ago.

Even in the middle of all this mess, eagerness and awe and respect for this place were beaming off him like sunlight.

Peter smiled. "Turn right and it's at the end of the hall on your left."

"Thank you, sir."

The country had been through worse crises. It would survive this.

He walked out onto Pennsylvania without looking back.

It was a chill April morning. The dogwoods were blooming. He had always thought they were cherry blossoms, and Rose had never succeeded in getting him to be able to tell the difference.

She was waiting, double-parked on G Street. "How'd it go?" she asked.

"Easy enough."

"And how are you doing?"

He thought about it for a moment. He'd been running on instinct for as long as he could remember, trying to answer for his father's crimes, to answer those voices calling out for help. And now, he had done his part. He had stood his watch. He was free. He and Rose were going to get in that old Benz and get out of DC. They didn't know what came next, but they would figure it out. They had time. They had each other.

"Great," he said, looking up at the porcelain-blue sky. "Did you see those cherry blossoms?"

Rose laughed and didn't take the bait. "You mind if we stop somewhere?"

"Sure."

She drove past the Naval Observatory and the National Cathedral to her aunt and uncle's house. They went inside.

It was spotless, the blood washed clean, like nothing had ever happened.

They stood in silence. Peter put his arm around her shoulders.

After about five minutes she shut her eyes and took a deep breath.

"You want some time alone?"

She nodded and squeezed his hand. He walked back to the driveway.

He heard her, just barely, in the moments the wind was still. She was singing an old Stevie Wonder tune, and her voice was beautiful, and clear, and strong.

She came out a few minutes later. She'd been crying, he could tell, but her face was full of relief. She offered him a bittersweet smile.

"Are you okay?"

"I am." She said it like it was news to her, then she wrapped her arms around him. "I am."

Acknowledgments

Thanks to my family, especially Ellen Quirk, my mother (and my high school journalism teacher), who's there for every draft. They turn each plot bind into an excuse to jump on the phone or take a hike, and never fail to crack me up and rescue me from my bad habits.

I made some career moves recently, trying something a little riskier with this book, and was absolutely overwhelmed by the generosity and support of the thriller-writing and publishing crowd. The murder and mayhem world is full of sweethearts paying it forward. Joseph Finder and Gregg Hurwitz offered invaluable help and advice, and saved the day as surely as the heroes in their pages. Thanks as well to Alex Berenson, Allison Brennan, Sean Chercover, Marcia Clark, Ben Coes, J. T. Ellison, Chris Holm, Joshua Hood, Jesse Kellerman, Michael Koryta, Brad Parks, Chris Pavone, and Marcus Sakey.

I had the great fortune to have Dan Conaway by my side on this story from the beginning. An unbelievably talented agent and editor and just a great guy, he is dedicated to his writers and books to a degree I hadn't imagined possible.

And I am still a little awestruck that I found a home with the wonderful team at William Morrow—Liate

Stehlik, Andy LeCount, Eliza Rosenberry, Kaitlin Harri, and Chloe Moffett—and had the opportunity to work with David Highfill, who believed in this novel and improved it tremendously. He's a pleasure to talk to and an artist with a red pen.

Thanks to all of my DC friends for keeping me sharp and letting this ex-reporter feel like he's still in the loop. I'll mention Adam Kushner, Mike Melia, Josh Green, Julian Sanchez, and Garrett Graff, though there are so many writers and journalists doing extraordinary work right now. Thanks to Allison Archambault and Steven Davis for putting a roof over my head in the District (and a walipini under my feet!). And to John MacGaffin and Peter Higgins for taking the time to talk about their careers at the FBI and CIA. I took some liberties with real-world details here and there in the text, including a few particulars of FBI roles and training.

Thanks to my wife, Heather Burke, for the best ten years of my life and for revealing herself as a national security sage, and to all of her classmates and professors at the Johns Hopkins School of Advanced International Studies for the good times in DC and abroad and the quiet work they do in their day jobs.

And finally, thanks to the friend of mine whose long nights inspired this book.

About the Author

MATTHEW QUIRK is the *New York Times* bestselling author of *The 500*, *The Directive*, *Dead Man Switch*, *Cold Barrel Zero*, and *The Night Agent*. He spent five years at *The Atlantic* magazine reporting on crime, private military contractors, terrorism prosecutions, and international gangs before turning to fiction. An Edgar Award finalist and winner of the ITW Thriller Award for Best First Novel, Quirk lives in San Diego.

@mquirk
matthewquirk.com